ALL
THE
FABULOUS
BEASTS

Priya Sharma

Praise for Priya Sharma

"Priya Sharma has been writing and publishing short stories for over a decade, and I'm delighted that she's finally receiving the recognition her work deserves. She's extremely skillful in creating characters with whom we can empathize—no matter their deeds—leading her readers down roads of beauty and horror. I especially love her award-winning novelette 'Fabulous Beasts,' a perfect piece of storytelling."
—Ellen Datlow, *Best Horror of the Year* series

"The only fault I find with Priya Sharma's work is that there's not more of it! Her stories range in theme and even style, but each is beautifully written. This debut collection is well worth having."
—Paula Guran, *The Year's Best Dark Fantasy & Horror* series

"Priya Sharma is a consummate storyteller. She writes from the heart, with passion, warmth and authority. Her stories, focusing largely on familial relationships and traditions, brim not only with ideas but with humanity, and her characters are so vividly and exquisitely wrought that they seem to live and breathe beyond the confines of the page. Like Stephen King and Alice Munro, she has the ability to convey so much in prose that is concise, elegant and unfussy, and as a result her stories offer you the best of both worlds: they are both instantly accessible and exhilaratingly profound."
—Mark Morris, Author of *The Obsidian Heart Trilogy* / Editor of *New Fears*

"Priya Sharma explores liminality and otherness with skill and verve in her engaging and haunting stories."
—Alison Moore, Author of the Man Booker-shortlisted *The Lighthouse*

ALL
THE
FABULOUS
BEASTS

PRIYA SHARMA

UNDERTOW
PUBLICATIONS

Publication History

"Small Town Stories" and "A Son of the Sea" are original to this collection.

"The Crow Palace" originally appeared in *Black Feathers*, Ellen Datlow, ed., 2017.

"Rag and Bone" originally appeared in *Tor.com*, 2013.

"The Anatomist's Mnemonic" originally appeared in *Black Static #32*, 2013.

"Egg" originally appeared in *Once Upon a Time*, Paula Guran ed., 2013.

"The Sunflower Seed Man" originally appeared in *Black Static #37*, 2013.

"The Ballad of Boomtown" originally appeared in *Black Static #28*, 2012.

"The Show" originally appeared in *Box of Delights*, John Kenny ed., 2011.

"Pearls" originally appeared in *Bourbon Penn #4*, 2012

"The Absent Shade" originally appeared in *Black Static #44*, 2015.

"Fish Skins" originally appeared in *Albedo One #42*, 2012.

"The Rising Tide" originally appeared in *Terror Tales of Wales*, Paul Finch, ed., 2014.

"The Englishman" originally appeared in *Libbon #3*, 2006.

"The Nature of Bees" originally appeared in *Albedo One #38*, 2010.

"Fabulous Beasts" originally appeared in *Tor.com*, 2015.

For Mark, who whistles. For everything.

CONTENTS

THE CROW PALACE

Birds are tricksters. Being small necessitates all kinds of wiles to survive but Corvidae, in all their glory as the raven, rook, jay, magpie, jackdaw, and crow have greater ambitions than that.

They have a plan.

○

I used to go into the garden with Dad and Pippa every morning, rain or shine, even on school days.

We lived in a house called The Beeches. Its three-acre garden had been parcelled off and flogged to developers before I was born, so it became one of a cluster of houses on an unadopted cul de sac.

Mature rhododendrons that flowered purple and red in spring lined the drive. The house was sheltered from prying eyes by tall hedges and the eponymous beech trees. Dad refused to cut them back despite neighbours' pleas for more light and less leaf fall in the autumn. *Dense foliage is perfect for nesting*, he'd say.

Our garden was an avian haven. Elsa, who lived opposite, would bring over hanging feeders full of fat balls and teach us about the blue tits and cheeky sparrows who hung from them as they gorged. Stone nymphs held up bowls that Dad kept filled. Starlings splashed about in them. When they took flight they shed drops of water that shone like discarded diamonds. The green and gold on their wings caught the sun.

Pippa and I played while Dad dug over his vegetable patch at the weekends. The bloody chested robin followed him, seeking the soft bodied and spineless in the freshly turned earth.

Dad had built a bird table, of all things, to celebrate our birth. It was a complex construction with different tiers. Our job was to lay out daily offerings of nuts and meal worms. At eight I could reach its lower levels but Pippa, my twin, needed a footstool and for Dad to hold her steady so that she didn't fall.

Elsa taught me to recognise our visitors and all their peculiarities and folklore. Sometimes there were jackdaws, rooks, and ravens but it was monopolised by crows, which is why I dubbed it the crow palace. Though not the largest of the Corvidae, they were strong and stout. I watched them see off interlopers, such as squirrels, who hoped to dine.

After leaving our offerings we'd withdraw to the sun room to watch them gather.

"Birdies," Pippa would say and clap.

The patio doors bore the brunt of her excitement; fogged breath and palm prints. Snot, if she had a cold. She touched my arm when she wanted to get my attention, which came out as a clumsy thump.

"I can see."

Hearing my tone, Pippa inched away, looking chastised.

Dad closed in on the other side with a forced, jovial, "You're quiet, what's up?"

It was always the same. *How are you feeling? What can I get you? Are you hungry? Did you have a bad dream last night?*

"I'm fine." Not a child's answer. I sounded uptight. I didn't have the emotional vocabulary to say, *Go away. Your anxiety's stifling me.*

I put my forehead against the glass. In the far corner of the garden was the pond, which Dad had covered with safety mesh, unfortunately too late to stop Mum drowning herself in it. That's where I found her, a jay perched on her back. It looked like it had pushed her in. That day the crow palace had been covered with carrion crows; bruisers whose shiny eyes were full of plots.

⊙

I sit in a traffic queue, radio on, but all I hear is Elsa's voice.

"Julie, it's Elsa. From Fenby."

As if I could forget the woman who brought us birthday presents, collected us from school, and who told me about bras, periods, and contraception (albeit in the sketchiest terms) when Dad was too squeamish for the task.

"Julie, you need to come home. I don't know how to say this, so I'll just come out with it. Your dad's dead." She paused. "He collapsed in the garden this morning. I'll stay with Pippa until you get here."

"Thank you."

"You will come, won't you?"

"Yes."

Ten years and they jerk me back with one phone call.

The journey takes an hour longer than I expected. Oh, England, my sceptred and congested isle. I'm not sure if I'm glad of the delay or it's making my dread worse.

The lane is in dire need of resurfacing so I have to slow down to navigate the potholes. I turn into the drive. It's lined by overgrown bushes. I stop out of view of the house and walk the rest of the way. I'm not ready for Pip and Elsa yet.

The Beeches should be handsome. It's crying out for love. Someone should chip off the salmon-pink stucco and take it back to its original red brick. The garden wraps around it on three sides, widest at the rear. I head there first.

The crow palace is the altar of the childhood rituals that bound us. It looks like Dad's lavished more love on it than the house. New levels have been added and parts of it replaced.

I stoop to pick something up from the ground. I frown as I turn it over and read the label. It's an empty syringe wrapper. Evidence of the paramedics' labours. The grass, which needs mowing, is trampled down. I think I can see where Dad lay.

A crow lands on the palace at my eye level. It struts back and forth with a long, confident stride as it inspects me. Its back is all the colours of the night. It raises its head and opens its beak wide.

Caw caw caw.

It's only then that the patio doors open and Elsa runs out, arms outstretched.

Job done, the crow takes flight.

⊙

Elsa fusses and clucks over me, fetching sweet tea, "For shock."

"What happened to him?"

"They think it was a heart attack. The coroner's officer wants to speak to you. I've left the number by the phone."

"How can they be sure? Don't they need to do a post-mortem?"

"They think it's likely. He's had two in the last three years."

"I didn't know."

"He wouldn't let me phone you." I don't know if I'm annoyed that she didn't call or relieved that she doesn't say *Perhaps, if you'd bothered to call him he might have told you himself.* "Your dad was a terrible patient. They told him he should have an operation to clear his arteries but he refused."

Elsa opens one of the kitchen cupboards. "Look."

I take out some of the boxes, shake them, read the leaflets. There's twelve months of medication here. Dad never took any of it. Aspirin, statins, nitrates, ace-inhibitors. Wonder drugs to unblock his stodgy arteries and keep his blood flowing through them.

I slam the door shut, making Elsa jump. It's the gesture of a petulant teenager. I can't help it. Dad's self-neglect is a good excuse to be angry at him for dying.

"We used to have terrible rows over it. I think it was his way of punishing himself." Elsa doesn't need to say *guilt over your mother.* She looks washed out. Her pale eyes, once arresting, look aged. "I don't think Pippa understands. Don't be hurt. She'll come out when she's ready."

Pippa had looked at me as I put my bag down in the hall and said, "Julieee," prolonging the last syllable as she always did when she was excited. Then she slid from the room, leaving me alone with Elsa.

Elsa's the one who doesn't understand, despite how long she's known Pippa.

Pip's cerebral palsy has damaged the parts of her brain that controls her speech. It's impaired her balance and muscle tone. It's robbed her of parts of her intellect but she's attuned to the world in other ways.

She understands what I feel. *She's* waiting for *me* to be ready, not the other way around.

Perhaps it's a twin thing.

Pippa stopped speaking for several years when she was a child. It was when she realised that she didn't sound like other children. That she couldn't find and shape the words as I did. Her development wasn't as arrested as everyone supposed. Dad, Elsa and her teachers all underestimated her.

I could've tried to help her. I could have acted as an interpreter as I've always understood her but I didn't. Instead, I watched her struggle.

⊙

And here she is, as if I've called out to her.

Pippa's small and twisted, muscle spasticity contorting her left side. That she's grey at the temples shocks me, despite the fact mine's the same but covered with dye. She's wearing leggings and a colourful sweatshirt; the sort of clothes Dad always bought for her. That she's unchanged yet older causes a pang in my chest, which I resent.

Pip looks at the world obliquely, as if scared to face it straight on. She stands in the doorway, weighing me up and then smiles, her pleasure at seeing me plain on her narrow face.

That's what makes me cry. For her. For myself. I've abandoned her again and again. As soon as I could walk, I walked away from her. As we grew older, my greatest unkindness towards her was my coldness. As a teenager, I never wanted to be seen with her. After our twenty-third birthday, I never came back.

"Julieee."

I put my arms around her. I've not asked Elsa if Pip was with Dad when he collapsed, if she sat beside him, if she saw the paramedics at work.

The onslaught of my tears and sudden embrace frighten her and I'm the one who feels abandoned when Pip pulls away.

⊙

Ten years since my last visit to The Beeches. Ten years since Dad and I argued. I drove home after spending the weekend here for our birthday.

Elsa had made a cake, a sugary creation piled up with candles that was more suitable for children.

Dad rang me when I got back to my flat in London.

"I'm disappointed, Julie."

"What?" I wasn't used to him speaking to me like that.

"You come down once in a blue moon and spend the whole time on the phone."

"I have to work." I was setting up my own recruitment agency. I was angry at Dad for not understanding that. I was angry that he thought I owed him an explanation. "I'm still getting things off the ground."

"Yes, I know your work's more important than we are."

"It's how I make a living. You sound like you want me to fail."

"Don't be preposterous. All I'm saying is that it would be nice for you to be *here* when you're actually here."

"I drove all the way to be there. It's my birthday too."

"You act like coming home is a chore. Pippa's your sister. You have a responsibility towards her."

"Yes, I'm her *sister*, not her mother. Aren't I allowed a life of my own? I thought you'd be happier that you've only got *one* dependent now."

"Don't talk about Pip like that."

"Like what?"

"Like you're angry at her. It's not her fault that your mother killed herself."

"No? Whose was it then? Yours?"

Those were my final words to him. I don't know why I said them now.

⊙

The following morning's a quiet relief. I wake long before Pippa. The house is familiar. The cups are where they've always lived. The spoons in the same drawer, the coffee kept in a red enamel canister as it always had been when I lived here. It's like returning to another country after years away. Even though I recognise its geography, customs, and language, I'll never again be intrinsic to its rhythms.

My mobile rings.

"Ju, it's me." Christopher.

"Hi."

I'm never sure what to call him. Boyfriend sounds childish, partner business-like and lover illicit.

"The new Moroccan place has opened. I wondered if you fancied coming with me tonight."

Not: Shall *we* go? There's *him* and *me* with all the freedom between *us* that I need.

"I can't. Take Cassie." There's no jealousy in that remark. Over the two years I've been seeing Chris, seeing other people too has worked well for us. It's precisely why I picked a man with form. A player won't want to cage me but Chris keeps coming back to me, just when I expect him to drift off with someone new.

"I stopped seeing her months ago. I told you."

I don't care. It makes no difference to me.

"My dad's dead," I say, just to try and change the subject.

"Oh God, Julie I'm so sorry. I'd just presumed he was already dead from the way you talked about him. What happened?"

"Heart attack."

"Where are you? I'll come and help."

"No need."

"I want to."

"And I don't want you to,"

"I'm not trying to crowd you, but may I call you? Just to see if you're okay."

"Sure. Of course." He can call. I may not answer.

I hang up.

"Julie."

Pippa sidles up to me. We're both still in our pyjamas. It's an effort but I manage a smile for her.

"Do you want breakfast, Pippa? Cereal?"

I'm not sure what she eats now. It used to be raspberry jam spread thickly on toast. She tugs on my sleeve and pulls me up.

A trio of swallows hang from her bedroom ceiling. It was sent one Christmas, like all my presents to her for the last ten years, chosen for being flat packed and easy to post. Pippa reaches up and sets the birds in motion as she passes.

It's the bedroom of a child. No, it's the bedroom of an innocent. It needs repainting. The realisation makes me wonder what I feel. Our future's a knife.

"Look," Pippa beams.

Her childhood collection has grown to dominate the room. It's housed in plastic craft drawers that are stacked on shelves to a height that Pippa can reach. Her models are lined up above the drawers, on higher shelves.

She used to make them in plasticine. They were crude lumps at first. Now she's graduated to clay. They must fire them at the day centre. Her years of practice are in the suggestive details. A square tail. The shape of the head with a pinched beak.

They're crows, over and over again.

Pippa opens one of the drawers and picks out buttons, one at a time, and drops them into my open hand. Each one's unique, only their colour in common. They're white plastic, mother of pearl, enamel, stained fabric, and horn. She laughs as they spill through my fingers. The rest of that block of drawers contains buttons, each separated by compartment for the rainbow.

"Pippa, are all these from the crow palace?"

"Yes, birdies." She mangles some of the syllables but she's definite.

She shows me more. Her collection is sorted by type of object, or by shape where Pippa was unsure. Coins and bottle tops. Odd earrings. Screws. Watch parts. The tiny bones of rodents, picked clean and bleached by time.

I used to have a collection of my own, the crows left us treasures on the crow palace in return for food. They came with presents every day. I threw mine out when I started high school.

I regret it now, as I sit here with Pippa.

"Here." She thrusts one of the drawers into my hands.

Something lonely rattles around inside. I tip it out. I hold it up between my forefinger and thumb. A ring designed as a feather that wraps around the finger. Despite the tarnish, it's lovely—the hard line of the shaft, the movement of the hundreds of vanes and downy barbs.

It's impossible that it's here because I'm sure Mum was buried with it. I watched Dad lay out the things for the undertaker: a silk blue dress, tights, a pair of leather heels, a lipstick, and this ring. He put her wedding band and diamond engagement ring in a box and placed it in his bedside drawer. *For you, when you get married,* as if this was a given.

The feather ring was kept to go with her into the grave. *We were on holiday when she realised she was expecting. She chose this from an antique shop in France the same day that she told me. I was thrilled. I think she'd want to wear this.*

I close my eyes. Had I imagined that? As I do, the ring finds its way onto the ring finger of my left hand, which goes cold. I can feel the blood in my wrist freezing. I yank it off before ice reaches my heart.

"Where did you get this?" My voice is shrill. "Pippa?"

"Crows," she says.

☉

I force myself to go into Dad's room. It's stifling. Being north facing and a dull day, the poor quality light brings out the green undertones in the patterned gold wallpaper. The dark, heavy furniture makes the room crowded and drab.

Everything's an effort. There's something about being back here that's put me in a stupor. I'm procrastinating about everything.

Looking through Dad's things should hurt but it doesn't. It's like rifling through a stranger's personal effects for clues. He was an unknown entity to me because I didn't care enough to want to find out who he was. Shouldn't blood call out to blood? Mine didn't. I felt more for Pip, my dead mother, and for Elsa. Dad's love was smothering and distant all at once as if I was something to be feared and guarded closely.

I pile his clothes in bin bags to take to the charity shop. I pause when I find box files full of football programmes. I never knew he was a fan. It looks like he went regularly before we were born. It crosses my mind that they might be worth something, but then I chuck them on the pile to get rid of.

It's only when I'm clearing out the second wardrobe that I find something that piques my interest. There's a steel box at the back with his initials on it, under a pile of moth eaten scarves. It's locked. I spend the next hour gathering together every key I can find, searching drawers and cupboards for them. Nothing fits.

I carry the box downstairs and put it on the kitchen table. It's too late in the day to take it to a locksmith. I'll go tomorrow.

☉

Who knew that death is so bureaucratic? I'm relieved there won't be a post-mortem but there's still the registering of Dad's death and meetings with the undertaker, bank and solicitors. Elsa's a brick, taking Pip to the day centre or over to her place if I have things to arrange.

The future leaves me in a stupor of indecision. I stare out of the kitchen window at where the pond used to be. Now it's a rockery in the same kidney shape.

What sort of people would have a pond with young children in the house?

The pond was where I found Mum's body, looking boneless as it slumped over the stones at the water's edge. I was four. I thought she'd just fallen over. I ran out to help her get up. A jay sat on her back. The bird is the shyest of all Corvids, flamboyant by comparison to its family, in pink, brown, and striped blue. It normally confines itself to the shelter of the woods.

I paused as the wind blew up her skirt, revealing the back of her thighs. Her head was turned to one side. The jay hopped down to look at her face, then pecked at one of her open, staring eyes.

The jay turned as I approached and let out a screech, blood on its beak. Or maybe I was the one screaming. I'd put my hands over my ears.

A shriek comes from the sun-room, next door. I drop my coffee cup, imagining Pippa has conjured the same image. She'd followed me out that day and seen Mum too. By the time my cup smashes on the floor and sends hot coffee up my legs and the cabinets I realise something's actually wrong.

Pippa's pressed against the window, shouting and banging with her fists.

"What is it?"

I grab her shoulders but she twists around to look outside again. From here we have an interrupted view of the back garden.

A magpie deposits something on the crow palace, then starts to make a racket. Its blue-black-white colouring reveals its affinities for the living and the dead.

Only then does the sudden whirring motion draw my gaze down to the lawn. The cat's bright pink collar contrasts with its grey fur. A second magpie is pinned by the cat's paw on its spread wing. Its other wing is a blur as it struggles. The magpie's mate flies down and the cat breaks its gaze with its prey and hisses.

I know it's the natural order of things but I'm sickened and trembling. I open the patio door and clap my hands as if such a banal gesture can end this life-and-death struggle. Pippa's more decisive, stumbling out and I hold her back for fear she'll be scratched.

Flat black shapes with ragged wings darken the sky. Ravens. One swoops, catching the cat's ear with its bill as fierce as pruning shears as it passes over. The cat contorts, blood on its fur, releasing the magpie which makes an attempt at broken flight.

The cat crouches, a growl in its throat. Its ears are flat to its head, its fur on end, doubling its size. The birds are coming down in black jets, from all directions. The cat raises a paw, claws unsheathed, to swipe at its assailants. The ravens take it by surprise with a group attack. One lands, talons clutching the nape of the cat's neck. It writhes and screams. The sound cuts through me. The birds are like streaks of rain. I can't see the cat anymore. It's been mobbed by darkness.

Pippa and I clutch one another. The cat's silent now. The ravens lift together into the sky and all that remains on the grass are steaks of blood and tufts of fur.

○

I remember later that the magpies left us a gift, a task which made them careless of their long collective memory of their past persecutions by gamekeepers and farmers.

The key they left on the crow palace shines as if calling to me. The metal's so cold that it hurts to hold it, as if it's just come out of a freezer.

I have the queasy feeling that I know what it's for. It slides into the padlock on the steel box with ease and I feel its teeth catch as I turn it.

Everything I know about Mum is distilled from scant memories. I'm shaking at the prospect of something concrete. I open the lid. Here's where Dad buried her significant remains.

It contains a random assortment. A lady's dress watch. A pair of pearl earrings. A silk patterned scarf. An empty perfume bottle. I open it and the stale fragrance brings Mum back to me on a drift of bluebells. I wipe my eyes. I'd forgotten she always wore that. There's a birthday card signed *With more than love, Karen.*

What is there that's more than love?

We weren't a photographed family. There aren't any happy snaps that feature Pip and me. This pile of photographs are of Mum and Dad when they were young, before we were born. I shuffle through them. Mum and Dad at the beach, on bicycles, another in formal dress. Their happiness grates. Why couldn't they have saved some of it for us?

The last thing out of the box is a handkerchief. Whatever's knotted within clinks as I lift it out. It's a pair of eggs. They're unnaturally heavy, as if made of stone. And they're warm.

I can't resist the impulse to crack one of them open. Fluid runs over my fingers. I sniff it. Fresh egg white.

A baby's curled up within, foetal like, her tender soles and toes, her genitals displayed. She's perfect. I don't know what she's made of. Something between rubber and wax that's the colour of putty.

I break open the second one. Another girl. This one's different. She has massive, dark eyes that are too wide set to be normal. There are sparse, matted feathers on her back. Faint scale cover her feet.

I carefully rewrap the pair, trying not to touch them, and put them back in the box.

O

My phone rings. Then stops. Starts again. There's nothing for it. I answer it.

"Chris." I try not to sound irritated.

"How are you?"

"Busy. You know."

"No, I don't. Tell me."

"Stuff to sort out. Dad and for my sister."

"You have a sister? What's her name?"

"Phillipa. We call her Pippa."

"What's she like?"

Pippa? She likes birds, me, the colour turquoise, chocolate, having a routine, crow gifts, sunshine. She gets frustrated when she can't make herself understood. Her eyes are hazel brown and she has eczema.

"She has cerebral palsy. My dad took care of her."

"Will I meet her at the funeral?"

I'm about to say *Of course she'll be at the funeral* but then I realise that Chris is assuming he's invited.

"Why do you want to come? You never met him."

"Not for him, for you. Tell me your address."

"I don't need you here."

I don't understand. It feels like an argument, full of unspoken baggage that I didn't even know we were carrying.

"Julie, what are we doing?"

His tone sets off an alarm bell in my head.

"You must know that I—" Don't say it. Don't say *I love you*. He falters, "You must know how much I care about you."

I feel sick. I thought we were alike. Just my luck to find a man who falls in love with the one woman who's not chasing him.

"I'm not talking about marriage or children."

Children. For all the carelessness of my affections there's never been a child.

"I told you at the start that I'm not like other people. You promised me that you understood completely."

"There's more to us than just sex."

I can't believe he's doing this.

"Don't you get it?" I should be angry but a column of coldness is solidifying inside me. "There *is* no more. I'm not broken, so you can't fix me. I don't love you because I can't love anyone."

"Julie, please..."

I hang up and bar his number.

☉

There's never been so many people in the house. I don't like it. I wanted it to be just us, but Elsa went on so much that I relented. I wish I hadn't now.

I forgot to pack a black dress so I had to buy one in a hurry. I took Pippa with me, there being nothing suitable in her wardrobe either. The shop assistant stared at her while she touched the expensive silks. The woman's tune changed when it was clear that I didn't have to look at the price tags.

I picked out a neat black dress myself and a black tunic, leggings and ankle boots for Pippa. On impulse, I took her to a salon to get her hair dyed and styled. She was more patient than I expected. She liked being somewhere new. My favourite part was Pippa's smile when the shampoo was massaged into her scalp.

It was a nice day.

Today isn't. When we went out to the funeral car, Elsa said, "Look at the two of you. Pippa, you look so grown up. And Julie, wonderful. Black suits you more than any other colour. You should wear it more."

Grief fucks people up.

The mourners come in, folding up their umbrellas like wings, dripping rain on the parquet floor.

"Elsa, are any of the neighbour's coming?"

"God, no. All the one's you'd know are dead or moved away."

I don't know the people here. Some used to work with Dad, apparently, others knew him from Pippa's day centre or through Elsa. They all greet her like she's long lost family.

It's unnerving that they line up to speak to me, something more suited to a wedding than a funeral.

The first is a tall, broad man, dressed in a shiny tight suit and winkle pickers. Spiv's clothes but he's gentle, paternal even. He takes my hand and looks right into my eyes, searching for something.

"My name's Charlie."

"Thank you for coming."

"I'm so very pleased to meet you, my dear. You're as lovely as I thought you'd be. I understand you're a smart lady too." Then as if he's just recalled why we're here, "I'm sorry for your loss."

A pair of elderly ladies are next. They're twins. Both have the same bob, cut into a bowl shape at the front, hooked noses and dowager's humps that marks their identically crumbling spines.

"Do you have children?" says the first one, which isn't the opener I expected.

The second one tuts and pushes her sister along. They're followed by a couple who call themselves Arthur and Megan. A first I think they're brother and sister as they're so alike, but the way he hovers around her suggests their relationship is more than familial. Her arm's in plaster.

"How did you know Dad?"

"Through my father." The man waves his hand in a vague gesture that he seems to think explains everything.

Young men, a few years younger than I am, come next. They're all in designer suits. Each is striking in his own way. They stand close to me as they introduce themselves. One even kisses my hand. The last one interests me the most. He's not the tallest or best looking but I like his quiet confidence and lively face. There's a yearning in his voice when he says my name that tugs at me. To smile at him seems weak, so I nod.

"My name is Ash."

"Ash." The word coats my tongue with want.

A woman edges him along.

"I'm Rosalie."

She has the manner of entitlement that only certain hard, beautiful women have. Her fingernails are painted black. The lacquer's like glass. She looks me up and down as she passes.

I sip my drink as more people introduce themselves, then go off to decimate the buffet and the wine boxes. I try not to look at Ash's every movement. It's a lovely agony. I close my eyes, the tannin in the red wine shrinking the inside of my mouth.

"How is Julie settling back in here?" It's Charlie.

"Well, she's here for now." I don't like Elsa's tone. She must be drunk too.

I open my eyes. Charlie's suit can't settle on a single shade of black.

"I'm sorry Elsa. You must be missing Michael."

I turn away a fraction, not wanting them to know I'm listening. From the periphery of my vision I see him embrace Elsa.

The young men congregate by the hearth. Rosalie's berating them for something. I catch her final words: "I don't see what's so special about her anyway."

I know she's talking about me because Ash looks over and keeps on looking even though he's caught me eavesdropping. "Don't you?" he replies with a smirk.

"I'm Stephanie." A woman gets in the way, just when I think he's going to walk over and join me. "You're Julie, yes?"

"Hello."

There's a long pause. I sigh inwardly. I'm going to have to try and make conversation with her. She's in her fifties. She's only wearing one earring and most of her hair's escaped from her bun.

"Where are you from?"

"From?" she says.

"Your accent…" Her pronunciation's off kilter, her phrasing odd.

"I've lived in lots of different places." She glances around the room. "I think Elsa would rather I hadn't come."

She reaches out and swipes a sandwich from a plate, gobbling it down in two mouthfuls. "These are delicious."

The volume of the chattering around us bothers me. I've drunk too much on an empty stomach.

"This place hasn't changed since your mother's funeral."

"You met her?"

"Tennis club."

Tennis. How little I knew about her.

"Such a gracious, joyous woman." Stephanie twitters on. "Want and need. How they undo us."

"Pardon?"

Stephanie blinks.

"There are so many crows in Fenby now. They've quite pushed out the cuckoos." She speaks in a comedy whisper, getting louder with each word. "Your mother guessed that they'd double-crossed her."

The chatter's dying. Everyone's watching us now.

"You know how it works, don't you? They laid one of their own in your mother's nest..."

Charlie comes over and puts an arm around her.

"Stephanie, what are you taking about? Julie doesn't want to hear this rubbish." He pulls a face at me. "It's time for you to go home."

"You can't push me around. I have a right to be here. We had a deal." She breaks away from him and seizes me in a hug.

"I'm sorry. For all of it," she whispers in my ear. "It's true. Look under the crow palace."

I want to ask her how she knows that's what we call the bird table but Ash comes and takes her arm.

"Aunt Steph, I'll see you home."

"I'm not your aunt."

"No, Ash, you should stay." Elsa joins us.

"It's fine." Ash kisses my cheek. My flesh ignites. "May I come and see you again? Tomorrow?"

"Yes." It's as easy at that.

"Until then." He steers Stephanie towards the door.

The noise starts up again in increments. Ash's departure has soured my mood.

Pippa can't settle. As the mourners gathered around Dad's grave she cringed and started to wail as if finally understanding that he's gone. Now she's wandering about, refusing to go to her room but flinching when any of our guests come near her. She stands, shifting her weight from foot to foot, in front of the twins who are perched in her favourite armchair.

"Oh for God's sake, just sit somewhere will you?" I snap.

Pippa's chin trembles. The room's silent again.

Elsa rushes over to her but Pippa shoves her away. Elsa grabs her wrist.

"Look at me, Pippa. It's just me. Just Elsa." She persists until Pippa stops shaking. "Better? See? Let's go outside for a little walk."

Pippa's face is screwed up but she lets Elsa take her out onto the patio.

I lock myself in the bathroom and cry, staying there until everyone leaves. I've no idea what I'm crying for.

☉

I wish this humidity would break. It' sticky, despite yesterday's rain. I feel hungover. Lack of sleep doesn't help.

I wave goodbye to Elsa and Pippa as they go out. Elsa's keen to be helpful. *I'll drop Pippa off, I'll be going that way to the shops. Why don't you go and get some fresh air on the lawn? You'll feel better.*

I can't face sorting out the last of Dad's clothes. The thought of the hideous green-gold wallpaper in there makes me want to heave. Instead, I take boxes of papers out to a blanket I've laid out on the lawn. It's prevarication. I'm pretending that I'm doing something useful when I should be sorting out our future.

All the ridiculous talk of swapped babies and symbolic eggs seems stupid now that I'm out in the fresh air.

I imagined it would be cut and dried when Dad died. Sell the house. Find somewhere residential for Pippa or pay Elsa to take care of her. Now I hate myself. I have all along, and have taken it out on Pip. She's the purest soul I know. There's such sweetness in her. How can I leave her to the mercy of others?

How can I love her so much yet can't bear to be near her sometimes? I fought everyone who tried to bully her at school. I became a terror, sniffing out weakness and reducing other children to tears. I started doing it just because I could. They hated me and in return and I felt nothing for them, not anger, not contempt. That's how damaged I am.

I'm afraid that everything people think of me is true, but I'm not afraid enough to change. I *am* selfish. I like my own silence and space. I hated Dad for saying, "You will look after Pippa won't you? The world's a terrible place."

Need. Nothing scares me more.

Then I look at Pippa, who is far more complete a human being than I am. She's no trouble, not really. I could work from here and go to London for meetings. All I need to run my business is a phone. It would only need a bit of will to make it work.

I pull papers from the box. It's an accumulation of crap. Receipts from electrical appliances, their warranties long outdated, bills, invitations and old business diaries.

It's so quiet. I lie back. There's not even the slightest breath of a breeze. I shield my eyes as I look up. The trees are full of Corvidae.

Birds don't roost at eleven in the morning, yet the rookeries are full. Sunlight reveals them as oil on water creatures with amethyst green on their foreheads and purple garnets on their cheeks.

Rooks, weather diviners with voices full of grit who sat on Odin's shoulders whispering of mind and memory in his ears.

How Elsa's lessons come back to me.

She taught me long ago to distinguish rooks from crows by their diamond shaped tails and the bushy feathers on their legs. I find these the strangest of all Corvidae, with their clumsy waddles and the warty, great patch around the base of their beaks. It's reptilian, Jurassic, even. A reminder that birds are flying dinosaurs, miniaturised and left to feed on insects and carrion.

I turn my head. Crows have gathered too, on the patio furniture, the bird baths, the roof and, of course, the crow palace. The washing line sags under their weight.

I daren't move for fear of scaring them. Perhaps I'm scared.

Ash walks through their silence. They're not unsettled by his presence. He's still wearing the same suit. His stride is long and unhurried.

He doesn't pay attention to social niceties. He falls to his knees. I lean up, but I'm not sure if it's in protest or welcome. It's as if he's summed me with a single glance when I'm not sure what I want myself. He presses his mouth against mine.

He pushes my hair out of the way so he can kiss the spot beneath my ear and then my throat. The directness of his desire is exhilarating, unlike Chris' tentative, questioning gestures.

He pulls open my dress. I unbutton his shirt. He pulls down my knickers with an intensity that borders on reverence.

His body on mine feels lighter than I expect, as if he's hollow boned.

When he's about to enter me he says, "Yes?"

I nod.

"Say it. I need to hear you say it. You have to agree."

"Yes, please, yes."

I'll die if he stops now. The friction of our flesh is delicious. It's as necessary as breathing.

When Ash shudders to a climax, he opens his mouth and *Caw, caw, caw* comes out.

⊙

I wake, fully dressed, lying on a heaped-up blanket beneath the crow palace. There's a dampness between my legs. I feel unsteady when I get up. The shadows have crept around to this side of the house. It must be late afternoon.

When I go in, Elsa's in the kitchen. She's cleaned up after yesterday.

"I'm sorry. I was going to do that…"

"It's okay." She doesn't turn to greet me.

"Where's Pippa?"

"Having a nap. We're all quite done in, aren't we?"

She turns to wipe down the worktops. She looks so at ease, here in Dad's kitchen.

"What happened to my mother?"

I have to take the damp cloth from her hand to make her stop and look at me.

"It's all on record."

"I want to hear what's not on record."

"Then why didn't you ask Michael while he was still alive?"

I've been expecting this but the anger and resentment in Elsa's voice still surprises me. I take a deep breath. Retaliation won't help my cause.

"Because he hated taking about her."

"Then it's not my place to tell you, is it?"

"Of course it's your place. You're the closest thing to a mother that either of us have ever had." I should've said it long ago, without strings. The tendons at Elsa's neck are taut. She's trying not to cry. I didn't just leave Dad and Pip. I left her too.

"You were born in this house. The midwife didn't come in time. Your father smoked cigarettes in the garden. Men didn't get involved in those days. I helped bring you both into the world. I love you both so much. Children fly away, it's expected. I just didn't realise it would take you so long to come back."

"I know you loved Dad too. Did he love you back?"

"He never loved me like he loved your mother." Poor Elsa. Always at hand when he needed her.

"You sacrificed a lot to be with him." Marriage. A family of her own.

"You've no idea." Her voice is thick with anger. "It's utterly changed me."

Then she bows her head. The right thing to do would be to comfort her. To hold her and let her weep on my shoulder. I don't though. It's a crucial moment when Elsa's emotions are wide open.

"The papers said Mum had postnatal depression and psychosis."

An illness that follows childbirth. A depression so deep that it produces bizarre beliefs.

"They were desperate for children. They would've done anything."

"Anything?"

"Fertility treatments weren't up to much back then."

"So what happened?"

"Well, you happened. A surprise, they told everyone. I remember holding you in my arms. It was such a precious moment."

"When did she get ill?"

"When it became clear that Pip wasn't doing so well. You were a thriving, healthy baby but Pippa was in and out of hospital because she was struggling to feed. She slept all the time. She never cried. You were smiling, then rolling over, then walking and she was falling further and further behind."

"And Mum couldn't cope?"

"The doctors became worried as she had all these strange ideas. And you were a real handful."

"Me?"

"I'm sorry, maybe I shouldn't say this."

"Tell me."

"You were just a little girl, trying to get their attention. You'd bite Pippa, steal her food. When you we big enough, you'd try and tip her from her high chair."

"And what exactly was it that Mum believed?"

"She insisted she'd been tricked by the birds. They'd helped her to conceive and then they went and swapped one of you for one of their own."

☉

I wake in the hours when the night turns from black to grey to something pale and cold. My mind's full. It's been working while I sleep.

Mum's insistence that she'd been tricked by birds. That they'd helped her to conceive.

They laid one of their own in your mother's nest…

Cuckoo tactics. Mimic the host's eggs and push out one of their own. Equip your chick for warfare. Once hatched, the hooks on its legs will help it to heave its rivals from the nest.

Look under the crow palace.

I pull on jeans and a sweatshirt. Dad kept his tools in his shed. I pull the shovel from the rack, fork and a trowel for more delicate work.

It's chilly. I leave footprints on the damp lawn. It takes a while because I go slowly. First I take up turf around the crow palace. Then I dig around the base. The post goes deep into the rich, dark soil. My arms ache.

I lean on the post, then pull it back and forth, trying to loosen it. It topples with a crash. I expect the neighbours to come running out but nobody does.

I have to be more careful with the next part of my excavation. I use the trowel, working slowly until I feel it scrape something. Then I use my hands.

I uncover a hard, white dome. Soil's stuck in the zigzag sutures and packed into the fontanelle. The skull eyes me with black orbits full of dirt that crawl with worms.

I clean off the skeleton, bit by bit. Its arms are folded over the delicate ribcage. Such tiny hands and feet. It's small. She's smaller than a newborn, pushed out into the cold far too early.

Mum and Stephanie were right. Here is my real sister, not the creature called Pippa.

Oh my God, you poor baby girl. What did they do to you?

⊙

"Are you okay?" Elsa ushers me into the kitchen. It's eight in the morning. She has her own key.

I can't bring myself to ask whether Pippa, my crow sister, is awake. How was the exchange made? Was it monstrous Pippa that heaved my real sister from my mother's womb? Was she strangled with her own umbilical cord? And who buried my blood sister? Was it Mum and Dad? No wonder they were undone.

"What happened to you?"

Elsa opens a cupboard and pulls out a bag of seed mix, rips it open and tips out a handful. When she eats, some of it spills down her front. She doesn't bother to brush it off. When she offers me some I'm hit by a wave of nausea that sends me across the room on rubbery legs to vomit in the bin.

"You've got yourself in a right old state." Elsa holds back my hair.

I take a deep breath and wipe my nose.

"Elsa, there's a baby buried in the garden."

She goes very still.

"You knew about it, didn't you?" I sit down.

She pulls a chair alongside mine, its legs scraping on the tiles. She grasps my hands.

"I didn't want you to know about it yet. I wish that cuckoo-brained Stephanie hadn't come to the funeral. And Arthur and Megan hadn't interfered with that damn key. You found the eggs, didn't you?"

I think I'm going to faint so I put my head on the table until it passes. Elsa rubs my back and carries on talking. When I sit up, Elsa's smiling, her head tilted at an odd angle. A gesture I don't recognise. "I'm actually relieved. It's easier that you know now you're staying."

"Elsa, I can't stay here."

"It's best for everyone. You've others to consider now."

I press my fists to my closed eyes. I can't consider anything. My mind's full of tiny bones.

"Mum knew that Pippa wasn't hers, didn't she?" I'm thinking of the human-bird-baby in its shell.

"Pippa?" Elsa's eyes are yellow in this light. "No, she knew that it was you that wasn't hers. She had to watch you like a hawk around Pip."

I vomit again. Clumps of semi digested food gets caught in my hair. Elsa dabs at my mouth with a tea towel. Her colours are the jay's—brown, pink and blue. Was it her, stood at Mum's back and pecking at her eye?

Pippa stands in the doorway looking from my face to Elsa's and back again. I've never seen Pip's gaze so direct.

Now I know why my heart's loveless. Pip's not the aberration, I am. I'm the daughter of crows, smuggled into the nest. Pippa is how she is because of my failed murder attempt. I affected her development when I tried to foist her from the womb.

It's all my fault.

Pippa edges around the room, giving the woman who raised her a wide berth. She tucks herself under my arm and puts a hand low down on my abdomen. She peers into my face, concerned, and says, "Birdies".

Rag and Bone

I leave Gabriel in the yard and go into town, taking my bag with the vials of skin and bone, flesh and blood, my regular delivery to Makin. The Peels are looking for body parts.

I love the grandeur of The Strand. High towers of ornate stone. The road's packed with wagons and carts. Boats choke the river. The Mersey is the city's blood and it runs rich. Liverpool lives again.

I can hear the stevedores' calls, those kings of distribution and balance, whose job it is to oversee the dockers loading the barges. The boats must be perfectly weighted for their journey up the Manchester Ship Canal. Guards check them to ensure no unlicensed man steals aboard. Farther along, at Albert Dock, there's a flock of white sails. The Hardman fleet's arrived, tall ships bringing cotton from America.

The Liver birds keep lookout. Never-never stone creatures that perch atop the Liver Building where all the families have agents. I keep my eyes fixed on the marble floor so that I don't have to look at the line of people desperate for an audience. Peels' man has the ground floor. The Peels' fortune came from real estate, small forays such as tenements at first, but money begets money. They took a punt when they redeveloped Liverpool's waterfront, a good investment that made them kings of the new world.

The other families have managers on other floors, all in close proximity as nothing's exclusive, business and bloodlines being interbred. The Hardmans are textile merchants, the Rathbones' wealth was made on soap, of all things, while the Moores are ship builders.

The outer offices contain rows of clerks at desks, shuffling columns of figures in ledgers. A boy, looking choked in his high-necked shirt, runs between them carrying messages. No one pays me any mind.

Makin's secretary keeps me waiting a full minute before he looks up, savouring this petty exercise of power. "He'll see you now."

Makin's at his desk. Ledgers are piled on shelves, the charts and maps on the walls are stuck with pins marking trade routes and Peel territories.

"Have a seat." He's always civil. "How did you fare today?"

"A few agreed."

I hand him the bag.

"They're reluctant?"

"Afraid."

There are already rumours. That the Peels, Hardmans, Rathbones and Moores, these wealthy people we never see, are monstrosities that live to a hundred years by feasting on Scousers' flesh and wearing our skins like suits when their own get worn out. Their hands drip with diamonds and the blood of the slaving classes. They lick their fingers clean with slavering tongues.

Makin taps the desk.

"Should we be paying more?"

"Then you'll have a line that stretches twice around the Mersey Wall consisting of drunken, syphilitic beggars."

"Do we have to order obligatory sampling of the healthy?"

"That's unwise."

His fingers stop drumming.

"Since when are rag and bone men the font of wisdom?"

I'm not scared of Makin but I need the money so I'm respectful. Besides, I like him.

"At least wait 'til it's cooler before you announce something like that or you'll have a riot."

That brings him up short.

"I'm feeling fractious today." He rubs the top of his head like a man full of unhappy thoughts. "Don't be offended."

"I'm not."

"You're a good sort. You work hard and don't harbour grudges. You speak your mind instead of the infernal yeses I always get. Come and work for me."

"Thank you but I hope you won't hold it against me if I say no."

"No, but think on it. The offer stands." Something else is bubbling up. "You and I aren't so different. I had to scramble too. I'm a Dingle man. My daughters are spoilt and innocent. My sons no better." His rueful smile reveals the pain of parenthood. "It's their mother's fault. They're not fit for the real world, so I must keep on scrambling."

I envy his children, wanting for nothing, this brutal life kept at arm's length. Makin must see something in my face because he puts the distance back between us with, "Have you heard any talk I should know about?"

He's still chewing on my unpalatable comment about riots.

"All I meant was that it's unseasonably hot and a while since the last high day or holiday. Steam builds up in these conditions."

I hear craziness in the ale houses all the time that I'm not going to share with him. Talk of seizing boats and sailing out of Liverpool Bay, north to Blundell Sands and Crosby to breathe rarefied air and storm the families' palaces. Toppling the merchant princes. A revolution of beheading, raping and redistribution of riches.

Tough talk. Despairing men with beer dreams of taking on armed guards.

"They can riot all they like. Justice will fall hard. Liverpool's peaceful. There'll be no unions here. We'll reward anyone who helps keep it that way."

I want to say, *The Peels aren't the law*, but then I remember that they are.

⊙

I cross Upper Parliament Street into Toxteth. My cart's loaded with a bag of threadbare coloured sheets which I'll sell for second-grade paper. I've a pile of bones that'll go for glue.

"Ra bon! Ra bon!" I shout.

Calls bring the kids who run alongside me. One reaches out to pat Gabriel, my hound, who curls his lip and growls.

"Not a pet, son. Steer clear."

When I stop, the children squat on the curb to watch. They're still too little for factory work.

"Tommy, can I have a sweet?"

"No, not unless you've something to trade and it's Tom, you cheeky blighter. Shouldn't you be in school?"

There are elementary classes in the big cathedral. I convinced Dad to let me attend until he decided it was too dangerous and taught me himself instead. Hundreds of us learnt our letters and numbers by rote, young voices raised in unison like fevered prayers that reached the cavernous vaults. The sad-eyed ministers promised God and Jerusalem right here in Liverpool and even then I could see they were as hungry as we were, for bread and something better.

"Are you the scrap man?" It's a darling girl with a face ravaged by pox. "My ma asked for you to come in."

"Don't touch my barrow," I tell the others. "After the dog's had you, I'll clobber you myself."

I wave my spike-tipped stick at them. It's not a serious threat. They respond with grins of broken teeth and scurvy sores. They're not so bad at this age. It's the older ones you have to watch for.

I follow the child inside. The terraces seethe and swelter in the summer. Five storeys from basement to attic, a family in every room. All bodies fodder to the belching factories and docks; bargemen, spinners, dockers, weavers and foundry workers. Dad reckoned Liverpool got shipping and industry when the boundaries were marked out and other places got chemicals, medicines, food production and suchlike. He said the walls and watchtowers around each county were the means by which the martial government quelled civil unrest over recession, then biting depression. It was just an excuse to divide the nation into biddable portions and keep those that had in control of those that didn't.

Dad also said his grandfather had a farm and it was a hard but cleaner living. No cotton fibres in the lungs, fewer machines to mangle limbs. Less disease and no production lines along which contagion can spread.

The girl darts into a room at the back. I stand at the door. The two women within are a pair of gems. One says, "Lolly," and the child runs to her. She looks like an angel, clutching the child to her that way.

"We've stuff to sell," says the other one with the diamond-hard stare. "I'm Sally and this is Kate."

Sally's dazzling. I take off my cap and pat down my hair.

They share the same profile, long hair fastened up. Sisters. Sally's still talking while Angel Kate puts a basket on the table. I catch her glance. This pitiful collection's worth won't meet their needs.

"Let's see." I clear my throat. "These gloves might fetch something. The forks too." The tines are so twisted that they're only worth scrap value. There's a jar of buttons and some horseshoe nails that look foraged from between cobbles. "I'll give you extra for the basket."

Kate looks at the money in my outstretched hand with hungry eyes but Sally's got the money in her pocket before I can change my mind.

"Are you both out of work?"

"Laid off." Sally makes a sour face.

"I'm sorry. Laid off from where?"

"Vicar's Buttons."

A good, safe place for nimble-fingered women.

"I'll let you know if anyone's hiring."

"Lolly, play outside." Lolly jumps to Kate's order, dispelling any doubt about which woman is Lolly's mother.

"We need more money." Mother Kate is fierce. "I've heard that you're looking to collect things for one of the families…"

"Which one?" Sally butts in.

"The Peels," I answer.

"The Peels have taken enough from us already."

I want to ask Sally what she means but I don't get a chance.

"*We need more money*, Sally. Peels, Vicars, Hardmans. What's the difference?"

"There is."

"No, there isn't, Sal." Kate sounds flat. "Lolly needs food and a roof. She comes above pride or principles."

Nothing could make me admire Kate more. I'm gawping at her.

"We'll get work."

"Not soon enough." Kate turns to me. "Tell me more."

"It's just in case one of the Peels get ill." I feel foolish trotting out this patter. "Should they need a little blood or skin, or bit of bone."

"Are they too proud to ask one another?" Sally's sharp. "I've heard that they take the bits they want and toss the rest of you to their lapdogs. And what if they want an eye or kidney?"

"They wouldn't want anything vital and the compensation would be in keeping, of course."

"Compensation?" Sally presses me. She's the sparring sort.

"That's up for discussion. Someone got granted leave to live outside Liverpool for their help."

Outside. Myth and mystery. That shuts her up.

"Yes, but what will you give me now?" Kate has more pressing concerns.

Both women are bright-eyed. They don't look like they buy backdoor poteen or have the sluggish, undernourished look of opium fiends. They've worked in a button factory, not a mill, so they've young unblemished lungs, engine hearts and flawless flesh, except for their worn hands. Just the sort I've been told to look for. I feel like a rat, gnawing on a dying man's toes.

Do whatever you need to survive, Dad would say. *Do whatever you need to be free.*

I put a silver coin on the table.

"I'll do it," Kate says.

"Don't." Sally's like a terrier. I don't know whether to kiss or kick her.

"We've queued for weeks with no luck."

The indignity of hiring pens and agency lines. At the respectable ones they just check hands and teeth. At others, they take women and boys around back for closer inspection.

"What if they want something from you? What then?" Sally sounds panicked.

"All they ask is a chance to speak to you. No one's forcing anyone." It's what I've been told to say, but the rich always have their way.

"Do it." Kate's firm.

I take off the bag strung across my chest and sit down at the table.

"What's your name?"

"Kate Harper."

Kate's hands are callused from factory work but her forearms are soft.

"It'll hurt." I remove the sampler's cap.

I put it over her arm and press down. I feel the tip bite flesh and hear the click as it chips off bone. It leaves a deep, oozing hole. Kate gasps but doesn't move. It's only ever men that shout and thrash about.

"I'll give you some ointment to help it heal. What about Lolly's father?" I try and make it sound like easy banter as I write her details in the log book and on the tube.

"He was a sailor on *The Triumph.*"

"You're Richard Harper's wife?" A name said with hushed reverence.

"Yes, and before you blather on about heroism, he didn't give us a second thought. Everything we'd saved went on his sailor's bond."

The Triumph was a Peel ship that landed in the Indies. You can't send men across the ocean on a boat and not expect them to want to get off on the other side and walk around. It's a foul practice to stop sailors absconding, resulting in cabin fever, brawling and sodomy. The crew of *The Triumph* mutinied.

The leader, Richard Harper, was a martyr for his part. The authorities tied him to the anchor before they dropped it. His sailor's bond, held with the port master, was forfeit.

"You were widowed young."

Kate's nod is a stiff movement from the neck. She tries to soften it with, "It's just us now."

"I understand. It used to be me and my dad until he died. He was a rag and bone man too." I'm overcome with the need to tell her everything, but I can't. "He wanted a horse instead of pulling the barrow himself. One day I'll get one, if I can save enough."

I'm trying to impress them. Sally sighs as if I'm tiresome but Kate pats my hand like an absentminded mother. Her unguarded kindness makes me want to cry. I want to put my head on Kate's knee and for her to stroke my hair.

Sally watches us.

"I won't do it. I don't trust them."

I realise that I want to touch Sally too, but in a different way. I have a fierce urge to press my mouth to the flesh on the inside of her wrist where the veins show through.

Sally stares me down and I want to say, *I'm not the enemy. I'm not a flesh-eating Peel up in an ivory tower*, but then I realise that I might as well be.

⊙

I sit in my room at The Baltic Fleet. Mother Kate's essence shouldn't be contained in a vial. I don't want anyone else to possess her. Not some sailor, bound and drowned, and definitely not a Peel. She should be free.

Times are hard. I've filled in a whole page of Makin's log book.

I go walking to clear my head, Gabriel at heel. Mrs Tsang, the publican, is stocking the bar with brown bottles of pale ale. She's good to me, just like she was good to Dad. She lets me the room and I keep my barrow in the yard under a tarp.

"Okay, poppet?" she asks as I pass.

On impulse I lean down and kiss her cheek. She swats me away, hiding her smile. Mrs Tsang's tiny but I've seen her bottle a man in the face for threatening her. The jagged glass tore his lips and nose.

The factories are out and everyone's heading home. Workers pile into the terraces. Some sun themselves on doorsteps. A tethered parrot squawks at me from its perch outside a door, talking of flights in warmer climes. Kids play football on the street.

I head to Otterspool Prom where I stand and consider, looking out at the river. Herring gulls scream at me for my foolishness. Gabriel lies down and covers his face with his paws.

I drop Kate's vial and stand on it. Then I kick every single fragment into the water and don't leave until the Mersey's taken it all away.

I pause outside Makin's office.

"I'd advise caution with his sort, sir." A stranger's voice.

"What's *his sort* then?" That's Makin.

"Loners, in my experience, are freaks or agitators."

"Tom's neither."

Behind me, someone clears his throat. I turn to find myself on the sharp end of a pointed look from Makin's secretary. No doubt he'll tell later.

"I told you to knock and go in." He opens the door.

"Ah, Tom, this is Mr Jessop."

Jessop's the most handsome man I've ever seen, with good teeth and all his hair. He's no gentleman. He has the swagger of the law, not a regular policeman but a special.

"Tom, we were just talking about you." He sounds like a Scouser now, a rough edge to his voice that was missing before. He must talk it up or down, depending on the company. "Can I see the log book that Mr Makin gave you?"

I look at Makin who nods. Mr Jessop flicks through it, checking against the ledger where a clerk copies the details.

"Is this address correct?"

It's Kate's.

"Yes." I shrug. "I filled it in at the time."

"Anyone else live there?"

"Her sister and daughter."

"And you broke one of the samplers that day?"

"Yes. An empty one. I'm a clumsy oaf." I try and sound like I'm still berating myself. "I dropped it and stepped on it. I reported it straight away, didn't I, Mr Makin? I offered to pay for it."

"No one's accusing you of anything, Tom."

"Do you know where Kate Harper is now?" Jessop doesn't let up.

"Isn't she there?"

I know she isn't. I knocked at her door and an old man answered. *Bugger off. I've no idea where they went.*

"No, but you know that already because you went back." Jessop smiles, the triumphant conniver. "You do know that she's Richard Harper's widow, don't you?"

"Yes, but what's that got to do with me?"

Jessop's hands are spotless. He must scrub them nightly to get out suspects' blood. Specials with manicured hands don't come in search of factory girls without reason.

Makin sits back, waiting. Of course. They're terrified of Harper. That his wife will be a rallying cry.

"I didn't know who she was until she gave the sample."

"And why would she do that?"

"She needed money."

"So she's not being looked after by her Trotsky pals?" Jessop won't let it go.

"I don't think so." I try and catch Makin's eye.

"Why did you go back?"

Makin's holding his breath, waiting.

"The thing is"—I shift about, embarrassed by the truth—"they were pretty and I wanted to see them again."

"There's no shame in that." Makin seems relieved. Thank God that good men like him can rise in this world that favours politicians who use smiles, wiles and outright lies.

I feel bad about lying to him.

"We need to speak to her," Jessop says.

"But I don't know where she is."

"But you'll tell us if you do find her?" His smile makes me want to bolt for the door. "You've never had a job, have you?"

"I work."

My dad would say, *We're free. Never subject to the tyranny of the clock. The dull terrors of the production line. No one will use us as they please.*

"Bone grubbing. Piss-poor way to make a living."

"Enough." Makin tuts.

"So sorry." Jessop's oily and insincere. "If you do find her, be a good lad and run up here and tell Mr Makin."

I want to say, *Shove your apology*, but keep my gob shut.

☉

The bastards follow me about all day. Jessop and his pals, got up like dockers. I pretend I've not seen them but they stand out. They're too clean to look real.

I look for Kate and Sally in the hiring lines, strolling past with my barrow as if on my way elsewhere. I wouldn't give her away. I just want to see her face. I ask the washerwomen at the water pumps and the old men standing around the fires at night.

Kate, Sally, Lolly. There's not a whiff of them.

I go up to the destitute courts of the Dingle, each court comprised of six houses set up around a central yard. The noxious stench from the shared privy is of liquid filth. I look through open doors: blooming damp patches on the plaster, crumbled in places to bare brick. I see faces made hard by deprivation. Infants squalling from drawers because they're hungry. It was a miracle that Makin clawed his way out of here.

"You."

A priest accosts me. He's on his rounds, demanding pennies from the poor to give to the even poorer.

"Come here."

Closer and he's unshaven and smells. He's ale addled. I feel for him, driven to despair and drink by the gargantuan task of saving so many lost souls. He follows me out of the court, onto the street.

"I've heard about you, Thomas Coster."

I tie Gabriel to the cart in case he goes for the man and wait for the rage of the righteous. I don't feel so well-disposed towards him now.

"You're in league with evil." He shoves his face into mine. Gabriel goes crazy. We're drawing quite an audience. "The Peels keep people in tanks like fish, cutting off the bits they want."

I'm panting from pushing the cart uphill and trying to outpace him. Jessop's up ahead, leaning against a wall.

"A man should be buried whole in consecrated ground."

The priest's enraged when the crowd laughs. Burial's expensive. The poor are cremated on pyres.

"You'll be damned. You'll suffer all hell's torments. You'll be flayed. The devil will sup on your gizzards and crack the marrow from your bones."

Jessop laughs under his breath as I pass.

☉

It's a rare day that a Peel comes to town.

The Peel factories have closed an hour early to mark the day. Men loiter on Hope Street, outside the Philharmonic pub. Rowdy clerks from the insurance offices and banks are out, seeking white-collar mayhem. One turns quickly and shoulder barges me as I pass. He's keen to prove he can push more than a pen. His friends laugh.

His mates all line up across the pavement to block my path. I step into the gutter. One of them steps down to join me. He's wearing ridiculous checked trousers and his hands are in his pockets. I wonder what's in there.

"You walked into my friend. You should apologise."

I open my mouth but someone's standing at my shoulder. It's Jessop.

"I think you're mistaken," Jessop says as he opens his jacket. Whatever's glinting within is enough to put this bunch off.

I glance around. Jessop's travelling in numbers, all of them in black suits.

"I'm sorry, sir."

Oh, to wield so much power that you don't have to exert it.

Jessop picks up his pace, looking back to give me a final grin. I follow in their wake, pushing through to the barrier. There's a big crowd. Lord Peel's here to give a special address to his foremen. They must be in need of bucking up if he's got to come down here to talk to them himself.

The doors of the assembly rooms open and a pair of specials come out, eyes scanning the crowd. The foremen follow, dressed in their Sunday best. They look uncertain as they emerge, blinking in the afternoon sunlight. Makin and his secretary follow. Makin looks stiff and starched. I'm used to seeing him with his shirtsleeves rolled up, fingers inky from his calculations.

Then Lord Peel steps out, the brim of his hat angled to shade his face. I realise there's silence. Not even the sound of shuffling feet.

Some lackey shoves a child forward and she holds up a bunch of pink roses. Peel turns his face as he takes them. He's a shocker close up. His nose and eyes are leonine. Thin lipped. Skin stretched to a sickening smoothness that rivals the silk of his cravat. His blue eyes are faded by age.

Then it begins. A low baritone from deep within the crowd.

The sea takes me from my love…

Another voice joins in, then another, then more so there's a choir.

The sea takes me from my love
It drops me on the ocean floor
The sea tempts me from my true love's arms
And I'll go home no more.

Peel smiles, thinking this impromptu serenade's for him. He doesn't know that each ship has its own shanties and ballads and this one's famed as *The Triumph's*.

Makin leans over and whispers in Peel's ear and his smile fades. There's another chorus and it sounds like the whole of Liverpool is singing.

The sea takes me from my love
It drops me on the ocean floor
The sea tempts me from my mother's knee
And I'll go home no more.

There are no jeers or shouts. Just the people's indignity dignified in song. The police don't know how to respond. They form a ring around Peel and his retinue. The foremen are outside this protective circle. Someone motions for Peel's carriage.

The air's filled with fluttering white sheets. They're being thrown down onto the street from the roof of the infirmary. Hands reach for them. Makin plucks at a sheet, reads it and crumples it in his fist. Peel's caught one too. He's angry. He turns to Makin and jabs at his chest with a gloved forefinger as if he's personally responsible.

I pick up one. It's *The Echo*, a dissident rag, printed on cheap, low-grade paper, the ink already smudging. It advocates minimum wages, safety measures and free health care. This edition's different. It bears the words *Lord Peel's Triumph*, with a drawing of Richard Harper floating on his anchor. It's the anniversary of his death. A bad day for Peel to show his face.

Once Peel's departed the police will demonstrate their displeasure for this display. Jessop's already giving orders. It's time to leave.

Peel's in the carriage as the singing continues. Makin turns as he climbs in and his gaze fixes on me, *The Echo* still clutched in my hand.

☉

It's an official match day, when the factories close for the machines to be serviced.

Football's a violent and anarchic game where passions are vented, on and off the pitch. The crowd wears the colours, red or blue. They're no longer just a dark mass of serge and twill that pour into the black factories.

Jessop and his sidekick are behind me. I try and lose them in the crush. The hoards of Everton, Toxteth, Kensington, and Dingle come together for this sliver of pleasure.

The constabulary are mounted, their horses stamping and pawing the cobbles. They'll tolerate fisticuffs amid the crowd to vent rising tensions. A good-natured kicking or black eye, as long as everyone's fit for work the following day no harm's done.

The coppers know if they weigh in the crowd will turn on them, but I can see in their eyes how they'd love to beat about with batons and hand out indiscriminate thrashings in the guise of peacekeeping.

I see my chance. A chanting group comes up the street towards Anfield's football pitch, waving Evertonian flags. Red banners are at my back. The two groups meet, posturing and jostling. I dart down an alley, ducking to avoid the lines of washing. Jessop's lost.

There's one place I've not looked for them. The dirty terraces where parlours of women wait for the game to end. It makes me shudder.

I peer into windows and am shocked by what's on show. It's just another factory, churning up girls, making fodder of their flesh. I go around the back. Women line the wall, waiting to be hired. My heart stops when I see her. I push past the other girls who try to lure me in with promises that make me blush.

"Where's Kate?"

"You." Sally looks tired and bored. "Are you paying?"

Hard and heartless. I rifle in my pocket, glancing up and down the street. "Here."

"It's double that." She scowls.

I give her more. We have to get indoors.

She leads me to a house. A room's free at the top of the stairs. It's painted an oppressive red that would look fashionable somewhere grand. The window's dirty. There's a bed with a sheet and pillow on it. A pitcher and bowl on the dresser. A headboard rattles on the other side of the wall.

"What are you doing, Sally?"

"Earning a living."

"Here?"

"I can't get work."

"And Kate?"

"Dead."

The mattress sinks even farther as I sit beside her. She moves away.

"When?" Then, "How?"

"A week ago. We moved in with a family in Croxteth. The woman was sick that day so Kate went to work in her place. She got her sleeve caught in a roller. It took her arm. They were too slow tying the stump off. She bled to death."

Sally's matter-of-fact. Her lip doesn't quiver. Her eyes are dry.

"I'm sorry." Words clog my throat. "Where's Lolly?"

"At home, where else?" She's glad of an excuse to be angry. "What sort do you think I am, to bring a child here?"

"The best sort." I try and soothe her.

Kate's dead. I wish I'd gone back to their terrace sooner but posthumous offers of help mean nothing to the dead.

"I'm the best sort, am I? Is that why you think you can buy me with a few coins? You men are all loathsome."

I'm angry too. I want to shut her up. I grip her head and cover her mouth with mine. She pulls away.

"Don't kiss me with your eyes shut and pretend I'm Kate. Fuck me for my own sake."

I don't relent. I'm too busy kissing Sally to correct her. The tension in her is like a wire.

We lie down. She's thin, a skeleton wrapped in skin. I'm not much better, but I take the weight of my large frame on my knees and elbows.

"This doesn't mean anything. Understand?"

She's wrong. It means everything.

"You're crying," she says.

"So are you."

She undoes my trousers and puts her hand between my legs. No one's ever touched me there before.

"Oh," she says. Then louder, "Oh."

I feel the wire snap, and her whole body relaxes. She kisses me, finally yielding. My whole life's been leading to this moment of sex and solace.

I want to say, *Thank you, thank you, thank you,* but I'm too breathless to speak.

⊙

Sally's head is on my chest. Sleep slows her breathing. My trousers are around my thighs, my shirt's undone. Her petticoat's rucked up around her waist. I don't move for fear of disturbing this lovely girl. The sudden roar from Anfield carries over the rooftops and into the room. It masks the quiet click of the door opening and closing.

Jessop stands at the end of the bed, chuckling. I leap up, struggling with my trousers.

"So Tom," he says, sarcastic. "Who's your pretty friend?"

I do up my fly. Sally retrieves her blouse from the floor and pulls it over her head. Jessop's sly look scares me. He takes off his jacket.

"We've all afternoon. Why don't you both lie down again?"

I go at him like a cornered dog. Dad used to say, *Fight if you're cornered.* I stick him in the throat with my pocket knife. Bubbles of blood mark the wound. I put my hand over his mouth to stop him crying out. He grips my wrist and twists. Sally's fishing about under the bed and I wonder what the hell she's doing, then I see the docker's hook. It's the weapon of choice in Liverpool. The handle sits snug in the palm, the hook protruding between the first and second fingers. She comes around behind him and plants it in his skull.

Jessop pitches into my arms. I lower him to the floor.

"Hold his legs."

I grab them to stop his boot heels from hammering on the floor.

48

Sally helps. How he clings to life. It seems like forever before he's still.

"Are you okay, Sal?" A woman's voice.

"Fine."

"Sure?"

Sally gets up. I wipe the blood spray from her face. She goes to the door and opens it a crack. She whispers something and the woman laughs. Then Sally locks the door.

"Who was he?"

"A special."

"Jesus. We'll both swing."

She's right. We'll go straight from the law courts to the noose in Victoria Square. But before that there'll be long days and nights in a cell with Jessop's friends queued outside.

I'd rather die.

"What did he want with you?"

"He was looking for Kate. They think she can lead them to trade unionists."

"That's crazy."

"Sally, we've not got much time. I'll deal with this. You need to go."

"No. We stay together."

"Get Lolly. Wait at The Baltic Fleet. Don't speak to anyone but Mrs Tsang. Tell her I sent you. You can trust her." It kills me to say this. I want to be a coward and say, *Yes, stay. Never leave my side.*

She kisses me. Why did I ever think her hard?

"I'm sorry that I got you involved with this." I usher her out. "Go on now, quickly." Once she's gone, I splash cold water on my face and button up my jacket to hide my bloodied shirt.

All the while I'm thinking of Sally. Of how my parting words were *I'm sorry that I got you involved with this,* when what I meant was *I'm sorry that you think I love Kate more.*

⊙

I roll Jessop under the bed and pull the rug over the stained floorboards. I'm thankful for the room's violent colour as it hides the blood sprayed across the walls.

The specials must be going house to house. I'm on the stairs when I hear outraged shouts from the room below. A pair of them come up the narrow stairs. I grapple with the first one and he knocks me down. The other tries to hold my thrashing legs. Like Jessop, I struggle against the inevitable.

A third clambers over us, pretty tangle that we are, and checks the rooms. There's a pause, then a hoarse shout. Jessop's been found.

"Take the bastard outside."

They've cleared the street. Faces peer from the window. Someone kicks my legs from under me. I land on my knees.

"Mike, remember what Makin said." The man holding my arm is young and nervous.

Mike, who's looking down on me, pauses, but then he decides I'm worth it. He kicks me in the chest. I feel the wind go out of me.

"Bugger Makin. He killed Jessop."

I curl up on the floor, hands over my head. My view's of the boots as they pile in. It doesn't matter. I've had a kicking before.

○

I'm in Makin's office. The clock sounds muffled and voices are distant. The hearing in my left ear's gone. The vision in my right eye's reduced to a slit. Breathing hurts.

Makin's furious.

"Get out."

"Sir, the man's a murderer," Mike whines.

"I gave specific orders. Tom wasn't to be harmed under any circumstances. You were to bring him straight to me if anything happened."

"Sir, Jessop…"

"Are you still here? Go before I have you posted to Seaforth."

Mike flees at the threat of Merseyside's hinterlands. Makin fetches a pair of glasses and a decanter. He pours out the port. It looks like molten rubies.

"Drink this. It'll steady you. I've called for a doctor."

I drain the glass, not tasting the contents. His sits, untouched.

"You're in serious trouble, Tom. I want to help you." The chair's legs scrape the floor as he pulls it closer and sits down. "Did you kill him?"

I nod. Then I start to cry.

"It happened so fast. He burst in. I was with a girl." I'm babbling. A stream of snot, tears and despair. "I'm not a trade unionist."

"Who was the girl?"

"Not Kate Harper, if that's what you're thinking. Jessop didn't do his job very well. She's dead. He should've checked the register."

"He did. The body didn't match the sample you gave me for her." Makin tips his head. "You have to trust me. Is Kate really dead or were you with her?"

"No. All I know is that she's dead."

"Who did the sample belong to? Was it the woman you were with?"

"Does it matter?"

He looks down at his hands. Ink stains his fingers. "More than you think."

He tops up my glass.

"Let's suppose Lord Peel's keen to find this woman, whoever it is. Let's say Lady Peel needs medical attention that requires a little blood or perhaps a bit of skin. It would be a wealth for this woman and a reward to whoever helps me find her." He lets this sink in. "Suppose Jessop got himself into a spot of bother with some girl. He played rough from what I've heard. There's no proof. The girl's long gone. An unsolved case."

My nose starts to bleed. Makin hands me his handkerchief. Blood stains the fine linen.

"You could do that?"

"I'll do what's necessary." Makin, not afraid to scramble.

"I want somewhere away from Liverpool. Out in the country. A farm with cows and chickens where nobody can bother me," I blurt out. "And I want to take a woman and child with me."

"That's a lot, just for information."

"It's more than that. Peel will be pleased. It'll make up for that day when he made his speech. But promise me first, that we have a deal."

Makin looks at me with narrowed eyes.

"A deal then, as long as you deliver her."

We shake hands.

"The sample's mine."

"That's not funny."

"I'm not joking."

He stares at me.

"Test me again and you'll see." I'm an odd-looking woman, but I make a passable man. I'm too big, too ungainly, too flat chested and broad shouldered. My hips narrow and features coarse. "I'm not trying to make a fool of you. I live this way."

"Why?"

"Sarah, my mother, got me when she was cornered on the factory floor by men who resented a woman who could work a metal press better than them. She swore she'd never go back. She became Saul after I was born."

Rag and bone men. We're free, Tom. Never subject to the tyranny of the clock. The dull terrors of the production lines. No man will use us as he pleases.

"What's your real name?"

"Tom." It's the only name I've ever had. "Do we still have a deal?"

"Yes. The girl you were with when you killed Jessop. Is she the one you want to take with you?"

His face is smooth now, hiding disgust or disappointment.

"Yes."

"I'll need to know who she is and where to find her if I'm going to get her out of Liverpool."

I tell him. When I say Sally's name he takes a deep breath but doesn't ask anything else.

I want to ask, *What do the Peels want from me?* But then I decide it's better not to know.

⊙

I've never been on a boat. I've never seen Liverpool from the sea. My stinking, teeming city's beautiful. I've never loved her more than I do now. I love the monumental Liver birds, even though they're indifferent to the suffering below. The colonnades and warehouses. Cathedrals and crack houses. The pubs and street lamps glowing in the fog. Workers, washerwomen, beggars, priests and princes. Rag and bone men. Liverpool is multitudes.

The boat's pitch and roll makes me sick. A guard follows me to the rail. He's not concerned about my health. He's scared I'll jump. I get a whiff of the Irish Sea proper. Land's a strip in the distance.

We don't moor at Southport but somewhere nearby. I'm marched down the rattling gangplank and onto a narrow jetty. Miles of dunes roll out before us. It's clean and empty. I've never known such quiet. There's only wind and shifting sands. I wonder if it's hell or paradise.

The dunes become long grass and then packed brown earth. I've never seen so many trees. Their fallen leaves are needles underfoot, faded from rich green to brown.

There's a hatch buried in the ground. One of my guards opens it and clambers down, waiting at the bottom.

"You next."

The corridor leads downwards. Our boots shed sand and needles on the tiles. There's the acrid smell of antiseptic.

"In here." One of them touches my arm.

The other's busy talking to someone I can't see because of the angle of an adjoining door. I catch the words, "Makin sent her this way. She'll need time to heal."

"Take your clothes off and put them in the bin. Turn this and water will come out here. Get clean under it." My guard's talking to me like I'm a child. "Soap's here. Towel's there. Put on this gown after."

I'm mortified, thinking they're going to watch, but they're keen to be away. I drop my clothes into the bin. I can still smell Sally on me but she doesn't stand a chance against the stream of hot water and rich suds.

A woman's leaning against the far wall, watching. I pull the towel about me and try to get dry. She looks like a china doll, with high, round cheeks and blue eyes. Her long yellow hair swings as she walks.

"Sit there."

She tuts as she touches my cheek where the skin's split. Then she checks my eyes and teeth. A needle punctures my vein. Blood works its way along a tube into a bottle. She takes scrapings from the inside of my mouth.

"Disrobe."

I stand up and let the towel drop to a puddle at my feet. I stare ahead of me. She walks around me like a carter considering a new horse. Her hand floats across the plane of my back, around the garland of yellow and purple bruises that run from back to front. She touches my breasts, my stomach, my thighs. From the steadfast way she avoids my gaze, I know there's more chance that the Liver birds will fly than of me leaving here.

I try and stay calm. I was dead from the moment Jessop opened the door of the red room. From the moment I put the sampler to my arm. It's either this or a jig at the end of a rope. There's no point in me going cold into the warm ground to rot when I can help Sally and Lolly. I hope they'll remember to take Gabriel with them.

Ink-fingered Makin, the artful scrambler, making his calculations. The possibility I've got him wrong is a cold, greasy knife in my belly. If I have, I've served up Sally, Lolly and Mrs Tsang into the constabulary's hands.

The woman seems satisfied. I want to say, *Look at me. Look me in the eye. I'm a person, not a piece of meat,* but then I realise I just might as well be. A piece of meat. Rag and bone.

THE ANATOMIST'S MNEMONIC

Samuel Wilson's life wasn't a search for love at every turn. There'd been girls he'd liked, with whom he'd managed fragile love affairs, but something was always lacking no matter how hard he tried. Something that failed to ignite.

Sam knew what it was. He knew that love and objectification weren't the same but he had a passion for hands. His arousal in every organ, the mind, the skin, the parts he'd once been told were made for sin, depended on the wrists, the palms, the fingertips.

Why don't we ask Sam to the party? I've invited Judith. We should introduce them.

Women were keen to intervene on his behalf.

Your Mother wants you to bring your friend, Sam, to Sunday lunch. She says he looks like he needs feeding up. Yes, your sister's also coming.

Colleagues, friends, friends' girlfriends, wives and mothers were all eager to help him along on a romantic quest.

What's Sam like? No, I don't fancy him. I only have eyes for you. I'm just curious. He's such a nice, unassuming guy. I don't get why he's single.

They were taken with his unconscious charm. He was a millpond of a man. They wanted to see what sort of woman would make him ripple. None guessed the secret so incongruous with the rest of him. The thing he'd denied himself.

Sam couldn't tell them for fear they'd make a tawdry fetish of the fundamentals of his happiness.

He couldn't tell them about the hands.

⊙

Sam, aged nineteen, had seen a fortune teller. There was a painted caravan on the outskirts of a funfair. He was close enough to childhood to find the fair childish, not old enough to enjoy its novelty with a pang of nostalgia. He wasn't having fun. His friends were raucous. Boorish. The whirling neon and cheap hotdogs made him feel sick. The quiet caravan seemed like a retreat. He was at the age and stage where he had queries about his life. Later the classmates he'd arrived with questioned his disappearance but he deflected them with vagaries and shrugs.

It was a formulative experience. The palm reader, twenty years his senior, took him in with a glance that measured his vitality. His every possibility. His diffidence hid his differences from his peers. The ardour and sensitivity overlooked by girls his own age.

Imogen (the palmist's real name) didn't go in for hoop earrings or headscarves. Her uniform was black and flattering, fit for funerals and seductions. Although her youth was behind her, Imogen was still young enough to want to feel it.

They sat on opposite sides of the table. Imogen was fleshy where expected of an older woman but with slender limbs. She used her hands and wrists to express everything.

Sam felt an unexpected thrill, the exact location of which was uncertain, when she leant across the table and seized his waiting hands in hers. He liked how she took charge despite her diminutive size. The way she examined him for clues. She dropped his left hand, having exhausted its information. It lay between them on the table, aching to be held again. Sam watched her pink tongue dart out between plum painted lips to wet the tip for her forefinger. She traced a damp circle around his palm, her face close so that she could peer into his future. Close enough to feel her breath on his skin. Close enough to see a single silver strand in the darkness of her parting.

She announced his hands were the instruments of fate and their message was explicit.

"Your heart line's unusual. It springs from Saturn. It's a chain pattern. Unforked. You're a sensual man. You'll have unique needs. Your line of affection shows a strong attachment, the sort that only happens once in a lifetime. You'll find true love because of her hands."

Most initiations involve fumbling and misunderstandings but this wasn't Imogen's first time with a first timer. As they lay together in the half light of her caravan, Imogen explained her trade to Sam using their own hands as primers.

"Life," she explained, "is laid out in lines: life, heart and head. The lines of destiny, affection and the sun." She traced each one out, stimulated every nerve.

"The whole universe is right here." She kissed his palms, his mounts of Venus, Mars, Mercury and the moon.

The next lesson was in the significance of fingers, after which she sucked each one in turn. She praised the nails that pinned down his nature, well formed, crescents rising at the base.

Sam didn't care about his own hands. They were whole and functional, fit for purpose. He was more concerned with hers. Imogen had the hands of Aphrodite. Her wrists were fine. Refined. He could encircle them with ease. Her hands touched him everywhere. They moved him. Not love but distilled desire. Eroticism crystallised.

Nineteen. A late age for imprinting but it was testament to Imogen's hands. The image of them roaming over him. She couldn't foresee the Pavlovian associations that would occur.

Whoever Sam loved would need hands as beautiful as hers.

⊙

Samuel had met with other hand worshippers. They were the reason for his reticence. He was puzzled by their games. The act of washing up became burlesque as hands were engulfed in suds. A game of *Rock, Paper, Scissors* was frank porn. They didn't care about hands the way he did. Hands were mystical, magical, not to be leered at as they went about their daily chores. Hands were delicate and complex. The ultimate Darwinian organ. The sign of a higher being. Opposable thumb above paw and claw. Why shouldn't they be the localisation of desire?

Sam decided, at thirty-two, he couldn't ignore his needs anymore. He copied the number he'd found onto a pad. It sat by the phone for weeks before he called.

"Hello."

"I'm sorry." He winced at this inauspicious beginning, unsure why he'd apologised. "Are you Beth Hurt? I found your website."

"I am." She sounded younger than he'd expected. He tried to imagine her face. Her hands.

"My name's Sam Wilson. I wonder if you can help me." He stalled. In the silence that followed he was afraid she'd hang up.

"Let me tell you a bit about what I do. I'm a medical illustrator. I have an anatomy degree as well as fine arts training. I do medical textbooks, teaching aids, exhibition posters and company brochures." He was thankful that Beth Hurt was gracious, trying to put him at ease.

"I need a drawing."

"What of?"

"A pair of hands. I work in advertising." This part was true. "I'm applying for a job with a rival agency so I can't go to my art department."

The last part was a lie. It was for a very different advert. A more personal one.

M, 32, single, solvent, sincere, seeks F to share music, books, food, film and the other fine things in life. Beautiful hands essential.

All he needed was an illustration.

"Tell me a bit more about what you want."

Sam discussed hand anthropometry. He specified dimensions. Palm to wrist ratio. Finger length. Shape of the nails. The glorious proportions of the flawless hand. "Most of all, they must be beautiful."

"All hands are beautiful," she mused. "They all tell a story."

Sam didn't know how to disabuse Beth Hurt of this. The subtleties of the mind, the sense of humour, the face and body were subjective. He had a non-judgemental approach to those and found their variations spectacular. Hands were different. Hands were absolutes.

"Beautiful to me then."

☉

Sam normally coped with the monotony of motorways by seizing on their differences. The ballet of the cars. The flowers that flourished on the verges. The flash of the central barrier. Graffiti that decorated the bridges overhead. Who blew, who sucked and other such stuff.

He didn't need to scrutinise the minutiae of the journey now. He had other things on his mind.

He turned off at Beth's junction onto a series of dual carriageways and roundabouts. Then a town. Trees. A school. A row of shops. People queued at a bus stop. Life went on around him unencumbered while he was overcome with hope.

Sam couldn't tell if Beth's street was on its way up or down. A handsome Georgian terrace past its prime. It exhibited signs of aspiration and neglect. Some of the basement flats paraded rows of geranium in pots while others had old sheets hung at the windows and peeling door paint.

He found the right house and examined the bells by the door. Beside Beth's was a brass plaque that bore her name and nothing else.

The voice that answered via the intercom wasn't hers. It was more melodic, lower in its range.

"Come up. Second floor. I'll leave the door open. Beth's on the phone."

The communal hall's flower prints and beige carpet gave no clue as to what waited upstairs. He took the stairs two at a time.

The door was ajar. Beth Hurt's hall was painted matte charcoal. A set of daguerreotypes hung upon one wall, formal portraits that were trapped beneath a silver skin. He liked these antique pictures from the past. Their eyes were alive in a way that eluded modern printing techniques. There were shelves loaded with curios. A set of opera glasses and a peacock fan. Metal syringes shining in their case. A porcelain phrenology head. A nautilus shell.

A navy surgeon's brass bound chest lay open against one wall. Sam read the label by each viscous instrument, designed for hasty amputations. The line drawing in the lid was a pictorial guide to removing a limb. There were clamp-like contraptions, a pair of petit tourniquets, to stem blood loss. An amputation knife, its curved blade designed to sweep around the limb's flesh and cut right down to bone. The zigzag teeth of the tendon and D-shaped saws looked like something from a joiner's bag.

A door at the end of the corridor opened. It was Beth Hurt.

"Sorry to keep you waiting, come through. Did Kate offer you a drink?"

"No, but don't worry. I'm Sam."

He held out a hand. She took it. Firm grip. Warm, soft skin. Her hair was short enough to allow its rightful curl around her face. It was a shade between brown and red.

"It's nice to finally meet you."

Sam felt a tug of something akin to recognition. He suppressed the urge to giggle. He knew from the wide spread of her smile that she did too. There was a softening around her eyes that drew him in.

"You've come a long way. Let me get you a drink. What would you like?"

"Go on then. A coffee would be great."

Beth opened the door and called out.

"Kate, kettle's on. Do you want one?"

"Love one," came the distant reply.

Kate. Friend, lover or just flatmate? It occurred to Sam that Beth had grown suspicious. Did she regret inviting him here instead of somewhere neutral? Had she rung around until she found a chaperone?

Sam waited in Beth's professional space, free to look around. It was a patchwork of diagrams and charts. Line drawings and sketches. Plastic models. Some of the words and pictures made him blush. A painting of a dissected heart hung over her desk. Bloodied meat and gaping valves. A fist of an organ, much misunderstood and mythologized. It was just a pump after all.

Sam was examining a set of photos of a dissected brain when Beth retuned carrying a tray. He caught the top note of her scent as she handed him a mug. A citrus smell that energised him. His eyes dropped to her hands.

They were too square, too fleshy to reveal a pleasing amount of the sinews beneath. Bitten nails. Ink stained flesh. Palms seamed and furrowed. Creases like bracelets at her wrists.

"Would you be more comfortable in another room?"

He took a final look at the brain photographs and grinned.

"No, it's only the sight of my own blood that makes me faint but if I feel funny I'll let you know."

"Do you think it's ghoulish?"

Sam sipped his coffee as he looked at a watercolour of a dissected leg.

"No. Your work's stunning."

"Would you believe that I wanted to be a children's illustrator? I used to make up stories and draw pictures to go with them for my sister after our mum died."

It was such a personal disclosure that made him embarrassed that he'd lied to her about his reasons for the commission. Her unguardedness disarmed him. She'd let him into her home. He felt he could tell her anything now that he was here.

"So what happened?"

"I took a job with a medical publisher because I was strapped for cash. The editor had loved my work on a book he read to his daughter at bedtime. He said it was just the right look."

"What sort of kid's book was that?"

They both laughed.

"Once I finished the job I knew I didn't want to do anything else. Isn't it strange how you know that you like something, right away?" She laid out the final drawing before him. "Is this what you had in mind?"

"It's brilliant." He meant it. One hand was partially folded against the other. They were elegant and tapered. Beth had made technical perfection seem informal. "You have real talent."

"Oh no, it's just about knowing the anatomy. It changes the structure of the work. May I?"

The way she took his hands made him dizzy.

"The finger bones are called the phalanges. Three to each finger. Two in the thumb."

She touched each one in his little finger and his thumb by way of demonstration. Sam felt the start of gnawing elation.

"Fascinating." He'd been preoccupied with aesthetics, not construction or mechanics, but her words thrilled him.

"And these are the metacarpal bones," Sam swallowed when she ran her finger across his palm. "At one end they form the knuckles and at the other they articulate with the wrist bones, which are my favourites."

"Why?" He relished her pleasure.

"They're interesting. Each one has a different shape and name but they fit together like a jigsaw."

She made him arch his thumb to reveal two taut lines along his wrist.

"This gap is called the anatomical snuffbox," she pointed to the space between the pair of tendons. "The bone which forms the floor is the scaphoid."

"Scaphoid," he repeated.

"The rest of the wrist bones are the lunate, triquetral, pisiform, trapezium, trapezoid, capitate and hamate." She worked her way over the wrist to show him where each bone was. "I like the hamate. It has a hook."

He felt like he was party to the arcane.

"How do you remember all that?" Sam wanted her to know he was impressed.

"Hard work. And mnemonics. Lots of mnemonics."

"The only mnemonic I know is 'Richard of York gave battle in vain' for the rainbow."

A spot of colour had appeared high on Beth's cheeks. It conjured up Beth Hurt in bed, post-coital, flushed and loose limbed. Intuition told him the reason for her flush.

"What's the mnemonic?"

"What?"

"For the wrist."

"Scared lovers try positions that they can't handle." Beth tried to sound unabashed.

The physiology of their attraction couldn't be faked. The symptoms of their chemistry. They were close. Sam's pupils dilated. It was hard to breathe. His heart no longer functioned as just a pump. His blood was hot. His throat was dry. Beth was a loadstone and he'd been magnetised. Their heads were tilted in sympathy. Lips parted in empathy.

He couldn't. Beth's hands were lacking.

"The picture," he moved away, "it's perfect."

"I hope you find what you want."

"Pardon?"

"Get what you want. The job." She sounded magnanimous in

rejection. Courageous. "I wish you the best of luck."

"I'll treasure this, no matter what. Not because of its anatomy but because you've pictured exactly what I described."

"I've a confession. It was easier than you think."

"What do you mean?"

"I had a model."

"A model?"

He'd imagined such hands could only be imagined.

"Yes, Kate, my sister. Do you want to meet her?"

☉

Sam could see the shades of sisterhood on their faces. Kate was at ease amid the depictions of flayed flesh and dismembered limbs. She was an elongated, elegant version of her sibling. Undeniably the better looking of the two, but with paler hair and skin. A less vivid version of Beth.

"I thought introductions were in order. Sam, Kate. Kate, Sam."

"Hi."

"Nice to meet you."

Sam searched her smile, this Madonna of the Hands, but all that it revealed was her teeth.

"Sam loves the picture. I thought you two should meet."

Kate's hands were partially covered by the cuffs of her jumper. The fine rib clung to her wrists. Her tapered fingers ended in short nails, painted with a dark polish. It should have tantalised him.

Sam thrust out a hand, desperate to connect. As she took it, Sam waited for the jolt of hormones. Instead of a spark there was just a seeping disappointment as her perfect hand lay in his.

"It's a good job you liked it," Kate thrust her hands back into her pockets, "Beth's promised me a modelling fee."

The trio laughed in unison.

"I'm going to get another drink." Beth glanced at him. "Coffee all round?"

She went, closing the door behind her with a careful click.

"Beth says the drawing's for a job interview. What's it for?"

"A hand cream campaign. I'm in advertising. What do you do?"

"I've just finished my degree. I'm a dietician."

"Your place is great."

"I wish it *were* mine. I'm just staying here until I can get somewhere."

Sam nodded. Of course it was Beth's.

"Beth's a diamond. She's always looked out for me."

It was Beth that Sam was thinking of. There wasn't enough of Kate, pleasant as she was, to fill the room. Her hands, though fabulous, couldn't compensate for Beth's absence.

Hands though, they were absolutes.

☉

Sam and Beth were bare beneath the sheets. It was her turn to be taught.

"Life," Sam explained, "is laid out in lines: life, heart and head. The lines of destiny, affection and the sun." Each one was traced out. Then there was the significance of fingers. The predictions of nails.

Imogen had been exorcised.

Scaphoid, lunate, triquetral, pisiform, trapezium, trapezoid, capitate, hamate.

The words Beth had taught him lingered in his mouth. He tried to pass them back to her, tongue to tongue. She was too weak to twist away.

Desire drove Sam. He didn't stop to consider the outrageousness of his demands. The flat was upended by his passions. The kitchen had become an impromptu theatre. The surgical instruments lay on the floor. Kate had been easily overcome. She lay where she'd fallen, in Beth's studio. Beth, though he'd surprised her, put up a greater fight. Sam kissed the bruise on her face, from the blow that had finally subdued her.

It was dirty work. Sam was glad that he'd been right that it was only his own blood that made him feel faint. The cuts he'd made with the amputation knife were ragged. The petit tourniquets were sound and stemmed Beth's bleeding. He'd not used them on Kate, not from unkindness but because there wasn't time.

Cautery was a more tricky matter. He'd improvised with a knife, heated on the hob until the blade glowed. He touched it to the places on Beth's bloody stumps that leaked.

64

Sam covered his clumsy suture work with wrappings of scarves. Kate's hands cooled quickly, despite their new attachment to Beth. It was a fleeting few hours that Sam couldn't hold onto for long enough. It left him hungry.

He put his lips to the perfect palms, to Beth's mouth. Her lips were pale. She shivered as he covered her body with his.

Beth whimpered, limp in the hands of fate.

EGG

I consider my egg; its speckled pattern, its curves, strange weighting and remarkable calcium formation that's both delicate and robust.

It hurts but I'm determined. The old hag promised. I put my egg inside me.

☉

Hot water soothes my skin. It plasters my hair to my scalp and runs in rivulets down my back. I nurse the heavy feeling in my lower abdomen with my hand. Then comes a different sort of deluge. Blood trickles down my thigh. Water carries it away and down the drain.

It's expected. I've already urinated on a stick this morning and it pronounced me *without child*. Disappointment has joined agony and blood on the same day of each month.

I drop my towel into the laundry basket and dress.

There's a sparrow on the balustrade. A blighted bird, one of many breeds decimated by predators, harsh winters and pestilence. The public were outraged by the loss of blue tits and robins but sparrows are too nondescript to feature on calendars and cards.

Another joins it, then a third. The trio perform an aerobatic display, as if they don't already have my attention. A fourth, now a fifth. More and they're a flock.

I step onto the terrace but they don't flee. They stay earthbound and hop around, leading me down the steps to the lower garden. Past the tennis courts to the fresh green avenue of limes. Over the stile and across the fields to the crumbling farm buildings at the edge of my estate.

The barn. The sparrows enter through a broken panel. The rusty hinges whine and creak as I pull the door open.

The old hag lives on a bed of mouldy hay, twigs, moss, newspaper and woollen tufts. She squats rather than sits. Her irises are covered with a milky shroud. She wears layers of white, each stained and torn, like a demented virgin bride.

A sparrow lands on her upturned hand. The hag brings it to her face and peers at it with opaque eyes, listening intently, as if to a song I can't hear, before it flies up to the beams above.

We have an audience up there. Blackbirds, starlings, jays, sparrows, falcons, and a variety of owls jostle together for space, having set aside their differences.

"Who are you?"

"That's a rude greeting for a guest." The hag's voice has a peculiar melody, rising and falling in the wrong places.

"Guest implies an invitation."

"I'm here at your request. I'm sick of you asking."

"Request? I've never seen you before. I'll have you thrown off for trespassing."

"You've been hard to ignore. You're crying out with want."

"I want for nothing."

"Liar. The ache's consuming you."

"There's nothing *you* can give me."

"Not even motherhood?"

"You can't give me that."

"Can't I?" Then a sly smile crosses her face. "You've tried the usual way?"

"It didn't work."

"Perhaps you didn't try hard enough."

I have, not lacking in partners and willing potential fathers.

"I have fibroids and severe endometriosis." I sound bitter. My pelvis contains a tangled mess of lumps and adherences that renders my reproductive tract defunct. I'm still outraged by my body's betrayal. It's failed in the most basic of female functions.

"Can't the quacks help?"

"What do you think?"

My specialist had stressed that my conditions were benign but I couldn't see the benevolence in what's caused me so much pain and robbed me of a child. My own salvaged eggs, fertilised and implanted, failed to take as if they'd fallen on stony ground.

"Adoption?"

I shake my head.

The hag must be able to see with those white eyes. She counts something on her fingers and calculation done says, "I'll help you but there'll be pain."

"Childbirth?" I ask hopefully.

"Much worse. Children drag you down and break your heart."

"No," I refute her jaundiced view of parenthood, "they lift you up and give you love."

"A survival trick of the young and vulnerable," the hag talks over me. "You'll love them and it'll kill you when they don't need you anymore."

"I'm strong. I'll take that pain."

"There'll be sacrifice. Your dreams will be subject to their needs."

"I've already achieved all I wanted to and more." Except this.

"Such success for one so young but everyone looks at you as if you're unnatural. Not having children is the price you've paid for having a man's ambition."

This rankles.

"I'm every inch a woman."

"Of course you are," she tries to soothe me. "I just want you to think this through. Children demand everything, even your name. You'll be mother first and last."

"And I'll be glad of it. I'll pay whatever it takes. I have the means."

"You will, never fear. There's also the thorny issue of expectation. You must love her for who she is, not who you want her to be."

"She?" I'm already enamoured of the notion.

"A daughter."

"What will she cost me?"

"We'll negotiate later."

"I don't do business that way."

"I won't ask for anything you can't give."

A reckless trade. I consider the depth of my desire.

"How?"

The hag shifts on her nest, reaches under her and pulls something out. She offers it to me in her scrawny, reptilian hand. I take the egg. It's warm.

She leans over me.

"May I be godmother?"

"Is that part of the payment?"

"No," she sniffs, sounding hurt, "I just thought it would be nice."

"No child of mine will be baptized." I want to laugh. I'm clutching an oversized egg, having accepted help from a mad squatter, and am rejecting religion as a fiction.

"That's probably wise, all things considered. Now, this is what you must do."

○

I consider my egg; its speckled pattern, its curves, strange weighting and remarkable calcium formation that's both delicate and robust.

More conundrums are hidden within. Viscous birth fluids designed to be consumed. The yolk, rich in unfulfilled life.

It hurts but I'm determined. I put my egg inside me. Its tip nestles into my cervix. Not for nine months. That would be ridiculous. Just long enough for my trembling DNA, fearing extinction, to permeate the shell and scramble the genes within.

Once retrieved I hold it up to the light but can't see the outline of a child inside.

Egg and I embark on a course of antenatal education. I read her Machiavelli and Chomsky. I play her Debussy and Chopin. We watch French films and listen to Cantonese language tapes. Egg will be more equipped for life than I.

Then finally.

Here she comes.

The shell cracks, the tiny life thumping its way out. Fragments come away, tethered by membrane. I pick up my featherless chick, who's pink from her labours. It *is* a girl, goose-pimpled skin as if plucked. I rub her and swaddle her in a warm towel. Her ribs are exquisite curves. Her nails miniscule and pliable.

Small for her age. Little Chick.

The hag's right. She said I'd have a mammalian response. My breasts engorge and leak. Chick's mouth puckers as she tries to plunder nourishment but she can't latch on. I prepare formula milk in a flap, fearing she'll starve. It dribbles down her chin as if it would poison her to keep it in.

I sit through the night, exhausted, waiting for the flood of love, the tugs of blood that will sustain me while she cries with hunger but nothing comes.

Chick has dark, bulbous eyes. Her hands are drawn up before her like useless appendages. I cry as I hold her, this culmination of all my wishes, and I know that she's not right.

⊙

I go back to the hag.

"You lied." I'm not so astute. I've been duped.

"You wanted a child. I gave you one." She peers into the bundle of blankets in my arms as if to see if Chick is a child after all.

"What's her name?"

"Eloise."

The hag makes a noncommittal noise.

"She's not..." I struggle with the word *normal*.

"Life's a lottery," she shrugs, "you can't swap her."

"I can't bring up a child like this."

"One that requires sacrifice?"

The clouded corneas don't conceal the mockery in her eyes. I can't stand her crowing and I won't concede defeat to a mad old crone but something makes me swallow my indignation.

"Help me." I hold Chick up. "She won't feed."

The hag beckons me over with a curled talon.

⊙

There's nothing for it. I cradle Chick in one arm and dig with my free hand. My manicured nails break. Earth clogs my diamond rings.

I hate worms. Eyeless, skinless, boneless, they inch along the ground. My excavation brings one up. It writhes in protest, clamped between my thumb and forefinger.

The longer I look at it, the harder it becomes. Chick's screams have faded to a mewl. She's fatiguing without food.

I put the worm in my mouth. Then I'm sick. I find another, this time gagging as it flails against my palette. I manage to keep it in despite the spasms of my throat. I chew.

I put my mouth to Chick's and drop the masticated mess in. Her eyes brighten with excitement. She all but sings.

More. More. More please Mummy. Chick gulps it down, her mouth open straight away in readiness the next portion. She won't be tricked by anything mashed up with a fork. It must be from my lips. I search for the bugs sheltering between the stones of the garden walls, for earthworms hiding in the flower beds. I hunt by torchlight for slugs that brave the paths by night. I retch and vomit. My little gannet's insatiable.

☉

"Where was your daughter born?"

"Abroad."

The new paediatrician seems satisfied with this answer.

"How old is she now?"

"Seven."

"And she doesn't talk at all?"

"No."

"Toilet trained?"

Couldn't you have read her records before you called us in? I want to snap at him for his indelicate questions but I've resolved to be less prickly. He's here to help. Allegedly.

"No."

Chick trembles as I undress her. The doctor measures her height, weight, and head circumference and then plots her poor development on a chart as if it wasn't self-evident.

"I see that no one's been able to identify Eloise as having any particular syndrome." He flicks through her file.

"No, but don't say it too loud. I haven't told her yet."

That makes him look at me. Chick, defying diagnosis, has been reduced to a list of problems in her medical records.

Poor growth. Mental retardation. Microcephaly.

"Pop Eloise on your knee."

Chick doesn't like to be held, even by me, but faced with a stranger she tries to hide her head under my arm. The doctor runs his hands around her ribcage to the hollow depression at the centre of her chest.

"Eloise is more than pigeon chested. Come and see."

Chick's chest X-ray reveals the white lines of her ribs sheltering the shadow of her heart and the dark hollows of her lungs beneath.

"Look at this."

"At what?"

"A furuncle."

"Pardon?"

"Here." He points with his pen. "Her clavicles are fused together. They should be attached to either of her sternum."

"In English please."

"She has a wishbone. Perhaps you should make a wish."

Then he looks at Chick, who's hiding under his desk and flushes.

☉

I make up a porridge of oats, seeds, and rice milk. Chick still gorges on worms but I've coaxed her onto other things, although there's still an exhausting list of what gives her diarrhoea, tummy pain, and hives.

Chick plays around my feet. *Play* is an exaggeration. She's not interested in toys. Not alphabet bricks, not the puzzles in bright plastic that are waiting to be solved, or her menagerie of stuffed toy animals. She wanders, unoccupied, then comes to stand beside me when she needs reassurance. Her tongue clicks when she wants my attention. Click, click, click. I hear the sound in my sleep.

Chick doesn't like cuddles. Once I thought she was trying to kiss me. I leant down, eager to receive it, and got a mouthful of chewed spider instead. Her attempt at affection.

She never looks at me directly. Sometimes I want to shake her and shout, just to make her meet my gaze.

I spoon the porridge into her small mouth, set in its receding jaw. Chick's face is narrow, her eyes large, ears low and her nose beaked. People find nothing endearing there. They either look away or simply stare.

I used to think, *Eloise will never be a business woman, a scientist or pilot. She'll never paint or write. She'll never be friend, lover, wife, or mother.*

Now I think, *Eloise will never feed herself, she'll never take herself to the toilet or dress herself. She'll always be at the mercy of others. She'll always need me.*

I try and imagine this life stretching out ahead of us. I'll wring the hag's neck if I ever see her again.

I wipe Chick's face and hands, sponge porridge from her hair. She hops around once freed from her chair.

Click, click, click.

The foil strip crackles as I pop out a tablet. I swallow down my daily dose of synthetic happiness with coffee, sweetened with synthetic sugar.

Click, click, click.

Chick's vocal this morning. She bumps against my legs. Her clicks have risen to a series of chirps. She hunches her shoulders and bobs her head.

I turn away. Chick's fed, watered, her nappy clean. I've met her needs.

I wonder what it would be like if I walked out. Nannies never last longer than an afternoon. *Eloise gets too upset without you. She just sits and cries. It's not fair to her.*

I imagine myself walking down the street. The luxury of going into a café to drink coffee and read a book.

Click click click click.

Even though I've folded back the kitchen's huge glass doors there's no breeze to ease the stifling heat.

Clickclickclickclickclick.

I could be picking out a dress and deciding where to go for dinner and with whom.

Chick's clicks become a sudden high-pitched squeal. I turn to see her cowering in the corner, a cat crouched before her. Scratch marks cross Chick's face. Blood wells up where the claws scored her skin.

The cat bats at her again with its paw. This hunter must have crept in while my back was turned. I shout and it looks over its shoulder, annoyed at being interrupted. It's a big, sleek tom, all black with white whiskers.

I shout again. It turns and stands its ground, back arched, spitting and hissing, unwilling to relinquish Chick. Her eyes bulge with fear, her mouth hangs open, bloodstained drool drips from her chin.

Chick's hurt cuts through my shock. I pick up a pan and fly at the cat, hissing back. I'm almost on it, screeching and stamping, when the cat decides I'm too much to take on. Its paws scramble on the tiled floor for purchase as flees between the legs of the kitchen table and chairs.

I pick up quivering Chick. Blood stains my dress. The worst thing's the sound. Her shapeless keening.

How could you let this happen to me?

The hag was right. It hurts.

☉

At twelve Chick still has a young child's body. There are no signs of puberty and, in truth, I'm glad that I don't have to deal with her having periods as well as everything else.

She *is* changing though.

Chick's acting strangely. Social Services would have a field day if they could see her. I've delayed her hospital appointment for fear that someone might examine her and see.

She's taken to climbing onto worktops, bookcases, and tables. She leaps and lands with a heavy thud, lying on the floor looking stunned. Her bruises are a spectacular range of colours, which never fail to make me wince. I'm exhausted from the constant vigilance supervising her requires.

That's not all. She's stopped eating, just like she did as a baby, as though sickening for something. I've tried bugs and worms again but she won't take them from me. She's listless. She won't splash about in her shallow bath. She doesn't click her tongue or follow me.

I undress her for bed. She's lost more weight. I remember holding her in my hands when she was born. I resolve to take her to the doctor in the morning, regardless of her bruises.

But that's not all.

There's her skin. I slip her nightdress on, over the thick, ugly hairs on her back that are so tough that they take pruning shears to cut through them. The cotton slips down to cover the fine down on her belly.

I lock the door and lie beside her on the mattress that I've put on the floor. It's the safest way, in case she gets up at night. There's nothing left in here for her to climb.

I'm woken intermittently by Chick who spends her sleep in motion. Her arms twitch and she wakes with a jerk as if falling, followed by a dialogue of clicks as if she's telling me her dreams.

The grey light of morning comes in. There's a sound at the window, like a pebble being thrown by some lothario below. I once had a lover who did such things, imagining himself romantic. Oh, the memory of sex. Chick used to get too upset if someone spent the night, or even an hour, while she slept. Afterwards she'd shy away from me as if I was tainted by a scent that ablutions couldn't remove.

The noise comes again, a series of short, sharp raps. A pecking on the glass that chills my skin. Something wanting to be let in.

I part the curtains. A shadow flutters against the pane, its wings a blur. Not a ghost but a sparrow.

The hag's back.

I listen to Chick's ragged breathing and I want to have it out with the old bitch.

I put a coat over my pyjamas and pull on boots. I put a sweater on Chick and swaddle her in a quilt. She's a featherweight when I pick her up. Her eyelids flutter, then open and she looks through me with dead eyes before she closes them.

The barn's cold. I can see the shape my breath. The hag's nest has been reduced by time to a rotting pile that reeks. She doesn't seem concerned. It's her throne.

"I want a word with you. You cheated me."

The hag hasn't aged where I feel the weight of the last twelve years. She still wears a riot of once-white rags.

"She's unique, isn't she?" The hag clucks and coos like a proud parent. "You can't remake her in your own image. She's herself entirely. That's children for you."

Chick's awake now. Alert. She wriggles, wanting to be put down.

"Eloise," the hag calls.

"She only answers to Chick."

The hag smiles at that.

"Chick, come here."

I hate that Chick goes to her without hesitation.

"She'll do nicely."

"For what?"

"Our bargain. You don't want her. I'll take her back as payment."

"No."

"Don't tell me you've never thought of smothering her with a pillow or drowning her in the bath."

I can't deny it.

The hag's fingers roam over Chick.

"She's a fair payment. She has what my other fledglings don't. A wishbone."

"I've been wishing on it for years," I laugh. "It's useless."

The hag's quick as a whip. Chick's across her knee, squirming and crying to be set free. "Wishbone's must be broken if the wishes are to work."

Chick's cry rises as the hag presses on her collarbone.

"Stop!"

"Really? I suppose you're right. Wishing shouldn't be an impulsive thing. And it's strongest when the bone's clean. I'll boil her in a barrel. Don't look put out. I'll be a sport. You can pull one end. That's a fifty-fifty chance on the greatest wish ever made. And Chick's hands and feet will make the finest divining bones."

"No."

"No?" The hag cocks her head on one side. "You could wish for a child. One that runs to you, arms out, when you call."

"Let her go."

"Ah, I see. You want it for yourself. Snap it and you could have a whole brood to comfort you in your dotage. Who'll hold your hand on your deathbed and bear your genes into the future. Children to praise your name and make you proud."

"I said let her go. Nothing of hers will be broken."

"Really?"

"You're hurting my daughter." I climb onto the nest.

"But you don't want her." She holds Chick out of reach.

"I do. Every inch of her is mine. I've paid in pain and sacrifice."

"Then why are you here?"

"Because you made her pay too. She's suffering and you can stop it."

"I can't make Chick different."

"That doesn't matter." I wouldn't tamper with a single cell of her. "I don't know what she's sickening for. You do."

"I can't tell you what she needs." The hag's stroking Chick now. Quieting her. "Do *you* know?"

The hag's white eyes stare through me. She's waiting.

I look at Chick. Here it is, mother's intuition, twelve years too late.

"Yes, I know."

When the hag stands she's eight feet tall, most of her length is spindly legs. She looks less haggard now. She leans down and passes Chick to me, then shakes herself out. The white tatters look like ruffled feathers. There's a sudden soft gloss about her.

"Up here."

I follow the hag up the rickety steps to the hayloft. She stoops to fit. A hole in the roof reveals clouds racing overhead. The birds have gathered up here, a panoply of breeds to bear witness to the glory of this morning. I can feel every thudding heartbeat.

Here it is. The biggest sacrifice.

There's no end of hurt.

I pull off Chick's jumper and nightdress. Her nappy. Her feathers have come in overnight. I'd be restless too if I had pinions pushing through my skin. Soft plumes cover her abdomen.

Her shoulder blades peel away from her back and unfold. Her wingspan is mighty considering she's so slight. No wonder Chick's clumsy on the ground. She's designed for flight.

Click, click, click.

Chick leaps up, her feet curling like claws around my forearm. I hold her up. She's heavy, held like this.

Click, click, click.

I'm fixed by my daughter's gaze. She's ferocious. Dignified. I bow my head. She doesn't need my limited definitions. She has her own possibilities and perfections.

Clickclickclick.

I launch my precious girl. She takes flight through the hole in the roof, going where I can't follow. She tilts and tips until she catches the wind and spirals upwards, a shadow on the sky.

How high she soars.

THE SUNFLOWER SEED MAN

Man, woman and child. Father, mother, daughter. They make slow progress along the lane. The houses thin out and the road markings disappear, the hamlet dissolving into countryside. Birds sing out in liquid notes, music pouring from their throats. There's a summer stillness, this golden day fixed in the sun's amber gaze.

"Are you tired?" Pip asks Jack. "We can go back if you're tired."

"No, I'm fine."

"Let me take Emma."

Pip takes the dosing toddler from him. As she does she steels herself in case her daughter wakes but the child sleeps on.

They pass a field where a bull basks in the sunshine and the adoration of his herd. He's covered in cream curls. The woolly monolith turns his head to watch them, the brass ring glinting in his nose.

Jack leans against the fence. "Lucky sod. Not a care in the world."

Pip looks at gaunt, grey Jack, his fists clenched in sudden resentment, jealous of the innocence of beasts. The bull senses the implied threat and gets to his feet. It seems to take an age for it to mobilise its weight. Finally there, the bull stands and glares.

"You're upsetting him." Pip is at Jack's elbow, pulling him away. What she means is *Don't be upset, not today.* A day so tranquil that the clock hands have slowed to a pace that undoes time. A day when they can pretend that all is well.

They walk on, joining another road. Emma is suddenly awake. Pip is looking down at her at the moment that she opens her eyes. The child lets out a long wail. The little body arches, rigid in protest.

"Come on, pumpkin. Stop now." Jack takes Emma when she refuses to settle for Pip. "Stop being a grump just because you've woken up."

Emma's like a monkey, clinging to Jack's neck. Pip doesn't like how the child looks at her over his shoulder, smug in ownership of her father's arms.

Jack stops abruptly, putting Emma down. He kneels and points. "Look, blackberries."

They nestle amid the nettles and the webs. He gathers the purple and black berries. Emma clutches at his leg.

"My mum always said wild blackberries are best."

He dispenses maternal wisdom and fruit. Pip tries to feed one to Emma but when the girl takes a bite she wails and spits it out. Jack bites one in half to check it's not too tart and then puts it in her mouth. She chews it, her smile dimpled.

Lips and fingers become stained. When they finish feasting, Jack takes up Emma again and carries her against his chest.

"Let me take her. You must be tired."

"I'm okay, Pip."

His smothered irritation makes her wince but she knows he's flagging.

"Let's go this way."

She starts off, making him follow, knowing that the other way will be a good mile. Ahead the road dips and curves into a field of rape.

"Have you ever seen so much yellow?" The intensity stuns Pip.

The mass of rape moves to and fro, a wind driven tide.

"Look at *that* beauty." Jack points to the solitary sunflower that navigates this floral sea. "I want a whole garden full of those."

Pip promises herself that she will grant this simple wish. She can't make him well but at least she can do this small thing to make him happy.

○

Pip and Jack lie in bed together. Their alarm clock marks time with its relentless ticks and tocks, a reminder of each minute lost. The moles on Jack's back are ink stains in the almost dark. The night has bleached the patterned quilt and prints upon the wall to shades of greys.

"Are you still awake?" Jack asks.

"Yes."

"Why do you always end up on my side of the bed? It's the same as yours."

"It's not. You're there."

She puts a hand to his mouth so that she can feel his smile.

"It was a nice afternoon, wasn't it?"

"Yes." She fears a ruse.

"We all enjoyed it, didn't we?"

She doesn't answer.

"Don't mind Emma at the moment. Toddlers are funny. She loves you. She's just that she's testing boundaries. She's all over me at the moment because she knows that something's wrong. Just be patient."

"You're so much better with her than I am. I don't think she likes me very much."

Pip's glad he can't see her face. The words sound petulant and bitter.

"I know you were upset when you found out you were pregnant but I'm glad you changed your mind."

"You mean you're glad that I didn't have an abortion?"

There. She's said the word.

"Yes. We made a choice, Pip. We made a choice, together."

No, I chose to have her because if I didn't I wouldn't have you.

"Pip, it's all right to be scared. Whatever happens, you and Em will always have each other."

She kisses him to stopper up his mouth before anything else spills out. She kisses and clings as though, at any moment, he might be washed away.

☉

The estate agent led them up the garden path. Tales to tell, houses to sell, his mouth moved in a constant narrative. As he pushed open the front door, sun fell upon the parquet floor.

The house was tired but clean. It was imprinted with the previous owners' love, which was palpable even though every room was bare. The agent left them in the living room, where bouquets fell endlessly on faded wallpaper. The view through the open patio doors was of the long, narrow lawn.

"*It needs a new kitchen. We'd have to knock through into the outhouse to make a proper utility room.*"

"*There's a railway line at the bottom of the garden.*"

"*And it needs central heating.*"

"*It'll take a long time to do up.*"

A litany of imperfections. Their fingers interlaced.

"*Yes?*"

"*Yes.*"

It was nine months later, lying in bed together, that Jack found the lumps sheltering in his groin. A row of lymph nodes, hard and hostile, beneath his skin.

⊙

Pip and Emma are in the garden together. It is long and narrow with tall hedges and shrubs that the estate agent had described as mature. *He means overgrown*, Jack had whispered in Pip's ear.

A train trundles past, slowing in its approach to the station. Pip imagines Jack alighting. Taking long strides along the platform, stooped, a habit owing to his height. In her mind he's loosening his tie. There's no end to wanting him.

Emma rushes past her into the house. Pip watches her go, pulling washing from the line. The final item is one of Jack's shirts, which she's taken to wearing. She holds it to her nose but there is nothing of him there. Only fabric conditioner and fresh air. The wicker basket creaks as she carries it inside on her hip.

"What is it?" Pip is sharp, making Emma cry all the more.

All Pip feels is exasperation, not remorse. She hasn't the energy to deal with Emma's outburst but she's learnt that anger will only make it worse. She exhales her impatience and starts again.

"Emma, what's the matter?"

Pip puts a stiff arm around her daughter's shoulders and waits for the shuddering sobs to subside.

"Emma, what's wrong?"

"It died."

"What? What died?"

"Daddy's sunflower." Emma shrinks from her. "I watered it, like you said. Are you angry?"

Oh God, how would Jack deal with this?

It comes to Pip, all at once. The way he'd sit beside Emma. What he'd say and how he'd say it.

"You don't know, do you?" Pip tries to sound teasing.

"What?" Solemn Emma, unaccustomed to maternal japery.

"The sunflower's secret."

Pip pulls Emma onto her lap even though she's getting too big. She squirms. Pip's knees are bony, not soft and dimpled, not built for mother comforts.

"Even though we love someone with all our heart and we'd do anything to protect them, sometimes they get sick. Or die." The word die feels like a stone in Pip's mouth. "They can't come back which makes us sad. But the sunflower is different. It has a secret."

Emma's arms snakes around Pip's neck. Weighing Pip down. Buoying her up. She carries Emma out to the garden, over the mossy grass that springs underfoot, past the lavender full of bees and the tubs of shameless pink fuchsias, to where the sunflower stands.

It towers over them, trunk thicker than Pip's forearm. Hand span leaves that are rough against the palm. The glorious yellow halo is now withered raffia. The bin lid face is no longer turned in worship to the sun. It looks down on them instead. The surface has started to dry out, the coarse brown velvet gone to seed.

Jack grew them first, then Pip, when he was ailing, his tired body failing. *One day you'll do this for me. Bury me in the ground.*

Pip plants them even though Jack's no longer here to watch them from the window. This year only one has flourished, bursting from the soil towards the sun.

I'll give anything. Pip remembers watching Emma playing with a skipping rope on the path while she patted the soil down to around the young plants. *Take Emma instead. Just give me Jack back.*

Recalling this appals Pip.

"Emma, do you remember how we made the sunflower?"

"We put it in the garden."

"That's right," Pip answers, "what did we put in the garden?"

"A baby sunflower."

"How did we grow the baby sunflower?"

Emma shrugs and hides her face in Pippa's neck. A gesture shocking in its childishness. *But she is a child.*

"That's all right, darling." Darling was what Jack called Emma. "We put something in a pot. Do you remember? It was a seed."

"Seed!"

Emma shouts out the word in unison with her and smiles into Pip's with joyful radiance. It fills up the cavity in Pip's chest, displacing the aching emptiness.

"Look," Pip points at the sunflower's head, "lots of seeds. We'll cut it down on Saturday and let the head dry out. We'll have all the baby seeds we need, waiting to be grown. That's the secret. We're sad the sunflower's gone, but it's left us something. A reason to be happy."

◉

They are in the kitchen, eating breakfast. Pip starts to tell Emma to stop humming and keep her swinging legs still but thinks better of it. Let her sing. Let her legs swing. She watches Emma chew her cereal, her small jaw working. Her face is obscured as she clutches her beaker in both hands to drain it. Details of her daughter that she's never noticed before.

Emma gets up and carries her bowl and beaker to the sink.

"Shall we make flapjacks tonight?" Pip feels a stab of shyness.

Emma nods as though making flapjacks is a regular event, her hand slipping into Pip's. Pip gives it a grateful squeeze in return.

◉

Pip locks the front door. A train rattles past. The noise elicits its normal Pavlovian response in Pip, the triggering of the sequence of thoughts that starts with Jack's journey to work. Him at his office. Pip imagines it's him when the telephone rings. *How's work at your end, Pip?* There are cherished seconds to be had before she answers. The impossible hope that it's him. Jack, whole, not ravaged by disease or the ills of chemotherapy. This train of thought terminates with the denial of his death. The bartering of grief. *Jack, come back to me. It doesn't matter how. Just come home.*

"It's gone." Emma pulls at the corner of Pip's coat and points.

They walk over to where the sunflower should be. Earth is scattered across the lawn in an arc. There is a hole where the giant flower had once stood. It looks like an empty grave. There are no fallen leaves or petals to indicate a struggle. Nothing else has been disturbed.

They walk to school, Emma, secure in their new found friendliness, badgers Pip with questions.

"Where is it? What about the baby sunflowers? Did a robber take them?"

A man with a swag bag and evil in mind.

"I don't know, do I?" Pip is harsh. "I don't want another word about the stupid flower."

Emma's face freezes. They've reached the school gates. The affair of the missing sunflower has made them late. Emma runs in to join the mass of children. There's squealing and laughter. Cat's cradle and skipping ropes. Coloured lines on the yard, markings for games Pip has long forgotten how to play.

○

There is no festooned incident tape to mark out the scene of the crime. Pip stands and looks, trying get inside the intruder's mind. There are no clues. No footprints. No fingerprints. No ransom note in blood or simple ink. No motive for the felony. Pip goes to her bedroom window, hoping the wider view will be more revealing.

Why would anyone take it?

Pip looks along the neighbours' gardens. A cat sleeps on a garage roof. Next door's washing flaps on the line. Nothing is amiss. She can see no other horticultural violations. No mutilated marigolds. No abducted conifers.

Pip's fury is sudden. She tears open the wardrobe, pulling at Jack's clothes. Striped shirts. Trousers, still on their hangers. They fall in untidy puddles on the floor. Never, since Jack's death, have they been treated with such disregard. Pip thrusts them into bin liners. The shirts. The suits. The lovely ties. She can't stand to look at them. She wants them out of the house. They are relegated to the bin by the back gate.

Why would anyone steal a flower?

Someone has come into her garden by night. Someone crept in after dark, snickering as they looked up at the hushed light of Pip's bedroom window. Someone has ripped her flower from the ground. No one would dare do this if she weren't alone. She's angry that Jack is not here. Pip is angry at Jack.

☉

Emma's hand is like dead wood in Pip's. Pip tells her about the chocolate that she's bought for the flapjacks but Emma says nothing.

Pip filled in the hole where the sunflower once stood that afternoon, slapping the soil down with the back of the spade to flatten it. She notices how Emma, stubborn child, doesn't look at the spot but keeps her eyes fixed on the ground ahead of her. There's a flush on her cheeks that Pip recognises as anger. She's not sure whether Emma's angry at her or the flower thief.

☉

Emma draws at the kitchen table while Pip cooks. The kettle boils, steam creeping along the underside of the wall cupboards. Pip dismembers vegetables. She stops chopping and glances over at the child's narrow back and bent head. Silence is their default state but now it bothers Pip.

"What are you doing?" Pip leans over Emma's shoulder.

Emma tilts her head and continues with her labours. She punishes the paper, pressing hard with her crayon to make thick, waxy lines. It's a sunflower. Pip sits beside her.

"I got angry this morning because I was frightened. I didn't know what happened to the flower."

Emma stops colouring and looks up at her, clutching the yellow crayon to her chest.

Pip tries again. "I got upset because we planted it for Daddy."

There's a knock at the door. A foreign sound. Pip's unsure if she's

88

annoyed at the interruption or relieved that she's been given a reprieve.

The knock comes again, a demand rather than a polite request. Pip thinks of the hole in the ground.

"Wait here," she tells Emma.

Pip sees the caller's silhouette through the frosted glass inserts of the front door. It's a man, tall, head bowed, one arm resting against the frame as if exhausted. She's startled by a noise behind her.

"Daddy?" It's Emma.

Pip's hands move of their own volition, reaching for the lock. The door swings open.

The figure unfurls to its full height. It fills up the doorway and casts a long shadow down the hall. The Sunflower Seed Man stoops to enter. The corridor can barely contain him.

His suit is crumpled from being balled up in the bin bag. The shirt and tie are a riot of clashing patterns and shades. Rustling foliage peeps out between his shirt buttons. Stems and roots protrude from sleeves and trouser legs, knotted up to make ankles and wrists, then splay out into feet and hands. Worms and soil are shed as he advances. His mane of withered petals is flattened back, like hair. Some of the seeds have fallen from his face in an approximation of a mouth.

Pip's adrenaline advises flight, not fight. She backs away, snatching at the hall stand and heaves it over, coats and all. It crashes against the side panel of the stairs, shattering the mirror and blocking the Sunflower Seed Man's path with a mess of coats and bags.

Pip runs into the kitchen, pushing Emma ahead of her. She rattles the backdoor key with sweaty fingers. There is the give of the lock but door only opens a fraction. It's not even enough to slide Emma through. Pip flings herself at it in desperation, bones slamming against the wood. Looking through the small pane of glass she can see the garden and the gate at its end. Pip stands on tiptoes to see what's blocking their escape. While she was collecting Emma from school, the Sunflower Seed Man has been busy. The contents of the outhouse, washer, dryer and a tangle of bicycles, have been heaped up against the kitchen door.

Pip grabs Emma's wrist and turns back to the hall. The Sunflower Seed Man is pulling at the upturned furniture, getting caught up in the winter wear. His head is visible over the top of this pile. His smile is terrible.

"Upstairs, Emma. Now."

There's nowhere else to go.

The Sunflower Seed Man has managed to climb over the hall stand. He's behind them now, closing the distance. Pip glances back. He takes the stairs on all fours. The jacket he's wearing rips along its back seam with the strain, revealing the flesh pink lining beneath the blue fabric. Pip feels his hand brush her ankle as she reaches the top step. It spurs her into a sprint for the bedroom, picking up Emma as she goes.

So close. The Sunflower Seed Man traps his grasping fingers in the door as she slams it behind her. There's a scream as he rips them free, a high pitch shrieking that shreds Pip's nerves. She gives thanks that she kept the door key for privacy. Jack had been exasperated. *For heaven's sake, Emma can't even walk properly yet.*

The door handle rattles and then falls quiet. There's only the sound of the alarm clock and Pip's panting. The floorboards creak beneath her as she moves, making her wince. Pushing up the window sash, she takes a deep breath and lets the fear out. She screams and screams.

The neighbour's cat is in residence upon the garage roof. Its head turns in a snap and it fixes her with its green glare for daring to disrupt the peace. Then he rolls onto his back, squirming as if scratching an itch. The wind carries off Pip's voice. No door opens. No one comes.

The floor boards creak again, this time from out on the landing. She needs a plan. She could knot sheets together and lower Emma down out of the window. Take Emma in her arms and jump. Or hide Emma in the wardrobe or under the bed.

There's a thud against the door. Pip is transfixed, Emma clutched against her. Time's run out. The Sunflower Seed Man is using a chair leg as a battering ram. The door frame won't yield but the door panels buckle and splinter.

Do something.

The wardrobe is old and deep. Pip lifts Emma up and puts her inside, behind the dresses that are hung up like martyrs in a row.

"No matter what you hear, stay put. Don't move. Don't make a sound."

Pip kisses her. The dresses fall back into place and she closes the wardrobe.

The Sunflower Seed Man has made a hole low down in the door. His arm comes through, then his head, followed by the other arm. In he crawls and Pip is rooted to the spot.

He stands, taking off the tattered jacket and throws it on the bed. The gesture has panache. Intent. That of a man who wants his wife. The Sunflower Seed Man undoes the tie's bungled knot and pulls at one end. It slides from under the collar in a way that makes her shudder. The shirt buttons are trickier. His foliage fingers lack dexterity. His damaged hand hampers him. Impatient, he rips the shirt open.

Pip bolts to the far side of the bed. He follows. She scrambles across the mattress but being nimble is no match for his long reach. She struggles to stay upright but he wrestles her down. The stems twine around her arms and legs. The Sunflower Seed Man's head nuzzles her face. His withered mane stands erect in halo around his head. She seizes at it trying to pull him off but the stuff comes away in handfuls. Her mouth and nose are filled with seeds.

I'm suffocating, Pip thinks.

The Sunflower Seed Man is heavier than seeds and leaves ought to be. Stronger too. His rough leaves grind against her skin. They leave bloody abrasions where they've been, her belly smeared and sore where her t-shirt has ridden up.

"You're not Jack."

Her words are full of his debris. He lifts his head, as if to hear her better. She spits bits of him out.

"You're not Jack."

The stems are barbed wire around her wrists and ankles. As she struggles they tighten, drawing blood. He lays a loving cheek on hers. He presses himself close. Pip cries, dry smothered rasps that pass as sobs.

"Mummy." Emma whimpers from the wardrobe.

Mummy. Not *daddy.* The Sunflower Seed Man turns his head, looking for the source of the sound.

"Look at me," Pip says.

The Sunflower Seed Man looks at Pip and back to the wardrobe.

"No, look at me." She kisses his gritty, grinning mouth.

She feels his hold slacken as his desire grows. Pip pulls her hands free and cradles his monstrous head with tenderness.

"You can't have her, she's mine."

Pip fumbles to finds the main stem that is the Sunflower Seed Man's neck. She grips it with both hands, hard as she can. He kicks and bucks, realising her ruse too late.

Jack's dead.

Her fingers sink into the stem, making it hard for him to prise them off. It feels fleshy and wet. The sap stings her skin.

Jack's dead. You're not Jack.

He pummels her with his fists, indiscriminate, panicked blows. Pip feels something in her left cheek crack but refuses to let go.

Jack's dead but I'm not. Neither is Emma.

Pip holds on long after the struggle has gone out of the Sunflower Seed Man. His great head flops to one side.

Pip cries as she lies there, clutching the carcass of the dead sunflower in her arms.

THE BALLAD OF BOOMTOWN

It's estimated that in 2011 there were 2,881 semi or unoccupied housing developments in Ireland.

○

There was a time when we put our faith in Euros, shares and the sanctity of brick. A time when we bought our books from stores as big as barns and ate strawberries from Andalusia, when only a generation before they'd been grown on farms up the road.

The wide avenues of Boomtown were named for trees when there was grand optimism for growth. Now nothing booms in Boomtown. It's bust and broken.

I miss you. You were a lick of cream. I can still taste you.

I walk to the village on Mondays. I pull my shopping trolley the three miles there and back along the lanes. I used to drive to the supermarket, just for a pint of milk, without a thought to the cost of fuel. It doesn't matter now. I like to walk.

Sheila-na-gigs look down on me from the church walls as I pass by. These stone carvings are of women with bulging eyes and gaping mouths, displaying their private parts. These wantons are a warning against lust. Or a medieval stone mason's dirty joke.

The shop's beside the church. Deceased, desiccated flies lie between the sun faded signs. There's a queue inside. I've heard all their grumbling about prices and supplies. They decry the current government, the one before, the banks and then apportion blame abroad. Despite the orderly line and polite chatter, I can imagine these women battling it out with their meaty fists if the last bag of flour in Ireland was at stake.

We're not so poor as yet that we can't afford a veneer of civilised behaviour.

I put my face to the glass as the shop owner takes the last slab of beef from the chilled counter and wraps it. I wish I'd got up earlier. I would've spent half my week's grocery allowance to smell the marbled flesh sizzling in a pan.

The bell jangles as I push the door open. A few heads turn. A woman leans towards her companion and whispers in his ear. I catch the words blow in. I'm a Boomtown interloper, buffeted by changing fortune. There's a pause before the man looks at me. His salacious glance suggests he's heard scandalous stories.

I've no doubt a few of them recall me from before, when I first came here to talk to them about my book. There was a certain glamour in talking to me.

I take my time considering the shelves' contents while the others pay and leave. There are budget brands with unappetising photos on the cans. Boxes of cheap smelling soap powder and white bread in plastic bags. I tip what I need into my basket.

"I want freshly ground coffee."

I can't help myself. I'm the Boomtown Bitch. It's cruel. The shop owner's never done me any harm. She always offers me a slow, sweet smile. It's fading now.

"We only have instant."

"Olives then." I want my city living, here in the country. I want delicatessens and coffee bars. Fresh pastries and artisan loaves.

She shakes her head.

"Anchovies, balsamic vinegar. Risotto rice." The world was once a cauldron of plenty.

"I only have what's on the shelves."

She's struggling to contain herself in the face of my ridiculous demands. I sling the basket on the counter where it lands with a metallic thud and slide. There's a dogged precision in how she enters the price of each item into the till. She doesn't speak but turns the display to show me the total, waiting as I load my shopping into the trolley. Her refusal to look at me isn't anger. There's glimmer of unshed tears. It's not her fault.

It's yours. It's mine.

I feel sick. Yet another thing that can't be undone. I try and catch her eye as I hand her a note but she's having none of it. I want to tell her that I'm sorry. It's shameful that I don't even know her name and now she'll believe the worst she's heard and won't ever smile at me again. She slides my change over the counter rather than putting it into my hand.

The bell above the door jangles as I leave.

⊙

The chieftain stood before the three sisters, flanked by men bearing swords and spears, and said, "This is my land now."

"We lived here long before you came," they replied.

"By what right do you claim it? Where's your army?"

"You can't own the land, it owns you." That was the eldest sister. "Rid yourself of such foolish desires."

"No. Everything you see belongs to me."

"Do you own that patch of sky?" the middle born said.

The chieftain was silent.

"Is that water yours?" That was the youngest. "See how it runs away from you."

"I want this land." The chieftain stamped his feet. "Look at my torque. Even metal submits to my will."

"You'll be choked by that gold around your throat." The eldest stepped forward. "You're master of ores and oxen, wheat and men alike, but not us. We're like the grass. We only bow our heads to the wind."

The chieftain looked at them, pale witches in rags with swathes of dark hair and there were the stirrings of a different sort of desire.

The chieftain and his men raped the sisters, one by one.

"See," he said, "I possess everything."

"We are ancient. We are one and we are three." The youngest covered herself with the tatters of her clothes. "We were there at the world's birth. We are wedded to the earth. We don't submit. We endure."

A cold wind came in carrying rain even though it was a summer's day.

"We curse you and your greed." The middle sibling swallowed her sobs and raised her chin. "It'll grow so large that it'll devour you and your kind."

Thunderbolts cracked the sky.

"We'll dog your children's steps from womb to tomb." The eldest had the final word. "When their fortune's in decline we'll rise again. No one will be spared our wrath. Then we'll go to heal what you've rent."

The eldest gathered up the other two and retreated to a place where the hills were at their backs and enfolded themselves in stone.

⊙

The Three Sisters are a group of three stones that occupy a small plateau on the eastern side of the _____ hills in County Meath. Their history has been retold for generations in the local village of _____. There are several variations of the tale. The one I've included here is the most detailed.

—*Songs of Stones: Collected Oral Traditions of Ireland's Standing Stones* by Grainne Kennedy

⊙

I drove us from Dublin. You directed. You kept glancing at my legs as they worked the pedals, which excited me. It felt like you were touching me. Sliding your hand between my knees.

"Turn right."

The indicator winked. We were on Oak Avenue.

"Does this all belong to Boom Developments?"

"Yes."

I whistled, wanting you to know I was impressed.

"Left here." Then, "This is Acacia Drive."

There were diggers, trucks, the cries and calls of men. We bumped along the unfinished road. Stones crunched under the tyres and ochre dust rose around us.

"Pull over here." You buzzed, happy amongst the evidence of your success. "I asked the lads to complete some of the houses up here first."

You ran up the road towards a group of men in jeans and T-shirts. The men looked at me when you'd turned away and I could tell they'd said something smutty from the way they sniggered.

You returned, carrying hard hats and keys. "Put this on."

I refused to be embarrassed by our audience. I piled up my hair and put my hat on, back arched in mock burlesque. You took my elbow with a light touch, as if unsure of yourself. I liked that you weren't adept with women when you seemed so proficient at the rest of life. You guided me towards a house.

"Here." You unlocked the door.

Our feet rang out on the bare boards. Fresh plaster dried in shades of pink and brown.

"This model's the best of the lot. It'll be done to the highest spec."

I followed you upstairs.

"Huge master bedroom. Nice en-suite too."

It was the view that I admired most. The hills, the open sky was spread out for us. I couldn't tell you that I'd been here before your burgeoning success scarred the land. That I'd trekked for miles under rotten skies that threatened rain, across open fields carrying my notebook, cameras and a tripod. I didn't want to spoil the moment by making it anything but yours.

You should've known though. If you'd looked at the copy of the book I'd given you, my own modest enterprise, you'd have seen. You weren't interested in history, not the ones of Ireland's standing stones, not even mine. I was a woman of the past. You were a man of the future.

"We could lie in bed together and look at this view." Your tone had changed from business to tenderness and I was beguiled by the use of *we*. "Don't feel pressured. Just think on it. You said you wanted to move somewhere quiet to write."

"I can't afford this."

"You're looking to buy outright. This would be yours at cost price."

"Can you do that?"

"I'm the MD," you laughed, "of course I can."

"I couldn't accept it."

"Grainne, you'd be helping me. Selling the first few will help to sell more. Things snowball. This property will treble in value over the next ten years, I promise."

I didn't enjoy this talk of values and assets. I did like the prospect of us sharing a bed that was ours.

"I'll think about a smaller one, at full price."

I'd always been careful not to take anything from you. Need's not erotic.

"It's cost price or nothing. Please, Grainne, it's the least that I can do for you.

○

The estate looks normal from this approach. There are cars on drives and curtains at windows. I can see a woman inside one of the houses. She bends down and comes back into a view with an infant on her hip. The portrait makes me wince. Madonna with child. She turns her back when she sees me.

I stop at Nancy's on Oak Avenue, the main artery of the estate.

"Have a drink with me." She ushers me in and shuffles along behind me.

Water rushes into the metallic belly of the kettle. I unload her groceries. UHT milk. Teabags. Canned sardines.

"Pay me next time."

Nancy snorts and forces money into my palm. "I'll come with you next week, if you don't mind taking it slow."

"It's a long walk."

"Don't cheek me." Her spark belies her age. She must've been a corker in her time. "I need to take the car out for a run. I'll drive us somewhere as a treat."

I wonder how long it'll take the village shopkeeper to forget my tantrum. Longer than a week.

Steaming water arcs into one mug, then the other.

"Grainne..." Her tone changes. "Lads are loitering about up here. Be careful."

When Nancy bends to add milk to the tea I can see her pink scalp through the fine white curls.

"I'm just going to come out and say this." She touches my hand. Her finger joints are large, hard knots. "You're neglecting yourself. You're losing weight. And your lovely hair…"

I can't recall when I last brushed it.

"You're not sleeping either. I've seen you, walking past at night."

"You're not sleeping either."

"That's my age."

Nancy sips her tea. I gulp mine down. It's my first drink of the day.

"You're all alone up at that end of the estate."

I can't answer. I've been too lonely to realise that I'm alone.

"Life's too sweet to throw away."

Then why does it taste so bitter?

She tries again, exasperated by my silence.

"What happened up there isn't my business but I can't bear to watch you punishing yourself."

I should be pilloried for my past. I should be stricken with shame but I can't tell Nancy that it's not remorse that's destroying me. It's pining for you.

"You're full of opinions." It comes out as a growl but there's no bite.

"You can stay here anytime. God knows I've room enough to spare."

She opens a pack of biscuits and makes me eat one.

"Be careful out there on the hills, Grainne. You could turn your ankle and die up there and no one would know."

⊙

I kept a well-made bed, dressed with cotton sheets. Worthy of the time we spent upon it. Sunlight moved across our bare bodies, which moved across one another. Hands and mouths roamed over necks, chest, breasts, stomachs, genitals and thighs, stoking a deep ache that only you could sate.

Afterward we lay like pashas on piles of pillows.

"I loved you from the first moment I saw you."

"That's a cliché." I meant to tease you but it sounded bitter.

"You don't believe me. You don't believe anything I say."

"I do."

I did believe you because I felt it too. From that first moment I wanted to open my arms to you. I wanted to open my legs to you. I promise it wasn't just lust because I wanted to open my heart to you too.

"I'm just someone you sleep with."

"Dan, don't play games to make yourself feel better."

"You don't need me, not that way I need you."

"Of course I do."

You thought yourself the more in love of the two of us. Not true. I hated sharing you. I hated not knowing when I'd see you or when you'd call.

"You've never asked me to leave her."

"Do you want me to?"

"Yes." You paused. "No." Then: "I don't know. I don't love her. I did once. I can't leave her now. Ben's still so young. But wait for me, Grainne. Our time will come. I promise."

"Don't make promises."

"I wish I'd met you first."

I wish it all the time, for so many reasons.

◉

The short cut to Acacia Drive goes through Boomtown's underbelly. There's a square that would've been a green but now it's the brown of churned mud. It should've been flanked by shops. Some are only foundations, others have been abandoned at hip height. A few have made it to the state of squatting skeletons. Piles of rotted timbers and broken breeze blocks litter the verges. An upturned hard hat is full of dirty rainwater. A portable toilet lies on its side and I get a whiff of its spilled contents.

I flip over a tin sign lying in the road and it lands with a clatter. I clean it with the hem of my shirt. Boom Developments, it exclaims. The symbol's a crouched tiger, its stripes orange, green and white.

I go straight to bed when I get home, leaving my shopping in the hall. The once pristine sheets are creased and grey. I push my nose against the pillowcase but can't smell you there, only my own unwashed hair. Frustrated, I strip the bed and lie down again. I touch myself in a ferocity of wanting but it's a hollow sham that ends in a dry spasm. I'll not be moved.

Not without you.

I put my walking boots and coat back on. I feel the reassuring weight of my torch in my pocket. My premium property backs onto open country. I open the gate at the bottom of my garden and walk out to where the land undulates and settles into long summer grasses that lean towards the hills.

Out here, away from the estate, nothing's inert. Buzzing insects stir the grass. The wind lifts my hair and drops it. A chill settles in and I wish I'd worn another layer. I cross the stream, sliding on wet stones and splashing water up my jeans. The stream's unconcerned. It has places to go.

The sun's sinking fast. The sky is broken by a string of emerging stars as night arrives.

The ground rises and I have to work harder until I'm climbing on all fours onto the plateau. The hills crowd around to protect the Three Sisters. This trio of stones are eternal, bathed in sun and rain, steeped in the ashes of our ancestors. They're more substantial than our bricks and mortar. They'll sing long after our sagas are exhausted. They outshine our light.

The Sisters cluster together. They're not angular, phallic slabs. Their Neolithic design looks daringly modernist, each shaped to suggest womanhood. The smallest, which I think of as the youngest, has a slender neck and sloping shoulders. The middle one has a jutting chin and a swell that marks breasts. The eldest has a narrow waist and flaring hips. I touch each in turn. They're rugged and covered in lichen. I put my ear against them, wanting to hear the sibilant whispers of their myths. I kiss their unyielding faces but they don't want my apologies for ancestral wrongs. There's only silence. They wait, of course, for us to abate.

I walk back home, not looking down, playing dare with the uneven ground. My torch stays in my pocket. You could turn your ankle and die up there and no one would know.

Death comes for me. It's a white, soundless shape on the wing. A moon faced barn owl, dome headed and flat faced. I'm transfixed. It swoops, a sudden, sharp trajectory led by outstretched claws. How small have I become that it thinks it can carry me away?

I've read that owls regurgitate their prey's remains as bone and gristle. I laugh, imagining myself a mouse sized casket devoid of life.

The owl swoops low over the grass and heads for Boomtown. I press my sleeve to my cheek. Dizziness makes me lie down. The long grass surrounds me, reducing the sky to a circle. I don't know how long I'm there but cold inflames my bones. Eventually I get up and walk home, coming up Acacia Drive from the far end where the houses are unfinished. The street lamps can't help, having never seen the light. I'm convinced it's whispering, not the wind that's walking through the bare bones of the houses. Now that I've survived the menace of the hills and fields, I allow myself my torch. What should be windows are soulless holes in my swinging yellow beam. The door frames are gaping mouths that will devour me.

I don't look at the house but I feel it trying to catch my eye.

There's something akin to relief when the road curves and I see the porch light of my home. It looks like the last house at the end of the world.

○

You were in the shower sluicing away all evidence of our afternoon. Your clothes were laid out on the back of a chair. You were careful to avoid a scramble that might crumple your shirt or crease your trousers.

The gush of water stopped and you came in, bare, damp, the hair of your chest and stomach darkened swirls. You'd left a trail of wet footprints on the carpet. You weren't shy. I enjoyed this view of you. The asymmetry of your collarbones and the soft, sparse hair on the small of your back. My fascination for you endured, as if I'd never seen a man before.

"When will they start work again?"

By *they* I'd meant the builders. The estate had fallen silent. No more stuttering engines, no more drills or shouting.

You'd been drying your chest. The towel paused, as if I'd struck you in the heart. I cursed my clumsiness.

"Soon. There's been a bit of a hiatus in our cash flow. People are just a bit nervous, that's all. Everything moves in cycles. Money will start flowing again."

"Of course it will." My optimism had a brittle ring.

You wrapped the towel around your waist in a sudden need to protect yourself, even from me.

O

I wake in the afternoon, having lost the natural demarcations of my day. My cheek smarts when I yawn. I pick at the parallel scabs.

My mobile's by my bed. I've stopped carrying it around. You never call. It's flashing a warning that its battery is low. I ignore its pleas for power and turn it off.

I did get through to your number once. There was the sound of breathing at the other end. It wasn't you.

"Kate," I said.

The breathing stopped and she hung up before I could say I'm sorry.

You haunt me. I see your footprints on the carpet where you once stood, shower fresh and dripping. I catch glimpses of you in the mirror and through the narrow angles of partially closed doors. These echoes are the essentials of my happiness. For that fraction of a second I can pretend you're here.

It's rained while I slept. Everything drips. The ground's too saturated to take all the water in. It's not cleansed Boomtown, just added another layer of grime.

From the spare bedroom I can see the street. I put my forehead against the window, savouring the coolness of the glass. I tilt my forehead so I can see Helen's house, further along the opposite side of Acacia Drive. The other house, the one where it happened, is out of sight, at the incomplete end of the road. It's defeated me so far.

I slip on my boots and snatch up my coat. I shut my front door and freeze, the key still in the lock. Something's behind me, eyes boring into my back. It waits, daring me to turn. I can feel it coming closer. I make a fist, my door key wedged between my ring and forefinger so that its point and ragged teeth are protruding. It's a poor weapon, especially as I've never thrown a punch in my life. I turn quickly to shock my assailant, only to find it's a cat shuddering in an ecstatic arch against the sharp corner of the garage wall. It's not like other strays. The uncollared, unneutered, incestuous brood that roam around Boomtown are shy. This ginger monster's not scared of anything. It fixes me with yellow eyes and hisses. It bares it fangs and postures. I hiss back but it stands its ground, leaving me to back away down the drive.

I find myself at Helen's, which is stupid because Helen doesn't live there anymore. The For Sale sign's been ripped down and trampled on.

I walk around the house, looking through windows. It's just a shell without Helen and her family but evidence that it was once a home remains. The lounge's wallpaper, a daring mix of black and gold. Tangled wind chimes hang from a hook by the kitchen door. There's a cloth by the sink, as though Helen's last act was to wipe down the worktops.

We used to stand and chat as her brood played in the road. When they got too boisterous she'd turn and shout, "Quit your squalling and yomping, you bunch of hooligans! Just wait until your dad gets back." Then she'd wink at me and say something like, "He's in Dubai this time. Not that they're scared of him, soft sod that he is."

I used to get the girls, Rosie and Anna, mixed up. Tom squealed as he chased his sisters. Patrick rode around us on his bike in circles that got tighter and tighter.

Patrick.

I'm sick of thinking about that day.

I'm sick of not thinking about it.

Today, I decide, today I'll go inside the house where it happened.

It's about twenty doors down from Helen's. The chain link fence that was set up around it has long since fallen down and been mounted by ivy intent on having its way. The Three Sisters are reclaiming what's theirs by attrition. There are lines of grass in the guttering of Boomtown, wasps' and birds' nests are uncontested in the eaves. Lilies flourish in ditches and foxes trot about like lonely monarchs. The Sisters will reclaim us too, our flesh, blood and bones.

I stand on the threshold of the past. A breeze moves through the house carrying a top note of mould and piss, then the threatening musk lingering beneath.

The house is gutless. One wall is bare plasterboard, the rest partition frames so I can see all the way through, even up into the gloom above.

There used to be ladders but they've been removed.

From the doorway I can see the stain on the concrete floor. It's a darkness that won't be moved. The blackest part gnashes its teeth at me.

I put a foot inside and then the other. I realise my mistake too late. I've already inhaled the shadows. They fill up my nose and clog my throat. I can't move. I can't breathe. My lungs seize up. Something's there. The darkness is moving.

The shadow rushes at me and takes my legs from under me. The ginger cat. It watches with yellow eyes as I land on my back. Everything goes black.

⊙

I roll onto my side and retch. Acidic vomit burns my nose and throat. When I put a hand to the back of my head I find a boggy swelling. My hair's matted and stuck to my scalp.

I stand, test my legs and find them sound. I get away from the house, to the middle of the road, but looking around I see I'm not alone. Company's coming up the street. A trio of creatures that are neither men nor boys. One throws his empty beer can away and fingers his crotch when he sees me.

"You," he says.

He's skinny, grown into his height but yet to fill out. It occurs to me that he expects me to run. His face is hard. He's gone passed being abused into abusing.

"You're the Boomtown Bitch."

I turn my back and walk away at a deliberate pace.

"I'm talking to you." I know without looking that he's lengthening his stride to catch me. "Pull down your knickers and show us what all the fuss is about."

My heart's a flailing hammer. He's done this before and is looking to initiate his friends, who seem less certain of themselves. I can see him reach out to grasp my shoulder in the far corner of my vision.

I strike before he can touch me. I jab at his eyes and rake at his face with dirty claws. I'm a moon faced owl. I'll regurgitate his carcass. I'm the feral feline who'll jab his corpse with my paws. The boy's screaming now but I don't stop. Even a chink of fear will let the others in and I can't fend off all three. My would-be rapist retreats. I must put him down before he gathers his wits and tries to save face. I advance, hissing and spitting like the ginger cat.

I am crazy, scarred and unkempt, a bloodied scalp and big eyes in the dark hollows of my face. I pick up a brick and run at him and to my relief, he sprints away.

They shout from a safe distance, taunts that I'm happy to ignore. I don't look back as I walk away in case they realise I'm weak.

○

I saw your outline through the glass of my front door. You were wearing your suit, even though it was a Saturday.

You weren't alone. A boy stood before you. Even though you had your hands on his shoulders it took me a moment to realise it was your son. Ben. You were there in the shape of his mouth and chin. The other parts must've been your wife. I resented this child, this scrap of you and her made flesh.

"Miss Kennedy—" you mouthed sorry at me over Ben's head "—I've come to see you about your complaint over the house."

I wanted to laugh. You were a terrible actor.

"That's good of you."

"Apologies, I had to bring my son. Say hello, Ben."

"Hello." He squirmed in your grasp.

"I had to let you know I'd not forgotten you. Shall we make an appointment for next week?"

"Would you both like a drink?" I knelt before Ben, hating him because he was getting in our way. "Would you like to play outside? It's a lovely day."

I stood up and raised a hand, a plan already formed. "Patrick, over here."

Helen's brood were on their drive. Patrick cycled over. The bike was too small for him and his knees stuck out at angles.

"Meet Ben. Can he play with you?"

"Sure." Patrick sat back on the saddle. He'd no need for deference, being older than Ben and on home turf. The other children stood on the far pavement, waiting to take their cue from their brother.

"As long it's okay with your father, of course." I couldn't look at you. Please say yes. My longing was indecent. Even the children would see it.

You hesitated.

Please say yes.

"Ben—" you put a hand on his head "—stay with the other children on this road. Don't stray."

I could tell that you were proud of Ben and wanted me to see him but a dull, creeping jealousy stole over me because of the trinity of Dan, Kate and Ben.

"This way," Patrick beckoned and Ben followed, glancing back at you.

"I can't stay long," you said as I closed the door.

We raced upstairs.

"Won't your neighbours wonder when they see Ben? Won't they guess?"

"Who cares?"

I didn't. I was too busy with your belt. There was a sudden shriek of laughter and I stopped you from going to the window by snatching at your tie and pulling you into the bedroom.

"Leave them. They're enjoying themselves. So are we."

You hesitated again and then undressed, your ardour cooled by the tug of parental love. I shoved you, ineffectual considering your size. Your carefully folded clothes enraged me. You'd brought your son to my door. You'd been honest about your life when you could've lied but you'd been a coward and made the decision mine.

I shoved you again.

You picked me up and threw me on the bed. We grappled and when you understood I meant to hurt you, you held my wrists so I couldn't mark you with my nails. You didn't kiss me for fear I'd bite. I wish I'd known it was the final time. I wish we'd taken it slow. I'd have savoured the slip and slide, then the sudden sensation of you inside.

You dozed. I watched. Your breathing changed to slower, deeper tones. I treasured the minutiae of you, the banal details that made you real, like how you took your coffee, brushed your teeth, the slackness of your face in sleep.

The doorbell rang, a sudden sequence of chimes that struggled to keep up with the finger on the bell. A fist hammered at the door, followed by shouts. It went through my mind that it was your wife, that she'd followed you here spoiling for a fight. Then I recognised Helen's voice. Its urgency boomed through the hall and up the stairs.

Silence. There'd been silence during our post-coital nap. No squeals or calls.

I snatched up my blouse, fingers stumbling over the buttons.

"Dan." I reached for my skirt. "Dan, wake up."

You sat up, dazed. "What is it?"

Helen, even in panic, saw the flagrant signs. The buttons of my blouse were done up wrong and I was bra-less beneath the sheer fabric. You'd followed me down the stairs with your tousled hair and bare feet.

"You'd better come. I've called an ambulance."

You pulled on the shoes that you'd discarded by the door. You and Helen were faster than I as she led us to the empty houses. Three of the children were outside one of them. Rosie and Anna were red faced from crying. Tom sat on the step beside them, staring at the ground.

"Stay here," Helen ordered them even though it was clear they weren't about to move.

I followed you from light into the shade of the house. It took a few moments for my eyes to readjust. The coolness inside felt pleasant for a second, as did the smell of cut timber.

You and Helen squatted by the shattered body on the floor. Ben's silhouette didn't make sense and I had to rearrange the pieces in my mind. His arms had been flung out on impact but it was his leg that confused me. It was folded under him at an impossible angle that revealed bone, so white that it looked unnatural against the torn red flesh. Ben was a small vessel, his integrity easily breached.

"He must've fallen from up there."

We looked up towards the eyrie that was the unfinished loft where Patrick perched astride a joist. A ladder spanned the full height of both floors which is how they must've climbed so high. Helen's husband was at the top, reaching for the whimpering boy.

A dark stain crept out from beneath Ben's head. His eyes stared at nothing. There was an appalling sound. A dog's howl, the scream of an abandoned child. The keening of something bereft and inconsolable. It grew until it filled the room. I realised it was you. I put a hand on your shoulder and said your name.

You shook me off.

⊙

I wake up on the sofa. It's early and the grey light of dawn creeps through the parted curtains. Sleep's not healed me. I smell of spoiling meat. There's a dull throb in my head but I can't locate whether it's in my eye, my teeth, or somewhere in between. I'm cold and clammy, as if in the aftermath of a drenching sweat.

I go to the mantel mirror. There's enough light now to see that the marks on my cheek are raised, the scabs lifted by lines of pus. I touch one and it gives under gentle pressure, bringing relief and yellow ooze. The back of my head feels like it belongs to someone else.

I eat a dry cracker, drink a pint of water and then vomit in the kitchen sink. There's a pounding now, at a different rate and rhythm to my headache. A drumming that escalates.

It's outside the house.

Hooves thunder on the earth. Something's racing through the grass, running towards the rising sun as if about to engage it in battle.

I go out to the road. Someone, perhaps my failed assailants from yesterday, have spray painted filthy graffiti across the front of my house. It doesn't matter. The wind's changed and is bringing something much fouler with it. Things left too long without light or laughter. Things nursing grudges and dwelling on outrages for too long. My heart pauses and restarts. The horse's gallop makes me gasp. Its cadence changes as it hits the tarmac.

This nightmare is gleaming black. Its rolling black eyes are wild. It tosses its head about and snorts. I can't look away. The mare slows to a canter as it approaches, circling me in rings that get tighter and tighter. It's big, a seventeen hander, heavily muscled. It hits my shoulder on its next pass. When it turns and comes again I have to dodge it to avoid being knocked down.

Adh Seidh. A bad spirit. I'd be safe from its malice if I'd led an upright life.

It flattens its ears and flares its nostrils, then rears up before me and paws at the air as if losing patience. I try to edge to the safety of my open door but it kicks out again, forcing me to retreat. It follows at a trot. Each step jolts my head but I turn and run. When I shout for help my voice is faint from lack of use. There's no one to hear it anyway.

I try and dart up Helen's driveway but the horse isn't confused by my sudden change in direction. It comes around me, right, then left. Lunging at me, kicking out if I stray. Herding me.

I'm panting. My chest's tight and the stitch in my side's a sharp knife. I want to lie down and die. To let it dance on me until I'm dust beneath its hooves.

I'm at the house now. The horse waits beyond the fallen chain link fence in case I try to bolt. I've been brought here to atone for my crimes. The only place I can go is that cold, dark hole.

Broken beer bottles and rubble crunches underfoot. Kids have been in here since my last visit. I feel hot again. Sweat stings my forehead. The past is too heavy. I can't carry it anymore. The stain accuses me. It rises from the floor and spreads itself across the wall. It's absolute, sucking all the light from the room. It smells my guilt and swells, emboldened. Its waiting is over. It's Ben. It's Kate. It's you. It's all the people I can't face. It's the Sisters, taken to the wing. They have hooves and paws studded with claws. They're done with waiting. They've risen up to smother us.

They're not out there on the hills. They're not walking through the dying summer grass. They're not lingering by the streams, fingers stirring the water.

They're not out there. They're in here.

THE SHOW

The camera crew struggled with the twisting, narrow stairs. Their kit was portable, steadicams being all the rage. They were lucky that the nature of their work did not require more light. Shadows added atmosphere. Dark corners added depth. It was cold down in the cellar. It turned their breath to mist, which gathered in the stark white pools shed by the bare bulbs overhead.

Martha smiled. It was sublime. Television gold.

Tonight there'd been a crowd. Word had got out. She'd have to find out who blabbed. There were only a few fans at the start but now they needed security to keep them back.

She'd joined the presenter, Philipa and her producer-husband Greg at the barrier. The three of them had posed for photographs and signed autographs. Philipa had been strict about that. Be nice to the public. The audience would make or break the show, not studio executives.

Martha laughed out loud when a woman produced a photo of Philipa and Greg in their previous incarnation as chat show hosts.

"Nice haircuts," she said as they both signed it. Their fashionable styles dated this period of fame but Martha was careful when she joked about their pasts. It was Philipa's new idea that had reinvented their careers.

Philipa was popular but it was really Martha the crowd wanted. She recognised the faithful amid the curious locals. The ones who wanted to touch her hand, as if it were a blessing. To ask her help to reach the dead, to say what they'd left unsaid.

A man reached out as Martha tried to leave, snatching at her coat sleeve.

"Good luck," he said. "May God keep you through the night."

☉

Martha leant against the cellar wall to watch Philipa in discussion with the team. She could tell Philipa was well pleased. The first part of the show comprised of interviews. The bar staff had been verbose in their remembering. The tall tales of the spooked. The cellar had fallen fallow. Too many broken beer bottles. Boxes overturned, alcopops leaking on the floor. Too many barmaids emerging with bruises flowering on their arms. Too many accusations. Too many resignations.

Yes, it was horrible down here. Its history appalled. The chill seeped from the floor, through her boot soles and crept into her feet. She fastened up her coat. Red cashmere. She'd decided to live a vivid life. She wouldn't exist in shades of grey. She'd no longer bow or obey. She'd promised herself good money. In the bank. Not tatty fivers from someone's housekeeping, like the ones her mother would take with embarrassment and stuff into the chipped teapot on the dresser. Iris never asked for more. Only barely enough. *You can't abuse the gift.* Cheap meat on Sundays as a treat. For Martha and her sister Suki, white knee socks gone grey, but still too good to throw away.

The second part of the show was a vigil. The team were busy setting up thermometers and motion sensors to add the illusion of science but it was Martha that added the something special to the mix.

"Don't forget," Philipa would say, face tight into the lens, "Martha, our psychic, doesn't know our destination. She'll be brought here and do a reading, blind."

Martha stamped her feet to expel the cold. Philipa was busy with her preparations. Vocal exercises. Shaking her limbs. If Martha channelled spirits, then Philipa channelled the audience. With the cameras on, Philipa (like Martha) became a true believer. Her range spanned from nervous to hysterical. Her tears of fear turned her heavy eye makeup to muddy pools. Her performance heightened suggestibility and atmosphere.

"Have you destroyed them?" Greg sidled up to Martha. He was talking about the copy of his research notes that he always gave her.

"Don't treat me like I'm an amateur. You know I learn them and then burn them."

These were hot readings, as they were called within the trade, when a medium was already primed. Martha would reveal the memorised histories of suicidal serving girls, murdered travellers and Victorian serial killers.

Martha's key was subtlety. She was frugal with the facts. Too direct and the show would be a pantomime. Too detailed and she'd be reciting by rote. And what couldn't be confirmed couldn't be denied, which was useful when the truth wasn't juicy enough to appeal. All Martha needed was a name, a date, a hard fact around which to embroider her yarns. Greg, who also played on-screen researcher, would fake surprise with widened eyes, saying such as, "Yes, Martha, there was a third son here by the name of Walter, but we can't corroborate there was a maid by the name Elaine whom he killed on Midsummer's Day."

"New coat?" Greg's fingers stroked her collar.

"Keep your paws off."

"Watch it. Philipa will think we're paying you too much."

Greg was clumsy where Philipa's angling had been more oblique. Martha had chosen to ignore her jibes and hints, having stuck to the deal made when they were all green and keen. She'd not allow Greg to change the terms.

"You're not and I'm worth every penny."

Worth a better time slot and channel. Worth another series.

"How many personal clients do you have now? How much for your last tour?"

A lot. The world was ripe. She'd weighed it in her palm.

"None of your business."

Martha was brisk. Even with her clients she was sharp. She'd not pander to their fantasies that mediums were soft and ethereal.

"Take care. We built you up and we can pull you down."

Her laughter echoed around the empty cellar. Philipa turned and stared at them.

"You won't. You can't."

To reveal Martha as a fraud was to expose them all. The true believers would be incensed. Most viewers though were sceptics, they would already suspect, but the fun lay in the possibility of doubt. The chance that Martha might be real. So, not perjury, not a lie to shatter worlds, but was it one to shatter careers?

"We can find someone new. You'd be easy to replace."

"Don't threaten me. I'll send you all to hell."

"Keep it down," Philipa stalked over. "Do you want everyone to hear? We'll talk about this later. Do you understand, Martha? There are things to be addressed. Now get ready, it's time to start the show."

☉

Martha had learnt from watching Iris and Suki. Both had reigned at Lamp Street, lumpish in their muddy coloured cardigans, giving readings to anyone who called. Muttering thanks to spirit guides. Turning tatty Tarot cards.

Martha had no claim to special gifts. She learnt to read the hands and face, the gestures that betrayed need and greed. The skill of deciphering a tic, interpreting a pause. Martha studied hard and learnt how to put on a show.

"Yes, David. Thanks."

Made-up-David helped Martha to the other side. A fictional spirit guide to help usher in an imaginary spectral presence or fake demonic possession. David was a friar. Shaman. Priest. Rabbi. Denomination was irrelevant. People seemed to find religious men more comforting in the afterlife than in the flesh. David was based on an engraving that Iris kept by her bed. A monk with his hand folded in prayer.

"What do you make of it?" Philipa asked, now in character.

"It's a big place." Martha sniffed. "It smells bad."

The low ceiling pressed down on them, while the walls stretched out into shadow. Martha rubbed her temples, where pain had started to gather. She walked to the opposite wall, as if in search of something. It was her trick. The camera was forced to follow and the others had to orbit her to stay in shot.

"Brother David, help me." Martha gained momentum. She covered her ears with flat hands. "Make them stop. They're deafening me."

"What is it?"

"Clanging. Fit to wake the dead. The sound of banging metal." She winced as if uncomfortable. Tonight had to be special. She had a point to prove. "It's claustrophobic. Too many souls in too small a space. A strong sense of punishment."

Philipa made a display of her excitement, trying to reclaim screen time for her and Greg. Greg also doubled as show historian. "Greg, can you tell us more?"

"It's a fascinating place. A gruesome history. It was a prison in the eighteenth century."

His eyes shone in the viewfinder.

"What about the clanging?" Philipa asked. More professional than Greg, she'd not prove a point at the show's expense.

"An inmate, Samuel Greenwood, was questioned by the prison board. One of them, shocked, recorded the interview in his diary. The main gates were locked but down here the doors were all open. New arrivals were greeted by the banging of the cell doors." He mimed a man clutching bars and rattling them. "An unholy din by all accounts."

Martha took off her gloves and trailed her fingers along the crumbling mortar of the wall, talking continually to David as she went. Her eyes closed in concentration. The camera loved the gesture.

"Of course. I see it now." She stopped and the spotlight overshot her. "There's so much misery here. Pain. Searing. Physical."

The cameraman tripped up on an empty crate. The world was upended as an explosion of panicked feathers went off in his face. Too stunned to scream, Philipa did it for him. The bird, in its eagerness to escape incarceration in the upturned crate, sprang up and hit the ceiling. It landed with a dull thud upon the floor. It jerked and flapped, a reflex of the fleshly dead, until finally it came to rest. Martha knelt and picked it up. It was a scrawny thing, its feet deformed, head lolling on its broken neck.

Philipa had stopped screaming, looking over Martha's shoulder.

"I wonder how it got down here. And how long ago."

Martha laid the carcass back on the crate. She shook her head in disbelief. Sickened by this small, crushed life, her headache was suddenly much worse. She'd never experienced a migraine but she recognised the signs. Lights danced at the periphery of her vision. Strange patterns hovered in the air. It interfered with coherent thought. She tried to reassert herself.

"This is no ordinary prison, is it, Greg? All these voices cry out but no-one comes. No-one keeps the peace."

"Samuel Greenwood said the inmates ran the place. The authorities didn't get in their way."

Martha tasted bile rising in her throat. *I'll not be sick. I'll not be sick.* Not a mantra but a command. She'd last vomited in childhood. Its associations were too painful to encounter. Not like this. Not here. Martha fought it back.

"There's uncontrolled rage within these walls. Frenzy. Violation." She turned on Greg as if he were to blame. "Men, women, children, all mixed in together."

"Yes," Greg's voice was serious and low. "Murderers and thieves," he savoured the words, "cheats and fraudsters."

Martha wasn't listening. The smell was getting worse. It was decaying flowers, fungi and burnt sugar. The pain in her head was punctuated by explosions. Monstrous white blooms contracted and expanded before her eyes. She clutched the wall with one hand, bent double, and threw her stomach contents upon the floor.

The sensation of muscles moving in her throat, of acid burning in her nose, evoked the shock and grief of that distant summer her father died. Passed over was the term they used at home. Martha despised this euphemism, even though it was part of her work's vocabulary. Not long after her father's sudden death, she had been burnt up by a fever. She'd vomited without relief. She had the same sensations now as then, like she'd died and was floating out of reach.

"Where's Daddy?" Hot and hallucinating, Martha was emphatic. She wanted her father, not her mother's comforts.

"Daddy's here," Iris replied. "He's in the room. He's telling you he loves you. Can't you hear?"

"No," Martha whimpered. Had there been a time when the world was full of voices? She couldn't recall.

"Oh, my sweetheart," and under her breath, Iris spoke the damaging, damning words that separated Martha from her tribe, "you used to be like us. You used to see but now you're blind."

So Martha was left in darkness, Iris and Suki in the light.

Martha dabbed her mouth, vomit dripping on her coat. Greg motioned for the filming to continue. Philipa ladled on concern.

"Are you okay?"

"I'm sorry. It's the smell."

"It's bad, isn't it? Maybe there's a dead bird or rat that's rotting." Then, because Martha's pallor couldn't be feigned, "Do you want us to stop?"

Martha clutched a crumpled tissue to her mouth to stem the swelling tide. She recognised the smell now. It was death. Bedridden Iris, nursed by her girls in the front parlour, had been rank with it. Devoured by the canker in her breast.

People still came, even at the end. To see her. Just for a minute. Just to ask advice. Women whose daughters followed Suki and Martha home from school. Hair pullers, name callers, shin kickers who loved to plague the pair of witches. These same mothers would sit and wait, watching the girls no older than their own, move around the unclean kitchen, washing their mother's soiled sheet in the sink. Not a single one offered aid.

Suki started reading to give Iris peace. So this wall-eyed girl who was clumsy at PE and hated school inherited her mother's mantle and the regulars. She stayed at home and read the cards, while Martha passed her exams and got into fights with anyone who looked at her askew.

"I'm dying, a little more each day. There's no need to be afraid." Iris had beckoned Martha over. "They're waiting for me on the other side. Suki will be just fine. She has the gift but what will become of you, Martha? What will you do?"

Yes, Martha was familiar with the smell. It was enough to make her turn and vomit once again before the floor rose up to meet her. She felt her bones crunch with the impact.

"Martha, can you hear me?"

She was shaken back to consciousness by rough, frightened hands. The pain had gone and left her empty headed, her brain replaced by cotton wool, her mouth with acid and sand.

"Thank God. What happened?" Greg motioned for the crew to stand back and give her air. She tried to sit.

"Just a faint."

In the seconds she was away the cellar had reassembled itself. She could see anew. The investigators were still there. The bare bulbs still shed their light but there was a whole world superimposed upon their own. A past that occupied the present, which shared their time and space. Figures moved around them, weak imprints on here and now. She had peeled back the skin of the world and was looking underneath. When one of these shadow prisoners walked through Martha, she shuddered. It felt like cobwebs were being brushed against her skin.

"There's a lot of residual energy here." The stock phrase had been given shape. Martha wanted to cry. Something locked away was liberated. Was this how Iris saw the world? She realised it has been six years since she last spoke with Suki. How much they had to share. "This place was a health hazard. They're all filthy."

Ragged figures milled around or else they squatted in huddles. Food was piled in troughs as though for swine. There was a gentle buzz. They were too afraid to speak up.

A group of convicts emerged from the far end of the prison, the overlords of this peculiar hell. These self-tattooed, beribboned demons strutted with such swagger that Martha quailed with fear. They singled out a shadow-boy for sport. They hauled him up and took their time at play. One swung his knife about and it passed through Martha's chest, making her gasp, even though it was only a projection of things past. Another one unfolded his razor and the boy's face was devastated. The crime he suffered for most was his prettiness.

"Martha, what is it?"

"A gang ran this place." She found her voice. She talked too loudly so she could hear herself above the shrieks and jeers.

"They kept the peace," Greg said.

"Not peace. I wouldn't call it that."

Martha struggled to her feet. She tipped and tilted until the horizon righted.

"Jimmy Bailey, Michael O'Connor, Kit Williams, Simeon Weaver..." Martha repeated the names as they were shouted at roll call.

"I don't have it here but there is a ledger..." Greg fumbled with his notes.

"Check if you want. They'll all be there."

Greg twitched. This was unexpected. She had raised the stakes. He hadn't thought she'd do her own research.

"Emma Parker," Martha's eyes were horrified. Emma lay on the floor. Slit from pubic bone to ribcage, her blood sprayed upon the walls. "They were animals. When she fell pregnant they opened her up with a knife. They cut out her womb and watched her bleed to death."

Greg frowned at her nasty embellishments. After all, it was a family show.

"The smell. It's death."

She walked back towards the twisted stairs. She had been shocked but now she was afraid. Something was missing from this nether, neither world. Someone was missing.

"There's something about this spot." She strained to listen to the henchman who stood beside the steps like a lackey at some royal court making proclamations. "Thomas the Knife, that's his name."

It sparked of recognition. The name in Greg's notes was Thomas Filcher. Where was he?

"Close. Thomas the Blade." Greg was glad of her return to the script. "He sat waiting for new inmates to be brought down. Tapping on his boot heel with a knife."

Martha pushed her fists against her eyes. Where was the architect of this regime? Why could she not see him?

The clearing of a throat. It was a quiet sound.

"Did you hear that?" Philipa piped up. "Who's there? We mean no harm. Give us a sign."

It came again. This time between a chuckle and a growl.

"Did you hear it?"

Greg was normally subtle in the projections of his voice, but in for a penny, in for a pound.

Cold trickled down Martha's spine. What did it mean that the others could hear him too? There came a laugh, cruel and amused. Martha held up a hand to silence Philipa. "Come out. Show yourself. Or else leave us well alone."

He rose to her challenge, stepping from shadow into light. Thomas the Knife stood before her, denser than the other shades. There was enough of him to trip a movement sensor. It called out in alarm.

"What is it?" Philipa hissed.

They can hear him, Martha thought, but they can't see him.

"Everyone, step back towards the stairs."

"Why?"

"Just do it." Martha could smell her own stale vomit and fear. "This isn't residual energy. It's active. He's here."

The crew started to retreat but Philipa hovered by her side. She'd not be upstaged.

"Martha, tell us what you see."

"He's tall. Handsome." Thomas smirked at that. "Well dressed and fed compared to the rest. A dandy in a blood splattered shirt."

He was gentleman butcher, linen stained by the evidence of his industry. Long hair tied back and boots up to his thighs. Even dead, he bristled with an energy Martha rarely saw in men. She watched him like he was a predator. Magnificent and unpredictable. Her eyes were fixed on him in retreat. She clasped Philipa's elbow but the presenter shook her off.

"He's King down here. He thrived. He sniffed out the proudest and the most delicate. Broke their spirit as if it were a game." Martha looked up, a line of girls crucified upon the bars, their modesty and disfigurements on display. "He's full of hate and it's women that he hates the most."

Martha knew the cleansing rituals, protective circles and holy chants. Iris had been most insistent that they learn, even if Martha wasn't blessed with special sight. Arrogant and adamant in her disbelief, she'd come down here totally unarmed.

"We have to get out now."

Too late. Too late. Thomas the Knife wanted company. His boots fell heavily on stone. Surprisingly loud, considering he was a ghost.

All the lights went out, leaving only sounds. Philipa's screaming and struggling. Greg shouting for her. The metallic crunch as a camera hit the ground. One of the bulbs shattered overhead, showering them in glass. Tiny fragments lodged in Martha's face. A dozen tiny stings.

"Leave her alone." Martha tried to help, calling over muffled cries.

"Please stop. Don't hurt her."

He did stop. Eventually. Then the movement sensors were set off one by one, marking Thomas' progress around the room. Martha found the wall and groped along it in the direction of the stairs. Greg shouted out, a single cry of pain.

The lights came on and the carnage was revealed. Greg was within Martha's reach, lying on the floor. She crouched beside him, dabbing at his wound. A neat line joined his ear to the corner of his mouth, blood oozing from the deep wedge of red flesh revealed.

"Where's Philipa?" Greg, dizzy and disorientated, struggled to lift his head.

They followed the soft sobbing to the corner. This was not Philipa's TV histrionics but the heartbreak of the truly wounded. Thomas stood back, well satisfied with his work.

Philipa was revealed in the dim circle of the lamp. She was curled against the wall, bare torso revealed. Thomas had remade her. When the blood crusted and the scabs fell off, she would be a work of art. That a single, common blade could carve such detail was remarkable. She was etched with arcane calligraphy. Profane flourishes. No plastic surgeon could eradicate his dirty graffiti. But that would be for later. For now she was slick and slippery with snot and tears and blood. Martha slipped her coat off to cover her. Greg moved to enclose her in his arms. Nothing could diminish her distress until the paramedics arrived and she slipped into the dreams of deep sedation.

⊙

The traffic was streaks of light. Neon discoloured the night. The police kept the crowds at bay. Greg went to where Martha stood alone. Her hair, soaked with perspiration, stuck to her head in unflattering curls.

"You did this, didn't you? When I find out how, I'll kill you."

A policeman came over, casting them a warning look.

"Miss Palmer. We're taking everyone in for questioning. It's time for you to come along with me."

"Greg, he says you got it wrong." Her last words to him. "It's Thomas the Knife. Not Thomas the Blade."

Martha settled into the slippery car seat. Her new travelling companion by her side. They stared at one another, neither speaking. Iris' lessons came to mind.

A medium must take care. The opening of consciousness is a special time in a girl's life. When a spirit guide is acquired. Don't be scared. I'll be here to keep you safe.

Suki had smirked when it was her time. The advent of Martha's menstruation seemed paltry by comparison.

You'll never want for company.

You'll never be alone.

For all those years, I believed all the things you said, Martha thought. *You're not the gifted one. You're not gifted.* It was always you and Suki, talking to voices I couldn't hear.

Talking to Dad.

If only you could see me now, Iris. If only you could see me now.

PEARLS

I sat in the park watching a couple who were like all lovers, only intent
on one another. The girl was a beauty ripe for harvest, her hair a golden
sheaf. The boy's desire was visible in the way he kissed her. I felt a pang. I,
too, had been lovely once and loved.

My hair made jealous noises in sympathy.

A man walked by and I could hear the furious beat that was piped
straight into his ears. His curious gaze slid over my sunglasses and cap,
then the sketches on my pad.

I loved the park. It had appeared in my work many times. I liked how
it muted the traffic's song and softened the steel and glass towers with a
shimmering heat haze. I felt sleepy and my pencil made loose, lazy marks
on the page but the coils that passed for my hair were invigorated by the
warmth. I hissed at them but the serpents twitched and jerked. They
refused to be stilled. They longed to creep and crawl, to enjoy sunlight on
their scales.

The young lovers were staring at me.

It was time to go so I packed my things away. Somehow, it was always
time to go.

⊙

I lived a quiet life, contained within three rooms. Sunshine flooded in
through long windows and fell upon the bed, whose sheets were stained
with turps and paint. Alone in my apartment I could let down my hair to
slither, unrestrained. Without the need for dark glasses, my eyes had to
readjust to the light.

My paintings covered the walls. They occupied tables and chairs.

They crowded out the clothes from my closet. Canvases were lined up in the plate rack. I filled a crate and sent it to the gallery when I needed funds. The pantheon of my former life was resurrected. Hermes riding the Staten Island ferry. The Graces shopping on Fifth Avenue. Bacchus drinking in a Brooklyn bar. Eros pimping in Harlem, wearing a ridiculous fur coat.

I adored the city but it rarely noticed me. Sometimes I'd hear a long low whistle or the call of *freak*. I'd even been stopped and dollar bills pressed into my palm. Either alms for needy or an invitation to spend a sweaty afternoon in a hotel room. I always declined and went home, filled with difficult wishes, to lie upon the shambles of my bed. When it got too much to bear I'd get up and occupy myself in a fury of oil paint. I'd work until the insomnia and hunger made me weak. Elation made the colours bright and the pictures came alive.

☉

I watched the night retreat from my window. I stood there until the shops' shutters rolled up to reveal their displays. A rainbow of plastic beads. Vintage handbags with creases etched into the leather. Indecent mannequins in wispy lace underwear.

I felt confined. I needed to be outside. I wound a scarf about my head to keep the serpents in check and selected a pair of dark glasses from the basket by the door.

There was a man on the stairs. He stared at me.

"I'm Paul." His proffered hand forced me to stop. "I've just moved in across the hall from you. I wondered when we'd meet."

I took his hand. After all, I'd no reason to be afraid.

"What's your name?"

"I'm Maddy." I'd forgotten the order of social niceties.

Paul peered into my darkened glasses as if trying to see through them. My hair made chattering noises.

"Did you say something?"

"No," I replied.

"This building echoes. I'm not used to it yet."

"Have we met before?"

"Now you come to mention it, you do seem familiar." Paul cocked his head on one side "Where are you from, Maddy? Where's home?"

☉

I was out of world and time. I'd sickened of home, my villa full of torch-light, shadows and statues. The mosaics of my courtyard were obscured by mud, where once they'd been swept clean each day. Broken urns collected rainwater. Fine tapestries rotted where they hung. I kept the remains of a silenced lyre, the strings long since snapped, beside the pile of rags that were my bed.

Home was dangerous. Men came with swords and spears, wanting fame and fortune, to feast and fornicate on the glory of the tale. The battles and vigils exhausted me. Arrows clattered on my breastplate. Javelins struck my shield. Sometimes they used a net as if that could hold me. Tall shadows fell on the walls and reached around corners to find me. There'd be whistles, shouts and the smash of stone as I sent one of them crashing to the floor. The air was fetid with fear. I could taste it on my forked tongue.

The supplicants were worse. They left dishes on milk on the veranda as if I were a pet. Then there was a tribute. A caged mouse. Ravenous, I shoved the wriggling rodent in my mouth and crunched down. Its lifeless tail hung from my lips. A little death compared with all the rest but it caused me so much shame that I ran away. I slithered into the dark, my green tail rattling a warning to worshippers. They fled around me into the trees. More than one stone effigy was found the following morning, immortalised in its own horror.

I sought the safety of the valley, home only to thorny bushes and bony goats. I meant to spend a night or two. To find a shaded hole full of snakes and sleep. To lie down without the stealthy whispers of swords being unsheathed. I must have been tired because I slept for over a thousand years.

☉

"You ask a lot of questions."

"I'm a curious man." Paul stroked his beard. "Have you ever been to California?"

"No, maybe one day."

We'd progressed to the front step of the building.

"You should. The Pacific's terrific. Would you have breakfast with me?" He didn't pause long enough for me to decline his invitation. "Are you doing anything special today?"

"Yes. No." I was taken aback by my own rashness. "Breakfast would be wonderful."

Paul's grin revealed uneven, ivory teeth.

We walked side by side. Paul had the rolling stride of a man at no-one's command.

"What do you do for a living?" I asked him.

"I trained as an oceanographer but I've done a few different things in my time."

"And what about now?"

"Antiquities dealer. Ancient Greece mainly." Paul smiled. "It's a passion of mine. I've quite a personal collection."

I'd thought all the believers, hunters and collectors were dead. That I'd managed to outlive them all. If Paul fell into any of these categories, then we should celebrate. One of us would soon be extinct.

"I like lost things," Paul continued. "I was a bit lost myself for a while. It made me reconsider what's important. Reconciliation. Forgiveness. That life must go on once grief and anger have gone."

"What caused that bout of introspection?"

"A woman. What else?"

I snorted.

"What have you lost, Maddy?"

We stopped at a crossing, the crush of bodies at our back.

"Everything," I replied, "everything that mattered. Some things were taken from me and the rest I threw away."

⊙

I awoke in a panic after my millennium of sleep. The weight of the world crushed me. I'd shed my skin while I'd slumbered and it had become a fibrous shroud. I'd regrown legs instead. My tongue was fused, not forked anymore. My overgrown fingernails had curled over on themselves and broke into strange brass spirals as I clawed at the earth. Villagers now inhabited my burial plot and saw me crawl out of the ground and stumble on unpliant legs. I tried to avert my eyes but they got in my way. I left the curious ones with more than feet of clay.

I had to find a means to travel. I had to get away. A travelling show was the only way to go. Home became a shabby caravan. Crowds queued to glimpse my reflection. They saw me in the looking glass, stripped to the waist except for a string of pearls. A mass of writhing serpents hung down from my head and covered my breasts. My eyes shocked them the most though. Yellow, the pupil's slits, not circles.

It was a living of a kind. It was a kind of life. I'd have gone on with but for the Lion Man who shook me from my apathy. He knocked on the door of my caravan and asked to come in. He kissed me, unaware of the incompatibility of our species. Or perhaps he didn't care. I didn't either. I had my spectacles on. His mane tickled my face.

"Don't you find me ugly?" I asked.

"You're the most gorgeous gorgon I've ever encountered."

It was my fault.

The Lion Man ripped off his shirt. My glasses fell to the floor. I was thrilled into forgetfulness by his warm flesh and opened my eyes, just for a moment. His erection was stone against my stomach. I was caught in his flinty embrace and had to wiggle free.

I laid him on my bed and covered him with a blanket. I made a bundle of my things. The extra sets of spectacles, spare clothes, my pearls and an apple I'd saved for supper. It was time to go. Somehow, it was always time to go.

☉

Paul and I ordered breakfast from a waitress who looked timeless in a black dress and white apron. Her smooth, dark hair was twisted into a bun. A waiter was writing the specials on a blackboard while another wiped down the marble counter.

"You never take your glasses off." Paul spoke between mouthfuls.

"I've a rare eye condition. My specialist's told me to keep my glasses on."

"I'm sorry." Paul looked at me as though he could diagnose the fault through my lenses.

"That's nice."

"What is?"

"Nice of you to be sorry." I stirred my cappuccino. The cocoa dust mingled with the froth. It looked like marbled paper.

"I love your style—the boots, the dreds, the headscarf. Where are you from?"

"Here and there. I've travelled a lot."

"Like?"

"Europe mostly." I tore open a croissant, scattering flakes.

"Doing what?"

"Painting. Dancing. Idling."

Paul's eyes were fixed on his empty plate. It occurred me that he might be bored. That he might want to leave and I'd spend another day alone.

"Hey, how about I show you some of my favourite places?"

"Aren't you busy?" He screwed up his napkin in his fist. "You must have things to do. Like painting. Dancing. Idling."

The mood had soured. I felt the unexpected sting of tears and was grateful for my glasses. "Of course. We'll go back."

"No," he covered my hand with his. "You can't go back. You can only go forward. Give me a tour."

⊙

I kept moving after the Lion Man. I danced, blindfolded, in a Parisian nightclub. I undulated under dimmed lights, moving in a stupor with all those eyes directly on me. My scanty costume itched. I told fortunes in Prague, my face hidden behind a veil. I was no prophet. I couldn't even see a future for myself but I tried to give solace to the hopeless. London followed with its smog, lamplight and piecework. I stitched gloves in a garret. I wearied of being treated as if diseased or as a victim. I was backed into an alley by a man with a scalpel. Such a dapper gent to be wreaking havoc on the flesh. I slipped off my specs and gave him a long, hard stare.

I was no stranger to brutality but the old world was depraved. Time to usher in the new. I sold some of my pearls to ensure comfortable passage. It was a long voyage spent confined to my cabin. The ship bobbed up and down in the swell like a bath toy of the gods. I lay on my bed listening as the water thumped the hull. Poseidon's heart beat in my ear.

The Statue of Liberty was as fine as any titan and it made my heart glad to see her green skin. I slid from the ship into the oily black water, my belongings towed behind me in a sealed oilskin bag. My serpents were limp with hypothermia by the time I crawled onto the banks of the Hudson.

My hate for Poseidon wouldn't abate but it grieved me to sell off his pearls, one by one. Each was a lustrous story. They'd fall from Poseidon's ears, nostrils and mouth whenever we quarrelled. It was his way of getting me to laugh and make up with him.

⊙

Paul and I sat in the atrium of the Frick Museum, chaperoned by an angel. She was an impassive creature carved in marble, her wings folded high on her back. Sunlight flooded through the glass ceiling. The fronds of the ferns were delicate under my fingers.

"I love it here because it looks like a home, not a stuffy museum." I remembered the Frick family. A cunning clan of robber barons who'd discovered gentility and art. They'd built this mansion overlooking the park. "I can imagine the Frick women sitting here, gossiping."

"You look sad." Paul was tender voiced.

Sad for my home that was like this, except that my courtyard was open to the elements so that the mosaic floor glistened underfoot when it rained. Water trickled from the dolphin spouts into the central cistern. I'd sit there with my sisters, Sthen and Euryale, sewing and talking.

Sthen would play that damn lyre of hers. She was never very good at it. Euryale giggled as she asked, "What's Poseidon like? Is he more salty than mortal men?"

Sthen tutted and blushed but listened, breath held for my answer.

○

I took Paul to Grand Central Station to view the crowds from the balcony. It was a grand ballet. People moved with such purpose that I felt tired just watching them.

"Let me show you The Whispering Gallery."

I'd read about it but had no-one with which to test the theory. I took Paul's hand and pulled him down the long, low steps. The spot was underground. Not a gallery at all but the junction of four subterranean walkways. The space was marked with four corner pillars which rose to meet at the apex of the tiled dome. I took Paul by the shoulders and put him facing one of the pillars like a child cornered for their naughtiness.

"Don't move." I went to the opposite pillar and spoke to it. "Can you hear me?"

"That's amazing." His voice came back to me. "Can anyone else hear us?"

"No, the sound transmits from one pillar to the opposite one, across the dome."

"You're beautiful." It sounded like we were in bed together and he was whispering in my ear.

"Isn't the acoustic design fantastic?"

"Don't ignore me."

"Easy flattery. How many women are you currently trying to seduce?"

"Just you."

"Directness. Good. Are you doing this for money or sport?"

"Doing what?"

"Hunting vulnerable women in search of trophies. Will you take my head for your collection?"

"It's not your head I'm after. And you're about as vulnerable as a bag of rattlesnakes"

"You say the nicest things."

"You don't cut men any slack, do you? Do you forgive or forget anything?"

○

I returned home, my tryst with Poseidon in every crevice and pore. There were bloody footprints on my porch as if a battle fresh army had trampled through the house. I followed the trail back to the carnage in the courtyard where I fell to the floor and howled.

My darling Sthen and Euryale. All Sthen had wanted was for Perseus to notice her. I could see her longing looks at his oiled curls and athlete's legs. Strutting Perseus and his friends had given both my sisters their full attention all afternoon. Then they'd cut their throats and laid them out with their arms about each other, like sleeping infants. Their hair, always curled and pinned, was loose about their pallid faces. Blood seeped from their wounded necks onto their tattered gowns.

And all because I said no to you, Perseus. All because you couldn't have me.

I ran to Poseidon's cliff top house. He held me while I screamed and shook. He stroked my hair and the sea below boiled in fury.

"I want him dead. Kill him for me."

"We can't, my love. Perseus is championed by Athena. On Zeus' orders."

"Since when do you care about Athena? I was one of her temple maidens when you seduced me. On her altar, no less."

"Let's not give her another reason to seek revenge."

"You said you hated her. You called her a battle hungry spinster. Why do you care what she thinks?"

"She's Zeus' daughter."

"So? You're Zeus' brother."

"Yes but Zeus is King of Olympus. There'd be war."

"Zeus would go to war with you over Perseus?"

"Perseus is his son."

"Son." Secrets and nepotism. Zeus, king of philanderers and begetter of bastards.

"We'll have revenge but we'll have to bide our time."

"You haven't seen what they did…"

"Listen to me, Medusa. I loved your sisters but we can't do anything. Not yet."

You gods are as treacherous as men. You all stick together. Blood,

Poseidon, is thicker than your precious water after all.

So I sought out a goddess where gods had failed me. Hera was Zeus' queen and consort. I threw myself on the ground before her. Hera shushed her sniggering court with a look and stepped down, dainty footed, from her dais.

"Poor dear, your sisters must be avenged." I could see her calculating the gains. A lesson for her errant husband and his illegitimate children. "I commend your loyalty and I think I can see a way. There's so much anger in those lovely eyes. The price would be very high though."

"Anything. I don't care. Just help me."

"Are you sure?" She held my hand, relishing the task ahead. "We poor weak women must do what brave men can't. I'll make them afraid to even look at you."

Goddesses, as treacherous as women. You should have told me to go home, Hera, and bury my sisters.

I didn't care what it cost me. I gloried in what she made of me. A tail replaced my shapely legs. I had snakes instead of locks. Their fangs bit me. I lay in the floor while Hera stepped over my convulsing body. I felt the pain with every heartbeat as waited to become immune. I didn't mind. I felt alive. Best of all was the fury in my eyes. There was no-one I couldn't petrify.

⊙

It was evening and the summer sky was dark blue and the moon hung low and yellow over the city skyline.

"That one, there." I pointed to a basement bar, the high stools and tables just visible from the street.

We drank whisky from heavy tumblers.

"You don't give much away." Paul gestured to the barman who refilled our empty glasses. "I know you paint. That you can walk me off my feet. Why's a girl like you single?"

"You make it sound like I'm incomplete as I am." I leant back, letting the whisky drain down my throat. It left a combination of peat and antiseptic in my mouth. I decided to stop sparring. "There was someone once."

"What happened?"

"He let me down."

"How?"

"He sided with his family."

"It's a mistake forcing people to chose. Invariably they never chose you."

"Whose side are you on?"

"See? You're doing it now. There has to be a side." Paul snorted into his glass, clouding it up with his breath. "Not everyone has the luxury of choice."

I put an ice cube in my mouth and crunched it up.

"Let's not talk about the past." Paul turned his body towards me. "I've not seen your eyes. I bet they're green. The green of glittering emeralds."

"Guess again."

"Brown, like chocolate."

"Nope."

"Blue, then. But what shade of blue?"

Blue as the deepest part of the ocean. That's what Poseidon, god of all the seas, said to me when we made love. I'd forgotten that.

Oh, Poseidon, you were running water in my hands.

"Do you want to see them?"

My dirty, yellow eyes.

"Oh, yes."

Paul reached out to remove my glasses but I stopped him.

"Not here. Let's go to your place."

☉

My courtship with Poseidon had been steeped in miracles. Marvels were mundane. He took my hand and we dived into the sea, encased in a bubble he'd made. I could breathe despite the fathoms that fell away. I could see the swirling surf above me when I looked up. Poseidon's kingdom was below. Jellyfish pulsed and throbbed. Rays flapped their fins like wings. Sharks stared at us as they patrolled. We were engulfed in a shoal of silver darts that went as quickly as they came.

There was a huge door set in the ocean floor.

"What's that?"

"A jail. It's a prisoner that I guard for Zeus."

"Who is it?"

"The Kraken."

The Kraken was a titan from the start of time who had dared to challenge Zeus. The Kraken appeared at the bars, having heard his name. All I could see was a giant eye. The rest of him was lost in the watery gloom. I smiled in sympathy and raised a hand. The eye blinked back.

"I didn't bring you down here to flirt with him," Poseidon chided. "I wanted you to see the water. It's just like your eyes. The darkest shade of blue that the ocean can possibly be."

⊙

Kissing was a distant memory that I associated with gods, lion men and calamity. Kissing Paul was discovering kissing anew. It reminded me of what I'd put away. Poseidon, a god among the waves but just like any other man in bed. Demanding to worship and to be worshipped in return.

"Come upstairs with me," Paul clutched my hand, "please."

We started to undress in the hall in his flat, amid the unpacked boxes. Paul's shirt lost its shape as he dropped it to the floor, unable to withstand the world without him. I traced the crookedness of his collarbones with my fingertips. The smattering of coarse hair on his chest.

"Where's your bedroom?" I said between kisses.

"There." He indicated a room behind me with a flick of his eyes. I walked backwards, leading him to it. I pulled my blouse over my head and threw it on a chair. Then I saw the picture Paul had hung over his bed. The canvas dominated the room. A fantasy within a Rococo-style frame.

It was one of mine. A self portrait of sorts. I'd sent it to the gallery as soon as it was finished as I couldn't bear to look at it. I'd remade the city as arcadia with Bryant Park at its heart. The grass was deep and lush. Trees had conquered concrete and glass. Poseidon and I were post-coital in this idyll. That was clear, not just from our nudity but glow. My head rested on his chest. His arm was around me. He looked down at my head of snakes and yellow eyes like I was the loveliest woman in the world.

"Don't you recognise me, Medusa?"

"Poseidon."

"I've been searching for you. I wasn't even sure you were still alive but when I saw the painting I knew I'd found you."

"Well, now you have. What do you want?"

"Forgiveness."

"That won't help my sisters."

"Nothing will help your sisters. It would help us though."

"I was just a plaything to you."

"That's not fair."

"Neither's life. You taught me that."

"I loved you. I still do. Why else do you think I'm here?"

I looked out of the window. Distant lights winked at me.

"It's too late. I'm tired. A tired, old murdering hag."

"And I'm a washed up, has-been deity."

"What became of Perseus?" I surprised myself. I couldn't recall when I'd last thought of him. He'd evaded me.

"Hera chose Perseus' bride as a sacrifice. She demanded the Kraken be released to do the deed. The Kraken was more interested in Perseus," Poseidon gave me a wry smile. "The Kraken liked you. He was glad to oblige."

I should've known to leave the gods to slug it out with one another I felt no satisfaction at the thought of Perseus fixed by the Kraken's slow blinking eye or dangling from its mouth.

I felt nothing.

"Do you really want to see me? See me as I am now?"

A mirror stood against the wall, waiting to be hung. I knelt before it. Poseidon joined me so that we were penitents before ourselves. I unwound my headscarf and took off my spectacles.

"This is me. I've nothing left, not even looks."

"There's still love. Life. We still have those." A pearl dropped from his nostril and rolled to a standstill on the far side of the room. Then another. A third spilled from his mouth. More from his ears. They fell, a percussion of pleading, as they bounced across the wooden floor. "You're beautiful to me. You always will be."

We were reflected in the mirror. A man with a crooked nose and a trimmed brown beard, speckled with silver. A woman with a sinuous coil of dark hair lying over one shoulder. Eyes, blue. The darkest shade of blue that the ocean can be.

"You see? Beautiful."

"Yes," I answered in wonderment, "yes, I am."

THE ABSENT SHADE

"Calm down now," Umbra said as she wiped away Thomas' tears. "Let's play a game. It's a secret though. You mustn't tell anyone about it."

After that Thomas wanted to play every night, so Umbra would get up from her roll up mattress on the floor beside his bed and move the lamps around to cast shadows on the wall behind them. Then she'd lie beside him and wrap her thin arms around him.

"You start," she'd say, "make me a shadow."

His hands were a muddle.

"What's that?" Umbra asked.

"A cat."

Her hands moulded his. The shadow formed a sinuous feline shape, Thomas' little finger sticking out to form its tail.

"My turn."

She placed one of her hands over the other and a dog appeared on the wall. He could see every detail of it, even though it was in silhouette; its shaggy fur, its lolling tongue, the wag of its tail. It cocked up its ears and chased the cat, leaping from wall to ceiling. Thomas squealed and clapped.

"What next?" she asked.

His hands wiggled.

"Is it a fish?"

He nodded, well pleased that she'd guessed.

"Let me see," Umbra mused as she gathered together the strands of scattered shadows in her fist and fashioned them into a seal that fell into a graceful arc as it dived, the boy's minnow in its mouth.

"Now, little man, copy me."

She taught him how to make shadow puppets. A rabbit with index and middle fingers for ears, a swan whose neck was formed from the curve of the wrist and feathers from fanned out fingers. Bears, ducks, turtles, even an elephant with tusks.

"This is my favourite," she said as she made a pair of birds on a bough. "Watch."

Her projections were as different to his as a child's plasticine figure is from an artist's carving. The bough was in flower and the birds cocked their heads as if listening to each other's song. Then the impossible: the birds divided and divided, becoming a flock that took flight. Fluttering wings covered the wall in an explosion of feathers.

"Now, that's enough." she kissed his forehead when the shadows had taken up their former shape. "Sleep now."

When he was older he thought about trying to tell someone about her but he knew that he wouldn't be believed, even though every part of it was true.

⊙

"Pleasure or business, Mr Leung?" The desk clerk smiles at Thomas.

"Business."

He used to work for a multinational that sent him to quell corporate uprisings, navigate difficult negotiations and strip out smaller companies. His wife, Viola, doesn't know that he has a new job, one that he's even better at than the last one. His wife calls him a cold fish which, he supposes, is why he's so good at this work.

"You're a new guest to us. Is this your first time in Hong Kong?"

"No." His English accent is the product of the finest International School that Hong Kong has to offer, which makes it difficult to place. "I grew up here."

It's the city where he lost his childhood, if that's what growing up is.

"Welcome home." The clerk hands him the key card.

Thomas has been here for two weeks already, staying in a third rate place under an alias while he gathers information. He's glad to be checking into somewhere more comfortable. The Ritz-Carlton Hotel occupies the top seventeen of the one hundred and eighteen floors of the International

Commerce Centre, the ICC, on Kowloon. His room has a view. It's spectacular.

Hong Kong is a city where peaks rise from the sea, layers of them that fade to soft greys in the distance. Thomas remembers Umbra telling him she'd never seen anything like it, a place where so many mountains had drowned. Tower blocks flourish amid the lush greenery. It's vertiginous as it lacks the space to sprawl.

From his window he looks out on Victoria Harbour. The water's busy with freighters coming in from the South China Sea, their cargo parcelled off onto smaller boats that are pulled along by sturdy tugs whose paths criss-cross cruise ships and ferries.

Enough. Time to work.

Thomas lays out his gear on the bed and assembles what he needs. He catches the Star Ferry over to Central, the part of Hong Kong island that's the bloodless, beating heart of the economy. Its towers are clad in gold, silver and copper facades that look burnished in the sun. The city reflects itself. He has dressed like all the other men who are piling out of work onto the elevated footbridges. The man Thomas is looking for, Mr Tsang, is crossing a bridge below him. He's nondescript for someone so powerful man, revelling in his anonymity.

He should be more careful, Thomas thinks.

He follows Mr Tsang to the escalators. There's eight hundred metres of them in segments, all covered, crossing the narrow streets on their ascension to Victoria Peak. They're a radical solution to the weariness of commuters who have to scale the steep hill.

Thomas has done his research. He knows where Mr Tsang is going. Thomas gets off at Hollywood Road and overtakes him. Instinctively, Thomas moves out of the sunshine and crosses over to shade where he feels less conspicuous. He walks with intent, ignoring the antique shop windows, crowded with curios and trinkets.

His destination is the Man Mo Temple. They are the gods of Literature and War, respectively. He finds temples less forbidding than churches, even though his family are Christian. People wander in and out, carrying shopping bags as though calling on an old friend. Discarded incense wrappers litter the ground around the trestle tables outside where they're being sold. Old fruit is dumped in bins, having once been left as offerings.

Thomas likes the gloomy red and gold interior. Giant incense spirals that take weeks to burn hang down from the ceiling. Sandalwood smoke stings his eyes. It's busy, filled with people who've come to pay their respects to their dead and disrespectful tourists taking photos. He lights incense for Umbra, not knowing if she's alive or dead. He owes her a lifetime of remorse. She owes him, too.

Mr Tsang enters. Thomas waits for him to finish, watching his mouth moving in a prayer. Then he follows him out onto the street, letting him walk along for a while. Mr Tsang's shadow stretches out along the pavement in front of him, his soul going ahead. Thomas closes the gap between them on silent shoes.

"Mr Tsang."

Mr Tsang turns, confused that Thomas is so close but he doesn't understand why. His eye will have seen what's odd and his subconscious will have registered it but his mind has yet to understand. Thomas doesn't give him time to think about it.

"Mr Tsang." Thomas seizes his hand like he's a friend that he's not seen in years. "Please accept my condolences. Your father was greatly respected."

Thomas presses his hand over their combined fists in a gesture of sympathy. "I met him in Beijing..."

The pressure of Thomas' hand triggers the mechanism on top of the gaudy ring he's wearing and the poison tipped spike is released from the band and punctures Mr Tsang's palm. It's a scratch but it'll suffice.

Mr Tsang flinches and pulls away, putting it to his mouth. All the better for Thomas' purpose.

"I'm sorry," Thomas says smoothly, glancing at his watch. "I must go, I'm late."

He turns and leaves before Mr Tsang has a chance to stop him. He'll be dead within the hour. Mr Tsang's assassination is a warning. Thomas doesn't know why. It's none of his business. The concoction he's used is so potent that he's taken the antidote, just in case he accidentally stabs himself. It'll be easily identified at toxicology but not so easily traced back to a source. This is his favourite kind of kill. He'll be well away before Mr Tsang's death throes start.

Thomas slips the ring off and puts it in a plastic case in his pocket.

He's well acquainted with all kinds of murder and how to hide them. Pseudo-suicides, sex games gone awry, allergic reactions. Mock muggings that leave him standing over a body in the gutter. Thomas dislikes the last one as it reminds him of what Umbra said.

⊙

"This is Umbra," Thomas' mother said. "She's here to help us."

Help. His mother, Mai Yuen, needed a lot of help. She would've had a flotilla of staff if she could. The staff themselves were cheap. The real luxury was having the space in which to keep them. By law imported servants had to live with their sponsors and so there was only enough space in the apartment for them and Umbra. Thomas' parents were affluent, not uber-wealthy, living in a city where extended families often lived in just one room.

Mai Yuen always complained about Umbra. She would've preferred what she had herself as a child, an amah, some Chinese spinster consigned to a life of drudgery. Instead she made do with a series of foreign domestic 'helpers'.

Mai Yuen had left Umbra at the door to Thomas' room. He looked up to see a woman, like all the others. Or nearly. Big dark eyes and bang straight hair. A velour tracksuit and flip flops. The scar on her left cheek marked her out as different. It was jagged and ugly.

"I don't want you," he shouted at her. "I want my daddy!"

The truth was that he didn't know what he wanted. At four, all he knew was that he was angry.

"He's not here," Umbra said, "and I don't know when he'll be back, he has to work, so stop this."

Umbra was impassive, just like his father. That stopped his screeching.

⊙

His mother would've tried to placate him with *He'll be back soon, I'm sure*, before she got bored and drifted away. A tear ran down his face. Umbra seized him and her hug was fierce, unlike his mother's limp, insipid embraces. Umbra made him utterly hers in that moment and ever after.

○

Umbra had been with them for three months when Thomas' father, Chun Hin, came home. It was his birthday.

The apartment was all clean lines, almost masculine. Mai Yuen's art books were arranged in piles, topped with antique lacquered boxes. A set of oil paintings from the gallery where she worked. Celadon pottery. There was hardly anything of Thomas' father there.

"Who's this?" his father asked.

"Umbra." Thomas was keen to show her off.

"Hello, Umbra."

Umbra put down the cake plates and forks.

Mai Yuen held the cake slice poised over the cake she'd bought. She was glossy, her hair smooth, lacquered nails and her lips painted. She looked like a polished stone.

"You can go to your room now, Umbra." Mai Yuen dismissed her.

"Where's Daddy's cake?" Thomas asked.

His mother had ordered a patisserie creation covered in whipped cream icing and decorated in gold sugared almonds. It was far too large for the small family.

"Look, this one has Daddy's name on it."

"No. Where's mine?"

He wanted the cake that Umbra had helped him to make. It was a misshapen heap of chocolate and sponge.

"Don't be silly." She widened her eyes at him.

He leant over and shoved her cake off the table. The stemmed cake platter shattered on the floor, the cake smashed up.

"Can't you control him?" That was Chun Hin.

Thomas shouted for Umbra. She hovered in the doorway.

Mai Yuen was wiping the cream that had splattered over her shoes and up her legs. His father was out of his seat, seizing Thomas' arm.

"I just wanted a nice night with my family. Is that too much to ask?" He was talking to Mai Yuen. "And you," his grip on Thomas tightened, "go to your room."

"I want Umbra."

"No." Chun Hin pointed at Umbra. "You, to your room too. Stay in there."

"She sleeps with him. It's the only way he'll settle." His mother's face looked blotchy.

Chun Hin rounded on her. "No wonder he acts like a baby if you treat him like this."

He threw Thomas on his bed and slammed the door. The boy shrieked and shrieked. When his mother came in she didn't look polished anymore.

"Stop it," she hissed. "You've ruined everything."

It only made him shriek more so his father came in an, took off his belt and hit him. It made a cracking sound as it made contact with his back. Thomas glared at him in shocked silence and then started to shriek once more. Chun Hin raised his arm again.

"Please, no more." Mai Yuen got down on her knees, her head bowed. "Not tonight."

He stared at her. Then he walked out, slowly, the belt still in his hand trailing on the floor behind him. She got up and followed him in silence. When he passed the door to Umbra's room which was in sight of Thomas' room, he opened the door.

"Go to him. Keep him quiet."

Umbra lay down on the floor beside Thomas.

"I want him to go."

"He'll leave soon enough. He's just another thing to be endured. I've seen much worse."

"I hate him."

"Calm down now," Umbra said as she wiped away his tears. "Let's play a game. It's a secret though. You mustn't tell anyone about it."

☉

Work's done. Time to play.

Thomas chooses a bar called Ciacada, overlooked by the escalators, its doors open wide to the street. He likes its lighting, diffuse and safe enough for him to feel comfortable.

There's a girl in the corner. She's not a dead ringer but she's close enough. He catches her eye. She says her name is Lunette, her glance flicking from his eyes to mouth and back again. He buys them Belgium beers and they talk. He makes her laugh. He knows how to pass as human. He does it every day.

They find a love hotel. Lunette picks a room from a laminated brochure while he pays. The Underwater Fantasy room is more tasteful than Thomas expects, despite the mermaid costume in the wardrobe. As he hands over a roll of bills to Lunette he remembers what Umbra said. *Better to be one man's whore than many's.*

Lunette strips down, bathed in soft blur light. She sits on the edge of the bed, open legged in bra and pants that are no more than gauzy triangles. He lets her unbutton his shirt and kiss his chest and stomach. A sigh comes from deep inside her, as though she genuinely desires him. She reaches for his fly but he stops her. He's not ready yet.

He slips his hands inside the thin pieces of fabric and works the flesh beneath. That distracts her. He pushes her back, tilting her head away from him. At that angle she looks more like Umbra which makes him suddenly hard. He tears open a condom packet and throws the empty wrapper on the floor. She reaches up to help him put it on.

"No, stay there," he whispers. "Just like that."

Lunette bites her lower lip as he plunges into her.

It's easier with her than his wife. Easier to imagine that it's Umbra beneath him. When Thomas climaxes he thinks he feels something but he's not entirely sure.

☉

"The next few days are very important."

Thomas sat opposite his mother. Mai Yuen had no idea just *how* important, how long a shadow those days would cast.

A row of low copper lampshades hung over the dining room table, casting soft, diffuse light. The city outside the window was vibrant in neon, rather than garish. A hierarchy existed on Hong Kong island. The closer to Victoria Peak the property, the higher up the social scale the owner was. The Leungs, who lived in Dragonfly Mansions, were sufficiently placed to have a view.

"Your father's coming home. He's back tomorrow night. There's an important dinner that we're going to on Monday evening."

Umbra brought out their meal, placing a bowl of broth before Mai Yuen who took it without thanks.

"You're sixteen, Thomas. It's time that you started to behave, especially when your father's back."

"I *do* behave."

"No, you provoke him." He watched as she took a spoonful of the clear liquid with soundless delicacy. "You're doing it now instead of listening. No wonder he never wants to come home."

She glared at Thomas as he slurped his noodles.

"Don't make him angry. I'm busy tomorrow at the gallery so I'll have to pick up some shoes to go with my new dress on Sunday." She put down her spoon as if laying down a weapon to negotiate a truce. "Come with me and I'll take you to the cinema on the understanding that you'll be good while he's here."

Umbra's shadow stretched along the floor. It gathered together the multiple, muted shadows cast by the various lights. Mai Yuen's shadow was transformed into a parody of a preening woman at a dressing table, as if she were no more than Umbra's puppet. Thomas didn't smile. He'd learnt to hide his amusement at Umbra's jokes.

Umbra's shadow reached out and ruffled Mai Yuen's shadow-hair until it came out of its smooth knot. It surprised Thomas. He hadn't realised that Umbra could exert such an effect because his mother turned to look in a mirror, frowning as she tried to smooth down her already perfect hair.

⊙

There's something that Thomas is putting off.

He sits in tatty dim sum restaurants that serve the finest food in the city. He drinks espresso martinis. He buys his wife expensive shoes that look exquisite and crippling. He's missed this king of cities. Its plazas and alleyways contain everything. As much as he understands its rhythms, he doesn't belong anymore.

He tells himself that he's looking for Umbra. He watches the crowd. Foreign bankers, men and women in suits that look the same regardless of whether they work in Hong Kong, London or New York. Then there are the young fashionistas. This season they're eschewing Gucci for Harris Tweed. The Chinese mainlanders that can afford to stay here are easy to distinguish because of their expensive, tasteless bling, having grown rich on corruption, mining and property speculation. Their wealth will be gone within a generation because of ridiculous spending. And finally there are the helpers, peripheral and unseen, wheeling prams and carrying shopping.

Wherever Thomas is in the world, he seeks Umbra's face. Or he hopes to find someone like her, someone with a denser shadow that could turn abruptly in his direction, recognising that he's different.

If he ever saw such a person he would ask them if they could fix him.

☉

Thomas's parents seemed so old to him when Umbra started to work for his family but his mother was only twenty-five and his father thirty-four. Thomas only knew him through the women in his life—Mother, Umbra and then Marcia. Chun Hin was a stranger that came in and out of the apartment in Dragonfly Mansions demanding to know why he wasn't doing better at school and making Mai Yuen more fractious than normal.

Thomas used to go to his father's closet, trying to fathom who he was. All his clothes were sealed in dry cleaner bags. He tore one open and put his face against Chun Hin's jacket but all he could smell were wool and chemicals.

The closest he'd ever been to his father was that weekend, when he was sixteen and he didn't even know Thomas was there.

Thomas had gone out to a Mandarin tutorial that morning but halfway there he'd called the man, claiming sickness. He felt unsettled and wanted a morning alone with Umbra while his mother was at the gallery and before his father's flight landed.

A mop and bucket were abandoned in the hall. His father's suitcases were close by. He was back earlier than expected.

Thomas slipped off his shoes and stood, listening. Nothing. He walked through the kitchen. A half-drunk cup of tea sat on the work top. Thomas put a hand around it. It was cold.

Umbra's door was ajar. Thomas could hear breathy moans and soft cries coming from within. In that narrow gap he could see his father. Chun Hin's white shirt was tangled around his torso, his trousers and shorts pushed down around his thighs. The muscles of his buttocks strained with each thrust. Umbra head was tilted at an angle that made the sinews of her neck taut. Her eyes were closed.

An involuntary thrill shot through Thomas' groin. When the sharp spasm passed a dull ache remained. He hated that watching them could make him feel that way, hated what his father was doing to Umbra and that she was allowing him to.

Thomas imagined himself a man because he'd had sex with older girls and drunk beer late into the night, but he wasn't yet man enough to understand the meaning of the shadows on the wall. Umbra's wasn't entwined with Chun Hin's but was sat in a corner with its arms wrapped around its drawn up knees.

☉

"Your mother wants you to go out with her today. Remember?" Umbra asked, as if Thomas could forget.

Umbra was laying out breakfast trays for his parents who were still in bed. It was Sunday and she would have to be gone before they got up.

"Yes." Thomas nodded, unhappy. He didn't know how to act with any of them after what he'd seen.

"He's only here until Thursday. The time will pass quickly."

"I don't care when he leaves."

"Don't upset them. It'll only make your mother unbearable for weeks."

"Will you always be there for me?" Thomas blurted out. "Will you promise that you'll never leave me?"

Will you always put me first?

"That's an odd question."

She was stalling, knowing that words like *always* and *never* should be handled with care.

When he was younger she would stand behind him whenever he was frightened or sad, her arms forming a protective circle around him and her chin resting on the top of his head.

He'd been too tall for this sort of comfort for some time but now he was sat down in front of a bowl and soggy, uneaten cereal, she held him. He could feel her breasts against his back, her warmth burning him, and it made him furious.

◉

Thomas stared out of the store window into the mall. Potted orange trees were festooned with red envelopes. A man played a piano under a herd of horses. It was a few weeks before the advent of the Year of the Horse. The largest one was twenty feet high, red velvet, with a golden bridle and saddle. The others were an array of sizes and colours, some satin, some mirror glass. A few had wings or a unicorn horn.

"Will these match my dress? I think they'll look nice with the earrings that your father wants me to wear. The diamond and pearl ones."

He turned to look at what his mother was wearing. Black ankle boots, the leather cut away in delicate patterns, the heels golden spikes. A shop assistant brought her more boxes. Mai Yuen tried on another pair, ignoring the girl because she was young and beautiful.

"What about these?"

The sandals were intricate constructions of straps and buckles that wound around her ankles.

She'd promised to take him to the cinema but now it was too late for the film he wanted to see. He wasn't interested in her shoes. He didn't really care about the film either. He cared that she made so few promises to him and never kept any of them. He kicked out at the wooden panelling. Everyone turned to stare.

Mai Yuen came over and shook him by the shoulders. "You're an ungrateful little brat. Now sit and wait."

His cheeks burnt at being reprimanded like a child, especially in front of the young, pretty assistants. His mother threw down the shoes that she was carrying. The girl knelt down to pick them up.

"I'll take the boots, the sandals and the grey suede pumps. I want them delivered. Tonight." They were approximately three thousand dollars a pair. Mai Yuen was a conspicuous spender.

The girl packaged the boxes with ribbons so that they looked like presents, not purchases.

Thomas left the shop ahead of his mother, willing himself not to cry. Her heels clipped along behind him. They left the mall, heading back to Dragonfly Mansions.

Thomas heard the collective sound of women when the mall doors slid open.

It was a hum, as though a great flock had gathered. Every Sunday, in every season, thousands of helpers were evicted from where they lived. They had a day off but nowhere to go so they communed all over Central's walkways and squares. They sat on corrugated cardboard or used it as windbreakers. They covered themselves with blankets. They knitted, they played cards, they sang and danced.

Thomas knew they were the reason why his mother hated shopping on Sundays. It was in the way that she held her head up, refusing to look at the women beneath her. *Pinoy girls*, she'd call them, a phrase for domestic servants from the Philippines that smacked of insult.

Among all those Pinoy girls was Umbra. Thomas stopped. She stood there with a young man, a year or two older than Thomas. He had Umbra's wide smile. He sat on a wall and she stood, her chin resting on the top of his head.

Thomas could feel his mother hovering at his elbow, her body turned in the same direction as his. She put a hand on his shoulder but he stepped away from her, unwilling to be comforted or consoled. Umbra was the only person who normally touched him and he didn't want to share her. Not with his father and not with her son.

☉

Mai Yuen's dying. She's been dying for years but now Thomas thinks it

149

will be very soon.

He can't put it off any longer. He flies out tomorrow.

⊙

The foyer attendant at Dragonfly Mansions watches him as he walks to the lifts. It's a relief to be inside the air-conditioned building after the humidity and the sun.

A helper lets him into the apartment.

His mother is on the sofa, swaddled in cashmere. The joints of her hands are blown out in gnarled lumps, her fingers slipping sideways at the knuckles. Rheumatoid disease has wracked her joints, her lungs and kidneys. She has an artificial knee and shoulder joint. The light's clarity is unkind to her thinning hair and papery skin but she's made an effort, all coiffed and made up. It occurs to Thomas that he could be kind and give her a death that's as quiet and comfortable as falling asleep but decides against it. One of his rules is that work should never be personal.

He hands the flowers—tea roses which are her favourites—to the helper. It's what people do in these circumstances.

"Come and kiss me."

Her perfume's an overpowering a mix of ambergris and jasmine, that she's worn in an attempt to mask the smell of her demise.

"How are you?" he asks.

She shrugs and he doesn't press her.

"Nice of you to come. It's been so long." At least two years. "How are Viola and the children?"

"Fine." Viola is so like his mother. Thomas wonders if that means he's like Chun Hin.

"And your father?" She can't help herself.

"I called him about six weeks ago but he was in Taiwan. I spoke to Marcia instead."

"Oh?"

"She's pregnant."

Mai Yuen looks out of the window, down on the other apartments and across the bay to Kowloon's waterfront.

"Men can do that, I suppose." Her eyes are hard and dry. She's bitter that, at ten years her senior, her ex-husband has a new life with a lovely young thing. "A father again at sixty. Well, it won't be him looking after it anyway. How's your work?"

"Excellent."

"That's something then. Do you like what I've done with the place?"

Thomas gives the apartment a cursory glance, deliberately disinterested in the décor as his mother is in him. Her flawless taste lacks personality. The neutral palette is accented with beiges and browns, colours dubbed *mocha* and *caramel* by the stores to make the prices more palatable.

They talk nonsense over tea. The machinations of the residents committee, the new developments on Kowloon and the unseasonable hot weather. All the while Thomas thinks about the desolation and destruction of family life. How they have trampled one another.

He waits until the visit's nearly done to make what he's really come here to ask her sound like a throw away comment. It's not from sensitivity. It's just that she'll be more likely to talk.

"Do you remember Umbra? Whatever happened to her?"

"Umbra?" She says the name as if it's of no consequence, and in her studied nonchalance is the full weight of her years of feeling alone.

"She had a son, didn't she?" He pours them both another cup of tea. "Where did *he* live?"

"No idea. It was a long time ago."

"It was my fault." He tries to disarm her with honesty. "I hid your earrings in her room."

"Of course you did. She had too much to lose to do something so stupid. You were furious that day when we saw her with her son. Did you imagine that you were the centre of her universe?"

"You sent her back, to somewhere dangerous, because Dad was sleeping with her."

"Yes but it wasn't just that. You always looked at her like *she* was your mother. You always wanted her, never me." She snorts. "We're a fine pair, aren't we?"

There was no solidarity in that comment. Even if there was, she was right. Thomas doesn't know how to let her in.

"You were such a precocious child. You remembered every slight. You bore grudges. You never liked to be with other children. All your rage disappeared when Umbra left. Your father said you became cold, like me."

"How would he know? He was never there?"

Thomas wasn't trying to make her happy but that pleased her.

"I love him. Or I did once. To the point of madness." It took Thomas a moment to realise that she was talking about his father. "I was too young to understand that he puts women in different compartments, one for pleasure and the other for procreation."

Thomas is his opposite, which is why Umbra has become everything. He's confused her in his mind even though she wasn't his mother, sister or lover. It's too many roles for one person but his every memory of emotion relates to her. He imagines her at forty-six and him at thirty. An age difference to cause comment but not an unimaginable one. Sometimes he marries her. Sometimes he kills her. He's used every connection that he has but he's never found her. He's even asked his father at one of their rare father-son lunches but Chun Hin's fork paused, then he continued to eat as though Thomas hadn't spoken.

The helper comes in and puts down a tray of pills and a tumbler of water.

"Later," Mai Yuen tells her.

"No," the woman insists. "Now."

Thomas is impressed at how his mother complies, the fine gold bangles tinkling on her bony wrist as she lifts the glass. She lets the helper arrange the cushions behind her.

At least his mother has her. He shouldn't begrudge her that.

○

Thomas lay on his bed, facing the wall.

Chun Hin had gone out hours before. He hadn't shouted or slammed doors, he'd simply walked away from them all, having somewhere more important to be. Oh, the luxury of just being able to get up and leave.

Mai Yuen sat in the lounge, still wearing her new dress with a deep plunge at the front and pattern cut boots. Her metallic eyeshadow was smeared by tears. She stared at the wall, the television muted and the colours bright in the darkened room.

Her earrings were on the coffee table. Each one was a diamond stud from which a pearl dangled by a gold chain.

Earlier, Thomas had hung about in the doorway of Mai Yuen's bedroom, drawn by the sound of slamming drawers. The room was wall-papered in embossed grey silk with mirrored wardrobes that reflected her. Her jewellery case was open and there were boxes piled up on the floor. She knelt on the floor, rummaging through boxes. Chun Hin was down-stairs in the lounge, on the phone.

"Have you seen my earrings?" she asked.

"Which ones?"

A ruse on Thomas' part.

"The pearl drops your father bought me from Japan." She opened another box and then threw it down in frustration. "He expects me to wear them."

Thomas shrugged. Then, Little Judas, he said, "Have you looked in Umbra's room?"

Mai Yuen froze, another box in her hand, looking at him. The idea gathered enough momentum to get his mother to her feet and send her marching from the room.

The earrings were there, in the folds of one of Umbra's cheap sweat-shirts. Glamorous and opulent, they were a ridiculous thing for a woman in her position to steal. Mai Yuen flew at her, screaming and pulling at fistfuls of Umbra's hair. Chun Hin had to pull her off.

"I didn't take them, I swear." Umbra addressed Chun Hin directly.

"You have to be gone in the morning." He still held Mai Yuen in his arms, his arms across her chest like iron bars. "It's out of my hands."

"Please."

"I can't." It almost sounded like an apology.

So, Thomas lay on his bed, having had a whole evening to reflect. Umbra's shadow slid under the door and squatted over him like a brooding succubus.

"I'm not a thief," her shadow said. "Your mother must've put them there."

"No, I did."

"I don't understand." Her shadow put its hand to her chest as though he'd just shot her through the heart.

He was sullen when he should've been ashamed.

"Thomas, why? Why would you do it? You're like a son to me."

"I'm not your son. You're a servant." How he envied her boy those Sundays. "And you already have a son. I saw him. You didn't tell me."

"My son…"

"You never told me. You're a liar and a whore." A recently acquired word that he thought he understood.

"What would you know, little man?" *Little man.* It was the first time he'd ever heard her say those words with anything other than tenderness.

"I saw you with my father."

"When?"

"On Saturday. Did he make you?"

"No. It's a fair trade. He's helped me to keep my son in this country. He's been true to his word."

"So, you've been fucking him all these years?"

"Better to be one man's whore than many's."

He should've told her that he was sorry. He should've turned off the lights. Her shadow wasn't soft and deep. It was sharp and cruel.

"You think you're gown up now? Are you grown up enough to know the truth about me? Where I come from, the world has fallen down." The Philippines, a beautiful and anarchic archipelago. "I lived with my mother in a village. One day a truck full of men arrived.

"'We've come to liberate you', the leader said.

"We didn't know that we weren't free.

"'We are the New People's Army.' The leader sat down in my mother's chair and slapped his knees with his bloated hands. The others leant against the wall.

"'Go to bed, Umbra,' my mother said, even though it was morning. She held me close, putting her mouth beside my ear.

"'Yes,' the leader said, 'to bed.'

"'Go out through the window and hide,' she whispered. 'Don't come back until they've gone.'

"Then she took my face in her hands and looked into my eyes the way she did when she told me not to play in the undergrowth because of snakes.

"The truck stayed all day. When I went back my mother was sat in her chair. I'd never seen her so still. I cast my shadow around the room as a troupe of monkeys, trying to make her laugh. When she eventually did get up to turn down the lamps the back of her skirt was ringed with stains."

If it was possible for a shadow to cry, then it was.

"We moved to the city. I was raped in a stairwell when I was fifteen. He cut my face to prove what he'd do if I didn't lie still.

"I didn't want to be like my mother, forever blank and empty. I decided that if he was going to take something from me then I'd have something from him in return. As he zipped up his fly I covered his shadow. I could feel it tear, ripping under the weight of mine. He staggered and then carried on walking.

"That made me understand how it is to violate another person. I felt powerful and controlling. I knew I'd changed him forever, just as he'd changed me. His life would be a dry and joyless thing.

"My country makes monsters of men and women. Now I have to go back there and take my son with me. He's too soft for that kind of life. I don't want him to die in a gutter, someone stood over his body. I don't want him to carry a gun. It's your fault. Yours and your family's."

Thomas could feel her shadow touching his. He wanted to push it off but couldn't.

"You're fierce, little man. I'll relieve you of those difficult feelings. I'm going to take your shadow and you'll never feel whole again. When you're older you'll wonder why you're different and I want you to remember that I did this to you."

Thomas didn't expect it to hurt.

☉

Thomas stands outside Dragonfly Mansions. A girl passes him, dressed in jeans and a Tiger Beer t-shirt. She pushes a toddler that isn't hers in a buggy. The child twists around to smile at her, his mother-servant. Thomas thinks of Umbra and for the first time he realises that he never knew her son's name.

Nothing warms him. Nothing fills him. It's because of Umbra. She's all the emotions that he remembers but no longer has, except in an abstract form; pity, lust and love. He's a remnant of himself, a shade of what he might have been.

Sometimes he thinks it's all so improbable, that he imagines it, but as he holds out his arms, the late afternoon sun on his back, he casts no shadow.

SMALL TOWN STORIES

I grew up in a small town during an era reigned by bank managers and mayors, when we all knew one another and one another's business. Few of us remain. Most of my alumni have fled to bigger houses in better places, having fulfilled their potential. Now Sandbach has been invaded by commuters due to its proximity to the M6.

I walk to the top of Park Lane. The name makes it sound grand, which it once seemed. The largest house belonged to Philip Ross, the mayor. He was a rum one. Accountant, embezzler and philanderer, who went with prostitutes in carparks. Mrs Ross was a prize; a primary school teacher with grace and lovely shoes. When I look through the window of the house where they used to live I can see her legs suspended in slow rotation, as they always are. She was still warm when they cut her down, skirt soiled, and her patent heels placed together carefully by the door.

Your Fiat is on the verge, between the oaks. Each time I think, *Don't look, don't look*, so I focus on where the tyres churned grass. It's easier in winter when the whole scene is shrouded in snow.

Where are you, Peter?

The noise is harder to block out. The trees aren't whispering in the autumn breeze. They're screaming.

☉

The Stapletons loved a party, as did Mum. She was the posh girl that married in but was liked because she lived it large.

Dad's brothers, Simon and Duncan, were there. Phil, the eldest was in prison for assault. There were various aunts, uncles and cousins. The men were in the lounge, gathered around the telly, roaring and shouting in exasperation. It was the European Cup Final, 1981, Liverpool versus Real Madrid.

We womenfolk had gravitated towards the back room where Mum and I had spent all morning laying out the spread; cans in buckets of iced water, bowls of prawn cocktail crisps, cubed cheese and pineapple on cocktail sticks and ham sandwiches.

Mum, in her sophistication, drank cocktails made with Pernod. Her head was close to Aunty Lilian's, whispering and both of them rocked with laughter. Aunt Lil was the matriarch, even though she was Nana Stapleton's younger sister, by virtue of her bearing, bullishness and a husband that robbed post offices. He'd had a heart attack at sixty. Lilian scared the shit out of me. She wasn't fond of kids.

I was in charge of music. At ten, Mum trusted me with her records. I slipped the vinyl from its sleeve, holding the black disc between my fingertips and placing it with care on the turntable. I don't like the purity of digital sound. I like the faint crackle of the needle in the groove.

I played The Beatles, The Carpenters, Simon and Garfunkel, and Abba. Sometimes we'd dance, sometimes we'd all sit and sing.

"Lil," Mum giggled, "read Cheryl's palm."

"She's only a kid," Nana Stapleton tutted.

Aunty Lily wouldn't be told what to do. She put down her stout. "Come on, girl."

Mum beckoned me with a tilt of her head when I hesitated. Lilian unfurled my hand and studied it, giving me the chance to study *her*. Her mouth, lined by sun and smoking, puckered in concentration. She wore a series of gold chains around her neck and sovereign rings on her fingers, legacies of the dead men in her life.

Her forefinger stopped and hovered. Then she held my hand in both of hers. I'd never known her capable of such tenderness.

"I'm sorry, Cheryl," she said, "it's there in the lines. Your soul will crack."

⊙

I'm going to hell when I die and it'll be Sandbach Motorway Services.

What was once a beacon of convenience for modern travellers is now a carbuncle. I'll be trapped in its soulless corridors, watching everyone else in transit to places I'll never see. My paper hat won't be able to keep the grease out of my hair, even in the afterlife.

I'm forty-two and I've been doing this job since I was nineteen.

It's Jake's last day. He's leaving for university soon. He talks about his parents with contempt for making him get a summer job, even though he's driving the brand-new Renault Clio they bought him. Ingrate. He shuts up when he remembers that it's not a summer job for me.

I've pretended that I've put my shitty old Fiesta in the garage for repairs. He jumped at the chance to offer me a lift. Now his glances make me self-conscious. He's doused himself in aftershave. He tries to talk to me properly, but it's a bit late in the day for us to be building a rapport.

"Thanks for going out of your way."

"No worries, it's not far."

Only a mile, from Sandbach to Elworth village.

"Once I've got a degree in Engineering and Mandarin, I'm going to work in China. Get some experience of the world."

"Life's not about what you gain. It's about what you lose."

I sound bitter. I wish I'd kept my mouth shut. You don't seduce someone with cynicism so I start again, coaxing him with questions about his exciting future.

"You've got nice eyes," he blurts out

"Let's have a drink to say goodbye." I move him away from banal flattery. "Let's go to your place."

"My Mum's in..." he blushes for both of us. I'm old enough to have given birth to him. I might feel seventeen inside, but that doesn't make it right.

"My place then."

We've both been waiting for this, so rather my place than never. I have a reputation, even though it's better than it used to be. Indiscriminate in my loneliness, I once had sex with a lad that looked like you, against the dumpster outside the kitchens. Everyone knew. The manager called me into his office and pawed me with his sweaty hands. I was glad when the dirty old bastard left.

I'm not Jake's first choice. He tried it on with Magda, one of the young Polish girls, but she's smarter than that.

"It's just here."

Jake pulls in. My flat's above a newsagent's.

"That used to be a bakery," I explain as if he cares. The shop's gone through many incarnations but I remember the pink-cheeked women and the flour-dusted loaves. I could tell him the smell of baking bread wakes me at five AM, but I don't. He follows me upstairs.

"Fucking hell."

My books are in orderly stacks; Greek classics, Russian, French, postmodern, gothic. People think I didn't go to university because I didn't get the grades. I got all As.

"Beer?"

"Yeah."

I get a couple of cans from the fridge. When I come back he's kneeling on the floor, flicking through the records.

"Don't touch those."

Some are Mum's and some are mine; the soundtrack of my youth. We drink the beer. Thank God for social lubrication. It helps us along.

I despair of teenagers. There's no joy of discovery, no mutual exploration. Jake's obviously seen a lot of internet porn and knows it all.

He doesn't ask about my inner thighs. In my early twenties I went through a phase of cutting that's left me with a web of silvery scars. The stigmata of survivor guilt.

I submit to his odder requests just to keep him here and wait for the flashes of recognition that brings *you* back to me. The shape of a bicep. A nipple. The texture and smell of a young man's skin. Brief seconds, but they'll have to do.

☉

I lie awake afterwards. I'm glad Jake doesn't linger. Under scrutiny, the flat's a dump with peeling paintwork and mould. I can afford better but it's a hair shirt I like wearing.

I get off the floor and climb into bed. It's two-thirty in the morning. The sound of trucks thundering past keeps me awake.

We were built on transport. Edwin Richard Foden invented the steam powered wagon in 1898. In the 1930s his partners at Foden's weren't impressed by the heavy chassis of his diesel-powered truck so Foden and his son left and took the idea one mile up the road from Sandbach to Elworth village to start a new company, ERF.

The entrance to each firm was decorated with flowerbeds. There were brass bands and civic pride. Mum's friend worked at Foden's. She said she met Peter Sutcliffe, who'd come to collect a truck. The Yorkshire Ripper, renowned killer of women, had immaculate manners, apparently.

Both sites are gone, given over to housing and a supermarket, but the phantom wheels thunder along. My flat quivers in the wake of juggernauts that no longer roll. Even industry dies.

☉

St Mark's Primary School seemed gigantic. I remember my first day, when Mum took me into Mrs Ross' classroom.

"Go and play, sweetheart."

"Where's Peter?" I looked up at her.

"He'll be along soon. How about you make some new friends?"

I couldn't recall a time when you weren't in my life. Mum said she put you down in my playpen and I grabbed you and held you close. I wished weekends away, waiting for your dad to drop you off on a Monday morning.

I didn't need new friends. I had you.

Women gravitated towards Mum. She no longer had fine clothes but with her provenance as Elsa Burnham, she still outranked most of them. Laughter rang out. She was quick to gossip and as bubbly as fizz.

"Hello, Cheryl, I'm Mrs Ross." She wore a full skirted dress. I reached out and touched the patterned fabric.

She knelt down to pull up my baggy, greying knee socks. I'll never forget that. Maybe she was thinking, *How standards slip, when you marry down*, but all I recall is unconscious kindness.

The adult buzz lessened. I looked around to see why. I ran to you but your mother kept you tethered by her side by a firm grip.

"Dr Stephens, welcome," Mrs Ross stood up.

Your mum wore you like a shield. You were angular, like her, with the same fine brown hair.

"I'm sorry, I can't stay." She shook Mrs Ross' hand. "Work."

Dr Stephens was a rarity in our community in the 1970s, a professional who worked full time after she had a child. She didn't encourage you in your attempts to make a mother of her.

"Don't worry, I'll keep an eye on Peter." Mum held out her hand and you went to her, eager for her to tickle you under the chin as she always did.

"Mrs Stapleton," your mum drew herself up, ignoring the looks that passed between the other mothers, "please take Peter home with you. I'll collect him at six."

There it was. Mum was just her child minder. Susan Stephens may have been a GP but Mum was both Burnham and Stapleton, and nobody would talk down to her, not in our town.

Mum said something under her breath and the women around her erupted in laughter, just as your mother reached the door.

☉

It's my day off. Elworth used to be pretty, with two primary schools, St Mark's church, a butcher's, baker's, a post office, and a hairdresser's. Most of the shops have gone and there's a remand centre for naughty boys. The park has plain, spiked railings. The original, graceful wrought iron gates have been removed and are probably on some councillor's house. Greedy sods, pushing brown envelopes about under tables.

The dead hedgehog is always outside St Mark's Primary School. It looks peculiar in the autumn sun, with its frosted, glittering spines and black eyes. How I cried for that tiny life when I was six, snuffed out during an unexpected cold snap. My heart ached for it when I first saw it again at seventeen, encumbered by the dead as I'd become.

As I walk to Sandbach, I pass your old house. It eclipsed the posh houses on Park Lane. It still has its tennis court that we never played on. I was never invited. Your mother saw to that. There's the same old bridge over the ornamental pond, like the one on willow pattern china plates that my mother collected. They all featured a pagoda and a bridge over a lake.

A pair of doves in flight. It represented the legend of the lowly servant who fell in love with the Mandarin's daughter. Love transformed them into doves, so they could escape and be together. Mum liked the romance of that.

○

I treat myself to some ground coffee from the deli. Wilson's is an institution that's survived many national financial crises. It's on Sandbach cobbles, a square with ankle turning terrain. The Saxon crosses at one end are a muddle of Christian iconography and Saxon motifs—the crucifixion and monsters with gaping jaws. Mercia's conversion wasn't bloodless. Christ cries, no matter what the weather. Tears run down his worn, ancient face.

I do my weekly shop at the supermarket, filling my basket with the value range. Marianne's in the freezer aisle. We nod at one another, our respect mutual. We are fabled. It's laughable really. We should be best friends.

There's a newborn in Marianne's trolley, lying on a bag of frozen chips. It's purple, with a gelid texture that makes me queasy. Shrunken genitals mark it as male. His eyes are screwed up and his mouth is open in a primal scream. Fortunately it's silent, or least to me.

Marianne's was a cautionary tale told to schoolgirls to scare them into keeping their legs closed. Oh, the shame, because in 1985 girls didn't get knocked up at fifteen and deliver their dead baby on their bedroom floor, then wrap it in newspaper for their dad to find in the dustbin.

Marianne. Soft-eyed, big-hearted and not all that bright. She's done alright for herself though. She's not buying economy brands. She married a builder who was much older than herself.

She doesn't deserve my bile. I think it's because I've seen them together. Man and wife, they dote on one another. Their daughter has Marianne's chestnut mane.

I like shopping here because my cousin, Raquel, works on the till. She's hard core Stapleton with a bad home dye job and a bloke that walks around with a dog snarling and straining on its harness.

The Stapletons haven't forgiven my rejection. They wanted to enfold me in their rough and loving bosom. And Raquel was always a bitch to me, even as a kid. Needling her at her place of work is the highlight of my week. Today I pack slowly, one item at a time, letting the queue build behind me.

"Twenty-four eighty-one."

I dole out the money in an exaggerated, deliberate fashion. She chucks the money in the till as I continue to pack. Her supervisor's looking over to see what the delay is. Raquel cracks first, snatching up a plastic bag and shoving things in, not caring about weight distribution or breakage. I'll repack it outside but now I can walk out with a smile.

Marianne's the only one in the queue who understands my victory. The other shoppers are interlopers, so they won't know. Raquel was a bitch to her too. Marianne winks at me. Or maybe she's just got something in her eye.

☉

Eventually primary school couldn't contain us. Soon we'd be divided, you to Sandbach School and me to Sandbach High School for Girls. The latter was a strange beast, an all-girls' comprehensive.

"You're wrong, thicko." You gave me a Chinese burn beneath the desk.

We were arguing over a maths problem but what we were *really* arguing over was that I'd gone off to play British Bulldog instead of playing football with you. I should've been outraged by your violent jealousy but I was secretly pleased. Just to show you that I wasn't to be bullied and that I wasn't going to share you either (not your freckles or hazel eyes), I stabbed you in the thigh with my sharpest pencil.

You yelped.

A board duster flew across the room. You were inches from concussion.

"Both of you. Outside. Now."

We held hands as we waited for our sentences. Mr Nelson, headmaster and tonsured despot, metered out harsh punishments for our own good. They involved a slap or a caning. Teachers used to be able to do that.

I understand that he retired early and went to Africa to terrorise children there with the threat of God.

☉

I go to the grave every week. St Mary's stands at the top of town, looking down. It's a dark and handsome church.

I carry an armful of flowers along the high street. Its commercial landscape has changed. This shop used to be Woolworths. That one a record shop which belonged to Neil Rivers, the guitar teacher. Now there are discount stores and places to buy e-cigarettes and mobile phones accessories. The wool shop is still by the church, which amazes me as Minnie must be at least seventy and no-one knits when you can buy a sweater in Asda for £8. She always waves me in when she sees me.

Your mum was a lovely woman. Consummate knitter.

Schoolgirls crowd the pavement. It's home time. I don't know if I envy or pity them. They've no idea what's ahead. I used to be haughty and immortal too, wearing the same uniform with the stylised Sandbach Cross design on the blazer pocket in blue, white and gold.

They're out in such numbers that I'm forced off the kerb. Blood sloshes over my boots. The town was granted rights to a Thursday market in Elizabethan times. An event, decimated by supermarkets, that was once the busiest day of the week. So many people. So many lorries coming through the town. Accidents were bound to happen. A woman went under an eight-wheeler. Bystanders were sprayed and splattered as her neck and chest were crushed. Her body flailed and twitched as it was dragged down the street. Her head was sent rolling. I read somewhere that an adult's body holds five litres of blood but that amount's been magnified by the drama of her death. Now the gutters run with it.

St Mary's Church is opposite the Old Hall Hotel, notorious for ghosts. It's been on television. I've been in there. The hauntings have been diminished by antiquity to pale, apologetic shades that I barely register.

In the cemetery I talk to mum as I change the flowers, even though she's not there to hear me. Her funeral was a blur, except for Grandma Burnham. She disapproved of Mum's marriage. She wouldn't have my dad, not at any price.

Grief needs blame. Grandma never shed a tear that day. She had an iron spine. Instead, she stared at the Stapletons who'd gathered on the opposite side of the grave as if it was them that shot Mum, not Dad.

☉

"Get that filthy thing off the table," Mum tutted at Dad.

It was March. I sat in the kitchen, studying for my A-level exams. Dad had put a toolbox before me.

"It's not filthy. It's brand new. It's for Cheryl."

He opened it and laid out its contents like a wise man presenting gifts; a bicycle repair kit, wire cutters, a wrench, nails and screws. A hammer. Batteries in various sizes.

"What will she want with all that?"

"It's for her to take to university."

"Oh, love, she doesn't want all that rubbish."

"It's not rubbish," he snarled at her.

I dropped my biro.

"Look, you'll need this stuff." He bent to retrieve the pen. "I've been thinking. When you've finished studying and come home, I'll teach you to drive. I'll have saved enough to get you a car. It'll be a banger but I'll get it running."

"She won't come back," Mum was still smarting from how he'd spoken to her, "not if she's got any sense."

"Just shut up, will you?"

"Don't you dare talk to me like that."

"But it's okay for you to talk to *me* anyway you want?"

I slipped out as their voices started to rise, and rang you.

"They're fighting again."

"I'll come and meet you. Where are you?"

"The phone box near The Limes. I don't know what's wrong with them. Dad scares me."

Dad couldn't afford to buy me a new car or lots of clothes but he taught me everything he could—how to mend a bicycle puncture, to check oil levels and tyre pressures on a car, change spark plugs, to pitch a tent.

Dad weighs heavily on me, despite his absent ghost. Yet it's shameful that for all my guilt it's you that fills my mind the most.

⊙

It was July. Hot. Dad was in t-shirt and shorts. The scar that wound around his right leg had healed in an ugly ridge, like a worm had burrowed under his skin and died there. The bone beneath had set but his limp curbed his career as a squaddie. Such are the caprices of motorbike accidents.

"Go and put some clothes on."

I'd climbed out of bed and come straight downstairs still wearing the t-shirt that I slept in. It fell to mid-thigh.

"I said get dressed. Don't parade around like that."

Mum carried in a plate of eggs and sausages.

"Don't go on at her all the time, eh, love?"

Dad loaded his fork with a disc of pink sausage and dipped it into a yolk. Yellow ran across the plate. "Michael's dropping his car off at six."

Michael—your father. Affable. He was the one who usually dropped you off at ours when you were little.

Dad sliced off a wedge of rubbery egg white.

"You haven't forgotten, have you?"

"Forgotten that he's too cheap to get it done at a garage?"

"Yeah, his Beamer will look shabby next to your Escort."

Mum, teaser and japer. Fun outside, biting indoors. Dad loved that Ford Escort RS2000. He'd done all the work on it himself. How she must have cut him.

Dad pushed his plate away and climbed into the overalls laid out on the back of the armchair.

"Dad, can I go out with Pete today?""

"No."

"Why not?" That was Mum. I wouldn't have dared. He'd become so touchy.

"Because I said." He smoothed down his hair.

"Cheryl's not got many friends. You know that."

"Mum!"

"It's good she's got Peter."

"I said no."

"They've known each other since they were kids."

"They're not kids anymore."

"He's a nice lad."

"Stop bloody contradicting me." He turned on her, the colour rising in his cheeks. He tried to soften it when he saw the look on my face. "I'll be back for six. Let's do something nice tonight. Get a chippie tea."

Mum made us toast after he'd gone.

"Go out with Peter. Just make sure you're back before your dad, okay? Otherwise my life won't be worth living."

"Thanks, Mum." I kissed her and ran upstairs to get ready. How selfish youth is.

☉

Summer has never lasted as long as that one, when we were young enough to have days to waste. A-levels were done and we were waiting for the results.

On the day I went behind Dad's back we lost our virginity beneath The Cloud. It's a phrase I loathe. I didn't lose my virginity. It was a gift to you.

Bosley Cloud, the hill that's at the Cheshire-Staffordshire border, rose above us. We lay in a sloping field, shaded by a copse of trees and hidden from the hikers above us on the hill. Insects buzzed about us in the long grass.

"So you didn't tell your dad you're with me?"

"He'd do his nut."

"Why does he hate me so much?"

"He hates everyone. Mum loves you though."

That made you smile. The adoration was mutual. You rolled from your side, onto your back. I put my head on your chest. Your breathing paused and then restarted.

In my sweetest dreams I'm there again, feeling your warmth on my cheek and the depth of your sigh. Such is your power over me, even in my sleep.

"Cheryl?"

"Yes?"

"We'll still see each other when you go away, won't we?"

"I won't be going anywhere if I don't get the grades." I had a place at Durham.

"Of course you will."

"Promise me that you won't run off with some girl from the bank?" You'd got a job at Barclays Bank on the high street.

"Never." You sounded so sincere. It's funny how we imagine that some things are unbreakable.

"It's not too late to change your mind. You could go to university too. Go through clearing."

"I'm not as smart as you."

"Yes, you are."

You were the only person I didn't want to get away from. The only one who didn't want to keep me in my place. You didn't care about my Stapleton and Burnham heritage. I was just Cheryl.

I kissed you, with all my belief in you. You kissed me back. We both pulled away, shocked by the act. The shadow of adolescence was still on you, but manhood had changed your mouth and skin. You touched my cheek and it made me gasp. Desire mounted. Our kisses grew more confident, firmer and deeper.

The weight of your body surprised me. It was delicious. You thought I couldn't breathe so you took your weight on your elbows. My body ran ahead of my mind, moving with yours. I thought I'd turn to water and run down the hill side.

Parts of you came in and out of focus. I couldn't take you all in. Eyelashes. Sinews. The taste of you. The line of your jaw. The sun through the trees dappling your skin.

We had sealed our promise to one another. Afterwards we were shy and courteous, as if seeing each other anew. We went up to the top of Bosley Cloud, the hill at the border, having crossed a border of our own, and looked down at the patchwork fields, the lanes and villages. Our green county. My heart spread out before you like the Cheshire plain.

How I long to feel that again. The connection of skin on skin, soul on soul. Except, I no longer know who I am. It's useless, fucking young men like Jake in search of you when I need to be looking for myself.

○

"We're going to be late."

"It's fine."

"No, it's *not* fine."

The inside of my chest felt cold. We hit every red light and got caught behind every slow driver on our way home from The Cloud.

"I'll come in and talk to him," you said.

"No, don't. Please. You don't know what he's like."

"He never used to be like that. He used to like me."

"Just drop me at the corner. Please."

We approached my road. As we turned I saw your dad's BMW that was in the drive. It was twenty to six.

"Just drop me here." I leant over for a kiss. "I'll call you."

"I might as well come in. My dad's here. I'll drive him home."

"No."

"I won't skulk around like we've done something wrong."

You followed me up the drive.

Your dad and my mum sat at the kitchen table. Mum wore a t-shirt and a denim skirt, which showed off well-shaped calves and ankles. Her throaty laugh filled the kitchen.

"Hello, what have you two been up to?" Your dad smiled at us.

My face burned as though he'd caught us out.

"We've been up on The Cloud."

"It's a lovely day, isn't it?" My mum looked at Michael, not us, as she said it.

"Yes, yes it is." Michael's face was bright and open. He looked cool in his crumpled linen shirt.

Mum didn't seem concerned that dad could be home at any moment. She seemed distracted.

The kitchen darkened, my dad at the window looking in. When he came in he kissed mum, full on the mouth. His overall was sweat stained at the small of his back and his armpits.

"Gavin," Michael nodded.

Dad stared at you.

"Mr Stapleton." Peter wouldn't be cowed.

"Peter's here to drive his dad home." Mum's lie was smooth.

"Yes, that's right." Michael's response didn't sound as convincing. Better he'd said nothing. "Thank you for doing this, Gavin, I appreciate it."

He put the car keys on the table.

"I think it's the alternator."

"Really?" Only I could see Dad's derision at Michael for trying to speak in the language of trades. Michael didn't know about Dad's hierarchy. Real men worked with tools, not in offices.

Mum got up and started to throw things into her handbag.

"Work phoned me. Nessa's rung in sick. I'll have to go in." She was a barmaid at The Red Fox. "Will you give me a lift, lads?"

○

I stood on the path with Dad.

"I'll drive." Michael held out his hands.

You threw the car keys over the bonnet and he caught them. Then you moved towards me but I stopped you with a frown and a slight shake of the head. The longing on your face made me feel naked. Now, I wish I'd run to you and threw my arms around you.

"Bye, Cheryl."

"Bye." Those were our last words to one another. I stuck my hands in my pockets.

You climbed into the back of the car. Michael held the passenger door open for Mum and closed it after her. Dad stood looking at the road long after you'd all gone. I went back inside.

When he finally followed, I was in the hall, gazing in the mirror, trying to see if I'd changed. What did Dad see on my unguarded face? Triumph? Pleasure? Could he tell that I wasn't his little girl anymore?

He ran upstairs, the sound uneven as he favoured his good leg. I heard wood splintering as he smashed in the false back on the wardrobe. When he came down he was carrying a shotgun. I didn't even know he had one. I stood in the corner of the hall, back to the corner.

"Stay here."

He yanked the phone from the socket and smashed it against the wall. The plastic shattered, sending shards across the carpet.

The Escort's engine roared into life, Dad revving too high. He was in pursuit of you. I knew that I had to move, to run to a neighbour and call the police, but I was rooted to the spot as if *Stay here* was a spell not an order. Dad's directions have kept me stuck in Sandbach and it was then that my soul cracked and the dead came pouring in.

⊙

Dad died on the floor of his prison cell. He had a fit and swallowed his own tongue.

The fit was caused by a meningioma. I looked it up after the inquest. It's a slow growing, benign brain tumour. Except it's only benign if it doesn't fucking kill you. It caused an insidious change in him, from the young optimist that mum married to someone unreasonable and aggressive. I'd be unreasonable too if I had a lump the size of a lemon squashing my brain.

Dad was dying and I was too busy with myself to see the change. He was dead from the minute he pulled the trigger. Or when he picked up the gun. No, it was when he ran upstairs to get the shotgun and I didn't do a thing to stop him.

⊙

Marianne must be waiting for me. We're in canned goods. Her daughter's not with her today. She steers her trolley towards me so quickly that I'm pinned against the tinned tomatoes. I try not to look at the squalling purple baby, without success. That look seems to decide her.

"Poor poppet," she says under her breath. "He never settles."

I drop the can I'm holding and she stoops to pick it up and hands it back to me. I'm not the only one who sees. Did her sight start when her water broke, or was it when she took her dead son in her arms?

"What's his name?" I ask.

"Ian." It contains all the love she bears him. How hard it's been for her, carting his ghost around with her all these years. I'd have gone mad, coward that I am. I've not dared to look at your car properly. Not even once.

○

The Fiat waits on Park Lane. The police said Dad had forced it off the road. The first blast went through the windscreen.

Fragments of shot and glass spread out, causing havoc with flesh and bone in its path. Sunlight catches the glass fragments that cover the interior, making the bloody splatters gleam. Each detail is fresh, as if it was only yesterday. The shot obliterated most of Mum's head. She's slumped sideways but her seatbelt keeps her upright. Her necklace is sticky and the front of her t-shirt is red and wet.

Michael's head is bowed, resting on his chest as if he's praying. His lower jaw had been blown off. That would have been you, if you'd been driving.

I walk around to the passenger window. You were sat behind your father. You're not in there. The living have no place in this tableau of the dead. The seat is blood-splattered and urine-stained. An involuntary action. Who can blame you, Dad staring at you with a shot gun over his arm?

Dad had time to kill you before the police car hurtled up Park Lane but he didn't. I was so worried that he'd realised what we'd done that I was blind. I thought the culpability was all mine. Mum, so scrupulous about her wedding and engagement rings. They were only ever on her finger or the ring dish by the sink. Now, as I look at her bare hands, I remember how her rings were in her handbag.

I blamed myself, thinking Dad was angry at me. He'd seen what I hadn't. The empty glasses on the table between Mum and Michael. Mum's flushed look. Her change of clothes. Her ringless fingers.

Mum let me go out that day just to get me out of her and Michael's way.

○

I saw you, you know. It was two years, four months and six days ago.

You came to the food counter at Sandbach Services. I was in the back but could see through the food rack. You were ordering from Magda. I struggle to keep your image clear in my mind, but I knew it was you straight away. You had your arm around a boy's shoulders, his head just above counter level. He didn't look like you, Peter. I thought he looked like your dad, with the same blonde wavy hair, or maybe I've imagined that.

All I could do was look at you. The right side of your face was scarred, my darling, peppered once by fragments of shot. I wanted to kiss it, to kiss those scars and stroke your face until it healed and you were perfect again.

No wonder you and your Mum got as far away from Sandbach as you could.

There was a moment when you looked up at me, right at me, but didn't see me. You stared through me like I was a ghost.

⊙

So here I am, stood on the verge beside a wrecked Fiat that's not there, crying my heart out. A group of school kids walk past me. One of them sniggers but the tallest girl in the group shoots them a dirty look and breaks away.

"Are you okay?" She can't be more than sixteen or seventeen. She pulls a mobile from a blazer pocket. "I can call my mum. She's a nurse."

I don't know why I'm so hard on them. Maybe it's because my time is past, my glowing moments gone and now it's their turn. I'm the outsider in Sandbach now.

I should move away. Move on. I've an untouched inheritance from Grandma Burnham. I could travel. Do a degree maybe.

As to Sandbach, it's not all bad. The commuters have stayed, and their children are rooted in the Cheshire soil. Buds that open in the sun. They'll make their own small stories, which is right and proper as this is only a small town.

FISH SKINS

My wife has brine instead of blood. She's full of the sea. I can taste it in her sweat, her tears, her sex. She's crafty and quick. She's lunar. She's tidal.

Men look at her. I don't need to see their wanting her to know that she's a catch.

○

I get up before dawn and go down to the harbour to help my brothers unload the haul. The creeping light is grey and the mist lingers on the water. I sit on the wall and wait for the boat, listening to the gulls and lapping water.

Then *Mercy*, our livelihood, lands. She's painted red and blue. I can make out the shapes of Robert and Michael moving around her deck and John, his arm raised to hail me from the bow.

The four of us sort the fresh, flapping fish. The shoals pour like molten silver into the crates, which are then loaded onto my cart. It judders on the cobbles as I push it, sending jolts up to my shoulders. John knows better than to offer to help me. This is my share of the family concern and I do it alone.

"I'll walk with you. I'm going to Silky's anyway."

John likes to play the patriarch now Dad's dead. He's taken on Dad's bearing, beard and Silky, the creaking, drunken widower who Dad looked out for.

"How are things with you?" John asks.

"Well enough."

The morning light's coming in strong now that it's decided to put in an appearance. I can see movement in kitchens and hallways as we pass through the uneven rows of homes. Stray cats lick their lips as they follow us, hoping for a fallen fish.

"Do you miss it?" John slows his step to match mine.

"Miss what?" I pick up my pace even though it hurts my leg, making John rush to catch up with me.

"The sea."

"The sea's there," I motion back towards the harbour, "every time I turn around."

"You know I mean *being* at sea."

"No. The pitch and roll of the boat makes my leg sore."

It does but that's not the real reason I won't take to the water. When I think of being out on the rolling vastness, on a pile of planks lashed together with tar and rope, my fingertips go numb and the breath's squeezed from my chest.

"Pete, do you remember any of it?"

It's over twenty years ago but John still asks me from time to time, as if reliving it will heal me. He blames himself for the loose boom that swung across the boat. I pushed John out of the way and it took me overboard instead.

I recall it all. The way John screamed my name into the gale. The sea sucked the air from my lungs. I twisted about, death's hook in my mouth. The waves rose around me and the unremitting cold froze my bones and made them brittle. My leg shattered as I smashed against the hull.

I can recall the black tug of the currents and the inquisitive fishes. My heart slowed and just when I thought the next beat wouldn't come, slim white limbs reached for me from the fathoms.

The doctor said it was the lack of air making me see things.

"I don't remember any of it."

"Never mind. Thank God for the fortune that washed you back ashore to us." John slaps my back in a gesture that's all our father. "I'll leave you here."

John, all caring and considerate, who doesn't understand what it's like to be afraid of the job you were born to do or the pain of having to learn to walk again when your leg's all smashed up. He takes the left fork in the street, up the alley to Silky's shack.

⊙

So it is that I'm a fishmonger, not a fisherman like the rest of my family. Having a market stall makes me feel like my own man.

The fish aisle isn't for the faint hearted. It's blood and carnage. The black and white tiles are an attempt to make the massacre sanitary. There are wet, staring eyes. Crustaceans crawl in pots, claws tied up to stop them snapping. There are suckered tentacles and armoured prawns. Smaller shell dwellers are laid out at the front. Inky blue mussels studded with barnacles. Cockles turned sideways look like ribbed hearts. Periwinkles contain sweet flesh but it's fat oysters I like best. Their rugged, ridged shells give no clue to the smooth enamel surface within.

I'm king here. No one's better with a knife or shucking blade. I'm swiftest to strip the heavy scale from bass or bream. I know the trick of moving the fish's tail, not the blade, as you pull the skin away. I understand the angles of filleting implicitly.

I lay the glistening darlings on my marble slab. I run my blade along their bellies, scoop out the innards and pack the cavities with ice. I look a sight in rubber boots with fish guts down my apron.

"Peter, I need those pollock." Marianne doesn't believe in preamble. "Don't forget the heads, bones and skins that are left. I'll use those for stock."

"How many people are we feeding?"

"You have a large family," she shrugs, "and it's our turn to cook for them this Sunday."

Marianne's accent is guttural and vague. I listen to the sailors that land here but can never find her voice in theirs.

"Do you want me to bring anything else home?"

"No."

Then she's gone.

"Your wife's not much of a talker, is she?" The flower seller sidles up to me. He looks like he's imagining what we do with all that silence when we're at home, alone. His salacious grin fades when I don't join in with his smuttiness. "Oh, well, I'll take two of them scabbard fish, if it's all the same to you."

⊙

I go home after the market closes, carrying fish and their remains. We live at the top of the town. Washing lines run across the alley, between the houses. Red seaweed hangs among our neighbours' sheets and shirts. Marianne snacks on the dried stuff. I was weaned on the sea but it's too much, even for me. The Dulse weed's too concentrated. Too salty and iodic.

Widow Howlett comes to her door and chucks a basin of dirty water at my feet. It splashes up my legs. She stares at me like I owe *her* an apology.

"Dulse on a washing line. I've never seen anything like it."

It's been twenty years and the old woman still treats Marianne like she's a foreigner.

Indoors, Marianne takes the baskets from me and presses me down into a chair.

"Your leg hurts."

She can always tell when it's bothering me.

Marianne's foraged foods fill our larder. The seashore's edible. Wild cabbage. Sea rocket. Samphire. Seabeet and purslane. Dinner's delicious. I eat the mussels first and then mop up the broth with homemade bread. Marianne favours the open textured sort that's like a sponge.

Middle aged, afternoon lovemaking follows our meal. Marianne wears an old red shirt that rides up her thighs when she reaches for me. The cloth's unbearably soft. I take it off.

When I draw her down on the bed I can feel the swell of her breasts against my chest as she sighs. There's a pause as if she's about to speak but then she doesn't. This is normal for Marianne but today there's something different in her face.

"What's the matter?" I tuck a strand of hair behind her ear.

I expect a perfunctory *nothing* so I'm surprised when she says, "Do you mind that there's never been a child?"

Marianne's wording goes astray when she's tired.

"No. Not ever."

She's thinking of my siblings and their prodigious children. I call the crowd that clamours around my knees *the minnows*. They pull me into games that involve charging and roaring but they dart away when Marianne puts out a hand to pat their heads.

"It's my fault."

"It takes two to make a baby." I take her face in my hands and make her look at me to be sure she's listening

We're not as young as we once were. Our bodies have altered. Her waist's thicker. I have a paunch. We're less vigorous in our pursuit of desire. None of that matters. I kiss her neck, her breasts, the scars behind her ears that look like defunct gills.

I think she's tired of me. She looks startled when she comes, as though I've called her back from somewhere far away.

☉

My wife's a beachcomber. Our house looks like the tide line. She brings all sorts back, except for dead seahorses which make her cry.

Fragments of sea glass are lined up on the window sill where they glow with light. Pebbles are piled in miniature cairns on the mantelpiece. Shells decorate the walls.

Marianne was ill soon after she first came to us. So ill that she couldn't get out of bed. She gripped the bedpost as if seasick and nothing calmed her fever.

"What can I do to help you?" I knelt beside her.

"The sea," was all she said in a broken voice.

She looked disappointed when I brought her a shell.

"They're dull once you've taken them from the water."

"Wait." I lifted it to her ear. "Listen."

Then she smiled.

☉

It's a feast day. The bell summons us to the white church on the hill. It smells of beeswax polish and stone until the priest swings the censer and fills it with incense. The candles are yellow columns of light. The stained glass casts coloured shadows on my hands.

We never miss the procession. John's one of the men carrying Our Lady this year. The Virgin's lifted from the altar and hoisted onto their shoulders. She's alabaster wrapped in flowing blue robes. Her lips are the shade of dead roses.

We follow Our Lady out onto the street where I can see the familiar view of dark slate rooftops, peppered with strutting herring gulls. I know the lineage of the people within each house. The stone dome of the market place is halfway down. The town hall's opposite. The statue that sits between the two looks like a toy soldier from up here. I can just make out *Mercy* bobbing in the harbour alongside the other boats. Then there's the expanse of shifting, sparkling sea beyond, with worlds unseen beneath. I've never left this town, never had to make a life for myself somewhere else.

When we reach the shore the bearers step into the water. Their trousers are stained dark, then their shirts as they go deeper. The water swelling around John's chest makes me uneasy. The Virgin's garlands float on the surface as she's submerged.

I clutch Marianne's hand. Her dress flutters around her legs. The fabric clings to her skin. My serge suit is hot and itchy.

It was on this very feast day, twenty years ago, that I was carried to the harbour on a chair to watch, my healing leg patched up with pins.

No one was looking at Our Lady that day. We were too busy staring at Marianne who lay naked on the shingle, a piece of jetsam cast up on the shore.

○

"Stop whistling." Marianne sits opposite me, peeling potatoes. She doesn't care for them but cooks a portion for me.

"I wasn't."

We seem to be falling over one another these days.

"You're getting on my nerves."

I pick up her discarded words to rub into the wound later.

"But I wasn't whistling."

"You were. Stop it. I can't think."

"What have you got to think about?" It's not fair but I say it anyway.

She gets up and grabs her coat. I let her go, the door left wide open so that everyone can look in and see me how she's abandoned me. Five minutes later I get up and close it.

I don't understand why I'm goading her.

⊙

Married love. My wife used to look at me with unconcealed adoration.

Marianne had no interest in bridal adornments, leaving my mother to stitch her gown and pick the flowers. She was so impatient with the rituals of marriage that she offended the priest who stared at her with bulbous eyes.

She was eager for our wedding night. Marianne pushed me back on the bed and put her hands wherever she liked. She wasn't a cypher for my desires. She had her own. We spent the following week entwined like seal pups in a pile.

Then there were the monthly irritations. She wept with each menstruation, as if womanhood was a revelation. I'd always thought it was sadness at not being pregnant.

⊙

I come home to an empty house. Murky soup's waiting on the stove. Pots and dishes are piled up in the sink. The floor's filthy.

I eat spoonfuls of cold soup straight from the pan and then start to clean. The feelings swelling in my chest don't abate with physical work. I'm on my knees with a scrubbing brush when the latch lifts behind me. Marianne's hanging up her coat and the duffle bag that she takes with her for beachcombing.

It's too mild a day for a coat. She always has to do something that marks her out as odd.

"Where've you been?"

"Out."

"Where?"

"Walking."

"And you're happy to leave this mess for me after I've been at work all morning?"

She looks confused. Today's no different from any other day after all.

"I work too."

She's right. We're an anomaly in how we live. My brothers' wives don't think I see them roll their eyes at one another when they visit. They shouldn't mind if our house is a state sometimes. Nor should I. Marianne understands the mysteries of molluscs. She brings the finest shell dwellers to the stall and it's doubled the income from which we all draw.

"I was going to do the floor later," she adds, defensive.

I know I'm being irrational. One of us gets to the chores eventually. It's never mattered who. We bump along together, managing the difficulties of domesticity.

"You haven't said where you've been."

"Nowhere special."

I fling the scrubbing brush in the bucket and kick the thing, slopping dirty suds on the clean flags. "And did you meet anyone while you were there?"

"Don't speak to me like that."

I follow her into the bedroom where she starts to brush her hair. It's her cure for melancholy, anger and vexation. "You talk to me anyway you like when you're in a mood."

I snatch the brush off her. The bristles dig into my palm. "Why can't I do the same?"

"Because…" Then she stops.

"Because what?"

"Because." She seizes her brush back.

"What?" I stand next to her but all I can smell on her is the ocean.

I expect an explosion but none comes. She can't be bothered to fight. She sounds weary.

"Because you're all I have."

John thinks himself wise.

I'm scrubbing down the marble slab. I stink of sweat and fish guts.

It's under my nails and in my pores. I'm tired. My leg's bothering me more than usual. I want to go home and smoke my pipe.

"What's on your mind?" I don't look up from my work.

John takes off his cap and twists it around in his hands.

"Not here. Let's take a walk."

I can't recall ever seeing him so uncertain of himself so I relent. "All right then, but not for long."

I match John's stride although it hurts. The town's quietening down. Shutters close and rocking chairs creak. There's a hushed chorus of voices behind a door. A boy kicks a ball against a wall until he's called to go in.

"Is Marianne well?"

It's the same tentative tone that all my family use when they talk about her. Her health's always been in question. *Marianne's not right.*

When we found her on the beach that day she couldn't speak. She clutched my arm and wouldn't let go. She only ate raw fish. It took all my mother's bullying to make her put on clothes.

"She's well enough." I don't want to hear what John has to say.

"Don't you still wonder where Marianne came from?"

Word was sent out with ships. Notices were posted in newspapers. No one came to claim her. She had no native tongue and no memory of herself. She didn't even have a name.

"She's my wife. That's all that matters now."

"Of course it is." John talks in the soothing tones, which only makes it worse.

"You can't stand that she chose a cripple like me over you, so she can't be right in her mind."

There. I've said it aloud.

"No one wants to take Marianne from you." John shakes his head, like he does when he thinks someone's being stupid. "Marianne only has eyes for you."

"It's not her I'm worried about."

"What's that supposed to mean?"

We're above the town now, approaching the cliff. I feel like we're climbing into the sun.

"You wanted her yourself." *You still do.*

John's lips are stretched so thin that they're colourless.

"It seems so long ago. We were all in love with her but she wanted you."

Me, a landlocked fisherman with a limp.

"And you hate that."

"Oh, for the love of God," he throws his hands up, "Pete, I swear there are times when I could knock you down."

"Big man. Come on then. Or are you worried what people will think if you do?"

"You know what? I'm sick of your self-pity. I'm sick of being sorry for my mistake, every day. You saved my life and I'm grateful. Don't you think I'm glad that you and Marianne are happy?"

"It doesn't matter now. We're not. She doesn't love me anymore." I'm as surprised at this admission as John is.

"Rubbish."

"I don't know what's happening to us. We used to be so close."

"That's just how it is. You can't be like young lovers all your lives. Love has to survive the mundane. You have to console each other with kindness when things get difficult. Let me tell you something. If Marianne had picked me, I'd treat her like a queen."

John, the wise one.

We've left the path and are crossing the green of the cliff tops. The sea's out there, the one certainty when everything else is unsure.

"Where are we going?"

"There's something you need to see."

"What?"

"I saw Marianne from the boat."

"So?"

"Trust me, you need to see."

We're at the cliff's curve, overlooking the cove. John squeezes my arm.

"I'm not doing this to make trouble. I'm doing this because I'm worried about her. About both of you."

Then he leaves me there.

Marianne's down below, lying on a bed of rocks. She's stunning, even though her hair's streaked with grey. She combs it as it streams over her breasts in waves. Pale skinned, as she doesn't weather like the rest of us. I can see the gentle curve of her stomach. The light catches the coating of sand on her arms.

Her legs are wrapped in a garment stitched from fish skins. A false tail begins at her hips and tapers to her ankles, then spreads out in a fin that flaps about as she moves her feet, concealed within.

Marianne sings her harsh song as she pretends to be a mermaid.

⊙

My wife loves being in water although I've never seen her swim. She pours sea salt into her bathwater and sings.

Sometimes she submerges herself, carrying on her song for a few seconds. The harsh quality in her voice is lost. Her waterlogged voicebox makes a glorious sound. She's a drowned angel, her hair spread out around her like drifting kelp.

Then Marianne sits up, spluttering and gasping, looking wounded and betrayed.

⊙

I don't go to sea anymore but my fingers are still skilled. All fishermen are dextrous with knots and nets.

The ocean's given me everything I have. I've enjoyed its gifts and witnessed its aquatic aberrations. Things caught in the nets that look too strange to live. I've heard the collective myths and memories of sailors, their tales of monsters large enough to swallow ships.

The ocean keeps secrets.

Worthy of pearls and all Marianne got was me. Just a boy when she deserved some God of the Sea.

I climb down the twisted steps to the cove. The receding tide's a foaming line in the distance. The basking seals see me and flee. I watch their bronzed heads bob about in the swell and then disappear. I strip off in the cold shadow of the cliffs. The shingle hurts my feet and I'm glad when it gives way to sand. There's a breeze on my bare skin.

I took what I needed from the stall and borrowed more from the others, who looked at me like I was addled. I use the finest needle I can thread. Sewing my legs into my fish skin tail is delicate work.

Marianne's made so many sacrifices for me. Her pale limbs reached for me from the gloom. She put her mouth to mine to help me breathe. She guided me to safety.

She left everything to follow me.

If I'm all she has then I must be everything I can be. For her. And I'll show her I'm thankful every day. I'll treat her like a queen.

I lie back, decked out in my merman's finery and wait for my wife to come.

THE RISING TIDE

Everything's wide at Newgale; the beach, the sky, but it's water that draws me. The sea goes on for miles.

The rising tide comes in, chasing and baiting. I scream at it, but it doesn't help. I still feel dead. The crash of the waves swallows up the sound.

I wander. Further up the beach are surfers who look as sleek as seals, dressed in neoprene as they brave the breakers. How free they must feel.

A figure walks towards me. A girl, with a dog that turns in circles around her. The animal crouches, belly to the ground, waiting for her to hurl the ball she's carrying. When she does the dog's off like a shot, making ripples and splashes on the water glistening on the sand.

Closer, and I see the girl more clearly. The sight of her shocks me to a stop. Her black hair streams out behind her in the wind. The girl's mouthing something. I think it's my name. Her dog bounds up to me, sniffing and licking, keen to be acquainted.

"Get down, you brute." She catches the dog's collar and hauls him back. "I'm so sorry."

I try to speak but my throat is tight. I'm choking on emotions that I can't swallow.

"Jessica?" The word comes out, faint and strangled.

It's not Jessica. There's no way it could be her. Not here. Not now. This isn't a teenager but a woman with straight, brunette hair, not Jessica's lively black curls.

"Are you okay?" The woman puts the dog on its leash. "Can I do anything to help you?"

I shake my head, tear stricken and mute. She lingers for a moment, looking awkward and uncertain, and I have to turn my back on her to make her go away.

⊙

"Have a seat."

My GP ushered me in. Pictures of children that I presumed were hers hung over her desk. There was the overwhelming odour of air freshener as if she'd sprayed away her last patient.

I explained why I'd come. She passed me a box of tissues when I started to cry.

"It sounds like a terrible situation for everyone." Her vague tone made me think that, having listened to my tale, that she'd already apportioned blame. "What's your mood like?"

She asked me the standard questions relating to my malady; poor sleep, inability to eat, mounting anxiety and loss of pleasure.

"Any thoughts of suicide?" She clutched the string of bright beads around her neck.

"No," I lied.

That wasn't true. I'd thought about getting on a train and running away. I'd thought about throwing myself under one.

"Could you fill this in for me?" It was a formal depression questionnaire. The modern NHS requires that everything be quantified, even misery.

She totted up my score.

"Right, I think we should start antidepressants." She was brisk. The use of *we* gave the process an illusion of democracy.

"Yes."

"Citalopram, twenty milligrams a day," she said.

Citalopram, a drug to keep my serotonin circulating. To bathe my brain in this happy chemical and make me well again. Or functional, at least.

"Do you need to see a counsellor?"

I shake my head.

"I'll write you a sick note."

"I can't go off sick."

"Nonsense. You're not well enough to work."

"I can manage."

"It's not just about you." She uncapped her pen. "It's about patient safety too. You need a clear head."

Patient safety. That stung, as it revealed what she, and everyone else, must have really thought of me.

⊙

Arosfa's the name of the hut that stands on the top of Treffgarne hill, near Lion's Rock, within sight of a cluster of houses and church that comprise the village.

Arosfa. An apt name given by my father. It means "remain here". That's all I want. To stay here and never have to face the world again. It's all I have left of Dad. We'd come here at weekends. He'd shrug off his overalls and roam as if set free. We'd walk and talk all day. I'd go with Dad while he went about his real vocation; a cleansing or a healing ritual.

Now Arosfa's windows are dirty and the floor unswept. Dad would be upset to see it so neglected.

When I get back from Newgale, the door's ajar. I stand, listening, sure that I'd locked it before I left. There are no signs that it's been forced. I push the door open. No one's there but I have the feeling of being only seconds too late to see who was standing there.

Nothing. Nothing but the stained and faded curtains, made in exchange for Dad's shingle cure, that hang in the window. Dad's empty whisky bottles, thick with dust, line the shelves. Each one was payment for a divination or a charm. His books are swollen with damp but look undisturbed. Piles of my clothes are left where I dropped them. Dirty cups and plates are all over the place. I should clean up.

Then I see the wet patches that stain the floorboards, making them darker. Footprints. Not the outline of shoes but heels and toes, fainter along the arches where the curve lifts away. I put my foot alongside them. The intruder's feet are smaller than mine.

⊙

My mobile's flashing at me. I've got a missed call.

"Cariad? It's Tom." There's a pause. There's a hard edge to his voice, like he's daring me to be furious at him for his defiance. "I know you said not to call but we need to talk. About the girl. About us."

The last thing I want to do is talk.

"Let me know you're okay, even if you don't want to see me."

More silence.

"Let me help you. You don't have to go through this alone." His anger rises. "The thing is, I love you. And I think you love me."

I wish he'd said it before Jessica. I wish I'd said it back. Not just because I'm too ashamed to face him now but because depression's a dark hole where no light goes. Your dearest wish becomes as inconsequential as crumbs.

I don't deserve Tom.

"Cariad, please…"

I turn off the phone, cutting him off mid-sentence.

⊙

I had met Tom on the first day of my new job in the Casualty department of Bronglais General Hospital, Aberystwyth. It was a new speciality to me, a new hospital and a new town. My orientation session had been curtailed after half an hour due to the department being busier than normal so I had no idea where anything was or who to ask for what. The staff were a hard, sardonic lot.

"Maria, would you mind looking at this X-ray? This bloke hurt his shoulder. I'm not sure if there's a hairline break of his …"

Dr Maria Callaghan, registrar, was our supervisor.

"Posterior or anterior?"

"Sorry?"

"What did they teach you at medical school? The force of injury," she enunciated each word, "was it posteriorly or anteriorly?"

"Oh, anterior. Head-on tackle."

She slapped the film onto a light box.

"No fracture. No dislocation."

Then she walked off.

I could feel the blotchy flush breaking out on my chest and face, the redness a beacon of upset, anger or embarrassment.

"Hey, don't let her get to you. I'm Ellen." Her badge said Nurse Practitioner. "Or, don't let her see when she does. If you need help, come and ask me."

If Maria was bad, the paramedics were worse. It takes a certain sort to survive the forefront of the frontline.

"We need you in our ambulance, now." A paramedic stopped me in the corridor. "I can't tell whether this guy's dead or not."

He ran out to his domain, parked in the ambulance bay. I followed thinking *How badly hurt is this man, that they're not bringing him inside?* Were they expecting me to perform heroics, such a chest drain or tracheostomy?

We got into the back of the ambulance.

"What do you think, love? Will he make it?" The paramedic roared with laughter.

The man on the trolley stared at me with a blank eye. The other side of his head was a nebulous hole full of crushed eye, shards of skull and macerated brain.

The door opened and a second paramedic addressed us.

"Piss off, Glynn. Let her alone."

I should've told Glynn to piss off myself but my mouth was too dry. Not that I was squeamish but it was surreal. I'd never seen a human head so decimated.

Glynn got out, still giggling, and the other man climbed in and closed the door.

"Sorry about him. I'm Tom." I must have looked particularly stupid because he asked if I knew how to verify a death. "I mean, you might as well do it now that you're here."

I nodded. Of course I did, but before Casualty I'd worked on a ward for the elderly where death occurred in bed or on the toilet.

"What happened to him?"

"Tyre blew out and he hit a tree at high speed. Poor lad didn't stand a chance."

Tom was tall. He stood back, not crowding me like Glynn had.

I checked the body, a pointless exercise to formalise the obvious. No heartbeat, no breath sounds, no pain response, the lone pupil fixed and dilated. Rest in peace.

"What's the C stand for Dr Evans?" Tom asked when I handed the form back to him.

"Cariad." Meaning darling, dearest.

"And are you?"

"What?"

"Beloved."

I scowled at him. It was only later that I realised he was flirting with me.

☉

I reinforce Arosfa's door with bolts from a shop in Haverfordwest. When I wake the next morning the light's mean and thin, unable to reach the corners of the room. The crows caw from the trees.

I get up and brush my teeth at the sink, not bothering to clear it of dirty dishes. I use bottled water as what's coming from the tap is brackish. I should get the electricity reconnected. It would be better than camping lanterns and torches.

I sit outside on the stone bench, wearing a jumper and coat over my pyjamas. The foil strip crackles as I pop out an antidepressant. I wonder what Dad would say about it as I swallow the pill.

Physician, heal thyself.

I remember lying on the camp bed in the dark. I was sixteen. Across Arosfa there was silence instead of Dad's breathing from the depth of dreaming. I looked at my watch. The luminous hands told me it was two in the morning.

"Dad?"

He was outside. There was no light pollution to nullify the night and hide the stars.

"Why are you up Cariad?" Dad took off his jacket and put it around me. He took a slug from his bottle of whisky. "Are you okay, chick?"

"Yes."

He touched the curve of my cheek where there was a bruise.

"Are you going to tell me then?"

"You've heard it all already."

"Yes, I've heard it from everyone. Just not you. Cariad, you're not one for scrapping. What made you go at that girl like that?"

"I hate her."

"I don't recall bringing you up to hate people. It's bad to wish ill on others. The universe will send it back to you, ten-fold."

I scowled.

"What did she say to get you so riled?"

"She said..." I struggled to say it. "She said that you were a piss artist that sold crap and empty promises."

"I've had worse said about me." I shot an angry look at him as he laughed. "I'm sorry." He nudged me. "Think about it. She didn't say that, Cariad. Emily Appleton's never had an original thought in her life. That's her dad talking. We've always agreed to ignore stuff like this. Why did you get so upset?"

"I just did."

He took a deep breath. I'd never spoken to him in that tone before.

"Cariad," he said slowly, "I think that you got so upset because you think she's right." Dad was wily. "It's okay, you know. Don't cry. This is how life works. You've got to find your own way."

"I'm not rejecting you." I wiped my face.

"When did you get so wise?" He laughed. "Will you promise me something?"

"What?"

"Keep a door open here, for possibilities." He tapped my forehead. "Don't close your mind to the idea that beneath what we know there's a whole world that we can only guess at. There are things in life that we *know* that we don't understand. The real danger is the stuff in the blind spot that we don't even know exists."

"That's a riddle."

"It's the long way of saying that what you don't know about is what bites you in the butt."

◉

"Sorry to keep you waiting."

Priya Sharma

I'd been seeing my GP for four months. I felt like she was sick of me. Or maybe I was sick of her. Or sick of still feeling the same.

"How are you?"

She was an expert in communication, having had special training. She knew exactly how to tell me that she didn't have much time without saying it aloud. Her gaze kept darting to her computer screen.

"Improved." I cut things short, knowing it was what she wanted to hear.

"Are you less tearful than last time?"

"Yes." That was true. I'd gone beyond crying.

"Are you sleeping?"

I nodded. I slept through afternoons, having spent the night lying awake. Two in the morning was the hardest time. The drowning hour where misery was at its deepest.

"Any idea when the inquest will be?"

"Not yet."

The thought was terrifying. I didn't want to face the family's anger and the Coroner's inquisition.

"Cariad," her face softened, "I'm not trying to rush you back to work but the longer you're off, the harder going back will be. When do *you* think you'll be ready to get back in the saddle?"

This from a woman who looked like she'd never fallen off the horse.

"Soon. Just not yet. I need a bit more time."

Before I hadn't wanted time off. Now I couldn't face going back.

"What will you do with yourself?"

"I'll go to my Dad's." I didn't mention that Dad was dead.

"Where's that?"

"Near Haverfordwest."

I wanted to be away. To leave Aberystwyth and drive along the blue of Cardigan Bay, past the painted houses of Aberaeron. I knew I was nearly at the Landsker line and home when I reached the Preseli Hills, whose blue stone made the inexplicable two hundred and fifty mile journey to the Salisbury Plain for the building of Stonehenge. The beautiful Preselis, whose hollows fill up with sun by day and at night the mist pours itself onto the road.

194

My GP's nails were bare but elegantly shaped, at the end of tapered fingers. I looked at her hands as she signed the sick note because I couldn't bear to look her in the face.

⊙

I sat beside Maria at the workstation, both of us writing in patients' records. She broke the silence. "You get upset easily, don't you Cariad?"

Any opportunity to undermine me.

"Do I?"

I tried not to sound defensive but I was strung out from self-doubt, stretched thin as an onion skin by the line of patients that never seemed to lessen. Sometimes I felt there was a whole wave of them about to crash down on me. Their fear made me fraught, as did their anger at being kept waiting. Waiting to be seen, waiting for test results, waiting for another doctor to come when a senior's opinion was needed.

"Yes, you should watch that," Maria continued. "Being too emotional is how you make mistakes. And you'll do no good trying to be everyone's friend. The nurses all tell me how caring you are, which is all very well, but it's only part of the job."

There was me, thinking it was the very essence of our vocation.

"Cariad, I'm not saying this to be hurtful. I'm trying to be supportive." Like all good bullies she knew how to couch her comments so as to avoid reprisal.

"Hello, my beauties." Glynn tapped the desk, the oily rag of a man eager for attention. "Which one of you is taking me out later?"

Tom hung back. We shared a smile that contained all that had passed between us. I looked away, unable to contain myself, only to see Maria staring at me, unhappy with what she'd seen.

⊙

The cliffs at Newgale are covered in sporadic patches of gorse, some of it bearing yellow blooms. *When gorse goes out of flower, love goes out of fashion.* Another piece of Dad's wisdom. The cliff face is spotted with pink thrift and white sea campion. The rock itself is layers of different coloured stripes, marking time's strata. This is what we are. Layers of history, one event laid down upon another. We are less consequential than sediment.

The tide has carved out caves. We imagine that we can do what stone can't; that we can hold back the rising tide and remain whole and unaffected. So much for my grandiose plans of helping people. I can't even help myself.

I squat in one of the caves. It smells of rocks and salt. I've come armed with one of Dad's empty whisky bottles. I half fill it with pebbles and then say her name over and over, *Jessica, Jessica,* into the bottle's mouth. I pray her in and then screw the cap on. I'm not sure if I've recalled it as Dad taught me. This was his legacy, this knowledge that's so at odds with everything else about me. I wish I'd listened more when Dad talked.

The match flares in the cave's cold shade and I hold a candle in the flame, letting wax drip around the bottle top to seal it.

I'll contain Jessica this way. I wade out into the cold water. The tide dragging at my thighs threatens to drag me down. I've not got a good throwing arm but I cast the bottle out as far as I can. It lands with a splash and then it's gone.

☉

I'd been working at Bronglais General for five months when I first met Jessica.

Saturdays were the worst. Inebriated brawlers and the hopeless attempting suicide were heaped upon victims of heart attacks and strokes. They threatened to overwhelm me. No matter how much I studied, I never knew enough. No matter how hard I worked, I couldn't keep up.

The girl in the cubicle was wrapped in a blanket. Her dark curls were stiff with brine. The woman that fussed over her was striking too. Like the girl, she had a beaked nose and black eyes but her hair was unruly and streaked with grey. She was taller, scrawnier, and her long black coat flapped around her as she moved.

"Hello Jessica." I read her name from the casualty card. "I'm Dr Evans. Are you Jessica's mum?"

The tall woman nodded. She hovered over me in a mix of anxiety and threat that I read as *Look after my girl.*

"What happened to you, Jessica?"

"I nearly drowned."

"Tell me what happened."

"My dog went into the water. We were on the beach." She smiled, rueful. "I went in after him and we got caught in a big wave."

"She was lucky," her mother's mouth became a thin line. "A group of lads were body boarding and one of them was close enough to reach her."

"How long were you in the water?"

"I don't know. It felt like forever."

"I'll bet. Did you black out at all?"

"No."

"Good. You must've been terrified."

Her mother started to cry. I envied Jessica that maternal love.

"I'm okay, Mum. Don't fuss."

I checked Jessica's chart. Her pulse and blood pressure were normal and she wasn't hypothermic.

"Come on, Jessica. Let's check you out."

She looked at me with admiring shyness, hesitating as if she wanted to say something. I paused, encouraging her to speak.

"I'm going into lower sixth in September. I want to study Medicine when I finish."

"Then we might work together one day. What do you think about that?"

I put my stethoscope to Jessica's chest and listened to the steady lub-dub of her heart as her atria and ventricles contracted in turn. Her lungs inflated normally, a healthy pair of bellows.

"Everything seems fine," I said. "How's the dog?"

"Damn the dog," her mother spat. "Leave the bloody thing to drown next time."

"He swam to shore in the end. Mum's friend took him to the vet."

The curtain twitched.

"Excuse me." Ellen pulled me from the cubicle. "Maria wants everyone in the resus bay now. There's been a pile up."

"One second," I told Ellen and went back in. "Sorry about that. Your chest X-ray is normal, Jessica. I think you're okay to go home. If you feel short of breath or get chest pains, a cough or fever, then we need to see you again."

I remember thinking, at that moment, that I'd hit my stride. My confidence was growing. I was finally playing my part.

"Are you sure?" her mother asked. "The vet's keeping the dog in for observation."

To which I replied, "Don't worry, Jessica will be fine."

⊙

Painful thoughts. They gnaw.

Everything's magnified by the unflinching lens of two AM, my every defect, fuck up and misstep that obliterates any modest successes.

Then, of course, there's the one act that negates everything. Even when I close my eyes, it's there.

I get up, sliding from my sleeping bag. When I put my feet down, they land in a cold puddle on the floor. I'll check that the roof's sound in the morning. Not that it matters. Damp permeates everything. It's in the walls. It's gathered on the window. Everything smells dank.

When I go outside the night's misted and murky. A gusting wind makes the low mist twist and swirl around me. It softens and blurs the lights of the houses. I need to pee but can't bear the idea of going to the ty-dach, the little house. The toilet drops into the neglected septic tank that's now rank. I don't want to be alone in there. Ivy has insinuated itself through the wall panels and crept up the inside. I walk out into the middle of the field instead.

Wet grass brushes my legs as I squat and relieve myself. Steam rises. A chill goes up my back which makes me feel exposed. There's a dense fog, blowing in fast over the hill. I'm vulnerable, unable to run and overcome by the idea that I'm going to die out here, knickers around my ankles, urine running down my leg.

I glance over my shoulder, wondering at the fullness of my bladder. The fog eddies and whirls in the wind, making shapes too fleeting for me to focus on.

My stream slows to a trickle. I hear something behind me, higher pitched than the hoot of an owl. I look back again, pulling up my pyjama bottoms. A black shadow is in the fog's depths. Something's coming out of the night.

It's taking shape, pulling itself together from pieces of darkness. It looks like a long-legged figure with straggly hair. A raven of a woman. Her long coat flaps around her. She's covering the ground between us in great strides.

It's the Gwrach-y-Rhibyn. The Hag in the Mist. She's a death omen.

I run. As I near Arosfa I hear a shriek and I stumble. My mistake is looking back. The hag's in flight, her coat transformed into great wings. I try and scramble to my feet but my trembling legs collapse and because of this she passes over me with a shrill scream of frustration that her clawed hands are empty.

She's circling but it's enough time for me to get to Arosfa. I slam the door behind me, lock it and throw the bolts. The hag hits the door with a thud. I upturn the table and put it against the door and then sit on the opposite side of the room. There's a strange fluttering sound outside, as if she's hovering in wait.

How long the night is. The wind picks up, rattling the roof. The hag taunts me. Just when I think she's gone, there's a sudden slapping sound against the door or one of the walls, followed by a flap, flap, flap as she prowls around Arosfa, trying to get in. I drag the bed to the centre of the room and sit with my legs drawn up and my arms wrapped around them.

Around dawn the wind drops and everything's quiet. I think the hag's gone. I doze off for an hour and then wake with puffy, swollen eyes. I pull the curtains and the clarity of the morning light mocks me, as does the torn black bin liner lying on Arosfa's step when I open the door.

☉

Jessica was rushed in the night after I saw her. Glynn pushed the trolley. Tom worked on her as they went.

"Bleep the crash team. Now."

Jessica's skin was white, her lips cyanosis blue. The rhythms of resuscitation failed to rouse her. I stood trembling instead of piling in and helping. I couldn't even muster the basic primer for survival. The ABC of airway, breathing and circulation.

Her mother stood by, her gangly limbs impotent as they hung by her side. We looked at one another.

"What's happened to Jessica?"

"She said she couldn't breathe. By the time the ambulance arrived, she'd collapsed."

More doctors and nurses ran in, answering the call. Ellen pulled the curtain across the bay so that Jessica's mother wouldn't have to witness the indignities required to save a life.

"We need to help Jessica now," Ellen spoke to her mum. "Go with Jamie and he'll get you a cup of tea. I'll come and get you when there's news."

"I want to stay."

"Let them help her." Jamie put an arm around her, gentle and insistent. He was the best member of staff at calming relatives and breaking bad news. "We'll only be around the corner when she needs you."

There were enough people with Jessica, I told myself. I'd just be in the way.

Maria found me later, in the staff toilets. She stood beside me as I washed my hands, removing smudged mascara with her little finger. She watched me in the mirror.

"You saw her yesterday, didn't you?" She didn't need to explain who she was talking about.

"Yes. How is she?"

"It doesn't look good. She went into the sea, right?"

"She was fine yesterday. Her chest x-ray was normal. I don't understand."

"Secondary drowning." She uncapped her lipstick and applied the coral bullet to her mouth. It was as though she was suddenly talking under water. I had to concentrate on the movements of her lips. I must've looked blank because she started to explain. "The surfactant that keeps the lungs open gets stripped off the lungs by sea water. Drowning follows within twenty-four hours."

Maria didn't need to tell me. I'd read about it, briefly. Without surfactant, her lungs had collapsed and she'd starved of oxygen. So Jessica had drowned on dry land.

"What were her blood gases like?" Maria tied her hair up in a knot. "That's the crucial bit."

Blood gases. A special measurement to check the gas profile in the blood. As soon as she said it I knew the yawning truth was that I hadn't done it. I didn't know I should have. Like my dad said, the most dangerous kind of ignorance isn't what we know that we don't know but what we have no inkling of.

Which is a long way of saying that what you don't know about is what bites you in the butt.

⊙

I wake from fitful sleep with a start. It's dark. The mattress is sodden with water that's level with the bed. I turn on my camping lantern but it doesn't reveal exactly where the water's coming in.

This isn't a leak. It's pouring down all four walls, flooding in faster than it can drain out.

I wade through the water that's up to my thighs, lighting the lanterns as I go. I unlock the door but the top bolt won't budge. It looks clogged up with decades of rust, not shiny and clean as he had been when I fitted only a few days ago. I get down, soaking myself, trying to force the bottom bolt but this is stuck too. I shoulder the door in frustration but all I get for my efforts is a jarring pain from shoulder to elbow.

I try and smash the window over the sink with a chair but it's reinforced with wire mesh. Sodden, I haul myself up onto the narrow draining board which creaks under my weight. I try and kick the glass out, not caring about my bare feet, without success.

Stop. Be calm. I find my mobile by the bed but it's too wet to summon help. What else? Preserve the light, move the lanterns to higher places to keep them dry. My waterproof torch is in my bag. I put its loop around my wrist.

The empty kettle floats. Plastic beakers and melamine plates bob past me. I'm flotsam and jetsam too. The room's filling up fast. I have to tread water.

Outside there's a frenzied barking. I shout, a waterlogged sound, hoping some nocturnal dog walker will hear me, but no.

The lanterns are submerged one by one. They glow momentarily making a ball of watery light, then they flicker and go out. Darkness magnifies the water's sound, the rush that's filling Arosfa up.

I turn on the torch. The white arc swings about, illuminating choppy water and the pale face in the corner.

Water's treacherous. It's brought Jessica to me. She's been baptised and now reborn. Her hair's plastered to her scalp. Her lips are dusky, her skin translucent and mottled from being submerged too long. Her neck and shoulders are bare. She glows, as if lit from within. Jessica opens her mouth and pebbles fall out. The bottle that I cast into the sea floats between us. The bottle top has been smashed off. Red wax still clings to the broken bottle's neck.

Jessica dips beneath the surface.

Fear's energising. I scream and thrash. Water slops into my mouth, drowning my shout. I taste brine, brine up here on Treffgarne hill.

There's churning, as if deep, vast undercurrents are about to pull me down. I feel a sharp tug at my pyjama leg. I kick out. Then Jessica yanks me down. I lose the torch in a panic. The beam of shrinking light descends.

Jessica's hand is clamped around my ankle as we follow the light into the depths. I might as well be out at open sea. Just when I think my chest will explode, she lets me go. I break the surface as if catapulted up, gasping and coughing. Waves buffet me about.

It's not mercy on Jessica's part. She's toying with me. This time I can feel her full weight, both arms around my calves like a clinging child. For someone so slight she's like a plummeting anchor taking me to the ocean floor.

This time we go further into the inky water. It doesn't make sense; we're too deep to be within Arosfa. It must be oxygen deprivation making me disorientated. I start to panic and struggle even more, desperate to inhale, even if it's just saltwater.

Jessica grants me another reprieve. Air has never seemed so sweet. I surface with aching lungs but all I can manage are shallow breaths. Not that there's much air left, only a few inches between the water level and the roof. I have to tip my head back to keep my mouth and nose clear.

It's not over though. Jessica comes up in front of me. I take a deep breath and tip my head so that I can keep her in sight. Her eyes are empty, like everything's been poured out of her. Her arms slide around me, like a lover's, her legs twine about mine. She's a dead weight. We sink like a stone.

The sea is vast. I'm weary of the struggle. I want to give in but the fear is physiological, my cells fighting to save themselves. The pain is surprising.

Then it comes. I have to gasp. I'm stunned as cold water floods my lungs, freezing me from within. Bubbles escape from my nose and mouth. Stars explode at the periphery of my vision.

Jessica releases me, which makes me sad because it's now that I want someone to hold me. I drift.

Being lost brings me a contrary clarity. My life returns to me. Mum, when she was still alive. It was dusk and I was in the garden of the cottage at Molleston, watching her as she stood at the sink. She looked up and saw me, giving me a broad smile.

I remember the afternoon sun sliding around a classroom. The algebraic symbols scrawled on the board finally rearranged themselves from a jumble into something I understood. In that moment I had the joy of intuition, of a knowledge as complex as my father's, and it thrilled me because it was mine.

I remember kissing Tom in a darkened room that was washed by the light of a mute television. Kissing him until my mouth felt bruised and swollen.

And Jessica's sweet, trusting smile.

The last bubbles escape into blackness.

Down at Newgale beach the sea is wide and the tide carries on rising.

THE ENGLISHMAN

*N*ever *has God been in such profusion as he is in India. He is in the dust, for every common man. He is in the bazaar, Shiva's hooded serpent, dancing in a basket; in Krishna's bony cow, lying in traffic; He is among the Dervishes as they whirl, sand flying from their skirts and He is in the stark white church, tended by wizened brown nuns in habits of navy polyester. He is in tiny shrines by the roadside and in the grand temples, carved from single mountains.*

God is everywhere. And once in your blood, India, like God, will never leave you.

⊙

The Englishman puts down his newspaper. He's irritated by the waiter, who stands before him, dithering, despite the Englishman's request in Hindi for another cup of coffee. Then the Englishman realises his mistake. He has the half-remembered, half-forgotten words mixed up. He repeats himself in English. "Another coffee, inside."

Embarrassment makes him brusque.

"Of course, Sir."

The waiter is a smooth, delicate creature in a Nehru jacket, tiny in contrast to the Englishman. The narrow man glides away, bearing the Englishman's empty cup and saucer aloft on a lacquered tray.

The Englishman leaves the veranda for the dining room. It's barely midmorning and there's already sheen of sweat on his forehead. As the doors swing shut behind him the cold blast from the air conditioning raises goosebumps on his arms.

Inside are wooden panels to waist height and a black and white diamond chequered floor, punctuated by potted palms. Only sixty years ago this was where the cream of English society took tea after polo. There had been music on a gramophone and dancing. The only Indians allowed would have been servants.

The Englishman surveys the social advancement around him; tourists in shorts, Indian businessmen having meetings and talking on their mobiles. Then he waits for his second cup of coffee and carries on reading. He is shocked by the stories. Kidnapped children. Brides burnt for dowries of washing machines and motorbikes. He hardly knows this India at all. He's not sure if he is more ashamed of her or himself. In his mind she is a place of genteel corruption and colour. When did she become so modern and brutal? In his memory India is vermillion and turquoise. She is orange and gold. She is a peacock of a country.

On his return, the Englishman was seated next to a girl on a gap year, her future on her bright face. She listened with eagerness as he told her about the colours. Together they peered from the window of the plane. Below, piled up matchboxes organised themselves into rickety shelters with corrugated roofs. As they lost altitude, the ants crawling over them became people. The Englishman realised that this impossible town was perched precariously on a rubbish dump. Its inhabitants scavenged with the gulls and dogs. The colour was somewhere between brown and grey.

The colour of Delhi was mud.

Stepping off the plane he was overcome by heat and moisture. It was saturated with smells that made him a child again. Humidity and dust. It was India. She lodged in his windpipe and he didn't think he would ever breathe again.

He's glad that Elsie hadn't seen this India. When they were in bed together, sharing a cigarette, she would say, *Tell me about India. Will I like it?*

He would pull the bed sheet over their heads, making a tent, through which the afternoon light would filter. In that place there was only the two of them. *Next year, Elsie. Next year I will take you. India is beautiful but not as beautiful as you.*

Her pale hair tumbled across his chest. There had always been a next year, until the years ran out.

Each morning the Englishman smiles as he passes the hotel guard, a man in khaki uniform, rifle tucked upright against his body. Looking back, the Englishman can see his hotel with its colonnaded verandas and grand portico.

He walks through the tree lined avenues of bungalows that are not-so-New Delhi, each building a chronicle of the Raj. The sunlight makes a heat blaze on the tarmac. He can see no order on the roads. Cars, lorries, buses packed beyond the comical to the precarious, all move in different directions. Weaving in and out of them are black and yellow auto-rickshaws and mopeds, carrying families stacked together like interlocking puzzle, the women perched side saddle in their saris. He recalls sitting in polite traffic queues on a Cheshire by-pass during his daily commute, taking for granted the calm, the sense of order, that had been such a wonderment to him as a young man.

As he walks, sweat pools in the crooks of his knees and elbows. He puts up his black umbrella for shade. As a child, his mother would sit him on a blanket. There was brightness and the feeling that his bones were always warm, not this oppressive heat, beating him down. Little wonder India is indolent at the height of summer, in temperatures that can kill a man.

The Englishman passes into Old Delhi, a different city. Here are the remnants of the Delhi Sultans and the Moghuls who left behind graceful minarets and stone latticework.

As he nears the bazaar, the street narrows and suddenly he is upon it. Or, rather, it is upon him, this swell of bodies, this riot of women in saris, coloured bindhis and eyeliner on their faces, who jostle and flirt with narrow hipped men, in nylon shirts over white vests.

There are fabrics, the colour of jewels, piled up in rolls. Spices are displayed in cloth sacks, their mouths ripped open, revealing dusts and powders in all the colours of the earth, from rich red turmeric to pale brown cinnamon. Tinsel garlands. Brass idols from the pantheon of Hindu gods. Men sell bottled Limka, a fizzy drink the colour of limes, from rusty fridges and cook fried parathas in blackened pans of oil.

On the floor sits a beggar, in a faded white mourning sari with glass bangles in a row upon one arm, looking impossibly small to fit over her bony, gnarled hands. They clink with the slightest movement. Before her is a piece of tatty cloth, containing a few lonely rupees. The hem of her sari is pulled down over her face and she bows her head, but the Englishman sees her chin continue onto her chest. She has no neck, just a lump in its place. The skin overlying it is stretched and ulcerated. The tumour is mottled, as though it is dying independently of its owner.

A woman nearby waves a shawl at him from the bundle at her feet. It is red shot through with gold. "For your wife. Twenty rupees. Very good price."

Elsie would have liked that, he thinks dully, *she loved bright colours. She made me laugh. She didn't mind my accent or strange cooking. She was my friend. I miss her.*

When she died the Englishman buried her in the ground at their local church. He converted, to please her family, even though she didn't want him to. She said it didn't matter. She was the only one to whom it didn't matter at all. Her father slapped him on the back and asked him what cricket team he supported, like it was a test. He walked through their town, with its cobbles and Tudor beams, the only brown face. Elsie always put her arm through his. People wouldn't look at them. Sometimes women spat at her. He thinks a lot about the nature of God these days. His father would come home from the post office where he worked. *Son,* he would say, *you can't be made a Hindu. You are born one. No matter where you go you can't turn away from it. Or India.*

Elsie didn't believe in God. She believed in love and laughter and having a smoke. She believed in seizing life and shaking it. She believed in herself, *because if I don't, no-one else will.*

I believe in you. He took her hand. *Marry me.*

The Englishman wonders whether he is being punished for turning away. From India. From his family. From Hinduism.

○

He passes a boarded up shop that smells strongly of urine and he turns his face away in disgust. He starts as a snake hisses, close to his eyes, curling off the shoulder of a man in tatty robes. Its tongue flicks in and out.

The man has three horizontal lines marked on his forehead, marks of Shiva, the Destroyer. The Lord of Death. His hair is long and matted, part of it tied up in a topknot. He is laughing, hoisting the giant serpent onto his shoulders and carrying it off. A laughing Shiva, walking through the streets. His throat is blue from drinking the poisoned oceans at the start of creation.

The Englishman feels dizzy.

"Come," Shiva beckons with a smile and a nod of the head.

The Englishman looks at the stone doorway he has indicated. He says its name. "Madir," and the words sound foreign in his mouth. *Madir, temple. Doorway to the heart.*

He slips off his shoes and stoops to enter.

Shiva smiles again. His mouth is red from chewing betel nut, the beloved Indian carcinogen. He lowers the cobra into a basket and then knocks the lid shut with a flourish. The walls are unplastered and the altar is made of rough hewn stone. On the floor is rush matting. Ganesha, the elephant-headed, pot-bellied son of Shiva sits on the altar.

"Ganesha."

"Yes," Shiva replies. "He is at the start of all journeys. How long have you been away from home, Englishman?"

"Twenty-five years."

Home. The Englishman thinks about the word. He has not been to India for twenty-five years. So where is home? In the house where he grew up in Jaipur? In the semi-detached he shared with Elsie? Washing his car on a Sunday, just like his neighbours. Investing in electricals, desirables, collectables. Being slapped on the back by his workmates. *You're just like us, aren't you Kris? A proper Englishman.*

When they ventured to a city they would encounter Indian faces that would look at the Englishman and his bride. He saw their features contort with disgust. *Coconut,* they would say in Hindi as they passed him by. *Brown on the outside and white on the inside.*

So, where is home?

"In Britain?" Shiva's guttural accent makes it sound exotic.

"Yes."

"What is your name, Englishman?"

"Krishna Sharma," replies the Englishman.

Just Kris, he would say. In England, their tongues would stumble over the extra syllable, the 'na' in his name that made it foreign.

"Your family? They are with you?"

"I'm a widower."

"Children?" Shiva's interrogation is merciless.

"No. No children. My wife. She was called Elsie." He feels like he is confessing.

"English then."

"Yes."

Shiva shrugs. "It doesn't matter. God can see her. He can see you. You are bound together. Die and be reborn together. That is the way it is. That is what it means to be on the wheel."

He laughs and when he does Krishna can see the sea churning in his mouth.

"All that love, it has to go somewhere. Like all energy in the universe, it can't just disappear. It changes, from one form into another. It is a good way, yes?" He puffs out his chest with pride, as though this is his personal plan.

Shiva takes the puja tray from the altar. It is stainless steel, containing dishes of rice, betel nut, tulsi leaves, honey and sandalwood paste. He takes his thumb and presses it into the paste and smears it across the Englishman's forehead. Three times into three horizontal lines.

"Bless you. For the start of your auspicious journey home, Krishna Sharma."

O

The Englishman stands outside the madir. He is crying. For Elsie. For India, who has so little and is so much. And England, whom he has come to love but is a void without his wife. For Krishna Sharma.

He has been given back his name.

To be reborn he has to die. That is the wheel.

Krishna walks through the crowd, not sure where he's going. If he has anywhere to go. The world is empty and full.

Children stand before him, little stick limbs jutting from ragged t-shirts. They are bare foot. The smallest one at the front holds out a hand, his black eyes liquid in his dusty face. "Please." He keeps his arm out straight, the other hand at the elbow locking it into position. They have formed a circle around him.

A girl in a ruffled, dirty skirt holds a naked baby at her hip. Her hair is plaited. At her elbows are patches of eczema, crusty from scratching.

On her forehead are three horizontal lines.

He gets out his wallet from his shirt pocket. First the little boy, then the girl with the baby. Encouraged, the others press in, pleading and crying in low moans that rise to a mourning wail. He empties out the money, passing the crumpled notes out as fast as he can to the eager little hands. They feel like soft cotton between his fingers as they are snatched away.

The baby clutches at his shirt front as the girl presses closer. He can feel the camera strap being cut, sliding from his neck and he catches a flash of sunlight on the casing as it is whisked away into unseen hands. *Never mind. Let them have it.*

There are more and more of the little bodies, all clamouring for him, a sea of them. A writhing mass, from which hissing tongues and dextrous hands dart. The Englishman feels his clothes being moved by tiny fingers. The flaps of pockets lift, as if by a breeze.

The watch falls from his wrist. The girl holds it in her hand, brazen, and then it's lost somewhere in the folds of her skirt.

Never mind, let her have it. It's just a watch. Nothing is irreplaceable.

Growing bolder, they fish under his waistband, pulling shamelessly at his money belt, like an insistent lover. It comes away. He feels lighter. *It's only money after all. Let them have all of it.*

The little hands slide around his belly, engulfing him, kneading him. One of them pinches the hanging flesh of his arms. He feels an experimental nip on his calf, drawing blood. He looks down to see a boy squatting by his leg, knees up by his ears. The girl, angry, bends down to slap the nibbler away.

She licks her lips.

Never mind, they look so hungry.

All this energy can't just disappear. One form into another.

As they lift him, he hears their groans, but they manage, being so many. The Englishman is carried away into the darkness of the alley.

Never mind, he thinks, *this is what it means to be on the wheel. Let them have me. Let them have all of me.*

THE NATURE OF BEES

Vivien Avery came into her summer late. She blossomed at the age of thirty-eight, a time when most women are past ripeness, their fruit sampled and discarded.

The men buzzed around her, enthralled.

⊙

The bee is praised by ancient Greeks and our own captains of industry for its philosophies of order and productivity. There is no self in this honeyed utopia, each member a willing sacrifice to its machinery.

As much as we would emulate its nature, we also emasculate it. The bee is reduced to a fuzzy bumbler, nectar drunk amid the blooms. We do not heed the warning of its colours. Such sweetness always comes with a sting.

⊙

When Vivien stepped inside the cottage she knew her choice to be correct. Built into the walls of an estate, it contained sunshine and shade, heavy oak and threadbare rugs. The manager showed her around without embarrassment at the stained hip bath beneath the dripping shower head, the tired Formica of the kitchen and the rattling windows. Vivien was happy to endure such deprivations. It had character.

He led her through the kitchen into the suntrap yard, the stone slabs warm. There was a washing line strung across it, wearing tea towels like a row of flags. There was a rotten door in the far wall, askew on its hinges.

"I keep meaning to fix this," for the first time he sounded like he was apologising.

"What's through there?"

"The orchard. The estate. It's better that you stay out unless they invite you." He stood and looked at her. "You will remember that, won't you? Only if they ask you to."

"Of course. Are you in charge of the estate?"

"Good God, no. Just this."

She followed him up the twisting stairs. From the windows under the slanting roof, she could see the yard, then hives scattered in the orchard, a kitchen garden and finally the roof of the mansion, made of crumbling ochre stone. She could see figures moving among the trees and between the rows of vegetables.

"You're not allergic to bee stings, are you?"

Vivien frowned.

"No, but I'm not fond of them either."

"This used to be a beekeeper's cottage." He nodded towards the big house. "They produce the caviar of honey."

He did not exaggerate. The estate's honey was a secret, kept by those who knew and didn't want to share. Medicinal and beautifying, it was sought by kings, media moguls and entertainment divas.

"They're very shy people. Filthy rich, apparently. Not that you'd know to look at them."

He stepped closer.

"The honey's very expensive. It's an aphrodisiac, you know."

The man lightly grasped her wrist and she pulled away. Undeterred, he went to the bed, seemingly to demonstrate the firmness of the mattress, patting the space beside him. Not looking her in the face made it an insipid invitation. He ploughed on.

"My wife. She doesn't understand me."

"Then perhaps you should make a better job of explaining yourself."

Vivien was shocked and excited, despite herself. Not by him but by the possibilities of the invitation. She had tried romance and found it fragile. This man was not offering her romance, but something entirely different.

She hid her smile behind pursed lips as she ushered the manager, who was baffled by his own audacity, out of the door.

☉

Long divorced, her marriage bewildering and brief, Vivien was an anomaly in her social circle. Being without husband or child, her personal and professional successes could be overlooked by her female friends. Being true friends, they never voiced their opinions that her manlessness had made her selfish and her childlessness had made her trivial. They never talked in pitying tones about her lonely nights of splendid isolation.

She became a pale shadow of herself in the company of the husbands, sons and lovers of these friends. Her failure with men blighted her side of the conversation. She was socially uncertain, diffident and eager, where another sort of woman might have become bolshy and bitter. She put them in mind of their brothers, the ones that were young enough to need their approval and not old enough to be a rival. Her attempts at flirtation were charming. Innocent and awkward enough to share with their wives, mothers and lovers.

It was this group of men that were the first to sense a change. They noticed her fingers lingering on the stem of her glass, that she no longer covered her mouth to stifle the laughter hidden there. There was nothing bitter in the tilt of her chin as she challenged their opinions. She teased them and it made them tingle. They did not share these exchanges with their wives, mothers or their lovers.

Vivien Avery was in flower.

☉

The queen is statuesque, bigger than any of her progeny who attend her. Her monarchy is two-fold. She is the only one of her tribe to reproduce and she has the power of chemical domination. Her prodigious pheromones keep the colony in supplication. The workers are her hand maidens, who clean and feed her from their own mouths with ambrosia, a viscous yellow milk that promises her abnormal longevity. So it is that for her entire life she is utterly theirs to adore, her residence a hexagonal cell that is both her throne and her prison.

☉

Later in her life, when Vivien had a surfeit of leisure to reflect, those early days at the cottage were the ones she remembered most. She had memories of basking in the yard, eating roast chicken with her fingers. The crisp skin melting between her tongue and palate. There was a square of unsullied blue above her and she wondered if it could have been as perfect or if she imagined it that way. There were afternoons with a muted radio and tatty paperback. Her life before was vague by comparison, barely tasted, lost and wasted.

Vivien also recalled when this life ended and her new one began.

The encounter with the manager had reminded her that her body had its own purpose, not just functions. Its need for satisfaction disturbed her sleep. By night she stood naked before the mirror in the bedroom, studying her tarnished image and invoking the jolt of his fist around her wrist. Her hoarding ovaries now threatened to release all her eggs at once. This rampant fecundity made her shine. Her pheromones were maddening. Vivien Avery didn't give a fig for procreation. Her state made her pleasure hungry. She longed to be a carnal adventurer.

She turned around, peering over her shoulder to view herself. The motion made one scapula take flight. There was the hollow of her back. The ample hips and fleshy bottom. Flesh on fire, she glowed in the dark.

The faint tapping startled her. It was a hesitant request for admission. She paused. It came again. Vivien pulled on clothes. The stairs creaked under her feet. She looked left to the soft shapes of the sofa. The rapping wasn't at the front of the cottage, but from the kitchen door. This was a backdoor caller.

The knocking came again. The trespasser had come through the estate and by the rotten door into her yard. She turned the key. The prospect of the manager didn't threaten her even though she had not decided what to do with him yet.

Vivien gaped. It was a woman. Tall and stooped. As naked as Vivien had been only moments before. Her silver hair was twisted into a rope over one shoulder. Her skin was taunt and uncreased on her aged face.

"Help me."

The old woman stepped inside. Her abdomen was revealed. Womanhood had ravaged her. The skin sagged as though once greatly distended and then emptied. The abdomen of a mother, many times over.

Her pubic hair was sparse and childish. Her breasts were like a beast's, damaged by the dragging suckling of a large and selfish litter. Her limbs were emaciated. Yet the skin had the same sheen as her face, cosmetic, youthful and unnatural. Bony hands snatched at Vivien as she collapsed into her arms.

Vivien lowered her to the ground, cradling her in her lap. The old woman smelled of honey. Her skin was thin satin slipping under Vivien's hands. It was as though she had been oiled to keep it supple.

"Please, help me." She touched Vivien's face, her fingers butterflies.

Figures loomed up from the darkness outside.

"Mother, we've been so worried."

They came as a pair, one enfolding the old lady in a blanket like she was an injured animal, pulling her from Vivien's embrace, the jealousy plain on her face.

"Mother," said the other, "we thought we'd lost you."

They clucked and fussed with palpable concern. They were shorter than their mother, solid country girls. Squat and square rather than curved. They were dressed in simple blouses and trousers that looked homemade.

"Do you want to bring her in? I'll light the fire and get some clothes."

"No, that's all right."

The taller one was brusque but the other one seemed more inclined to conversation.

"This is our mother," the girl said as though it weren't obvious. "She's never wandered off like this before."

"Your mother's lucky to have such a caring family."

"Oh, thank you. Thank you very much." The girl beamed at her, pleased by the comment. Vivien saw that she wasn't a girl at all, but a woman. Her lack of grooming, the unplucked eyebrows and the faint moustache, made her look younger. She lingered as her stocky sister lifted their frail parent in her arms.

"Hadn't you better help them?"

"She's very strong." Her hand loitered on the door frame, as if to stop Vivien from shutting her out. "We look after her. She's very old now.

What's your name?"

"Vivien."

"I'm Bea." She pointed to Vivien's arm. A bee had landed there. Insects could be as insomniac as old ladies. Bea lifted it off with care. She held it up and it took flight. "They like you."

"Is that good?"

"Oh, yes."

"Well, nice to meet you." Vivien started to close the door.

"You're very kind to have helped us."

"It's nothing."

"Most people wouldn't have answered the door. How much longer are you staying?"

"Another week."

"Are you with your husband?"

"No," Vivien hesitated, "I'm not married."

Bea leaned in. She seemed to be deciding something.

"Will you come to see us? I think my family will like you. We can thank you properly."

"That's not necessary."

"Please. It would mean so much to all of us. Through there, tomorrow afternoon then," she pointed back to where she'd come from, "and if you don't come, we'll have to come and get you."

○

It is appropriate that the workers are female, their passion not for themselves, but for the greater good. They are supple creatures, young and unfeminine, relishing their roles as cleaners, guards and builders, as hunter-gatherers and factory workers.

These workers forage among the flowers, curling tongues sucking nectar from blooms into their rosebud mouths. They hurry back to the hive with this delivery, where other workers wait with eager, open mouths.

They show blind devotion to the queen. They smother her with mother love which is touching as they are sterile.

A life of toil, doting on their queen, sweet and incestuous honeyed kisses, mass murder and the production of a spoon of honey are the best that they can hope for.

○

Vivien pushed open the door to the orchard. The wood was crumbling splinters against her palms. There was a sound on the air, a hum between the trees, a buzz, the Om that underlies the universe. It hung before her, sound given body.

It was a swarm.

He came through the bees as if invincible. Vivien was won over immediately, enchanted by his entrance. She admired the broadness of his chest and shoulders. The sinews of his forearms made her shudder. He wasn't pretty, which was good, as she distrusted prettiness. She'd made altars of beautiful men only to have tear them down again. Her ex-husband was one such man. She'd become indifferent to his sculpted face. By the end she found it vacuous. They was no chemistry, no urgency between them. Give her an ugly, charismatic man any day. She imagined them to be more attentive lovers.

"You're quite safe," his molten voice poured right through her, "they're not interested in you."

The man lingered in the swarm. When he opened his mouth bees flew onto his tongue. She gasped as they crowded his mouth. She imagined kisses, full of stings. Swollen tongues and bruised lips. He blew gently, sending them on their way.

"You must be Vivien. I'm Tom."

"Hello." She was shy. The shyness that is loaded with expectation, that showed her thoughts were giving her cause to blush. She was determined to enjoy this game. After all, it was her summer and nothing would be as sweet again.

Tom carried an enamel pail. He dipped his fingers in and they came out coated, dripping honey. Tom offered himself to her and she took them in her mouth.

He tasted exquisite.

○

"Come and join us. There's a picnic in your honour."

They walked together through the orchard. The boughs leaned towards them, laden with gifts. Several women were at work, harvesting the fruit. There was singing, the sound of wassailing and cider, of garlands and maidens. They were dressed in simple homemade clothes, like the women who'd come in the night. They turned as Tom and Vivien approached, eyes full of appraisal.

The kitchen garden opened up before them. Here more women were at labour, rearing rows of brassica and pulling up potatoes. Ferny carrot stalks spilled from their trugs. One woman had her face buried in a lavender bush, grasping it like a lover's face. She surfaced, glowing with pleasure. There was that song again.

They walked around to the front of the house whose leaded panes stretched above them, winking in the sun. The doors were treble height, unassailable and carved with bees.

The lawn spread out under the sun, blankets laid upon it and men laid out upon them. They turned their heads, they smiled at her and some even stood up but were waved back down by Tom.

"Here." Tom directed her to an empty woollen square and handed her a glass. His spoon clinked needlessly upon the glass as though he needed this to get everyone's attention. "I'd like to introduce Vivien."

Glasses were raised amid murmurs of welcome.

"Thank you." Vivien would not be flustered. Be it a coven, cult or clan, she would stand her own ground. No harm had come to her so far. It was just a plate of sandwiches and drinks.

Tom lay down, reclining like a sultan on a nest of cushions. He patted the space next to him. There was nothing insipid about this invitation.

Vivien sipped her drink, musing on the order of things before her. The women worked, the men looked on. Sunshine smiled upon them. A paradise for men and bees. The women's arms were always full: a spade, a tray, a plate or jug. Cult indeed. Subjugated, sexless women with hairy legs and industrious hands.

No wonder I'm in such demand. Vivien shocked herself with such an unsisterly thought.

Bea's hand fell on her shoulder.

"I'm so happy to see you." She kissed Vivien's cheek.

"How's your mother?"

Vivien had been so distracted by Tom that she hadn't asked him about the old woman and Vivien now wondered if she was his mother too.

"Not well," Bea's face fell. "Not well at all."

"I'm sorry."

"She's not been well for a while." There was a cropping sound as Tom ripped up grass. "Why don't you leave us alone?"

He addressed Bea as she stood over him like a servant bearing a plate of fruit in one hand.

"Are you always so rude?"

"Don't worry," Bea was radiant. Vivien had taken her side. "I'll get him back."

"Tom," Vivien put a hand upon his shoulder. The fabric of his shirt slipped over his skin. "Don't be so unsociable. Bea can join us if she likes."

"Whatever you want." Tom shrugged and looked away.

"I can't, but thank you. I have things to do. I'll give you some privacy." Bea eyed Tom, her mouth close to Vivien's ear. "My brother likes you."

"Are all these men your brothers?" Vivien called after her. "Surely not."

Bea did not turn to answer, leaving Vivien to be more direct.

"Are you all related?"

"Yes, we are. This is my family."

The occupied women and men at leisure were busy listening.

"And you all live here together?"

"Our family are direct descendants of the original beekeepers that lived in your cottage. There's always been bees, so there's always been us."

"So where were you born?" Vivien asked Tom. She was determined to find them out.

"Here. Bred and reared."

"And you grew up here?"

"I've never lived anywhere else."

"Really?"

"Yes. Why would I want to live anywhere else?"

Why indeed?

"But haven't you ever wanted to get away?"

"Not at all," he looked troubled, "it's a simple life but I don't know how much longer it can last, especially now with our mother being so ill. I love how we live. It satisfies me. In most things."

He handed her a piece of apple. It had arrived already sliced. The flesh was white beneath the skin.

"Most things?" She bit into it. Tart juices flooded her mouth.

"Nearly," he smirked at her, "but not everything."

Vivien stifled a giggle. A colony of inbred beekeepers living in arcadia. Tom's sauciness appealed. A simple man, a simple life, what was there not to like?

⊙

The drones are hedonists. These spoilt boys exist to feed and fornicate, a golden life which culminates in mating with their monarch. They have no inkling that this will herald their demise, hence their surprise when their servant-sisters, the jealous workers, rise up in pre-ordained revolution to starve, brutalise and slaughter the consorts of their beloved queen.

⊙

After the picnic, Tom and Vivien retraced their steps across the man-littered lawn, through the falling dusk of the kitchen garden, past the hives and trees to the back of the cottage. There was a large, yellow moon in the darkened sky. It was low enough for Vivien to draw it down and put it in her pocket.

The rotten door was as she left it, half pushed open.

"What are these?"

Vivien saw what she'd missed earlier that day. The side of the wall facing the orchard was a series of niches. Some were empty, some containing the last glimmer of candles. It looked like a shrine.

"They used to contain bee bowls."

"Bowls?"

"Straw baskets. An early form of the beehive."

"Oh."

Neither of them could be still. Their bodies, one electrified by the other, were in constant motion. She twirled from side to side on one heel; he twiddled a long stalk of grass between his fingers, put it in his mouth and took it out again.

"Bee bowls," she arched her back, "I've never heard of them before."

They had moved into the yard.

"15th century." His eyes flickered from her eyes to her mouth and back again.

"As old as that?" She unlocked the kitchen door, eager for him to continue her education inside. They came close enough to raise the hairs upon her arms.

"There's always been bees here. That's how we began. Wax used to be how the estate paid their taxes."

"A wax tax?"

"As candles for the church," he frowned, the idea displeased him, "before we were excommunicated for heresy."

"Really?"

"Persecuted for witchcraft. As they did with anyone with knowledge of birds and bees."

She trailed her fingers down her neck. His frown softened and faded.

"Tom, are you trying to convert me?"

They had reached the stairs. Vivien was on the first step. Tom caressed the newel post with his palm.

"Convert you?"

"To your religion. To bees."

He laughed. She entwined a strand of hair around her forefinger.

"It's not a religion. A way of living, maybe."

He leaned towards her. They had reached the top of the stairs. His clothes seemed wrong on his large frame. She wanted to take them off.

"I've no intention of being one of your little women, waiting on you hand and foot."

This part jest, part test made Tom suddenly tender.

"Is that what you think I want?"

"I don't know."

"Look at me. Tell me what it is you think I want from you. And more importantly, what do you want from me?"

Everything.

⊙

Sex with Tom, clothes half on, half off, left her breathless and invigorated. She didn't imagine herself to be in love. She knew herself to be in lust. Desire was a means to its own end. Tom was vigorous and selfish, making Vivien claw back satisfaction with her teeth and nails. It left her sore and satiated. She didn't chide herself for such recklessness. Her time of having regrets had passed, or so she thought. She lay back on the pillows, Tom beside her, close but not touching, nursing the feeling inside her, of wanting, of taking but not needing.

⊙

The lovers slept with the bedroom window open. A swarm of males stood among the trees in vigil, gazing up to where she lay. They could smell her. Her fertility was fragrant. It carried on the breeze.

They were in rapture.

⊙

"Vivien, wake up."

There was a gentle voice and clammy hand upon her shoulder.

"Vivien, please."

There was breath against her cheek. It smelt of honey. Her eyes snapped open. She was naked and chilled, the bed sheets twisted at her feet. Vivien's hand roamed across the mattress. The space beside her, the place that Tom had filled, was empty.

It was Bea, her hair tied up in a yellow ribbon, a school girl's decoration. It brushed against Vivien's skin and she pushed it away, her other hand snatching at the sheets. For all her new powers, she wasn't ready for such exposure yet.

"Vivien, it's our mother."

"What's wrong?"

"She's ill. Will you come?"

"Shouldn't you call a doctor?"

"We have." Bea blinked. "Tom asked me to come for you."

"He sent you?"

"Yes," Bea was too old to look so sulky, "but I wanted you to come too."

Whatever for? Vivien nearly said but stopped herself. "Tom has taken such a shine to you." It was a sly lure.

"All right." Vivien swung her legs over the edge. "Turn around." She retrieved her discarded clothes that lay in puddles on the floor. Bea watched in the looking glass, a pale figure glowing in the mirror.

Vivien was luminous.

☉

They were on the threshold. The carved doors were ajar, the innards of the house reduced to a long strip of shadow and greasy yellow light. Bea turned to Vivien.

"Not just anyone can come here."

"I know."

"Are you absolutely sure that you don't mind me fetching you?"

Vivien looked at her with irritation.

"It's just that I like you. So does Tom. We've all agreed how special you are. That we can trust you."

"I'm not sure what it is you think I can do to help."

"You've brought us so much comfort, just by being here. Come in now, Vivien, and be our willing guest."

Vivien followed her into the entrance hall. She expected the same evidence of industry that she'd seen in the garden and orchard but in the gloom of the electric lights everything was shabbiness and neglect. The wooden panelling was dulled by dust and she could smell the mildew in the walls. The tiled floor was tacky underfoot. She could hear the wavering, nasal hum of air conditioning, a ridiculous thing in such a tatty old pile.

"Where's Tom?"

His sudden presence calmed her. He came to her with outstretched hands. His face was tears.

"I knew you'd come." He enfolded her in an embrace, which she returned. "Didn't I say she'd come?"

"So did I." Bea's eyes were angry hollows. "Don't make out that I ever doubted her."

"Is she very ill?" Vivien looked at Tom, wanting Bea to leave them to each other.

"She's dying." His mouth was compressed. "It's no surprise. She's so old."

"I'm sorry."

Still enfolded in him, she rubbed his back, feeling the strength in his muscle and bone. His mother was dying and he pulsed with life. The thought inflamed her. Inappropriate but an affirmation of life all the same. She wanted him again and could tell he wanted her too. Before she wouldn't have known such a thing and it thrilled her that she knew with such certainty.

"It doesn't matter," he whispered in her ear, "you're here now and nothing else matters."

○

The corridor they walked along was kinder to the house. Lit only by candle, the dirt and decay was lost in their warm glow. Bea and Tom walked beside Vivien.

"We've been waiting such a long time for you."

"Shut up, Bea."

"No. Shut up yourself."

Vivien halted. The corridor seemed very narrow suddenly. "What do you mean?"

"Once our mother's dead we'd have to leave here. I've no idea what we'd do. Thank God you're here."

"I don't understand."

"None of us could ever replace her. We were so relieved when we met you."

"Relieved?"

Tom had taken her arm. She shook him off.

"Vivian, we'll take such good care of you. We'll be your girls. You'll want for nothing. Mother never had to lift a finger, we'd never let her. Let us show you how good we can be. You'll have to stay then. You'll see how much we love you."

Her relief and sorrow paralysed Vivien. Tom put his arms around her. Holding her. Restraining her. She was overcome, overwhelmed by their love. It brought bile up in her throat and made her limbs like lead.

Not so heavy though that they couldn't lift her.

⊙

Here in the great hall was the sound she'd mistaken for air conditioning. It was a buzz. A hum. An Om. The sound that underlies the universe. The hive was humming.

The sun was rising, spilling through the long windows. Vivien could see the room had been made fit for their purpose. The walls were lined with honeycomb, a construct of man sized hexagons. The honey within made the growing light liquid amber. Some of the chambers were darkened by the figure curled up, grub-like, foetal-style, within.

On the wall opposite was the old woman's bower, where she was kept safe, even from herself. The honey light made her look jaundiced. She was a queen lying in state. The hive sensed her dying. She was withered, drying, desiccating, her chemicals waning.

Vivien saw that she hadn't yet expired. Her ribcage heaved, erratic gasps as she tired of the task of respiration. Her eyes rolled and her heart threatened failure. The hive was in the act of entombing her in this state of semi life, of packing her in wax. She would be an effigy within her cell for Vivien to gaze upon. This was the old woman's fate, her successor had come too late for her to abdicate.

Vivien had her own cell. Disrobed by a multitude of hands, her hair let loose, her rings and earrings were removed. She would be adored without the need of such adornments.

Bea patted her hair and then sniffed at it. As if invigorated by the smell, she did a little dance of celebration and kissed one of her sisters full on the mouth. These grinning, buzzing women were no longer comical. They were monstrous. They all wanted to be near her, to touch her.

The men hung back. Crooning, swaying, waiting creatures. Vivien could not see Tom. She'd heard his shouts and then his silence. The women swept him up and carried him off to where he wouldn't be in the way.

She felt distant from the proceedings. They'd filled her up with ambrosia. They made her gorge on it. She would soon sicken of the taste and texture clogging up her throat. Sickened but she would wait for it, this addictive sedative, its arrival marking the divisions of her day.

It was getting darker instead of lighter as the morning became midday. Bees had lined the windows, crowding the panes, blocking out the light. The building crawled with them but they would not enter uninvited. They were excited. They wished to witness this rare spectacle. The coronation of the queen.

☉

The mating flight is not polite. It is an orgy, during which the queen is serviced by the drones. This is no gentle love making, no prelude to a lifetime of tenderness together but the panicked ejaculation of the selfish gene. The drones will deposit a lifetime of sperm, distending their queen's abdomen with thousands of fertilised eggs that will keep her hive bound and bearing baby bees, both workers and more drones, for the glorification of the hive.

☉

Vivien Avery came into her summer late. As she blossomed, the men buzzed around her, enthralled.

A SON OF THE SEA

Cadogan stood at the end of the bed.
    "Feeling better? Good. Now, ground rules. Scream and I'll
stuff rags in your mouth and break your legs. And you eat and drink or
I'll make you." He pulled a funnel and a hose from a bag to demonstrate.

After we talked I lay on my side trying to get comfortable, and eventually fell asleep. I dreamt of the sea.

I stood on the shore, the rim of the aquatic world. Its shallows were
pale and translucent. I wanted to be further out, in its dark depths. The
surf rushed up to me, covered my feet and ankles in welcome, then rushed
off again. I waded in until I was waist deep. A wave broke against the
underwater slope, sending up spray that looked like a fan of molten glass.

In my dream, as in life, just looking in the water, just knowing I was
going in was enough. My body readied itself. It relaxed. I took three deep
breaths, working the muscles in my stomach and chest. Then I started
packing, the act of gulping air, forcing it into my lungs.

The housemaster at one of my boarding schools once said to me,
"Leave before you're expelled, you lanky streak of piss."

He wasn't to know the ways in which I'm made for water.

All the wonders that have blessed my eyes, they were there in my
dream, when I needed them most.

○

I've always sought the ocean. Rivers are insufficient. I need water in the
thrall of the moon. I need tides not just currents.

I'd spent six months working as a barman in Greece when Cadogan
found me. "Mick's Shack" was a concrete box with plastic tables and chairs

but I liked it because it was on the beach. I had a sea view as I poured drinks.

We were getting ready to open for the evening. In an hour we'd be heaving with island hoppers, pumped up on pheromones and their own immortality. It never occurred to me that I wasn't that much older than them but I'd never had a night of drinking, pill popping, and fucking, followed by a day lying on the beach cooking a melanoma.

I was bringing up crates of beer from the cellar. I could see Suzie's flip flops as I came up the steps, her feet skimmed by her thin, long skirt. She was talking to someone. One look told me he wasn't looking for work. He was in his fifties and his hands were spread on the bar in a proprietorial manner that made me dislike him straight away.

"Thomas Briggs." It was a statement, not a question.

"Who's asking?" I felt like he was about to arrest me.

"I'm Paul Cadogan. I need to talk to you."

"Do I need to talk to you?"

"It's important."

"Still not interested." I picked up a cloth and wiped down the bar, making him move his hands.

"In that case, I'll have a beer."

Suzie went to the fridge but I pulled a warm bottle from the crate I'd just brought up and levered it against the bottle opener on the bar. The cap dropped into the bin beneath with a tinkling sound.

"Ten euros."

His laugh was sour. He shook his head as he pulled out his wallet. "It's all on expenses anyway."

Knowing what I do now I would've made that beer ice cold and gratis but I was thorny because I suspected he had something to do with my father.

"You were difficult to locate. Why don't you get a bloody mobile and a Facebook page like the rest of the world?"

"Because nobody gives a fuck where I am."

"Poor little lost boy."

"I'm not lost."

"If you say so. You're certainly not poor anymore." Cadogan took a long deliberate pull from the bottle. "That got your attention, didn't it? Why don't we go outside?"

I followed him out to the chairs and tables under the canopy, not because of the prospect of a fortune but because I thought I might as well get it over with.

"Your father's solicitor been anxious to find you. Your father's dead."

"How?"

"Diving in Mauritius. He had a heart attack. It happened two months ago. We couldn't find you in time for the funeral."

I looked towards the sparkling, dark blue waves. The Mediterranean is relatively placid, being a landlocked sea. It calmed me.

"How did you find me now?"

"You cashed one of your father's cheques."

"Oh, right."

"You're wealthy." He couldn't keep all his bitterness from his voice, not entirely. All he saw was a twenty-five-year-old who'd piss a fortune he hadn't made up the wall.

He slid something across the table at me.

"What's this?" I picked up the business card.

"It's how you cash in. She's your father's solicitor."

"Where was Dad buried?"

"In Sussex."

"Did many people go?"

"A lot."

"Did you know him?" I tried to sound casual.

"Never met him but I did a lot of research about you two when I was trying to find you. Did you know that he kept the apartment in Hong Kong where you both lived? Perhaps you should go. You might find out more about him."

I made a non-committal sound. Cadogan had done his homework. He knew Dad and I barely spoke.

"It's on Ma Wan, the island where your mother was from."

I stared at the card, turning it over in my fingers, angry that I'd learnt more about my mother from an ape like Cadogan than my father had ever told me.

☉

"You're leaving, aren't you?"

Suzie threw her bag down on the sand and sat beside me. The bar had closed and the punters had taken the party out onto the beach. They gathered in the firelight. I sat apart, where I could hear the waves.

"How do you know?"

"I can just tell. Are you in trouble?"

"My father died."

"I'm so sorry." Suzie meant it.

"It's okay. I didn't know him."

She didn't press me. I liked that about her. She knew when to leave things alone. She clutched at the rough grass that pushed up through the sand in clumps, pulling the coarse blades through her fingers.

"I'm sorry you're going. This is going to sound selfish but you're the only person here that I'm comfortable with. Everyone else thinks I'm bossy and stuck up."

By everyone, she meant the other staff.

"I reckon we're a lot alike."

"Are we?" I tried not to frown. I didn't want to hurt her.

"I was carted about as a kid," she said. "Army brat. Never settling makes you seem more self-reliant than you are. What's your story?"

"Boarding schools. Lots of them." I didn't elaborate.

"I knew it. I could tell. You're different to all the others."

I *was* different but not in the way she thought. "We're all misfits, Suzie. We can't outrun ourselves."

"No, I suppose not." She sounded disappointed at that. "You don't care what people think of you, do you?"

I shrugged. I had no idea if I cared whether people liked me or not anymore. Loneliness was a constant friend. I nurtured it.

Suzie poured sand from palm to palm. "I envy you. You're comfortable in your own skin."

There was always one in the group, wherever I went. I was a blank canvas on which they projected their own desires and hopes. Suzie dusted the sand off her hands and reached for my beer bottle. She drained it.

Her face told me everything she wanted from me. I envied her ability to make herself that plain. She pulled her t-shirt over her head, revealing her bikini top. Her skirt sat low on her hips and she leant back, forming a long curve from her ribcage to her waistband.

I reached out and touched the tattoo on her side, tracing it with my forefinger. It was perfectly formed from its coronet to its curled tail. Suzie had spent proper money on it. The fins were picked out in fine lines and the shape of the armour beneath the skin gave it substance. Its colours were delicate yellows. Seahorses give me heartache. Little fishes of surreal grace. Ground up for medicine as a panacea for asthma, skin issues, heart disease, and erectile dysfunction. Taken from the wild and sold as pets only to die within a few weeks without expert care. Weight for weight, they command the same price as gold in some quarters.

"Do you like it?"

"It's beautiful."

She thought I meant her, in a roundabout way. I hadn't noticed how she'd closed the gap between us. She mistook my concentration for sexual tension, letting out a gasp as her mouth found mine. My hand drifted to her waistband. I could smell the monoi oil on her neck. Her hands crept inside my t-shirt and examined the hard edges of my shoulder blades.

I envied Suzie's hunger. It stoked something inside me. I wanted her sex, her seahorse tattoo. I wanted relief from the sudden ache that had sprung up in my groin.

Maybe, just maybe, this time will be different, I thought.

I undid her bikini top and ran my fingertip around one areolar and then the other. I sucked each nipple until she stifled a cry, her hand in her mouth. Her skirt was tangled around her legs and I pushed it up around her waist. Suzie fumbled with the buttons of my fly. She reached into her bag and pulled out a packet of condoms. I recognised the brand from the vending machine in the bar's toilets.

"I don't want you to think that I do this all the time. I got them for us. Not that I assumed…"

"I know." I kissed her, just to shut her up. Talking would make things more likely to go wrong.

I pulled at the side tie of her bikini bottoms. Suzie pressed her lips together as I ripped the packet open and rolled on the condom. The smell of the lubricant and the oily texture made me feel sick. I didn't want to be distracted. I needed to stay in the moment. I pushed her down and she opened her legs. We moved against each other, mouths and groin joined. I nudged my way into her, towards the heat within her.

Instead of the mounting excitement I was overcome by the feeling that something was wrong. Something was missing. So it was, yet again, that I failed to make a success of sex. I wilted with each thrust, getting rougher as I got softer until I lay flaccid against her thigh.

"It's okay." Suzie kissed my cheek. "Just lie here with me. Let's just be together."

"It's not okay."

What would've happened if I'd stayed there, in her arms? Instead, I got up and ran to the water, plunging into the safety of the waves.

☉

I was dreaming of the sea.

The average person can stay underwater for forty seconds. The best free divers can manage six minutes.

I can stay under for half an hour.

In my dream, I felt my heart beating; one slow boom after another. My diaphragm twitched. It was just a reflex, my body trying to make me breathe but I ignored it.

My dreaming seabed was a drowned land with hills and valleys. It was punctuated by ship wrecks reclaimed by coral and anemones, by eels and fishes.

I crossed a field of moon jelly fish. They numbered in millions. These ethereal, pulsing creatures were a dense carpet of alien blooms. There shouldn't have be so many. They thrive on pollution. It's our fault, not theirs. Like all living things, they procreate while they may.

☉

Cadogan had made all the arrangements for my trip to Hong Kong. He handed me a wallet containing ticket and instructions.

"It's first class all the way for you." His grin revealed yellowed teeth.

Cadogan had even arranged someone to collect me from the airport. The driver wore a black suit, cut like something from GQ magazine. The man insisted on carrying my rucksack and opened the rear passenger seat of the Mercedes for me. People kept looking at my jeans and scruffy boots, wondering if I was a film star or singer they should recognise.

I sank back into the leather seats. We emerged from an underpass. Hong Kong's islands arose from the South China Sea. High rises clung to their lower slopes and green covered the peaks. It was beautiful but I wanted more. I wanted the frisson of recognition.

"Tsing Ma bridge." The driver was embarrassed by his lack of English. He needn't have been. I knew no Cantonese. Not even *please* or *thank you*.

It was a suspension bridge, stretching out across the water with its graceful arcs and angles. A tanker passed under us, a floating monolith shepherded along by smaller tugs.

There was another island to our left. I could see wooden houses on stilts along the shoreline and boats stacked up beneath them.

"Ma Wan." I didn't know if the driver had noticed my interest or was just announcing that we were close. Then he added, "Old part. Here is new part. Park Island."

Park Island Apartment Complex was coming into view. Tower block after tower block. We took the slip road down towards it.

"What's that?"

"It's a—", he paused, searching for the correct word, "Noah's Ark. For tourists."

A theme park for the evangelical, with the Ark beached in the bridge's shadow. Life sized model animals poured from its hull in pairs, into the garden below.

At least it wasn't the crucifixion.

"No cars allowed beyond this." He pulled up by an escalator.

I refused his help with my rucksack and he refused payment, not even a tip. Cadogan had dealt with everything.

The escalator came out onto a plaza. This was something familiar. The suspension bridge bisected the sea and sky. Tsing Yi Island rose ahead of me. A ferry was docked at the terminal, topped by a clock tower. Suddenly, the small child inside me was turning circles in the sun. I had run around the plaza on a day like this.

I found the right apartment block and rung the buzzer. The man at the desk gave me a toothy smile when he saw me and let me in. He wore the concierge uniform; grey trousers, white shirt, and a blue and orange striped tie. I showed him my passport, as instructed by Cadogan, and in return received a set of keys. I was trembling as he called the lift for me. I looked at the man's shoes while we waited. They were polished to a high shine. He took pride in his work.

The hall of my father's apartment. The walls were white, marked with nails where pictures had once hung. I put down my rucksack and pulled off my boots. There was a stillness and I had the oddest idea that someone was waiting for me. I expected to go into the lounge and find Dad there, the same distant look on his face as when I'd last seen him in a restaurant in Barcelona. We'd both been passing through.

He wasn't there, of course. There was a dark grey, L-shaped sofa, the minimalist sort that always looks modern and uncomfortable. The coffee table was glass-topped. The bookshelves were empty. Each surface was polished which made me feel sadder, somehow. I went through the kitchen cupboards. They'd been fully stocked. Fresh milk was in the fridge. Cadogan's efficiency.

The cleaner had made up the master bedroom for me. The wardrobes and bedside tables were empty. I slammed the doors shut, seething at the fruitlessness of travelling half way around the world because of a throwaway comment from Cadogan. Stupid.

There was a second bedroom. A nautical-themed frieze ran around the walls. Sea creatures bobbed along with the boats. An orange octopus smiled despite being sun-faded. A purple octopus wore a sailor's hat at a jaunty angle. It was a child's room. My room.

I was exhausted. I pulled a cushion from the rattan chair, lay down on the rug of thick, blue pile, and feel asleep in the square of sun.

⊙

I went out for breakfast, even though there was plenty of food in the apartment. The coffee was strong, covered in a layer of foam, coated with cocoa dust. I ate a croissant and then a second, realising that I was hungry.

Park Island had a manicured, artificial feel. The pathways between the buildings were covered so you could walk the length of the complex without being bothered by rain or sun. Gardeners tended the borders and cleaners emptied litter bins.

I read the notices regarding the consultation on the ferry fees while I waited for the lift. The concierge bowed to someone. As the lift doors opened the mirrored walls reflected the woman behind me. She followed me in and turned on her heel. I leant over and pressed the button, looking at her enquiringly.

"Same floor."

She was stylish in tight khaki trousers and a well cut white shirt. She looked at me with unconcealed curiosity. I looked right back. She was in her late sixties and from Hong Kong, I thought. Her hair was bobbed and she had flat cheekbones.

On impulse I reached out and touched the charms on her bracelet. Each one was marine—a sea urchin, a manta ray, a starfish, and a seahorse.

"I'm sorry."

"Don't be."

She wasn't unnerved by my breach of her personal space.

"I love it," she said. "Do you love it?"

"Yes."

As the lift doors opened at our floor I extended an arm. *After you.* She turned right and then left. We found ourselves outside neighbouring doors. She burst out laughing. I didn't understand why.

"You're Jonathan Brigg's son, Thomas."

She took my face in her hands. I could hardly object. The charms tinkled as she moved. I got a waft of whatever perfume she wore. There were notes of brine, algae and dry driftwood. I resisted rubbing my nose against her wrist.

"You don't remember me, do you? I'm Darla."

"No, I'm sorry."

"You're handsome. You have your dad's jaw." Her face changed as if she just remembered Dad was dead. "Should I be saying how sorry I am for your loss?"

"You can't mourn what you didn't know."

"You have the look of someone who's been mourning his entire life."

My smile was the bitter curve of being understood far too late in life for it to make a difference.

"Are you in a rush? Why don't you come in and tell me what you've been doing all these years?"

⊙

Darla's apartment mirrored Dad's but it had been remodelled. One of the bedrooms had been removed to make the lounge larger. The white walls were covered in swathes of blue canvas.

"What do you think of them?"

"They're wonderful."

"I did them."

Darla went off to fix us a drink without asking what I wanted. I admired her work while I waited. Blue, the most nuanced colour. All her paintings were abstracts, ranging from stormy greys, through brooding indigos and onto playful aquamarines and greens. The movement of the oil paint reflected the moods of each shade.

There were gallery catalogues and monographs on the coffee table. Darla wasn't an amateur dauber. Each one was about her work.

She put a tray down and passed me a chunky glass tumbler. I took a sip. Whisky and soda.

"What's with Noah's Ark?" I asked. We looked down on it from her window.

"One of the brothers who developed the island built it when he found God."

"It doesn't look like it could save a pair of everything."

"Token atonement for his sins. I say we need a great flood. Wouldn't that be a good thing?" Such a strange thing to say but before I could ask her more she went on, "I tried to find you. I know Jonathan went to Germany but what about you?"

"I was sent to boarding school in England. Lots of them. I kept getting expelled. When I was twelve I went to Texas. One of Dad's cousins offered to take me in. Did you keep in touch with Dad?"

"No. He was a busy man. Very in demand. Brilliant engineer from what I gathered. Good business brain too. He made a lot of clever investments. The family you lived with, were they good to you?"

"It was just Uncle Paul and Aunty Jean. And yes, they were. Why do you care?"

"You were such a lonely, sad little boy. I like to think that someone was kind to you. Do you still see them?"

"No. I'm not a very good human being."

"That's okay. Neither am I."

I didn't want to remember my last conversation with Paul and Jean. I called them before I left for Hong Kong. It was the first time in over a year.

We've been so worried about you. Not a single reproach for missing Dad's funeral, just concern and sympathy.

Paul and Jean didn't deserve my shoddy treatment. They put our awkward interactions down to their inexperience with children and adolescents and to my rootless, unloved state. The real issue was that I was strange. It wasn't their fault. They weren't to know what the problem was when I barely knew myself. The arid vista outside my window unsettled me. There was no water to salve the endless land.

"Did you see much of your dad?"

"No. He used to phone once a month but the time between calls got longer and longer, and the calls themselves got shorter and shorter."

"What happened to you after Texas?"

"I left when I was eighteen. I worked in bars and restaurants. Between what I made and Dad's allowance, I managed."

I didn't use much of what Dad sent me but I wanted my lack of ambition and education to piss Dad off. If Darla judged me, she gave no sign.

◯

I tried to explore the city.

I queued with the commuters at the ferry terminal on Ma Wan

island. There were people dressed for city jobs. Children in a variety of different school uniforms that looked like something from 1940s Britain. The younger ones were shepherded along by helpers, the maids-of-all-work imported from Bangladesh and the Philippines.

Water sprayed the window as we headed into choppy straights, crossed by a tanker that made us bob up and down like a toy in a tub. Most of the passengers didn't even look up, intent on their phones or tablets.

After fifteen minutes the ferry curved around the islands and Central came into view. This was the financial heart of Hong Kong; The Bank of China, HSBC, Standard Chartered, all sought to dominate one another. Their success was manifest in steel and glass. Its wealth was crushing. People teemed along the waterfront.

I stayed on the ferry and went back to Ma Wan.

⊙

I was dreaming of the sea.

Except everything was mixed up, as if one ocean had run into another. Sea creatures that should never meet swam alongside one another. Many were out of their normal depths.

The dolphins were puzzled. They didn't know whether I was fish or mammal. They were frustrated when I didn't join in with their chatter so they abandoned me.

I dove deeper. That far down my lungs were compressed to the size of clenched fists. Below thirty metres my eardrums should burst but they never do. I'm made of more pliable stuff. My concavities and my long, spidery limbs give me negative buoyancy.

Fishes followed me. The water was dense with them. There were silver sardines, open-mouthed. Tropical colours and spots darted around me, in the most electric of blues, the yellows neon. Tuna and swordfish cut through them.

The human view of beauty is arbitrary. The Atlantic seabass was a joy, muscular in its velvet grey. Its light smattering of gold scales were elegant and tasteful.

And rays. Finally, the rays. They covered me with the friendly flap of their wings. They looped-the-loop for me, revealing smiling white undersides. They're an amiable sort. They have grinding plates, not teeth.

Eels that lurked in holes revealed themselves. They came rippling out like black ribbons. Their secret is extra-terrestrial in its nature. A second set of jaws complete with teeth, as if one isn't enough.

In my dream, I felt the shift, my blood moving inward to prevent my organs collapsing. The familiar feeling was like a balm. It comforted me. I accepted the ocean's pressure and its depths in a kind of meditation.

☉

Darla is the closest I've ever had to a real friend.

She cooked me delicacies for purists, not the standard fare dished up for tourists. We trekked the dragon's back, a ridge running around Shek O Country Park. We followed the dragon's undulating spine, the sea on one side of us and the hills on the others, covered in blazing azaleas. The heat and the humidity were stifling but it was worth it to plunge into the cool waters of Big Wave Bay at the end.

There weren't any big waves but it was a proper beach, not like the artificial one on Ma Wan which was a strip of sand that was raked each morning.

Darla was a strong and graceful swimmer. I fought the urge to overtake her, to go far out and then dive until I reached the bottom. To stay there until I was sated. I resolved to return alone, when the beach was quieter.

Afterwards we stretched out on towels. Darla was striking in a navy halter-neck swimsuit and cherry red nail varnish on her finger and toenails. We drew looks from people who strolled by, curious about the nature of our relationship.

A group of young women unfurled a blanket nearby and started laying out a feast. They seemed happy in a way I'd never known, attractive because everything was ahead of them.

Darla's careless sophistication drew them, just as it had drawn me. One of the women came over and offered her a fancy pastry from a carton. Darla refused with a wave of the hand but gave her a big smile. I followed suit. The young woman nodded, suddenly shy at her own forwardness, but her gaze sought me again when she'd returned to her circle of friends.

"Shall I get her back for you?" Darla asked. She sensed my hesitation. "Do you prefer men?"

"Women might as well be a different species to me. Men are no better." I'd tried both without success. "Darla, are you my mother?"

"No, silly boy, I'm far too old."

"You don't look it." I rolled onto my back, shielding my eyes from the sun with my forearm. "I'm disappointed."

"I'm not sure whether I'm flattered or not."

"Do you have any family?"

"Not children. But I'm responsible for a large extended family. Totally self-appointed, of course, because somebody has to make the difficult decisions."

"You make it sound like a military operation."

"It's about survival."

I'd never seen her so serious. It added years to her face. "Darla, do you know anything about my mother?"

"Very little." She sighed.

"Am I being tiresome?

"No, never. You might not like what you hear though. She left you at reception in a cardboard box with strict instructions to call your father's apartment. Except he was at a meeting with investors. It was for his land reclamation project."

Land is king. Kowloon waterfront, which sits across the bay from Central, was once submerged.

"They heard you squalling and called me instead. I looked after you until he came back."

"What was her name?"

"I don't know. I only ever saw her at a distance. I think your father met her on one of his evening walks. She lived in the fishing village on the other side of the island. She was from one of the old families."

"I saw it from the bridge on my way here."

"You should take a closer look. Not many people live there now. Most of them have relocated. It'll get knocked down eventually to build luxury apartments. That's progress."

"Tell me about the old families."

Darla sat up and put sun cream on her arms. I watched as she rubbed it in.

"They were a different breed, those fishermen and women. Some of their daughters became pearl divers." She chuckled. "I don't know if they were people who adapted to the sea or fish that had learnt to live on land. I swear, they'd stay underwater for quarter of an hour in one go. I used to time them."

It was only then that I realised I'd been holding my breath.

⊙

I needed to be outside the confines of the apartment. I was staying in a space that would normally house an extended family in Hong Kong and yet it chafed.

I headed for the service road that circumnavigated the island. It was lined with letting agents, hairdressers, and low-rise flats. Darla had said that was where many of the villagers had moved to.

Does my mother live there?

I doubt it. I never saw her again after she left you.

I crossed over and kept going. There was a path that led into the trees. I stepped aside to let a runner pass. He was breathing hard as he took the incline towards me. Sweat marked his top. He was what people here called *gweilo*. A term for foreigners, literally translated as *foreign devil*.

Only mad dogs and Englishmen go out in the midday sun.

I was a *gweilo* too, only it didn't matter where I was. In Britain and in the States it was the same. Even when people didn't give a damn where I was from I felt like an outsider. Here in Hong Kong I looked like a native but it didn't take long for people to realise that I wasn't when they tried to talk to me in Cantonese.

The path forked and I had an overwhelming urge to follow the left one. It led into the narrow corridors of trees.

I emerged into the light. There it was, Ma Wan proper, laid out before me. I walked along abandoned streets. Weeds pushed up through the crack in the concrete to reclaim the land. Some of the houses were blocked off with chain link fences. Others were accessible. I went into a few of them. Faded imprints of life remained within. Torn wallpaper. A rotting mattress. Piles of cardboard boxes and bags covered in dust and rubble. There were empty shops and open-fronted sheds. Washing hung on lines, stiff from continual cycles of being rain-drenched and then sun-dried. Litter gathered where the wind had left it.

Slogans had been painted on walls in red. Banners were hung over doors. I didn't need to be able to read them to know that they were protest calls. Not everyone wanted to leave here. Some had remained. Somebody had left vases of chrysanthemums and incense sticks burning in pots of sand. Little gifts for silent gods.

One side of the village overlooked the water. There was everything a community needed. I looked through the window of a building marked as the "Ma Wan Rural Committee". Chairs were stacked up in the hall. On one wall there were photographs and yellowed notices. There was a school house further along and a playground that comprised a slide and a frame missing its swings.

Along the shore line were stacks of plastic pipes. The suspension bridge loomed over me. I'd reached the houses on stilts. They were rotten. The rooves had collapsed in on some of them. Struts had given way.

I followed the shore to the very edge of Ma Wan. A house stood alone on a promontory and it looked out onto the South China Sea. It was close to the water. Perfect.

The front door and window frames were missing. The building was unrendered. The concrete floor had been swept clean but it was stained. The plastered walls were unpainted. There wasn't a stick of furniture inside but I couldn't see beyond the tattered, yellow curtain that divided the room. Somebody had planned a life here that never materialised.

I could be happy here, I thought.

I stepped inside. It was as though I'd stepped into a vacuum. The roaring in my ears wasn't the rush of blood. It sounded like the sea. It was so loud that I crumpled to the floor. Shadow rushed at me and then receded. It was too much. I panicked, as I never had at open sea. My chest was tight. I couldn't breathe.

Then the world went black.

⊙

I was dreaming of the sea.

Great white sharks circled me. Thousands of years of unthinking history looked out from eyes that offered neither pity nor remorse. Their smiles were serrated.

They're psychopaths, designed for survival. The sand shark will eat its siblings in utero. Their personality issues are no excuse for what we do to them. I've seen them hauled onto boats, fins hacked off while they're still alive, then they're thrown back in. Rudderless, they fall through the water. Death comes slowly by suffocation, exsanguination, or they're eaten alive by other fishes.

Man must consume a small part of the mighty and discard the major portion like it's garbage. We will have dominion over everything.

We will have soup.

⊙

When I woke, I was on the other side of the yellow curtain. It was cool. I heard a woman humming. The metal bedframe creaked as I sat up. I could feel its springs through the cheap mattress. This end of the room had been tiled in white. It felt oddly clinical. Cupboards ran along one wall and a sink was set in the worktop at one end.

"You scared me. You took quite a turn."

A woman sat down at one end of the bed. She was a pearl. Luminous. "Drink." She handed me a bottle of water.

"How long have I been here?"

"Half an hour." Her accent was French.

She wore shorts and a t-shirt. Her hair was black and straight, her irises so dark that I couldn't make out her pupils. She shifted, pulling a bag onto the bed between us.

"Here," she rummaged inside and pulled out a bar of chocolate. "You should eat something."

The first bite made me realise that I was ravenous. The chocolate was bitter and restorative. She leant back on the head of the bed and watched me eat. There were bottles of water lined up on the worktop and a bag of apples. A red dress and coat hung on a peg. A suitcase lay open on one corner of the floor.

"Feeling better?" she asked.

"Much. Do you live here?"

"I'm squatting."

She pulled her hair into a loose knot and fixed it with a hairband from her wrist. The dark strands were matted, as if she'd been swimming in the sea and not rinsed it out with freshwater afterwards.

"I'm Tom."

"Simone."

I held out my hand to shake hers but it was really an excuse to touch her. I'd never felt the need to do that before, not with anyone. Her hand lingered in mine as if in answer to a question that I didn't know I'd asked.

Simone took the water from me and tipped her head back to drain what remained in the bottle. I could see the muscles of her throat working. It reminded me of Suzie, just before she kissed me.

I didn't want to be reminded of the disappointments of that night.

"Where are you from?"

"Paris." She tossed the empty bottle on the floor. "My father was a diplomat so we travelled a lot. My mother died when I was six. She was from Hong Kong so I always wanted to see it."

"I see you're doing it in style."

"I do everything with style," she laughed. "My father disagrees about what style is. I inherited some money from my aunt. It's not a huge amount, so I'm economising. To be honest, I don't need posh hotels. It's more important for me to be by the sea. I die inside if I can't see it."

"Me too. I lived in Texas when I was younger, near the desert. I couldn't breathe."

"What about you?"

"My father died recently. My mum was from Ma Wan. I never knew her. I came here to find out who I am."

I'd never said that aloud before.

"I've no idea who I am either, or where I belong." She made it sound inconsequential. Funny, even. "My father stopped loving me when my mother died."

"*My* father *never* loved me. He never wanted me. Apparently he had me tested to check I was actually his."

We laughed, incredulous at how our fathers had scarred us.

"Have you found anything worthwhile here?" The sound of my own voice shocked me. I realised I was flirting with her.

She responded with an honesty that floored me, as if she'd misunderstood the question.

"That I can't escape myself. Wherever I go, I'm already there."

My heart leapt and twisted, like a fish with a hook in its mouth. She had me with that line.

"I can't make friends, Tom, not the way other people do." She shrugged, embarrassed. "There's always someone who singles me out, who thinks that I need saving or that I can save them. Fellow freaks, maybe."

"And they scare you because you're not like them and you don't know how to be what they want—"

"—because I have no idea how to be myself."

The hairs on my arms stood on end.

"Tom, I need to be in the water. Naked. Will you swim with me?"

Her lips were parted. I was acutely aware of the rise and fall of her chest. It was the most earnest and erotic invitation of my life, made sweeter by our sudden empathy.

"Yes."

⊙

Simone stood on the rocks, not caring about the spray from the waves or who saw her. She stripped off her t-shirt and shorts. Then her underwear. Naked, she was made anew. Every muscle tensed as she stood on tip-toe, arms stretched out. She was tanned and sleek with a slight belly. She dived, a knife that sliced the surface.

I tore off my clothes as I followed her. My heart was hammering. The ocean enveloped me. Water filled by vision. Simone's hair floated around her like seaweed as she rolled onto her back, baring her neck and chest to the sun like a basking seal. I trod water beside her.

"I'm happiest here. So are you." She didn't look at me to gauge my reaction. She knew she was right. Then she kissed me. I kissed her back. When I held her there was no softness beneath her skin as if she were armoured underneath it. I was so hard that I thought I'd burst.

"Shall we?"

I nodded, already knowing what she was asking. My breathing was slowing and deepening. Down we went.

We twisted around one another, sometimes only an inch apart but never touching. Drifting out with the current, we went closer to the sea bed. A shoal of tiny fishes moved around us like slivers of silver. I could see the crab crawling along the bottom. I could sense the microscopic plankton that fuels the world.

We broke the surface in unison. Here she was, the person that wouldn't find me wanting. For once, I was in the moment, not trying to guess at what was required of me. Thought could be suspended and everything would be right. All those unsatisfied nights. I thought the joy of Simone would break me, right then.

We floated further out. Ma Wan looked miniature. I packed my lungs as much as I could. *Let her see. Let her know the man I really am.*

We spiralled back down, corkscrewing around one another. My breathing was controlled enough, my exhalations deep enough to give me the negative buoyancy to make giant strides along the sea bed.

Simone matched me, step for step until she wrapped her ankle around a drift of sea weed to anchor herself. I did the same. She put her forehead to mine. Her hands were on my shoulders. Mine were at her hips. She shifted to let me inside her.

There it was. The great mystery. We were synchronised. Our rhythm was primal. Tidal. Something in me rose. I could feel Simone tightening around me. I was clamped, the tip of my penis sucked and messaged by her cervix. I was so close to coming that it was painful. She gripped me tighter. My own orgasm was a dry spasm as she ejaculated inside me.

It was like breaking up and dissolving, every particle of Thomas Briggs dispersed on the currents.

〇

Simone and I walked back to the house, naked and dripping, carrying our clothes in bundles. I reached for her hand but she moved away.

We dressed in silence, me into what I'd been wearing and Simone into the red dress on the peg. I watched, throat clogged, as it slipped over her slight, bare breasts and then over the triangle of dark hair between her legs.

"Simone."

"You should leave."

She sounded angry. I reached out to touch her shoulder but she stepped back.

"Please, Simone. I've been waiting for you my whole life."

"Then you're stupid."

"What have I done? What's wrong?"

"Don't you get it?" She pushed me away, both hands on my chest, not hard, but it hurt all the same. "I don't want you. It was a mistake. Get out. Go on, go."

◉

I didn't want to sit alone in my father's apartment. I knocked on Darla's door. Cadogan answered. I stared at him, taking a moment to register it was really him.

"What have you done with Darla?" I pushed him out of the way. The lounge was empty. Nothing was out of place.

I was angry. I wanted to fight with someone who'd fight back. Let him kick the shit out of me. It didn't matter.

"Where's Darla?" I pushed him again. "Darla?"

"She's in there." He pointed to the bedroom. "I'll wait here, if it's all the same to you. And she said to shut the door after you."

I'd never been in Darla's bedroom.

There wasn't a bed in there. A footed bath occupied the space where a bed should've been. It was giant, with clawed feet. The floor was marble and ornate drains were set into the floor at regular intervals. It was a giant wet room. The tap dripped at regular intervals. It landed in the water below with a heavy splash.

One wall was covered in a huge canvas, just like the lounge. This was an angry, swirling blue, as if from an abyss.

A strangled, sucking sound came from the depths of the bathtub.

What was in there was at least eight feet long. Its skin was like hide, a mottled brown colour. Its gills moved as it squirmed with pleasure, its underbelly revealed. I could see patches of human skin.

The eel was thick around the jaw. It had Darla's face and when she opened her mouth to speak I could see the thick spikes that she had for teeth and the second set further down her throat.

The sea within the canvas writhed in fury.

"Thomas," Darla said and all the pounding water came pouring out.

○

I woke on the bed in the little house on the promontory. Simone was dabbing at my face with a cool, damp cloth.

"Darla, she's…"

Simone shook her head. Her lips pinched together, leeching them of colour. Her eyes were pink and tear-stung.

Fever raised beads of sweat on my head and neck. A sudden chill went through me and my teeth started to chatter. I didn't trust that Simone was there after all. I reached for her but a chain rattled, restraining me. I was tethered to the bed frame.

"Simone." My voice was hoarse. I followed her gaze to the corner of the room.

It was Darla. Darla as I'd always known her, dressed in linen and looking refined.

"Let me go."

"I can't. Not now." Darla was the one in charge.

"I want to go home."

"You *are* home. I've been calling you all back here, one by one."

I tried to sit up but slumped back, exhausted. My every joint ached. Every muscle felt weak.

"He looks really sick. I think we should get a doctor."

"And say what?" Darla asked sharply. All I could hear was their breathing.

"Good." Darla had taken Simone's silence for acquiescence.

"I can't do this anymore." Simone was trembling.

"You've done it before and you'll do it again because it's what you were born for. You can't help yourself. Like draws like. Something in your father found something in your mother. It was the same for him." Darla motioned to me. "A recessive gene, to be sure, but mixed together and becoming more manifest with each generation. You're a daughter of the sea, just like Thomas is a son. And you're all coming back to replenish what's been lost."

☉

I was dreaming of the sea.

I reached a coral reef. Sea horses were on the ocean floor, a grazing herd. They anchored themselves where they could; on coral, sea grass. One wrapped its tail around another's neck. Elsewhere they were knotted together in what looked like an orgy. Their prehensile tails were sinuous.

They rose to greet me when they saw me. They varied in size, some as long as my hand.

Their delicate, translucent fins were like fragile propellers. All they could manage was a drunken canter but they danced for me. A chorus line of prancing seahorses.

Emboldened, they came closer. Close enough for me to see their eyes moving independently of one another. That their snouts made a constant sucking motion. Lacking a stomach means that they must feed perpetually.

I pity their poor cousins, pipe fish, who lack the seahorse's equine angles. Such elegance. They bowed to me, even though they were the ones with coronets.

I felt like my chest would burst with their sweetness.

☉

Darla and Simone left. My fever settled as I slept.

Cadogan stood at the end of the bed.

"Feeling better? Good. Now, ground rules. Scream and I'll stuff rags in your mouth and break your legs. And you eat and drink or I'll make you." He pulled a funnel and a hose from a bag to demonstrate.

"I thought you worked for Dad's solicitor."

"I work for lots of people. That's the fun of being freelance."

"Conflict of interest doesn't bother you, then?"

"Clearly not. You're mixed up in some weird crap here, aren't you?"

"Can I have a drink?" Talking hurt. My mouth was dry.

He smiled as he handed me a plastic bottle of tepid water. What I wouldn't have given for a glass of cold beer, cold enough to make my teeth ache.

I looked at the curtain, moving in the breeze. Simone's things were gone.

He pulled back the yellow curtain a fraction so I could see the water.

"Was Simone worth it?" He didn't wait for an answer. "My dad used to say killing and fucking are what makes a man."

"What about parenthood?" The thought surprised me.

"He knew bugger all about that and never bothered to learn. Any idiot can father a child."

"Yes, it takes a real man to raise one." I was thinking of my own father as I said it.

"Yes, I reckon you're right there." When Cadogan looked at me then I felt like he was seeing me for the first time.

"You have children, don't you? Sons."

"Yes."

○

Cadogan changed my bedding, helping me back from the chair where I'd slumped. He tucked me in, pulling an extra blanket and pillow from a carrier bag to make me more comfortable.

"Is that better?"

"Thank you."

He reattached the shackles to the bedframe, letting the chains out a little more so it was easier for me to turn over.

"I've brought you soup."

My hands clattered the spoon against the bowl and he took it from me, spooning the goodness into me.

"Can you manage some more?"

Half remained. I shook my head. The freezing feeling was creeping back over me again, sooner than I expected. Cadogan put a hand on my forehead.

"Please, not the gag." I called out when my temperature plummeted and rose. "I'll try not to shout this time, I promise."

"I'll try not to use it. I'll be here with you, don't worry. I'll see you through it."

That was probably because there'd be repercussions if he didn't keep me alive but I felt better when he said that.

Cadogan had helped me through every indignity. He'd held a bucket for me to vomit into. He'd helped me on and off the commode and then the bedpan, when I became too weak, carrying off my putrid filth.

"Cadogan," I croaked.

"What is it?"

"Do your sons love you? I bet you're a great dad." I meant it. In those moments of outrageous intimacy he did more for me than my own father ever had.

I didn't know if I was hallucinating again, but it looked like Cadogan was crying.

☉

I was dreaming of the sea.

The fall was exquisite. I reached one hundred and twenty-five metres. It was dark and cold. Such silence. I didn't know if I was at the bottom of the ocean or in outer space. I didn't know if it was joy or just my heart being compressed. Infinity overcame me.

☉

I've been dreaming of the sea.

When I wake my groin's wet and I'm panting, straining at the chains.

"I need to be in the water."

Cadogan looks at me for a full minute before deciding. I'm off the bed before the last manacle has clattered to the floor. Genetics are imperative. My body knows what it must do. Cadogan tries to help me across the rocks as I flail and stagger, pulling off clothes as I go.

I plunge in, the momentary shock of cold water a distraction from the pain in my lower abdomen. I try to pee but nothing comes. A spasm doubles me over. I thrash, coming up for air, fighting to control my breathing. I take a lungful and dive, swimming out as far as I can before the first contraction.

Blood jets from the tip of my penis. It stains the water in a black cloud.

How willingly complicit we are in our own downfall.

Then I ejaculate. It's a gush of tiny lives. Sea horse fry. Hundreds of them float up around me, moving in streams. They're all bulbous eyes and tails at this stage.

My little ones. They can't all survive. The currents will buffet them until some die from exhaustion, poor swimmers that they are.

One of them twines its tail in my chest hair.

The spasms come again. More babies escape me. As I pump out young the brood pouch low on my abdomen flattens. My penis bleeds continually now and it feels like there's broken glass in my urethra.

All the things I've never felt. I've been accused of being cold-blooded but it's not blood in my veins but brine. Each spasm is a perverse happiness. I'm suspended in a cloud of tiny seahorses.

I sink into the ocean's infinite arms. I'm not just a son of the sea. I am a father.

FABULOUS BEASTS

"Eliza, tell me your secret."

Sometimes I'm cornered at parties by someone who's been watching me from across the room as they drain their glass. They think I don't know what's been said about me.

Eliza's odd looking but she has something, don't you think? Une jolie laide. A French term meaning ugly-beautiful. Only the intelligentsia can insult you with panache.

I always know when they're about to come over. It's in the pause before they walk, as though they're ordering their thoughts. Then they stride over, purposeful, through the throng of actors, journalists, and politicians, ignoring anyone who tries to engage them for fear of losing their nerve.

"Eliza, tell me your secret."

"I'm a princess."

Such a ridiculous thing to say and I surprise myself by using Kenny's term for us, even though I am now forty-something and Kenny was twenty-four years ago. I edge past, scanning the crowd for Georgia, so I can tell her that I've had enough and am going home. Maybe she'll come with me.

My interrogator doesn't look convinced. Nor should they be. I'm not even called Eliza. My real name is Lola and I'm no princess. I'm a monster.

○

We, Kenny's princesses, lived in a tower.

Kath, my mum, had a flat on the thirteenth floor of Laird Tower, in

255

a northern town long past its prime. Two hundred and seventeen miles from London and twenty-four years ago. A whole world away, or it might as well be.

Ami, Kath's younger sister, lived two floors down. Kath and I went round to see her the day that she came home from the hospital. She answered the door wearing a black velour tracksuit, the bottoms slung low on her hips. The top rose up to reveal the wrinkled skin that had been taut over her baby bump the day before.

"Hiya," she opened the door wide to let us in.

Ami only spoke to Kath, never to me. She had a way of ignoring people that fascinated men and infuriated women.

Kath and I leant over the Moses basket.

"What a diamond," Kath cooed.

She was right. Some new babies are wizened, but not Tallulah. She looked like something from the front of one of Kath's knitting patterns. Perfect. I knew, even at that age, that I didn't look like everyone else; flat nose with too much nostril exposed, small eyelids and small ears that were squashed against my skull. I felt a pang of jealousy.

"What's her name, Ami?"

"Tallulah Rose." Ami laid her head on Kath's shoulder. "I wish you'd been there."

"I wanted to be there too. I'm sorry, darling. There was nobody to mind Lola. And Mikey was with you." Kath must have been genuinely sorry because normally she said Mikey's name like she was sniffing sour milk. "Where is he now?"

"Out, wetting the baby's head."

Kath's expression suggested that she thought he was doing more than toasting his newborn. He was always hanging around Ami. *Just looking after you, like Kenny wants,* he'd say, as if he was only doing his duty. Except now that there were shitty nappies to change and formula milk to prepare he was off, getting his end away.

Ami wasn't quite ready to let Kath's absence go.

"You could've left Lola with one of my friends."

Ami knew better. Kath never let anyone look after me, not even her.

"Let's not fight now, pet. You're tired."

Ami's gaze was like being doused in ice water. It contained every-thing she couldn't say to me. *Fucking ugly, little runt. You're always in the way.*

"You must be starvin'. Let me get you a cuppa and a sandwich and then you can get some sleep."

We stood and looked at the baby when Ami had gone to bed.

"Don't get any ideas. You don't want to be like your aunt, with a baby at sixteen. You don't want to be like either of us."

Kathy always spoke to me like I was twenty-four, not four.

Tallulah stirred and stretched, arms jerking outwards as if she was in freefall. She opened her eyes. There was no squinting or screaming.

"The little scrap's going to need our help."

Kath lifted her out and laid her on her knee for inspection. I put my nose against the soft spot on her skull. I fell in love with her right then.

"What do you wish for her?" Kath asked, smiling.

Chocolate. Barbies. A bike. A pet snake. Everything my childish heart could bestow.

☉

Saturdays were for shopping. Kathy and I walked down Cathcart Street towards town. We'd pass a row of grimy Victorian mansions on our way that served as a reminder of once great wealth, now carved up into flats for social housing or filled with squatters who lay in their damp dens with needles in their arms.

After these were the terraces, joined by a network of alleyways that made for easy assaults and getaways. This model of housing was for the civic minded when everyone here had a trade, due to our proximity to the city of Liverpool. The ship-building yards lay empty, and the 1980s brought container ships that did away with the demand for dockers. The life inside spilled out into the sun; women sat on their steps in pyjama bottoms and vest tops, even though it was lunchtime. Fags in hand, they'd whisper to one another as Kathy passed, afraid to meet her gaze. A man wore just shorts, his pale beer belly pinking up in the sun. He saluted when he saw Kathy. She ignored him.

I followed Kathy, her trolley wheels squeaking. The sound got worse as it was filled with vegetables, cheap meat shrink wrapped on Styrofoam trays, and bags of broken biscuits.

Kathy stopped to talk to a woman with rotten, tea stained teeth. I was bored. We were at the outskirts of town, where the shops were most shabby. House clearance stores and a refurbished washing machine outlet. I wandered along the pavement a way until something stopped me. The peeling sign over the shop window read "Ricky's Reptiles". The display was full of tanks. Most were empty, but the one at the front contained a pile of terrapins struggling to climb over one another in a dish of water.

The shop door was open, revealing the lino floor that curled up at the corners. It was a shade of blue that verged on grey, or maybe it was just dirty. I could see the lights from the tanks. The fish were darting flashes of wild colour or else they drifted on gossamer fins. I was drawn in. The man behind the counter looked up and smiled, but to his credit he didn't try and talk to me, otherwise I would've run.

Then I saw it, a long tank along the back wall. I went closer. The snake was magnificent, from the pale skin on her belly to the brown scales on her back.

She slithered closer, eyeing me and then raised her head and the front third of her body lifted up as if suspended on invisible thread. I put my forehead against the glass.

"She likes you," the man murmured.

She moved up the side of the tank. I realised that I was swaying in time with her, feeling unity in the motion. I was aware of her body, each muscle moving beneath her skin, her very skeleton. I looked into the snake's black eyes and could see out of them into my own. The world was on the tip of her forked tongue; my curiosity, the shopkeeper's sweat and kindness, the soft flavour of the mice in the tank behind the counter.

A hand gripped my shoulder, hard, jerking me back to myself. It was Kathy.

"Get away from that thing." Her fingers were digging into me. "Don't you ever come in here again, understand?"

She looked at the snake, shuddering. "God, it's disgusting. What's wrong with you?"

She shouted at me all the way home, for putting the wind up her, letting her think some pervert had taken me. I didn't realise just how afraid she was. That she was looking at me like she didn't know what she'd birthed.

⊙

The novelty of motherhood soon wore off. Ami sat in the armchair of our flat, her toenails painted in the same tangerine shade as her maxi dress. She was sunbed fresh and her lips were demarcated in an unflatteringly pale shade of pink. Her hair was in fat rollers ready for her evening out.

"Guess where I went today?" she asked, her voice bright and brittle.

"Where, doll?" Kath puffed on her cigarette, blowing a stream of smoke away from us.

If Ami was slim, Kath was scrawny. The skin on her neck and chest was wrinkled from the lack of padding and twenty-five cigarettes a day. She wore a series of gold chains and her hands were rough and red from perpetual cleaning. Her face was unbalanced: nose too small and large ears that stuck out. Round eyes that never saw make-up. I forget sometimes, that she was only twenty-four then.

"To see Kenny."

Tallulah got up and I thought she was leaving me for Ami but she was just fetching her teddy. When she sat back down next to me, she wriggled against me to get comfortable. Ami bought Tallulah's clothes. Ridiculous, expensive things to dress a toddler in, old fashioned and frilly.

"Kenny always asks after you." Ami filled the silence.

"Does he?" Kath tipped the ash from her cigarette into the empty packet. God love her, she didn't have many vices.

"He never says but he's hurt. It's all over his face when I walk in and you're not with me. You're not showing him much respect or loyalty. All he wants to do is look after you and Lola, like he looks after me and Tallulah."

"I don't want Kenny's money. He's not Robin Hood. He beat a man to death."

"He's our *brother*."

Which was funny, because I didn't know that I had an uncle.

Kath's face was a shutter slamming shut.

"He loves to see pictures of Lola."

"Photos? You showed him photos?" Kath was blowing herself for a fight.

"I only showed him some pictures. He wanted to see her. What's up with you?"

"Lola's *my* business. No one else's."

"Well, I'm taking Tallulah for him to see next time."

"No, you're not. Not to a prison."

"She's mine. I'll take her where the fuck I want."

"You've done well to remember you've got a daughter."

"What's that mean?"

"You're always out with your bloody mates. You treat me like an unpaid baby sitter. She spends more time here than with you and then you've got the cheek to tell me to mind my own."

"So it's about money?"

"No," Kath threw up her hands, "it's about you being a selfish, spoilt brat. I'm your *sister*, not your mum. And it's about how you treat Tallulah."

"At least I know who her dad is."

Kath slapped her face. A sudden bolt that silenced them both. It left a red flush on Ami's cheek. Whenever I asked about my dad, Kath told me that she'd found me in a skip.

"I'm sorry, Ami..." Kath put out her hands. "I didn't mean to. I mean..."

"Tallulah," Ami snapped, holding out her hand.

Tallulah looked from me to Kath, her eyes wide. Ami pulled her up by the arm. She screamed.

"Be careful with her."

"Or what, Kath?" Ami lifted Tallulah up, putting her under one arm like she was a parcel. "Are you going to call Social Services? Fuck off."

Calling Social Services was a crime akin to calling the police.

Tallulah was in a full on tantrum by then, back arched and legs kicking. Fierce for her size, she proved too much for Ami who threw her down on the sofa. She lay there, tear stained and rigid. Ami had started to cry too. "Stay here then, see if I sodding care."

☉

There are times when I feel lost, even to myself, and that what looks out from behind my eyes isn't human.

I'm reminded of it each day as I go to work at the School of Tropical Medicine.

Peter, one of the biochemists from the lab downstairs has come up for a batch of venom. He watches me milk the snakes when he can overcome his revulsion.

Michael, my assistant, tips the green mamba out of her box. I pin her down with a forked metal stick, while Michael does the same, further along her body. I clamp a hand just beneath her neck, thanking her silently for enduring the indignity of this charade. If it were just the two of us, she'd come to me without all this manhandling. I'll make it up to her later with mice and kisses. She's gorgeous in an intense shade of green, her head pointed.

"You have to stop that work when you get too old," says Peter, "you know, reflexes getting slow and all that."

The deaths of herpetologist are as fabled as snakes are touchy. There's no room for lax habits or slowness. Handled safely for years, a snake can turn on you, resulting in a blackened, withered limb, blood pouring from every orifice, paralysis and blindness, if not death.

Peter's a predator. He's been a swine to me since I knocked him back. I turn to him with the snake still in my hand. She hisses at him and he shrinks away.

I hook the mamba's mouth over the edge of the glass and apply gentle pressure. The venom runs down the side and collects in a pool.

What Peter doesn't know is that when my darlings and I are alone I hold them in my arms and let them wind around my neck. Our adoration is mutual. They're the easy part of my job.

"They like Eliza," Michael is offended on my behalf. There's not been a bite since I've been here.

"Concentrate." I snap at him as he brings the mamba's box to me. I regret my churlishness straight away. Michael is always pleasant with me. He never takes offence at my lack of social graces but someday he will.

Snakes are easy. It's people that I don't know how to charm.

○

Tallulah trailed along beside me. She looked like a doll in her school uniform; pleated skirt and leather buckled shoes. I didn't begrudge her the lovely clothes that Ami bought her. She jumped, a kittenish leap, and then she took my hand. We swung arms as we walked.

We turned onto Cathcart Street. Laird Tower was ahead of us, dwarfing the bungalows opposite. Those used by the elderly or infirm were marked out by white grab handles and key safes.

A pair of girls sat on a wall. They jumped down when they saw us. School celebrities, these playground queens, who knew how to bruise you with a word. They'd hurt you for not being like them, or not wanting to be like them.

"Is she your sister?" Jade, the shorter one asked Tallulah.

"No," Tallulah began, "she's…"

"Of course not," Jade cut across her, keen to get out the rehearsed speech. Jade didn't like my prowess in lessons. I tried to hide it, but it occasionally burst out of me. I liked the teacher. I liked homework. I even liked the school, built in red brick, that managed to still look like a Victorian poorhouse.

Jade was sly enough not to goad me for that, going for my weakness, not my strength. "You're too pretty to be Lola's sister. Look at her ugly mug."

It was true. I remained resolutely strange; my features had failed to rearrange themselves into something that would pass for normal. Also, my sight had rapidly deteriorated in the last few months and my thick lenses magnified my eyes

"Be careful." Jade leant down into Tallulah's face. "You'll catch her ugliness."

Tallulah pushed her, hard, both of her small hands on her chest. Jade fell backwards a few steps, surprised by the attack. She raised a fist to hit Tallulah.

My blood was set alight, venom rising. Water brash filled my mouth as if I were about to be sick. I snatched at Jade's hand and sunk my teeth into her meaty forearm, drawing blood. I could taste her shock and fear. If she was screaming, I couldn't hear her. I only let go when her friend punched me on the ear.

☉

After I'd apologised I sat in the corner of the room while Kath and Pauline, Jade's mum, talked.

"I thought it would be good if we sorted it out between us, like grown-ups," Pauline said.

Social Services had already been round to confirm that I was the culprit.

Has she ever done anything like this before?

No, Kathy was calm and firm, *Lola wasn't brought up that way.*

"I'm so sorry about what happened." Pauline lifted her mug of tea, her hand trembling a fraction. She took a sip and set it down, not picking it up again.

"Why?" Kath sat up straighter. "Lola bit Jade. *I'm* sorry and I'll make sure that she is too by the time I'm done with her."

"Yes, but Jade was picking on her."

"That's no excuse for what Lola did. She should've just walked away."

"It's time that someone cut Jade down to size."

"My daughter *bit* yours." Exasperation raised Kathy's voice a full octave.

"She was asking for it."

Kathy shook her head. Then, "How is she?"

Jade had lain on the pavement, twitching. Red marks streaked up her arm, marking the veins.

"She's doing okay," Pauline swallowed. "She's on antibiotics. She's a bit off colour, that's all."

"The police and Social Services came round earlier."

"I've not complained. I'm not a nark. I'd never do that."

"I didn't say you had."

"You'll tell Kenny, won't you? We're not grasses. We won't cause you any bother. I'll skin Jade if she comes near your girls again." We were

263

known as Kathy's girls.

"Kenny?" Kathy repeated dully.

"Please. Will you talk to him?"

Kath was about to say something but then deflated in the chair.

"Ami's says she's visiting him soon, so I'll make sure he gets the message."

☉

Kathy closed the door after Pauline had gone.

"What did you do to her?" It was the first time she'd looked at me properly since it had happened.

"It wasn't her fault." Tallulah stood between us. "She was going to hit me."

"What did you do to her?" Kathy pushed her aside. "Her arm swelled up and she's got blood poisoning."

"I don't know," I stammered. "It just happened."

She slapped me. I put my hands out to stop her but she carried on, backing me into the bedroom. She pushed me down on the floor. I curled my hands over my head.

"I didn't bring you up to be like that." Her strength now was focused in a fist. Kathy had hit me before, but never like that. "I swear I'll kill you if you ever do anything like that again. You fucking little monster."

She was sobbing and shrieking. Tallulah was crying and trying to pull her off. Kathy continued to punch me until her arm grew tired. "You're a monster, just like your father."

☉

We stayed in our bedroom that night, Tallulah and I. We could hear Kathy banging about the flat. First, the vacuum hitting the skirting boards as she pulled it around. A neighbour thumped on the wall and she shouted back, but turned it off and took to the bathroom. She'd be at it all night, until her hands were raw. The smell of bleach was a signal of her distress. There were times when I thought I'd choke on the stench.

The skin on my face felt tight and sore, as if shrunken by tears.

Tallulah rolled up my t-shirt to inspect the bruises on my back. There was a change coming, fast, as the shock of Kathy's onslaught wore off.

It hurt when Tallulah touched me. It wasn't just the skin on my face that felt wrong. It was all over. I rubbed my head against the carpet, an instinctual movement as I felt I'd got a cowl covering my face. The skin ripped.

"I'll get Kathy."

"No, wait." I grabbed her wrist. "Stay with me." My skin had become a fibrous sheath, my very bones remoulding. My ribs shrank and my slim pelvis and limbs became vestigial. My paired organs rearranged themselves, one pushed below the other except my lungs. I gasped as one of those collapsed. I could feel my diaphragm tearing; the wrenching of it doubled me over.

I writhed on the floor. There was no blood. What came away in the harsh lamplight was translucent. Tallulah held me as I sloughed off my skin which fell away to reveal scales. She gathered the coils of me into her lap. We lay down and I curled around her.

I couldn't move. I could barely breathe. When I put out my forked tongue I could taste Tallulah's every molecule in the air.

☉

The morning light came through the thin curtain. Tallulah was beside me. I had legs again. I put a hand to my mouth. My tongue was whole. My flesh felt new. More than that, I could see. When I put my glasses on the world became blurred. I didn't need them anymore. The very surface of my eyes had been reborn.

My shed skin felt fibrous and hard. I bundled it up into a plastic bag and stuffed it in my wardrobe. Tallulah stretched as she watched me, her hands and feet splayed.

"Tallulah, what am I? Am I a monster?"

She sat up and leant against me, her chin on my shoulder.

"Yes, you're *my* monster."

☉

I ache for the splendid shabbiness of my former life, when it was just Kath, Tallulah, and me in the flat, the curtains drawn against the world and the telly droning on in the background. Tallulah and I would dance around Kath, while she swatted us away. The smell of bleach and furniture polish is forever home. Kath complaining when I kept turning the heating up. Being cold made me sluggish.

Endless, innocuous days and nights that I should've savoured more.

"How was your test?"

"Crap." Tallulah threw down her bag. "Hi, Kath."

"Hi, love," Kathy shouted back from the kitchen.

Tallulah, school uniformed, big diva hair so blonde that it was almost white, a flick of kohl expertly applied at the corner of her eyes.

"I'm thick, not like you." She kicked off her shoes.

"You're not thick. Just lazy."

She laughed and lay on her belly beside me, in front of the TV. She smelt of candy floss scent that she'd stolen from her mum. Tallulah was the sweetest thing.

There was the sound of the key in the door. I looked at Tallulah. Only her mum had a key. We could hear Ami's voice, followed by a man's laugh. A foreign sound in the flat. Kathy came out of the kitchen, tea towel in hand.

Ami stood in the doorway, flushed and excited, as if she was about to present a visiting dignitary.

"Kath, there's someone here to see you."

She stood aside. I didn't recognise the man. He was bald and scarred. Kathy sat down on the sofa arm, looking the colour of a dirty dishrag.

"Oh, God," he said, "aren't you a bunch of princesses?"

"Kenny, when did you get out?" Kath asked.

"A little while ago." He took off his jacket and threw it down. A snake tattoo coiled up his arm and disappeared under the sleeve of his t-shirt. It wasn't the kind of body art I was used to. This hadn't been driven into the skin in a fit of self-loathing or by a ham fisted amateur. It was faded but beautiful. It rippled as Kenny moved, invigorated by his muscles.

"Come and hug me, Kath."

She got up, robotic, and went to him, tolerating his embrace, her arms stiff by her sides.

"I've brought us something to celebrate."

He handed her a plastic bag and she pulled out a bottle of vodka and a packet of Jammy Dodgers.

"Just like when we were kids, eh?" he grinned.

"See, Kenny's got no hard feelings about you staying away." Ami was keen to be involved. "He's just glad to be home."

They both ignored her.

"Now, girls, come and kiss your uncle. You first, Tallulah."

"Well, go on." Ami gave her a shove.

She pecked his cheek and then shot away, which seemed to amuse him. Then it was my turn. Kath stood close to us while Kenny held me at arm's length.

"How old are you now, girl?"

"Eighteen."

"You were born after I went inside." He sighed. "You've got the family's ugly gene like me and your mum but you'll do."

For what? I thought.

Kenny put his fleshy hand around Kath's neck and pressed his forehead against hers. Kathy, who didn't like kisses or cuddles from anyone, flinched. I'd never seen her touched so much.

"I'm home now. We'll not talk about these past, dark years. It'll be how it was before. Better. You'll see. Us taking care of each other."

○

Georgia's unusual for a photographer in that she's more beautiful than her models. They're gap toothed, gawky things that only find luminosity through the lens. Georgia's arresting in the flesh.

I hover beside our host who's introducing me to everyone as though I'm a curio. We approach a group who talk too loudly, as if they're the epicentre of the party.

"I find Georgia distant. And ambitious."

"She lives on Martin's Heath. In one of the old houses."

"Bloody hell, is that family money?"

"Rosie, you've modelled for Georgia. Have you been there?"

"No."

Rosie sounds so quiet and reflective that the pain of her unrequited love is palpable. At least I hope it's unrequited.

"Have you seen her girlfriend?"

"Everyone, meet Eliza," our host steps in before they have a chance to pronounce judgement on me within my earshot, "Georgia's partner."

I shake hands with each of them.

"Georgia's last shoot made waves. And I didn't realise that she was such a stunner."

We all look over at Georgia. Among all the overdressed butterflies, she wears black trousers, a white shirt, and oxblood brogues.

"Don't tell her that," I smile. "She doesn't like it."

"Why? Doesn't every woman want that?" The man falters, as if he's just remembered that I'm a woman too.

These people with their interminable words. I came from a place where a slap sufficed.

"Don't be dull," I put him down. "She's much more than her face."

"What do you do, Eliza?" another one of them asks, unperturbed by my rudeness.

"I'm a herpetologist."

They shudder with delicious revulsion.

I glance back to Georgia. A man with long blonde hair reaches out to touch her forearm and he shows her something on his tablet.

I'm a pretender in my own life, in this relationship. I know how my jealousy will play out when we get home. I'll struggle to circumvavigate all the gentility and civility that makes me want to scream.

Eventually Georgia will say, *What's the matter? Just tell me instead of trying to pick a fight.*

She'll never be provoked, this gracious woman, to display any savagery of feeling. I should know better than to try and measure the breadth and depth of love by its noise and dramas but there are times that I crave it, as if it's proof that love is alive.

○

Ami took Tallulah away with her the first night that Kenny came to the flat.

"But it's a school night. And all my stuff's here."

"You're not going to school tomorrow." Ami picked up her handbag. "We're going out with Kenny."

Tallulah didn't move.

"Mind your mum, there's a good girl." Kenny didn't even look up.

After the front door closed, Kathy locked and chained it.

"Get your rucksack. Put some clothes in a bag. Don't pack anything you don't need."

"Why?" I followed her into her bedroom.

"We're leaving."

"Why?"

"Just get your stuff."

"What about college?"

Kathy tipped out drawers, rifling through the untidy piles that she'd made on the floor.

"What about Tallulah?"

She sank down on the bed.

"There's always someone that I have to stay for. Mum. Ami. Tallulah." She slammed her fist down on the duvet. "If it had been just us, we'd have been gone long ago."

"Stay?"

She wasn't listening to me anymore.

"I waited too long. I should've run when I had the chance. Fuck everyone."

She lay down, her face to the wall. I tried to put my arms around her but she shrunk from me, which she always did when I touched her and which never failed to hurt me.

O

If we were his princesses then Kenny considered himself king.

"Kath, stop fussing and come and sit down. It's good to be back among women. Without women, men are uncivilised creatures." He winked at me. "Tell me about Ma's funeral again, Kath."

Ami sat beside him, looking up at him.

"There were black horses with plumes and brasses. Her casket was in a glass carriage." Kath's delivery was wooden.

"And all the boys were there?"

"Yes, Kenny. All the men, in their suits, gold sovereign rings, and tattoos."

"Good," he said, "I would've been offended otherwise. Those boys owe me and they know it. I did time for them. Do you know the story?"

"Bits," Tallulah said.

"I told her, Kenny." Ami was keen to show her allegiance.

"You were what, twelve?" He snorted. "You remember nothing. We did a job in Liverpool. A jeweller who lived in one of those massive houses around Sefton Park. We heard he was dealing in stolen diamonds. I went in first," he thumped his chest. "At twenty-three I was much thinner back then, could get into all sorts of tight spots. I let the others in afterwards. We found his money but he kept insisting the diamonds were hidden in the fireplace, but his hidey hole was empty. He kept acting all surprised. He wouldn't tell, no matter what." Kenny shrugged. "Someone grassed. A copper picked me up near home. Under my coat, my shirt was covered in his blood. I kept my trap shut and did the time. The others were safe. Eighteen years inside. My only regret is what happened to Ma. And missing her funeral."

"There were white flowers, everywhere, spelling out her name." Ami said. He patted her arm in an absent way, like she was a cat mithering for strokes.

"I wish they'd let me out for it. Ma was a proper princess, girls. She was touched, God bless her, but she was a princess."

Kath sat with her hands folded on her knees.

"Do you remember what Dad said when he was dying?"

Kath stayed quiet.

"He said, *You're the man of the house, Kenny. And you're the mother, Kathy. Kenny, you have to look after these girls.* Poor Ma, so fragile. When I heard about her stroke, I was beside myself. It was the shock of me being sent down that did it. Whoever grassed me up has to pay for that, too. I should've been here, taking care of you all."

"I managed," Kathy squeezed the words out.

"I know. I hate to think of you, nursing Ma when you also had a baby to look after. You were meant for better things. We didn't always live in this shithole, girls. We grew up in a big rambling house. You won't remember much of it, Ami. Dad bred snakes. He was a specialist. And Ma, she was a real lady. They were educated people, not like 'round here."

The words stuck in my gut. 'Round here was all I knew.

"Happy days, weren't they, Mouse?" Kenny looked directly at Kathy, waiting.

"Mouse," Ami laughed like she'd only just noticed Kathy's big eyes and protruding ears, "I'd forgotten that."

Mouse. A nickname that diminished her.

"What's *my* pet name?" Ami pouted.

"You're just Ami." He said it like she was something flat and dead, not shifting his gaze from Kathy.

There it was. Even then, I could see that Kathy was at the centre of everything and Ami was just the means to reach her.

○

There's a photograph in our bedroom that Georgia took of me while we were travelling around South America. It embarrasses me because of its dimensions and scares me, because Georgia has managed to make me look like some kind of modern Eve, desirable in a way that I'll never be again. My hair is loose and uncombed and the python around my shoulders is handsome in dappled, autumnal shades. My expression is of unguarded pleasure.

"Let's stay here, forever," I said to her when she put the lens cap back on, "It's paradise."

What I was really thinking was *What would it be like to change, forever, and have the whole jungle as my domain?*

"Do you love it that much?" Georgia replied in a way that suggested she didn't. "And put him down. Poor thing. If he's caught he'll end up as a handbag."

So it is that serpents are reviled when it's man that is repulsive.

○

I got off the bus at the end of Argyll Street and walked towards home. Kenny was sat on a plastic chair outside The Saddle pub, drinking a pint. He was waiting for me.

"What have you been doing today?" He abandoned his drink and followed me.

"Biology." I was at college, in town.

"Clever girl. That's from your grandparents. I used to be smart like that. You wouldn't think it to look at me."

There was an odd, puppyish eagerness to Kenny as he bounced along beside me. I darted across the road when there was a gap in the traffic. The railway line was on the other side of the fence, down a steep bank. Part way down the embankment was a rolled up carpet, wet and rotted, and the shopping trolley that it had been transported in.

"Let me carry your bag. It looks heavy."

"I can manage."

"I wasn't always like this. I had to change for us to survive. Fighting and stealing," he shook his head, embarrassed. "I only became brutal to stop us being brutalised. Do you understand?"

The sky had darkened. Rain was on its way.

"We lost everything when Dad died. The house. The money. Your grandma lost her mind. It was the shock of having to live here. We were posh and we paid for that. On our first day at school a lad was picking on Kathy. Do you know what I did? I bit him, Lola. Right on the face. He swelled up like a red balloon. He nearly choked. Nobody picks on my princesses."

Nobody except him.

"Are you special, Lola?"

"I don't know what you mean."

I dodged him as he tried to block my path. Tallulah wouldn't have told him anything. Ami though, she had told him to prevent Pauline and Jade getting a battering.

"I can wait," he didn't pursue me, just stood there in the drizzle. "We have lots of time now."

"We're going for a ride today." Kenny followed Kath into the kitchen. He'd started turning up at the flat every day.

"I can't, Kenny, I've got loads to do."

"It can all wait."

Kenny had the last word.

"Where are we going?" Tallulah asked.

"You're not going anywhere except to Ami's. She needs to get her house in order. A girl needs her mum. She's sorting your bedroom, so you're going to live with her. Properly."

"I don't want to."

"Want's not in it."

Kathy stood between them. He pushed her aside.

"I live *here*." Tallulah wouldn't be moved.

"You live where I tell you." He had this way of standing close to you, to make himself seem more imposing, and lowering his voice. "You act like you're something with that pretty little face of yours. Well, I'm here to tell you that you're not special. You're fucking Mikey Flynn's daughter. And he's a piece of dead scum."

Poor Mikey Flynn, rumoured to have done a runner. I wondered where Kenny had him buried.

"Go home, Tallulah." Kathy raised her chin. "Kenny's right. You're not my girl. You should be with your own mother."

Tallulah's eyes widened. I could see the tears starting to pool there.

"Go on, then," Kathy carried on, "you don't belong here."

"Mum," I opened my mouth.

"Shut it." Kathy turned on me. "I've been soft on you pair for too long. Now help Tallulah take her stuff to Ami's."

"No," Kenny put a hand on my arm, "Lola stays with us."

☉

As Kenny drove, the terraces changed to semis and then detached houses. Finally there were open fields. It felt like he'd taken us hours away but it wasn't more than thirty minutes. We turned up an overgrown drive. Branches whipped the windscreen as Kenny drove.

"Kenny." Kath's voice was ripped from her throat. He patted her hand.

The drive ended at a large house, dark bricked with tall windows. It might as well have been a castle for all its unfamiliar grandeur. Overgrown rhododendrons crowded around it, shedding pink and red blossoms that were long past their best.

"Come on."

Kenny got out, not looking back to see if we were following.

Kath stood at the bottom of the steps, looking up at the open front door. There were plenty of window bars and metal shutters where I grew up, but the windows here were protected by wrought iron foliage in which metal snakes were entwined. The interior was dim. I could hear Kenny's footsteps as he walked inside.

"This is where we used to live." Kathy's face was blank. She went in, a sleep walker in her own life. I followed her.

"Welcome home." Kenny was behind the door. He locked it and put the key on a chain around his neck.

○

Kenny showed us from room to room as if we were prospective buyers, not prisoners. Every door had a lock and every window was decorated in the same metal lattice work.

I stopped at a set of double doors but Kenny steered me away from it. "Later. Look through here, Kathy. Do you remember the old Aga? Shame they ripped it out. I thought we could get a new one."

He led us on to the lounge, waving his arm with a flourish.

"I couldn't bring you here without buying *some* new furniture." He kept glancing at Kathy. "What do you think?"

The room smelt of new carpet. It was a dusky pink, to match the sofa, and the curtains were heavy cream with rose buds on them. Things an old woman might have picked.

"Lovely, Kenny."

"I bought it for us." He slung his arm around her neck. It looked like a noose. "You and me, here again, no interference." His face was soft. "I've plenty of money. I can get more."

"Go and play," Kath said to me.

274

It'll shame me forever that I was angry at her for talking to me like I was a child when all she was trying to do was get me out of his way.

I went, then crawled back on my belly to watch them through the gap in the door.

Kath broke away from him and sat down. Kenny followed her, sinking down to lay his head on her knee. Her hand hovered over him, the muscles in her throat moving as she swallowed hard. Then she stroked his head. He buried his face in her lap, moaning.

"What happened to us, Mouse?"

Mouse. He'd swallow her whole. He'd crush her.

"You said you can get more money. Do you mean the money from the job in Liverpool?"

He moved quickly, sitting beside Kathy with his thigh wedged against the length of hers.

"Yes." He interfaced their fingers, making their hands a single fist. "I want you to know that I didn't kill anyone."

"You didn't? You were covered in blood."

"It was Barry's son, Carl. He always had a screw loose. The man wouldn't tell us where the diamonds were and Carl just freaked. He kept on beating him."

"But you admitted it."

"Who would believe me if I denied it? I did the time. Barry was very grateful. I knew it would set us up for life. I hated waiting for you. I imagined slipping out between the bars to come to you. I was tempted so many times. I hated the parole board. There *were* diamonds, Kath. I took them before I let the others in. I stopped here and buried them under the wall at the bottom of the garden. I nearly got caught doing it. Then the police picked me up, on my way back to you. That's why I had to do the stretch, so nobody would suspect. They're safe, now. Shankly's looking after what's left of them." He laughed at his own cryptic comment. Every Merseysider knew the deceased Bill Shankly, iconic once-manager of Liverpool Football Club. "Did I do right, Kath?"

Then she did something surprising. She kissed him. He writhed under her touch.

"Mouse, was there anyone else while I was inside?"

Priya Sharma

"No, Kenny. There's never been anybody else."

He basked in that.

"It'll be just like I said."

I sensed her hesitation. So did he.

"What's wrong?"

"It won't be like we said though, will it?"

"Why?"

"It should be just us two." She leant closer to him. "Lola's grown up now. She can look after herself."

"Lola's just a kid."

"I was a mother at her age." She put her hand on his arm.

"No, she stays."

Her hand dropped.

"Lola," Kenny called out. "Never let me catch you eavesdropping again. Understand?"

☉

"I'll just say goodnight to Lola." Kath stood in the doorway to my new bedroom, as if this game of fucked-up families was natural.

"Don't be long."

I sat on the bed. The new quilt cover and pillow case smelt funny. Kenny had put them on straight out of the packaging without washing them first. They still bore the sharp creases of their confinement.

"Lola," Kathy pulled me up and whispered to me. "He said to me, when we were kids, 'I'm going to put a baby in you and it's going to be special, like me and Dad,' as if I had nothing to do with it. I can't stand him touching me. When I felt you moving inside me, I was terrified you'd be a squirming snake, but you were *mine*. I'd do anything to get him away from us and Ami. I was the one who told the police."

Uncle. Father. Any wonder that I'm monstrous?

"Kenny's always been wrong. He thought it was from Dad, although he never saw him do it. It's from Mum. It drove her mad, holding it in. She nearly turned when she had her stroke. I have to know, can you do it too?"

"What?"

276

"We can't waste time. Can you turn into," she hesitated, "a snake?"

"Yes." I couldn't meet her gaze.

"Good. Do it as soon as I leave." She opened the window. "Go out through the bars. Will you fit?"

"I don't know if I can. I'm not sure that I can do it at will."

"Try. Get out of here."

Panic rose in my chest. "What about you?"

"I'm going to do what I should've done a long time ago." She showed me the paring knife in her back pocket and then pulled her baggy sweater back over it. It must've been all she had time to grab. "I won't be far behind you."

"What if you're not?"

"Don't ask stupid questions," she paused, "I'm sorry for not being stronger. I'm sorry for not getting you away from here."

"Kathy," Kenny's voice boomed from the corridor, "time for bed."

After she left I heard the key turn in the lock.

☉

I went through the drawers and wardrobe. Kenny had filled them with clothes. I didn't want to touch anything that had come from him. There was nothing that I could use as a weapon or to help me escape.

I'd not changed since the time I'd bitten Jade. I lay down, trying to slow my breathing and concentrate. Nothing happened. The silence filled my mind along with all the things he would be doing to Kathy.

I dozed, somewhere towards early morning, wakening frequently in the unfamiliar room. I missed Tallulah beside me in the bed we'd shared since childhood. I missed her warmth and tangle of hair.

When Kenny let me out it was late afternoon.

"Where's my mum?"

"Down here."

There was a chest freezer in the basement. Kenny lifted the lid. Kathy was inside, frozen in a slumped position, arms crossed over her middle. Frozen blood glittered on the gash in her head and frosted one side of her face.

Kenny put his hand on my shoulder like we were mourners at a wake.

I should've been kicking and screaming, but I was as frozen as she was.

One of Kathy's wrists was contorted at an unnatural angle.

"She betrayed me. I always knew it, in my heart." He shut the lid. "Now it's just you and me, kid."

He took me up through the house, to the room at the back with the double doors. There were dozens of tanks that cast a glow. Some contained a single serpent, others several that were coiled together like heaps of intestines.

"My beauties. I'll start breeding them."

There were corn snakes, ball pythons, ribbon snakes, though I had no names for them back then, all of which make good pets. I stopped at one tank. He had a broad head with a blunted snout

"Ah, meet Shankly." Kenny put his hand against the glass. "He was hard to come by. They're called cottonmouths because they open their mouths so wide to show their fangs that you see all the white lining inside."

The cottonmouth must have been young. I remember his olive green colour and the clear banded pattern on his back, which he would lose as he got older.

"Are you special, Kathy?"

"I'm Lola."

"Yes, of course you are. Are you like me?"

"I'm nothing like you. Leave me alone."

"I'll look after you. Like you're a princess. You'll want for nothing. And you'll look after me because that's how it works."

"Don't fucking touch me."

Kenny pressed my face against the tank. Shankly showed me his pale underbelly as he slid towards me.

"Be afraid of him," Kenny nodded at the snake, "he still has his fangs. I'll make a mint from his venom."

Shankly climbed up a branch in his tank and settled there.

Kenny pushed me down with one hand and undid his belt buckle with the other.

"I'm your daughter." It was my last defence.

"I know."

Then he put his forked tongue in my mouth.

☉

I couldn't move. The place between my legs was numb. I'd already tried sex with a boy from college. I knew what it was about. We'd fumbled and fallen in a heap in the bushes by the old boating lake one afternoon. It wasn't an experience to set the world alight but it was satisfactory enough.

This wasn't just a sex crime, it was a power crime. Kenny wanted my fear. I shrunk into the distant corners of myself trying to retreat where he couldn't follow. His orgasm was grudging, delivered with a short, gratified moan.

Afterwards he sat with his trousers open, watching me like he was waiting for me to do something. I was frozen. I'm not sure I even blinked. That was how Kathy must have felt, forever stuck in that single moment of inertia and shock that kept her in the same spot for a lifetime. She was right. She should have run while she had the chance. Fuck her mother. And Ami, for all the good she'd done her.

Kenny stood up. I thought, *It's going to happen again and then he's going to dump me in the freezer.* Instead, he went upstairs, his tread heavy with disappointment.

"Don't stay up too late, pet."

I think I was waiting for something too, when I should've been searching for something sharp to stick between his ribs. I couldn't summon anything; I was still too deep inside myself.

I was colder than I'd ever been before, even though the summer night was stifling. The room felt airless despite the window being wide open and butting up against the grille. Sometimes, when Georgia's away, I feel that cold.

Get up, get up before he remembers you and comes back down for more.

"Lola." A voice carried through the window.

It was Tallulah, a pale ghost beyond the glass. Her mouth was moving as she clutched at the bars.

I turned my face away, in the childish way of *if I can't see her, then she can't see me.* I didn't want her to see me like this. It occurred to me that she might have been a witness to the whole thing. I turned back but she'd gone, so I closed my eyes.

I should've known that Tallulah would never leave me. The snakes swayed in their tanks, enraptured. Tallulah was long and white, with pale yellow markings. Slender and magnificent. She glided over me and lay on my chest, rearing up. I couldn't breathe because she took my breath away. I could feel her muscles contracting and her smooth belly scales against my bare chest.

Get up, get up, or he'll come down and find her like this.

Are you special?

Her tongue flicked out and touched my lips. I had no choice. I had to do it, for her. There was the rush of lubricant that loosened the top layer of my skin. The change was fast, my boyish body, with its flat chest and narrow hips perfectly suited to the transformation.

I crawled out of my human mantle. Moulting was good. I shed every cell of myself that Kenny had touched.

⊙

Both Tallulah and I are unidentifiable among my extensive research of snakes, bearing properties of several species at once. We made a perfect pair for hunting. The pits on my face were heat sensitive, able to detect a variation of a thousandth of a degree, feeding information into my optic nerves. I saw the world in thermal. Kenny's heart was luminous in the dark. I slid up the side of his bed and hovered over his pillow. Tallulah lay beside him on the mattress, waiting.

Look at your princesses, Kenny. See how special we are.

Kenny snored, a gentle, almost purring noise.

It's a myth that snakes dislocate their jaws.

I opened my mouth as wide as I could, stretching the flexible ligament that joined my lower jaw to my skull. I covered his crown in slow increments. He snorted and twitched. I slipped down over his eyes, his lashes tickling the inside of my throat. He reached up to touch his head.

Tallulah struck him, sinking her fangs into his neck. He started and tried to sit up, limbs flailing, which was a mistake as his accelerating heartbeat sent the venom further around his circulation.

Trying to cover his nose was the hardest part, despite my reconfigured mouth. I thought my head would split open. I wasn't sure how much more I could stomach. Not that it mattered. I wasn't trying to swallow him whole. A fraction more and I was over his nostrils completely.

There was only one way to save himself. I recognised the undulations he was making. I could feel the change on my tongue, his skin becoming fibrous. I had to stop him. I couldn't imagine what he'd become.

He was weakening with Tallulah's neurotoxins, slumping back on the bed, shaking in an exquisite fit. He'd wet himself. I stretched my flesh further and covered his mouth and waited until long after he was still.

⊙

I woke up on the floor beside Tallulah. We were naked. My throat and neck were sore. The corners of my mouth were crusted with dried blood. We lay on our sides, looking at one another without speaking. We were the same, after all.

"How did you find me?" I was hoarse.

"I had to wait until Ami went out. I found the house details in her bedroom drawer. I didn't have any money so I had to get a bus and walk the rest of the way. I'm sorry that I didn't get here sooner."

"It doesn't matter now."

Tallulah picked up our clothes and then our skins which lay like shrouds. It was disconcerting to see how they were moulds of us, even down to the contours of our faces.

"I'll take these with us. We can burn them later."

I went upstairs. I edged into the darkened room as if Kenny might sit up at any moment. He was a purple, bloated corpse with fang marks in his neck. I fumbled with the chain around his neck, not wanting to touch him.

"Where's Kathy?" Tallulah asked.

I told her.

"Show me."

"No, I don't want you to remember her like that." I seized Tallulah's face in my hands. "You do know that she didn't mean what she said, about you not belonging with us? She was trying to protect you."

Tallulah nodded, her mouth a line. She didn't cry.

"We have to bury her."

"We can't. Tallulah, we have to get out of here. Do you understand? Ami will come for you when she realises you've gone. There's something else."

I put my hand in the cottonmouth's tank. It curled up my arm and I lifted it out, holding it up to my cheek. He nudged my face.

"Lift out the bottom."

Tallulah pulled out bits of twisted branch and foliage, then pulled up the false base. She gasped. Out came bundles of notes and cloth bags. She tipped the contents out on her palm. More diamonds than I could hold in my cupped hands.

We loaded the money into Kenny's rucksack and tucked the diamonds in our pockets.

"What about the snakes?"

We opened the tanks and carried them outside. I watched them disappear into the undergrowth. Except for Shankly. I put him in a carrier bag and took him with us.

○

There are days when I wake and I can't remember who I am, like a disorientated traveller who can't recall which hotel room of which country they're in.

I'm hurt that Georgia didn't want me to collect her from the airport.

There's been a delay. I won't get in until late. Go to bed, I'll get a cab.

I wished now that I'd ignored her and gone anyway instead of lying here in the dark. The harsh fluorescent lights and the near empty corridors of the airport are preferable to the vast darkness of our empty bed.

Not going is a stupid test with which I've only hurt myself. I've resolutely taken her consideration for indifference. I want her to be upset that I wasn't there, as if she secretly wanted me there all along.

See, I confuse even myself.

The front door opens and closes. I should get up and go to her. She comes in, marked by the unzipping of her boots and the soft sound of her shedding clothes.

Love isn't just what you feel for someone when you look at them. It's how they make you feel about yourself when they look back at you.

Georgia is the coolest, most poised woman that I know. We're older now and our hearts and flesh aren't so easily moved but I still wonder what she sees when she looks at me.

"Do you love me?" It's easier to ask it with the lights off and my head turned away from her.

Everything about us is wrong. We're lovers, sisters, freaks.

She answers in a way that I have to respond to. I glide across the floor towards her and we become a writhing knot. We hunt mice in our grandiose pile and in the morning we are back here in our bed, entwined together in our nest.

When we wake again as human beings she says, "Of course I love you, monster."

When we shed the disguises that are Georgia and Eliza, and then the skins that are Lola and Tallulah, we *are* monsters. Fabulous beasts.

ACKNOWLEDGEMENTS

I have so many people to thank for believing in my work.

Mike Kelly, for his excellent advice and hard work in putting this collection together. C7 Shiina and Jeffrey Alan Love for the use of their beautiful artwork. Vince Haig for impeccable design.

Ellen Datlow and Paula Guran. I'm not sure thanks are sufficient.

Andy Cox at TTA, Mark Lord at Alt Hist and the team at *Albedo One* for taking so many of my stories.

Michelle Noble, nee Coles, whom I've known since we were four years old, and her husband Hadrian Noble. Thank you for our small town stories, tales of bloated corpses and malicious ghosts.

Sara and Dave Moore for the Arosfa and Newgale beach. When gorse goes out of flower, love goes out of fashion.

Cait Taylor, Natalie Tsang, Paula and John Halliday for friendship.

Andy and Melanie Flanagan for showing me parts of the world I might never have seen and that have bled into my fiction.

The writing community in the UK has been a revelation in how welcoming it is to new writers. And tonnes of fun. I've made friends, even though I only see them a few times a year. You know who you are. A special thanks to Simon and Cate Bestwick for their awesomeness. Without them I wouldn't have dared ventured into the world of cons.

Dev Agarwal who has been tremendously supportive in many ways.

Roy Gray for being an unsung hero and always helping fledglings.

Julie Travis and Sean Demory for their correspondence in all its forms.

Priya Sharma

And finally...

Veronica, Krishan and Ravi Sharma, my parents and brother for stories in all their guises and for your unconditional love. I am what I am because of you.

And Mark Greenwood, who whistles. For everything.

ABOUT THE AUTHOR

Priya Sharma is a doctor from the UK who also writes short fiction. Her work has appeared in *Interzone*, *Black Static*, *Albedo One* and *Tor.com*, among others. She's been anthologised in various annual *Best of* anthologies by editors like Ellen Datlow, Paula Guran, Jonathan Strahan and Johnny Mains. Her story "Fabulous Beasts" was on the Shirley Jackson Award shortlist and won a British Fantasy Award.

More about her can be found at www.priyasharmafiction.wordpress. com. For more information about this book, visit www.facebook.com/ AllTheFabulousBeasts/

CPSIA information can be obtained
at www.ICGtesting.com
Printed in the USA
BVHW030656071220
595077BV00040B/342